UN...

TORI...

AND

MIDNIGHT
RESOLUTIONS

BY
KATHLEEN O'REILLY

MILLS &
BOON

Dear Reader,

Wouldn't it be nice if everything were either black or white? Good or evil? Wrong or right? Honestly, though, don't you think it would also be unbearably boring? It's one of the reasons we take great thrill in exploring the shades of gray that come between.

In *Unbridled*, hot, suspended Marine Carter Southard (from *Branded*) is cleared by sexy defense attorney Laney Cartwright of a civilian crime he didn't commit, but he still must jump through military hoops if he hopes to be reinstated. As out of his league as Laney may be, he can't help wanting to mess up her pristine existence just a little bit. But when steamy, no-strings sex evolves into much, much more, they must wrestle with their preconceptions of each other…as well as their own misconceptions of themselves.

We hope you enjoy Carter and Laney's sizzling and sometimes heart-wrenching journey toward sexily-ever-after. We'd love to hear what you think. Contact us at P.O. Box 12271, Toledo, OH 43612, USA (we'll respond with a signed bookplate, newsletter and bookmark), or visit us on the web at www.toricarrington.net.

Here's wishing you love, romance and *hot* reading.

Lori and *Tony Karayianni*
aka *Tori Carrington*

UNBRIDLED

BY
TORI CARRINGTON

First published in Great Britain 2010
Harlequin Mills & Boon Limited,
Eton House, 18-24 Paradise Road, Richmond, Surrey TW9 1SR

© Lori and Tony Karayianni 2009

ISBN: 978 0 263 88151 6

14-1210

Harlequin Mills & Boon policy is to use papers that are natural, renewable
and recyclable products and made from wood grown in sustainable forests.
The logging and manufacturing processes conform to the legal environmental
regulations of the country of origin.

Printed and bound in Spain
by Litografia Rosés S.A., Barcelona

We dedicate this book to the fellow shades-of-gray travelers everywhere: enjoy the journey!

And, as always, to our editor extraordinaire, Brenda Chin, who has a knack for seeing the forest and the trees.

Prologue

FREEDOM WAS JUST a word…until you lost it. After you were put into a steel box and stripped of your personal belongings and your name, owning nothing more than a number and the crime for which you were charged.

"Inmate 55687, collect your things. You've been given your wings."

Carter Southard stared at the guard from where he lay on the hard top bunk in the four-by-nine-foot cell in the San Antonio County Jail. The words couldn't be meant for anyone else, because his bunk mate had been moved to a different cell the day before. Still, he couldn't help considering the imagery. He'd just been given his wings.

He closed the Steinbeck novel he was reading and got to his feet. He'd stopped even hoping for his release two days into his incarceration five days ago. Since he'd been wrongfully accused of a crime, there was no reason to believe things would be set right. Not so long as he was locked away, unable to prove his innocence.

And that had been the most difficult part. Not the injustice. Not that he'd been set up to pay for someone else's crime. But the loss of his freedom. Of his inability to fight back against an unseen enemy. Especially since his career in the Marines had always presented him with an identifiable target.

He gathered his few prison-issue toiletries and put them in the bag the guard provided and then stood Marine straight at the cell door. The guard motioned toward the block controller. The lock buzzed and the bars slid to the left. Carter turned so the guard could slap handcuffs on him and then turned around again.

Nearby inmates hooted and hollered as Carter followed the guard down the cell block. He kept his gaze forward, concentrating on the neat line of the other man's neck, urging him to speed up his steps. He wanted to get clear of the building before someone realized they'd made a mistake and locked him back in that damned cell.

What seemed like a lifetime later, a door was opened and the guard stepped aside, motioning Carter to precede him in. Carter was only too happy to oblige, keeping his eyes down.

Almost there…almost there…

The first thing he spotted was a pair of shiny beige high heels. Not the kind that strippers wore, but conservative, neat ones that had the height, but none of the zing.

The legs that belonged to the shoes, on the other hand, were nothing short of spectacular.

"Clear a path, inmate," the guard behind him ordered with a nudge of his nightstick.

Carter hadn't realized he'd stopped moving. He continued forward, the cuffs chafing his wrists behind his back. When he looked up, the woman was staring at him. And he felt as if the guard had just used that stick to whack him in the stomach.

He'd known women he'd trust at his side in a combat situation, something they were not legally permitted to do. But the woman in front of him was the complete opposite of any he'd find itching for a chance to fight on the front lines. She looked like a Kewpie doll, like the type of pinup girl men who had served in the Second World War might have taped inside their lockers. She had short, wavy blond hair, a perfectly oval face and flawless porcelain skin. Her bright blue eyes were wide, and her lips were shaped as if they were forever in pucker mode, waiting to be kissed.

Okay, it was official: he was losing it. He'd just spent the past five days swearing off all women. And he knew from experience that women like this one were exactly the kind to avoid at all costs. This bird would stick her bloodred talons straight into a man's chest and rip his heart out with arteries still fully attached.

The guard nudged him to turn and face him. He did, glad when the cuffs were removed. He absently rubbed his wrists and squinted at the woman, positive he was seeing things. Yes. Right now he was back in his cell, the Steinbeck novel in his hands, the woman before him a product of his imagination, an image sprung from the pages onto the blank wall of his unconscious mind.

Only not even his imagination was capable of conjuring the sweet smell of magnolias that engulfed him as she neared.

"Mr. Southard, I'm Laney Cartwright. Your attorney." She smiled. "I hope they treated you well."

His attorney? A couple of days ago he'd met with some snot-nosed public defender who'd looked as if he were two days out of grad school.

"I'm sorry—I've confused you," she said as the guard put the bag containing his belongings down on the counter next to the box of the clothes and watch and dog tags he'd been wearing, confiscated upon his arrest. "I've been hired by Trace Armstrong and a certain JoEllen Atchison to make sure you were released properly."

Carter stiffened at the mention of the couple responsible for his incarceration.

Miss June 1942 smiled again. "The real rapist has been caught. You're a free man, Mr. Southard."

Oh, yeah? If he was so free, why did he feel as if he'd gladly trade one prison cell for another so long as the leggy blonde was in it with him?

She looked at him a little too long. He tilted his head. She averted her gaze and then reached into her briefcase for something. She handed him what looked like the ring holding the key for his Harley.

"Mr. Armstrong arranged for your transportation to be delivered. It's outside now."

Carter raised his brows. If he didn't know better, Ms. Cartwright was as intrigued by him as he was by her. Which surprised him. While he'd come across his fair share of uptown women happy to slum it for a night or two, the attorney type barely looked twice at a man like him.

"Oh, here," she said, reaching into her briefcase again. "This is a letter of apology from Mr. Armstrong and Ms. Atchison. And while our business appears complete, should you need anything, this is my card with my office number in Dallas."

Dallas. Exactly where he was going.

Was it him, or did she put special emphasis on the word *anything?*

He grinned.

"As your attorney, it's my duty to strongly advise you to stay out of trouble, Mr. Southard."

She turned to walk away. Carter watched her go. He enjoyed the suggestive sway of her hips in the beige designer suit she wore, the long line of her legs and those naughty heels. He shook his head.

The last thing he needed in his life now was a woman. The most recent one had nearly proved to be the end of him.

"Way out of your league, Southard," the guard said, mirroring his own thoughts.

Carter slapped Ms. Cartwright's business card on the desk and swapped it for his personal effects. "Pass that on to someone who is in her league, won't you?"

And he turned toward the doors on his way to figure out the rest of his life. A life that would never include a woman like Laney Cartwright.

1

WHAT A DIFFERENCE two months made.

Or, rather, it was noteworthy how much the passage of time had affected Carter Southard's view of reality. He no longer woke up abruptly looking for a wall of bars that blocked him from the rest of the world. He didn't tense up when he passed a patrol officer on the road while driving his Harley, checking his rearview mirror to make sure the officer hadn't turned to follow him.

One thing that hadn't changed was the image of sexy Laney Cartwright standing in the jail's property room, handing him the freedom that had been ripped from him through no fault of his own. Her face was what he saw the moment he opened his eyes in the morning, and the last thing he thought about when he nodded off at night. And he wasn't granted a reprieve even then because his subconscious was given free rein over his unsatisfied desires and tortured him with fantasies involving the straitlaced defense attorney, fueling even more erotic images.

He hadn't seen her since then. But at least five times a day he thought about reasons he could use to do just that. Partly because he hoped another face-to-face might knock some of the air out of his almost too perfect memory of her. Mostly because he hoped it wouldn't.

Stupid. He knew it was. His recent experiences aside, inviting a woman into his life just now was probably the worst thing he could do.

Carter rolled over in the narrow bed. An ancient clattering fan doing little to cool the hot air in the small, two-bedroom bungalow outside the city.

Then a rancid smell made him draw back. He opened his eyes to stare into the droopy face of the neighbor's old hound that sat next to his bed, watching him expectantly.

"Damn." Carter sat up and grabbed his windup alarm clock. Just after eight-thirty in the morning. "How in the hell did you get in here again, Blue?"

All things being equal, Blue was as much his dog as his neighbor's, but Carter couldn't remember letting him in the house last night. He rubbed his face. Probably he'd left the back door open again. While he'd repaired the screen on the outer door a few days ago, it wouldn't take much for a determined dog to undo his handiwork if he put his mind to it.

Carter pulled on his jeans and walked to the small kitchen. Old Blue had definitely put his mind to it.

The hound's nails clacked against the wood floor as he followed him. He barked once, a half howl that could wake all the neighbors. Of course, at eight-thirty most were probably already up.

"All right, all right. Hush now. I'll get your breakfast in a minute."

The dog's only response was to tilt his head to the side. Which was about as good as it got with him.

Carter washed his face in the kitchen sink and shook out his hands before pouring the last of the sludge in the coffeemaker into a cup and putting it into the microwave. Then he filled the food and water bowls for Blue and took both out to the back porch, where the puddle of slobber the hound would leave behind wouldn't be as much of a nuisance as it was inside.

He stood next to the dog, looking around the three acres of land that had been in his family for more than a hundred years. The property had once been a couple of thousand acres, but after four generations, the parcel had been chopped up many times for inheritance purposes, and much of it sold off, so all that remained was the piece of land around him. And he was all that remained in the area of the original family. The brush was overgrown, fences were in disrepair. If he needed any further proof of that, he just had to look at the horse grazing in the distance. Another animal that belonged to one of his neighbors, this time the one to the west.

The microwave dinged. Carter let himself back into the kitchen, considering Blue's handiwork as he did, and took the cup out, downing half the scalding contents before picking up the single telephone on the wall. He put a call through to the Jacksons to tell them to collect their horse before it wandered off where they wouldn't find it.

"Thanks, Carter," Julia Jackson said after a long sigh. "I'll go right out and collect her. Damn horse. She'll never learn that the grass doesn't taste any better on your side of the fence."

Carter hung up the receiver and downed the rest of the coffee, his gaze drawn to the calendar on the wall. It was one of those given away by insurance companies, the pictures horrible, the paper already yellow although it was only August. But it showed the days and that was all that mattered.

Carter looked to where his right hand still rested on the telephone receiver. Then, before he knew he was going to do it, he picked it back up and dialed a number he'd memorized two months ago.

"Gavin, Ewing and Clairmont, Attorneys," a receptionist said in a cheery voice that set Carter's teeth on edge.

"Yeah. Give me Laney Cartwright."

2

LANEY CARTWRIGHT GAZED OUT her tenth-floor office window. It was lunchtime and Bryan Street bustled with life. Life that would vanish after five when everyone scrambled to their homes in the suburbs, leaving Dallas a ghost town dotted with the few tourists and conventioneers who dared peek outside their hotels.

She hadn't been in the windowed office very long. For the past three years she'd worked in a glorified cubicle on the open floor, one of many associate attorneys competing for a shot at the few offices that went up for grabs. Despite her impeccable résumé, she'd worked long and hard for this promotion to junior firm attorney. Eighty-hour weeks, carrying the load of three, burning the candle at both ends and the middle so that she barely had time to sleep, much less have a personal life.

Maybe that was the reason she'd been preoccupied ever since the legal secretary she shared with two other attorneys told her that a certain Mr. Carter Southard had called that morning to make an appointment. Violet had said there was nothing open, but he'd persisted, saying he needed no more than a couple of minutes and that it was important.

Important.

So Laney had told her to pencil something in during the lunch hour. Seeing Carter would at least keep her from thinking too much about the menacing note she'd received that morning.

Now she swiveled her desk chair away from the window and considered the case file open in front of her. When was the last time she'd had sex?

She twisted her lips. That was it, wasn't it? The fact that her love life had been nonexistent for so long was allowing her to daydream about what it might be like to act on that spark of attraction she'd felt two months ago, even though the jail jumpsuit and unshaven appearance of Carter Southard should have been enough to turn her off.

But it hadn't. Instead, in the first two weeks following their meeting, she found herself drifting off mid-conversation during social dinners and even phone calls, her concentration broken by the brief flash of Carter's strong hands. The granite set of his jaw. The half grin he'd given her when he apparently realized she returned the interest he displayed, however reluctantly.

What was she talking about? The sensation had taken her so much by surprise, there hadn't been a chance for her to be reluctant about anything.

Besides, she wouldn't be seeing him again. So what was the harm in returning his smile, letting him see what she was thinking? Saying without words, "Gee, Carter, another time, another place, you and me might have had a good time together. A very good time, indeed."

Laney swallowed hard, realizing that this was another time. And another place. And she was actually looking forward to seeing if that potential for a good time still existed. Oh, she didn't intend to act on it. But that brief interaction with Carter had been enough to fuel some interesting late-night sessions alone up until…well, even last night.

The intercom button buzzed. Laney picked up the phone. "Yes?"

The forty-five-year-old secretary said, "Your father on line one. He wants to know why you canceled lunch."

"Tell him I have an important meeting."

Silence.

Laney sighed. "I'll talk to him." She pressed the button for the correct line and then leaned back in her chair. "Hi, Daddy."

"Hi, yourself. So what's this I hear you've canceled our lunch today?"

"Sorry about that. A new development on the Mac-Gregor case came up and I've scheduled a strategy lunch to work it out."

Laney didn't lie to her father often. Mostly because he knew her better than anyone and immediately spotted an untruth. He would never go so far as to say it, but the few times she had relied on deception to hide her intentions had always ended with them both knowing where they stood.

She supposed that's what happened when you were

so close. After her mother passed away when she was twelve, Laney and her father had formed a bond that transcended parent and child. He was her best friend.

"What's the development?"

Laney blanched. Exhibit A on why she should never lie to her father.

Of course, he knew everything that was happening with *State v. MacGregor,* the case that had dominated her life for the past two months. The case that had also dominated the local and statewide news media, what with her young client accused of first-degree murder during an armed robbery.

The crime itself wasn't so much what garnered interest. Rather it was the fact that Devon MacGregor came from one of the wealthiest families in Texas.

"I received an interesting note this morning," she said quietly.

"Note?"

Laney hadn't planned on saying anything about it just then, but she figured she would have told her father sooner or later, so she might as well use it to her benefit now.

"Yes. Plain block letters. 'Drop MacGregor. Or else.'"

"Or else what?"

Laney sighed and fished out the note she'd placed in a Ziploc bag from the papers on her desk. "Your guess is as good as mine," she said.

"Have you given it to the police?"

"I have a call in. I was told a detective will stop by sometime this afternoon."

"Good."

There was a brief knock on the door. "Your twelve o'clock is here," Violet said.

Laney felt as if her stomach were full of a thousand butterflies flapping their wings to get out.

"Look, Daddy, people are beginning to arrive for the meeting."

She quickly said her goodbyes, hoping that she wasn't being too transparent, then left both hands on the telephone after she'd hung up.

"Hello again," Carter said from the open doorway.

Laney nearly knocked the receiver from its cradle and she fumbled to right it again.

She looked at the man responsible for her duplicity…and discovered that the hectic sensation she'd experienced two months ago was nothing compared with the one the cleaned-up version of Carter Southard made on her now.

What he wore was nothing special—a denim shirt, jeans and cowboy boots. It was the details that did Laney in. The way his sleeves were rolled up over his corded forearms. The cocky way he stood that pulled his well-worn jeans just so across his groin. The scuffed boots that proved he was a man who didn't wear them just for show, but had earned every last speck of Texas dust fused to the old leather.

In Carter's case, he wore the clothes—the clothes didn't wear him.

She looked up to find him grinning knowingly and

the bottom dropped out of her stomach altogether, freeing the butterflies there.

Oh, boy. It looked as though she was going to have to get used to her father's concerned reaction because she had the feeling that she was going to be doing a whole hell of a lot of lying in the foreseeable future.

3

OH, YES. This was exactly what Carter was looking for. Laney Cartwright's heated reaction to his appearance would stroke any man's ego; to his, it was a much-needed boost.

It wasn't often his path crossed with women of her class. Just seeing her sitting behind that expensive desk in her navy blue suit, her white-blond hair slicked back into some kind of neat do, baring her pale, elegant neck and what he suspected were real pearls at her delicate lobes—it all spoke of someone used to the better things in life.

Merely looking at her made him feel as if he'd soiled her somehow.

His grin widened. Oh, how he wanted to get her even dirtier still.

Laney looked as if she'd forgotten something and quickly got to her feet. She edged around the desk to face him, wiping her palms on her pencil-thin skirt before extending her right hand. "Where are my manners?" she said with a smile. "Hello, Mr. Southard." She gave his hand a quick shake, but Carter held on to hers a heartbeat longer. "It's good to see you again," she said.

He cocked a brow. "Is it?"

He watched as her initial surprise melted into something much different. Much more dangerous. Although to whom, he couldn't say.

She leaned against the edge of her desk and crossed her arms over her chest, drawing his gaze there and down to the long line of her legs in another pair of naughty high heels. She pursed her pink lips and considered him with the same naked suggestion that he knew was in his eyes.

Huh. A woman who liked a challenge.

While Carter could honestly say he'd never dated anyone with so much schooling, he had dated a woman or two who engaged him on more than a physical level. And Laney looked as if she could easily wipe them from his memory, set a new benchmark for those who would come after her.

She obviously enjoyed the sexual game of cat and mouse, where it was never quite clear who was the cat and who the mouse, with each of them easily sliding into either role to achieve some undefined objective.

Undefined? Carter took in the expression on Laney's beautiful face. Oh, no, there was nothing undefined there. Both of them were in it for the kill.

"Violet said you had something important to discuss?" she asked.

"Mmm. Yes. Important."

He stepped nearer to her, catching the subtle scent of magnolias. She smelled like heaven and he wanted to visit for a while. He reached out and fingered a soft curl that had escaped her do, then met her gaze, moving in closer still. He watched with a mixture of amusement and fascination as her pupils dilated in her blue, blue eyes. He guessed she wasn't used to such bold moves, and he liked that he'd still managed to knock her slightly off-kilter. Although he didn't expect her to remain that way for long.

He lowered his chin and then brought it up slowly, making it evident that he was smelling her…and that he liked what he found. The top of his nose brushed against her cheek and she gasped slightly.

He stepped back, holding her gaze captive with his. "I'm a man who always honors his debts and I've come to pay mine."

Laney blinked. "Debt…oh." She appeared to have momentarily forgotten the circumstances of their first meeting. "All expenses surrounding your release have been taken care of."

"Too vague. Who took care of the debt, Laney?"

"Mr. Armstrong."

"And your connection to him would be?"

"Client."

"Strictly?"

She smiled. "I don't see how that impacts the situation, Mr. Southard."

"Carter, please." He was tempted to press his thigh between her legs, force her skirt up and pin her against that expensive desk of hers right there before the window. But he planned to drag the hot anticipation out as long as he could.

Besides, he wasn't sure how far he could push her before she picked up the phone and called for security.

"Answer my question," he insisted. "Brother?"

A corner of her mouth turned up. "Cousin."

"Judging from your name, I'm guessing your mother's side?" He cleared his throat. "Unless Cartwright is your married name."

The other side of her mouth edged up until she was nearly smiling. "My mother's side."

He enjoyed the way she answered the question without answering the question.

Was she married? She wore no ring, but he'd met plenty of women who didn't. Whether it was a barmaid trying to encourage better tips from customers who thought she was single and therefore free game, or a taxi driver who didn't want to risk losing her ring at gunpoint, there were all sorts of reasons why women chose not to advertise their marital status.

Of course, a woman like Laney Cartwright wouldn't want to promote it because the less you knew about her, the better leverage she had.

Carter looked forward to compromising that power in every way that he could.

Laney seemed to realize that the scales were tipped a little too heavily in his favor. So he wasn't surprised when she walked back to the other side of her desk, breaking eye contact with him.

He half expected her to end the meeting. To give up the ghost and realize that indulging in a sexual duel with him benefited her not at all. Instead, she said, "I was about to head for lunch. Would you like to join me?"

He squinted at her.

She pressed the intercom button before he responded. "Violet? Have Raphael's ready a table for two for lunch, please."

And just like that the scales tipped back to her.

LANEY GREETED the maître d' with a kiss to both cheeks, as if seeing an old friend. Which, in essence, she was, since she took so many of her meals at the exclusive French restaurant.

"Miss Laney, how especially beautiful you look today. I was afraid I would not see you after your secretary called earlier to cancel your luncheon plans."

Pierre darted glances Carter's way, as if half hoping that during the conversation Carter would disappear.

"I have your favorite table all ready for you, Ms. Cartwright."

Laney swept her hand toward Carter. "Pierre, this is Mr. Southard. He'll be dining with me today."

She didn't need to say more. Pierre looked as if someone had just hit him in his snobbish head with a two-foot-long salami. And Carter stared back at him as if he didn't know whether to greet Pierre or hit him. He appeared prepared for both.

Laney hid her smile as Pierre explained to Carter that the restaurant had a dress code and asked if he wouldn't mind choosing a suitable jacket from an array they had in the cloakroom.

Laney twisted her lips, pretending that she didn't notice Carter's discomfort while challenging him to react in the way he'd like to. Namely, storm out of the uptight place.

Instead, he motioned for Pierre to lead the way.

Moments later, he came out wearing a bright green blazer bearing the crest of an exclusive club on the breast pocket and a bright yellow tie. Laney couldn't help laughing behind her hand. Not just at the garish combination, but at Pierre's chagrin and Carter's wide grin.

Pierre appeared exasperated as he led them to a table to the left, away from the kitchen and in front of the window, but he could do nothing as he watched Carter take the seat smack-dab where anyone passing could see him.

"Thank you, Pierre," Laney said after he pulled out the other chair for her.

He usually thanked her back or at the very least told her to enjoy her lunch. This time, he just gave her a little bow and then scurried away as fast as his fashionably decked feet could carry him.

The waiter came immediately, not indicating one way or another whether Carter's purposely chosen attire affronted him as he offered the wine list. Carter didn't bother reading it but handed it back and requested a beer in a frosted glass.

Laney did the same.

"I'm impressed," she said quietly, fingering the rim of her water glass and ignoring the stares from neighboring tables. "I figured you would have turned and left the instant Pierre informed you that you weren't dressed properly."

"Then it takes little to impress you."

She enjoyed it when people acted contrary to her expectations. So few did. She could usually predict exactly what a person would say. And was disappointed when they did. So when she came across the odd man like Carter, she liked to linger in his company. Just to see what he would do next.

The waiter served their beer and then informed them of the specials. Laney didn't have to look at the menu he handed her. She already knew every dish listed and what she would have. She was surprised when Carter didn't bother to open his menu, either, instead holding her gaze as the waiter finished with the specials and looked to her.

She ordered salmon with rice and then raised her brow when it was Carter's turn. He didn't even blink as he said, "Give me a strip steak, grilled. Baked potato and salad with vinegar and oil. No gravies, no funny stuff I can't identify. Just give it to me straight up."

The waiter bowed slightly, took back the menus and disappeared.

If Laney had hoped to outmaneuver him by bringing him here, she'd failed. And she couldn't have been happier.

"So," she said, taking a sip of her water, "how is it that you know my cousin Trace?"

Carter grimaced and looked around the nicely appointed room, giving a small finger salute to an older woman nearby who openly stared at him. "He shot me."

Laney nearly spewed her water over the table. "Pardon me?"

Carter's grin returned. "I said he shot me." He formed a gun with his fingers and pulled the trigger. "I have to say that if our positions had been reversed, I'd have done the same thing to him. But I would have hit him so he wouldn't get back up."

Laney had heard stories about her mother's side of the family. "A bunch of rowdy cowboys," her father would say before launching into a story about rustled cattle or gunfights or land feuds involving the branch of her family that came from the southwest part of the state.

Blake Cartwright was never flippant when telling the tales that had undoubtedly grown longer and longer over the years. Rather, he usually looked envious of a way of life so different from his own upbringing chasing oil with his father. Although occasionally guns had been involved, there had been no real honor in any of the clashes. All the disputes had revolved around money and who would be walking away with it. And it was usually Laney's grandfather.

Which explained why Laney had never had to worry about anything. She could have attended the best Ivy League colleges in the world, but had instead chosen to go to the University of Texas. Her father had been proud of the move, when she had expected him to argue with her.

Then again, her father had never acted the way she anticipated, either. Much like the man across from her.

Their salads arrived.

"To be honest with you, Ms. Cartwright—"

"Laney, please."

"Any outstanding debt is only part of the reason why I requested to see you today."

She folded a few spinach leaves onto her fork with the aid of her knife. "Oh?"

Carter took a bite of his salad, and then wiped his mouth with his napkin, resting his elbow on the table as he chased the greens with water. "Christ, they're feeding me cow food. I feel like I should be grazing."

She laughed.

He pushed his plate away and took a bread roll instead, slathering it with butter. Laney found her gaze riveted as he put the extra large bite into his mouth, chewing without much regard for etiquette. A man who was obviously hungry for more than what was on the table in front of him.

"I want you to help get me reinstated into the Corps."

4

"I DON'T NORMALLY HANDLE military cases," Laney had told him when they'd walked back to her office building a couple of blocks away from the restaurant.

"Define 'normally.'"

"Never."

Carter had figured as much. He was already working with a JAG attorney and understood the way the military worked. Especially in his case, after he'd been diagnosed with post-traumatic stress disorder, essentially a rubber stamp they used to cover every personnel problem they encountered. Mouth off to a rookie captain who couldn't tell his ass from an IED—improvised explosive device—and find yourself suspended for an amount of time to be determined by other glorified civilians who were even more clueless than the ones who had diagnosed him in the first place. Men who had no idea what it was to spend days on end in a shit-ridden sandbox without supplies and adequate protection, where everyone and no one could be your enemy, where ultimately your only friends were your weapon and your balls.

Things were just going far too slow for his liking.

Still, Laney had agreed to look into his case. See if there was something she could do to help expedite matters.

Sweat dripped from Carter's forehead, landing on the tile of his kitchen floor where he was on this second set of one hundred push-ups. Old Blue lay nearby, his head on his paws, his droopy eyes shifting up and then down as he followed Carter's movements.

It was after dark and outside the cicadas were kicking up a ruckus as they claimed the night.

This was Carter's least favorite time of day. Darkness yawned in front of him like a murky, endless ditch that no amount of dirt in the world could fill in, no matter how hard he shoveled. Shadows claimed the corners of the small, old house and lengthened, the few lamps and lightbulbs stopping them from swallowing the rooms altogether.

Carter usually did one of two things right about now. Either he sat in front of the old television set with a twelve-pack next to one ankle while Blue rested against the other. Or he hit a nearby roadhouse, seeking temporary companionship and ultimately escape in a welcoming woman's arms.

Neither option seemed palatable to him just now. Mostly because the only arms he could seem to concentrate on belonged to Laney Cartwright.

His muscles trembled as he pushed them beyond their limits. He finally collapsed to the floor, his cheek resting against the cool tile, his lungs on fire. But he paid attention to nothing outside the image of Laney's surprised and happy smile earlier at the restaurant when she realized he wasn't going anywhere.

The closest he'd come to meeting his match in a woman was JoEllen Atchison. He winced. At least that's what he liked to tell himself. It turned out JoEllen must not have returned the sentiment or else she would never have believed him capable of trying to rape her two months ago. Still, before then, he'd been convinced that they had been simpatico, two jarheads who didn't require foreplay but went straight to the deed when the need hit, their only real relationship being with the U.S. Marine Corps.

Carter rolled over and stared at the ceiling. Now with the wisdom that came with hindsight, he realized that what he and JoEllen had had was nothing but a handful of one-night stands that had occasionally included a weekend locked away in a seedy motel room with a box of pizza and a case of beer. And that somewhere down the line he had mistaken that for a relationship.

Of course, it was hard to understand the difference, because he had never really had a steady relationship with a woman. When he was younger, he'd been too busy being a Marine commander's son. There had been no real time for the usual teenage stuff outside his positions as varsity football cornerback and team captain, the roles nothing more to him than warm-up for what he would do once he enlisted in the Marines when he was eighteen.

Girls…oh, they'd been there. Lifting up their pretty

skirts and kissing him with their cherry-flavored lip gloss. But he'd never seen one of them more than three times, and even then not necessarily in a row, since he went out with other girls in between. He hadn't fooled himself into thinking that the reason he got away with such bad behavior had to do with his good looks. As his father had liked to tell him, he looked two licks shy of a full tongue bath.

No, he knew his status as football captain allowed him certain privileges. Liberties he hadn't been extended in the Corps, where one Marine was treated no different than a hundred others.

His mother…well, his mother lived down in Austin with another family. One she'd started after leaving Carter with his father when he was five, marrying another man and going on to have four more children that were no more like Carter than the sun was like the moon.

Heaving himself up from the floor, he opened the refrigerator, staring at the half-dozen bottles of beer in there, and reached for the water bottle instead. Unscrewing the top, he went to stand at the back doorway, staring out at the dark sky as he guzzled a good portion of cold water.

It wasn't often that he wondered how life would have turned out for him had his mother taken him with her instead of leaving him with his father. Only every now and again when he found himself drifting in a sea of uncertainty. As he was now.

Would he have been a lawyer like Laney? A doctor?

All four of his half siblings either boasted advanced degrees or were in the process of earning them.

Instead, the reason his mother had left his father had become a way of life for Carter, as well: the Corps.

And he had holes in his stomach knowing that they no longer wanted him.

Blue whined at his feet. Carter looked down at the old hound licking his drooping chops.

"What is it, boy?" He lifted the water bottle. "You want some of this?"

He opened the back door and led the way out onto the porch, where he poured a good portion into the dog's bowl. The hound lapped it up.

Carter dropped to sit on the edge of the small landing, letting his feet dangle over the side. On the kitchen table his M16 assault rifle lay partially disassembled where he'd been cleaning it, next to a half-eaten burger he'd picked up from a nearby diner earlier.

He spotted the waxing quarter moon rising from the other side of the trees and thought again of Laney Cartwright. Wondered what she was doing right about then.

Wondered if she was thinking about him.

LANEY LAY BACK against the down pillows piled up against her headboard, her feet tucked under the soft Egyptian cotton sheets because they always got cold with the air conditioner on. The grandfather clock her father had bought her a couple of years ago chimed the hour in the front room of her two-bedroom penthouse apartment as she leafed through the MacGregor case file, trying to figure out who might want to threaten her. Laughter caught her attention and she looked up to try to catch the joke she'd just missed on her DVD of the third season of *Sex and the City*. It wasn't long before her wandering attention wandered farther still and she was thinking about Carter Southard and the time they'd spent together earlier in the day.

So Carter Southard was a Marine.

She didn't know why she was surprised. He fit all the physical requirements of the job. And certainly the mental criteria, as well.

Still, somehow she imagined him doing something else. Say, drilling for oil. Or running a cattle ranch. Something that required him to be out in the sun all day toiling away.

Of course, he could do that as a Marine, but…

She sighed. Okay, her thoughts were veering toward the ridiculous. All because she was trying to ignore the fact that she was so enormously attracted to him she'd nearly blown off her afternoon agenda on the MacGregor case and called him. Not for social reasons. But to get the name of his JAG attorney, which he'd promised to supply.

Not for social reasons, indeed.

Although that wasn't far off the mark. She didn't want to take him to a garden party or a symphony benefit. She wanted to share her bed with him.

Laughter caught her attention again and she forced herself to look down at the file resting against the easel formed by her knees. She should be thinking about the brief meeting she'd had with a police detective after lunch. About his questions on the MacGregor case and who might want to send her the threatening note. But she hadn't been able to help him. MacGregor hadn't had an accomplice. He was being charged as the lone gunman in a convenience store robbery that had left a male clerk dead.

So who would want to warn her off the case?

Well, she certainly wasn't going to solve the mystery tonight. Not with her mind wandering to Carter every two seconds.

She closed the file and put it on the bedside table, then reached for the bottle of lotion there, smoothing a good squirt over her arms and knees before sliding farther down under the sheets.

"Do you make a habit of picking up strays?" Carter had asked her as they'd walked back to the office after lunch.

"What?"

He'd shrugged. "I can't help wondering if taking on strange cases is something you do on a regular basis, or if I'm the exception."

She'd stopped in front of the building and faced him, watching the way he squinted against the midday sun, causing fine lines to fan out from his granite eyes.

"Oh, you're definitely an exception, Carter Southard," she'd said. "And I have the feeling that this isn't the only rule you're going to inspire me to break."

Laney found herself smiling faintly at the memory.

It was more than Carter's unpredictability that engaged her; it was also the way she felt when she was around him. In a life full of dull days, he'd lit a fire she couldn't help being drawn to.

But if he'd been strictly fantasy material before, now he was very real.

She found that her hand had made its way down the silk of her nightgown, sliding over her hip bone and then back up again. Just thinking about him made her feel sexy, alive. Merely knowing that all she had to do was pick up the phone and make what her friends termed a "booty call" and he'd be over made her feel naughty for even considering it.

She bit her bottom lip. God, the way she was reacting to him, you'd think she was a virgin locked away from the world for the first twenty-eight years of her life. Not a woman who'd experienced her share of orgasms, although not as often as she'd like. Sue her, but she'd yet to find a man capable of supplying her with more than one or two. Usually after a couple of dates, the men either wanted to start staying over or wanted her to sleep at their place. And she hadn't been interested in either.

That, or they'd expected her to fawn over them, turning from a no-nonsense, ambitious attorney to a woman who could think of nothing else but making them happy, a woman with nothing but wedding dates and dinner parties on her mind.

It didn't take long for them to figure out that she didn't fit into the normal Southern girl mold. At least not yet, her father occasionally liked to joke, reminding her that time had a way of changing even the strongest, career-minded women.

She couldn't imagine herself changing, ever.

Still, even she admitted to pain when she'd spot her most recent ex with another woman. He'd make sure to introduce her to his latest conquest, who appeared to be just up his alley.

Carrie Bradshaw made a quip about men that normally would have amused her. Now she reached for the remote and shut off the television, then turned off the light, wondering if the rest of the world was out of sync with her. Or if she was out of sync with the world.

5

"So, TELL ME. Who is he?" Blake Cartwright asked.

Laney was suddenly incapable of swallowing the thinly sliced beef in her mouth. It had been two days since she'd lunched at Raphael's with Carter. Still, that didn't stop her from glancing toward the table she had sat at with him, barely seeing the older couple now lunching there.

She drank deeply from her water glass to help the food go down. "Pardon me?"

Blake pointed at her with his fork. "No pardon granted." He took a bite of his trout and then put his utensils down and dabbed at his mouth with his napkin. Her father was so different from Carter in that he'd eaten at this and similar restaurants hundreds of times and proper protocol was second nature to him. His suit was tailored, his shirt snow-white and freshly starched, his tie silk and pierced with a clip, his hair neatly trimmed. But his question and follow-up response proved that he had more in common with Carter when it came to seeing through her.

He narrowed his gaze. "You've been distracted ever since you came in. By now I usually know as many details about your latest case as your associates do, as well as what you've had for dinner the night before."

Laney's mouth dropped open. Thankfully there was nothing in it to fall out. "I can't possibly talk all that much."

Her father's grin warmed her. "Maybe not all that much. But enough for me to know today's quiet is out of character."

Laney readjusted her napkin in her lap. "I'm just a little distracted, is all. I went to see MacGregor at the county jail this morning before today's hearing." She gave a slight shiver, always uncomfortable with her visits to places where iron bars were the dominant décor. "He has no idea who might have sent me that note."

"Have you heard from the detective you gave it to?"

"Yes. No fingerprints. No unique characteristics."

"No reason to further pursue the matter."

"His words exactly."

Her father folded his hands on the edge of the table. "Would you like me to look into it?"

Blake Cartwright had had big shoes to fill, following Laney's legendary grandfather. But he had never really looked at it that way. Perhaps once he might have, but that would have been long before Laney was old enough to notice. Most men with inherited wealth were happy to accept a token role in the family business, allowing their money to make money for them. Not her father. He wanted to leave his own unique mark. And he was doing just that by establishing himself as a very successful venture capitalist.

In the past ten years alone, Laney could count fifteen of his schemes that had taken off, adding significantly to his wealth, most of them in green technology. Of course, he'd had to invest in a hundred to score on those fifteen, and she'd enjoyed hearing about every one of them, including the wacky idea of a hat that allowed advertisers to buy space on it when the owner registered with the mother Web site.

Laney realized her father was waiting for an answer, so she shook her head. "Thanks, but no. I don't feel I'm at any great risk."

"Sounds like famous last words to me."

She smiled. "God, I hope not. I didn't get into this line of work to put my life at risk. If I had wanted to do that, I would have become a police officer."

"Honest work."

"Honest work that gets you shot in the ass."

Blake laughed loudly and sat back, oblivious to the looks he got. "You know, you never did answer my question."

"What question?" She pretended an interest in finishing her meal.

"You know very well what question. I heard you were in here with another man the other day. You know, the one when you canceled your luncheon date with me so you could conduct an emergency meeting on the MacGregor case."

Laney frowned. "How could I forget how small this big city can be?"

How stupid! She should have known that word would get back to her father. Especially considering the interest that Carter had garnered. There were probably people in the room even now whom she might not know personally but who knew her father. And while none of them would openly gossip about Carter's questionable appearance (it wasn't the Texan thing to do), they would politely ask after him in a way that would get their unspoken meaning across.

"So are you planning to tell me?" her father asked again.

Laney shook her head. "No. Because he's of no concern."

And he wasn't, was he? At least not to her father. She hadn't heard from Carter since that day and was beginning to accept the fact that she might not. Which meant that there was zero chance that she'd ever introduce him to her father.

She caught herself wistfully fingering the hair at the nape of her neck and stopped, smiling at her father, who watched her curiously.

"I see," he said.

She opened her mouth to ask him what he saw, then thought better of it. She knew not to ask her father anything she wasn't ready to hear the answer to.

"Anyway, my love life is dismally boring compared to yours," she said, lobbing the conversation back in his direction.

His expression shifted as if to say, "That's more like

it," and he chuckled. "At least you're admitting to having a love life."

She didn't. But despite Carter's silence, she held out a slim hope that might change.

LANEY USUALLY TOOK the McKinney Avenue tram back and forth to work. It was convenient and fast. But in this heat, it also meant that she'd be soaked with sweat before she got to the office. So she'd taken to driving.

If her new habit had anything to do with the threatening note she'd received, she wasn't saying.

Besides, if she didn't drive to work, when else would she get to enjoy her Infiniti hybrid? The luxury vehicle was designed to please, and she liked being behind the wheel, feeling in control of her world as the city buildings loomed outside her windows.

She pressed the elevator button to take her to the garage level and then looked at her watch. After seven. Most everyone else in the company had gone home for the day. As usual, she'd let time get away from her while working out the MacGregor defense, and when she'd finally looked up, the sun was a huge, orange ball on the western horizon.

The bell dinged and the elevator doors opened. She stepped out, her footsteps echoing in the nearly empty chamber. She slowed, giving a little shiver and gripping her briefcase more tightly. If need be, she could use it as a weapon.

She rolled her eyes and took a deep breath. And just

who, exactly, was she expecting to accost her? The janitor with a broom demanding she hand over her thousand-dollar Jimmy Choos?

She was tired, that's all. And the lack of sleep was amplifying the fear that lingered in the wake of that threatening note. She didn't have anything to worry about. She hadn't committed any crime. Wronged anyone else. She was merely defending her innocent client.

And she did believe that Devon MacGregor was innocent, didn't she? While she didn't think she was an expert, she considered herself a pretty good judge of human behavior. And Devon MacGregor's pleas for her to believe him and the supporting, if meager, evidence told her that her client had been wrongfully accused.

Which meant that the real culprit was still out there somewhere.

God. Of course. That was it. Whoever had committed the crimes was probably very interested in letting Devon serve the time for them.

The thought had crossed her mind before, but she'd dismissed it. She wasn't interested in pointing the finger at anyone else, merely turning the fingers pointing at her client away from him.

The elevator dinged and she jumped.

Okay, she really needed to get a grip.

Still, she looked over her shoulder, watching to see who got out.

No one did.

The elevator doors slid shut again.

Now, that wasn't a figment of her imagination. That was just downright creepy.

Palming her key ring, she picked up her pace. Only a hundred feet separated her from her car. She kept to the middle of the floor, away from shadowy pillars, her gaze darting around for any activity. At this time of day there was none. Her quickened footsteps seemed to taunt her. She considered lightening her footfalls so she could hear if there were others. At this rate, she wouldn't hear a car engine above the sound of her own heartbeat.

She turned the corner and someone stepped out of the shadows. She cried out and swung her briefcase, simultaneously trying to figure out the safest escape route. The stranger was between her and her car, so that was out. It was a long way back to the elevator and the stairs. The closest route was the spiraling ramp leading out onto the street.

"Whoa."

A man's voice. A familiar man's voice.

She stared into Carter Southard's handsomely surprised face when he righted himself after ducking.

"Jesus," Laney said, leaning her hand against the trunk of her car. "What are you trying to do? Scare the spirits out of me?"

He reached out and took her briefcase from her other hand, setting it closer to the car door. "Was that the best you could do? Swing your bag?"

Laney managed to get her breathing under control

and stood straight. "You mean you were deliberately trying to frighten me? To see what I would do?"

He grinned. "No. I wasn't. But in hindsight, I suppose my stepping out like that probably wasn't the smartest move."

"You can say that again."

"I think once is enough."

"Funny. Very funny." Laney rubbed her arms. "What are you doing here, anyway?"

He tucked his hands into his front jeans pockets. "I wanted to get you that information I promised. Sorry it's so late. But I told my neighbor that I'd help him repair his fence. Turned into a two-day job and I just finally knocked off." He glanced toward the elevator. "I figured you as the workaholic type, so I thought it was a pretty good bet you'd still be here. And since the lobby was closed, this was my best chance for entry."

"Yes, well," she said, looking around at shadows that didn't seem as sinister with Carter at her side. "I'll have to have a talk with management about this."

"Might be a good idea. At least they could make sure the parking attendant doesn't think sleeping with his feet up on the counter is part of his job description."

"How did you know this was my car?"

"Educated guess." He gestured toward the luxury vehicle. "But that's not what drew me over this way. I'd planned to come up to the office."

She grimaced at him as he stepped to the side, revealing the flat front tire.

"Great," she said, exasperated, wondering if her auto service could gain access to the garage.

"That wouldn't be so bad," Carter said, "if the other tire wasn't flat, too. One flat tire, fate. Two? Someone wanted to make it difficult for you to get home tonight."

Laney slowly walked toward the front of the car, considering the damage.

"See that," Carter said, pointing to the sidewall. "Looks like a knife slash."

Laney shuddered, feeling as if a knife-wielding stranger was in front of her instead of long gone.

"What's this?" she said.

She leaned forward, spotting a note under the wiper, not unlike the one she'd received in the mail a couple of days ago. She pulled it out.

"Drop the MacGregor case. Now." Next to the words was the number two.

"That doesn't look good to me," Carter said, his voice low and gravelly. "That doesn't look good to me at all."

6

AN HOUR LATER, the police had come and gone, assuring her that the detective who had taken her earlier report would be informed of the latest development; Laney's tires had been replaced by her auto service, and Carter stood facing her once again, blessedly alone. And without a briefcase being swung at his head.

He resisted the desire to reach out and push back a few strands of errant hair. Aw, hell, who was he kidding? He'd never been the best at restraint, and he saw no real benefit in starting now. She appeared shaken, in need of protection. Yet just under the surface shone hard steel, telling him that she was much stronger than she looked. It would take more, much more, than a couple of threatening notes to knock her over.

Laney looked down but didn't pull away as he rubbed the baby-soft strands of her hair between his thumb and forefinger. Then he brushed them away from her milky cheek and tucked them behind her ear, wondering at the delicate shell and the sight of his dark hand against her light skin.

"Thanks for staying," she said quietly. "I really appreciate it." She briefly bit the side of her bottom lip and looked around, apparently still seeing ghosts. "But if it's all the same to you, I'd prefer not to spend another minute more than I have to in this garage."

Carter smiled. "I understand." He gestured to his bike. "Let me follow you home."

"That's not necessary," she said a little too quickly, then her gaze lingered on his. "Really, it isn't. I don't think I'll be finding another note tonight." She looked into the cavernous depths of the garage. "At least I hope not."

"I'd feel better if I saw you home. Where do you live?"

She told him. He raised a brow at the downtown address. He'd expected something in one of the swanky Texas subdivisions. Not that Dallas didn't boast more than a few high-rent condos downtown, but somehow he figured her for an estate development.

"Apartment building?" he asked.

She nodded.

"Front doorman?"

"Yes. And closed-circuit cameras and the latest in security."

That made him feel better. At least marginally. "Good. But let's get you there first. Have you had anything to eat?"

"What? Um, no."

He opened the driver's door of her car, indicating that she should climb in.

"Lead the way," he said.

WOULD HE WANT to come in? Laney wondered. Did she dare invite him up?

Her palms grew damp against the steering wheel. The classical station her car radio was tuned in to was failing to capture her attention. She drifted into the opposite lane twice since she was more focused on watching Carter in her rearview mirror than on the road in front of her.

Only an hour ago, she had thought he was gone from her life, that he had no plan to follow up on his request for help. Then he'd appeared out of nowhere, nearly scaring the socks off her.

Now he was following her on his Harley, looking particularly hot in his snug black T-shirt and sunglasses, his longish dark hair blowing in the wind. Knowing a bit about his military background, he could have been out for a ride or on his way to the front line.

The thought of him looking after her like this made her hot, and she squeezed her thighs together.

When was the last time she'd felt this way? Had she ever felt this way? She couldn't say. What she did know was that none of the suited, professional men she'd briefly dated over the past couple of years had made her mouth go this dry. And her heart beat in an uneven rhythm in her chest at the thought that the man on the motorcycle wanted her.

Of course, part of her response could be attributed to her tires being slashed. The violent act had opened her eyes to the seriousness of the threat in a way the first note had not.

Still, she couldn't think about that now. She seemed utterly incapable of thinking about anything but the man behind her.

She pulled in front of her apartment building and began to roll down her window. To thank him or invite him up—she wasn't sure which. Instead, he took the decision out of her hands by offering a brief wave and roaring down the street.

Interesting…

Okay, maybe this unpredictability wasn't as attractive as she'd first thought. She'd never considered he would merely drive off.

Laney watched the back of his bike. Despite her disappointment, she couldn't help thinking he looked as good going as he did coming. She reluctantly got out of her car, deciding to ask the doorman to arrange for the Infiniti to be parked in the underground garage. She didn't have the stomach right now to do it herself.

A short time later, she'd showered and was in her robe in her penthouse apartment, considering the contents of her refrigerator, when the apartment intercom buzzed.

"Yes, Roger?" she asked the front doorman.

There was a pause, making her wonder if something else had happened.

"Sorry to bother you, Ms. Cartwright, but there's a Mr. Southard here to see you."

Roger's pause hadn't been reluctance to share bad news, but grudging acceptance that he'd have to introduce a man who must look incredibly out of place in the upscale lobby.

Laney swallowed hard. Carter had come back?

"Ms. Cartwright?"

"What? Oh. Yes. Yes, Roger. Send him right up."

"Very good, miss."

Laney rushed toward her bedroom to put something on, but there wasn't time for that. So she rushed back and collected her shoes and jacket from the floor and chair near the door and tossed both into the closet. She'd just closed the door when the bell rang. She leaned against the wall for a few moments, taking deep breaths. Then she affixed a smile to her face and opened the front door.

"Hope you like anchovies," Carter said, entering with a box of pizza and a six-pack of beer.

OH, WHEN LANEY OPENED the door, she'd tried to act as if everything were all right. But Carter knew better. She'd been shaken by the incident in the parking garage more than she would admit.

Not that he could blame her. The office neighborhood wasn't the type where random tire slashings by juveniles were a regular occurrence. Besides, juveniles didn't normally leave threatening notes behind.

Laney had told him that this was the second such note. Not that she'd had to. Both her reaction to it, and the number two written on it, had told him as much.

He didn't make it a point to keep up with local news. He watched it, but absorbed very little beyond the weather report. If rain was forecast, he had to put away his bike and take out the old pickup he sometimes drove. But when she told him the threats were connected to the MacGregor case, he knew what she was referring to. He had seen the broadcast videos of the kid in the mask robbing the convenience store and shooting the clerk, who had already handed over the money, his death meaningless. The grainy footage had been run no more than a dozen times the night it was released to the media.

Laney had excused herself after putting the pizza on the counter that separated the kitchen from the living room and the beer in the fridge, and had emerged from what he guessed was her bedroom in a pair of snug white slacks and clingy top. The same color that was everywhere he looked.

He wished she had stayed in the short, white silk robe. Then again, if she had, he probably wouldn't have had the fortitude to sit talking with her at the counter, but would have given in to the desire to ravish her in five minutes flat.

He watched with a raised brow as she polished off her third piece of pizza and chased it with the rest of her second beer.

She seemed to read his thoughts and stopped chewing. It took her a moment to swallow what was in her mouth. "Oh my God. I'm a pig."

He'd figured she hadn't been paying much attention as she talked. About nothing in particular and everything in general.

"I'm going to have to call my trainer to come an extra day this week."

"Trainer?"

She put another piece of pizza on his plate and then wiped her hands. "Yes. Travis. He comes over at six in the morning three days a week to help me work out."

Carter wasn't sure how he felt about a man being around her for that much time, much less getting to see her sweat.

"Usually he takes me running, and then we stop by the gym up the street where he works out a strength training routine."

He gave her a once-over. That would certainly explain why she was so slender and fit. And he fully admitted the desire to see exactly how fit. Without the too-white clothes she wore.

Carter took a swig from his bottle and looked around the place. The penthouse. He wasn't surprised. He'd pretty much nailed Ms. Laney Cartwright's entitled background from the instant he laid eyes on her. And everything he'd seen since only confirmed that.

"Been here long?" he asked.

"Three years. No, wait. Four."

"I take it you like white?"

She laughed. "Daddy's house has always been such a bachelor pad—dark paneling, dark leather furniture—that I couldn't wait to get my own place and lighten things up."

Ah, a daddy's girl. "Bachelor?"

"Mmm. My mom died when I was twelve. He's been

single ever since." She smiled as she absently folded her napkin. "He says that's because he was afraid I'd chase off any other woman, but it's not true. I can't even remember him bringing anyone home."

"And now?"

She threaded her fingers through curls that were soft and white blond and then leaned her head against the heel of her hand. "My, aren't you the curious one."

She had no idea.

"As for Daddy…I guess you could say that we're both kind of serial daters."

Now that her mind was no longer on the pizza and she'd emptied her head of all the apparently random information floating around there, she grew still. Too still. And focused on him with a laser intensity.

She was sexy when she was eating.

She was drop-dead gorgeous when she was looking at him like she was now. As if she wanted to eat him.

Carter cleared his throat and eyed the piece of pizza. He suspected he wouldn't be able to swallow a bite. His jeans were already growing unbearably tight. And the desire to kiss Laney's decadent mouth was growing right along with other strategic areas.

"So…" Laney practically purred, crossing her legs.

Carter watched the way she wrapped one leg around the other, rubbing the top of her bare foot against her other calf.

"So, admit it. Now that I'm acting like a damsel in distress, you're looking to take advantage."

"The thought had crossed my mind."

But he was battling it for all he was worth. A woman had caused him all sorts of trouble two months ago. He wasn't in the market for that kind of trouble again. At least not so soon.

Before he knew that's what he was going to do, he'd grabbed her hips and hauled her so that she was sitting on top of the counter in front of him. He swept the pizza box and beer bottles off to the side.

So much for good intentions.

Laney gasped, apparently surprised by his actions. And pleased, if her sparkling, provocative eyes and catlike grin were any indication.

If they weren't, the way she positioned her feet on either side of his hips was.

"Mmm," Laney hummed, her pupils growing large. "I would never have guessed."

Carter tightened his hands on her hips, raking his gaze over her beautiful face, down to her breasts and farther still to the vee of her crotch.

"I'd say you have a lot to learn about me, then," he said as he leaned in and finally sampled the mouth that had been driving him crazy since the first time he'd laid eyes on it.

7

FOR REASONS SHE COULDN'T QUITE put her finger on, Laney felt as if she'd just taken a deep breath of air, and when she exhaled, all the anxiety and uneasiness connected with the tire slashing were gone. A languid, almost intoxicating responsiveness flowed through her, making her überaware of Carter wedged between her thighs.

Thighs that were clothed and yearning to be otherwise.

Laney entwined her fingers in his hair, finding it slightly curly as it grew out of what was probably a crew cut. With any other man, she might have found Carter's spontaneous action a bit too forward. But not with him. She knew on a fundamental level that they'd been building toward this from the moment they first met. And there was a breathless beauty in allowing it to unfold naturally.

Carter squeezed her hips, pressing her more insistently against his hardness. Laney licked her lips even as she eyed his full mouth, mere inches away from hers.

"You seem awfully confident," she whispered.

His knowing grin made her womanhood throb. "Let's just say I'm an expert when it comes to recon."

He worked his fingers under her top and skimmed his left hand up until the material bunched on her chest. He cupped her breast. She lost the ability to draw a breath.

"And what does your fact-finding mission prove?"

The rough pad of his thumb flicked over her taut nipple through the fabric of her bra. "That you're very amenable to any…invasion I might like to stage."

Laney shifted, the tension curling in her stomach nearly unbearable as he tunneled his fingers under her bra cup. "And do you?"

He reached around and easily popped her bra catch, causing the material to slip forward, leaving her semibare to his gaze. "Do I what?"

"Want to stage an invasion?"

His focus shifted from her breasts to her face. "I want to conquer everything in my sight."

Laney brazenly challenged him. "So what's stopping you?"

Later, she wouldn't be able to recount exactly what had happened. One moment they'd been locked in an unspoken battle of gazes, the next he claimed her mouth completely, plundering the depths with his tongue, demanding a surrender she refused to grant. Instead, she gave back, planning her own line of attack as she reached for his T-shirt and pulled the cotton up over his head. His skin drew tight over well-developed muscles, indicating that he hadn't been exactly sedentary since he'd been released from service. While she'd never dated a slouch, she'd also never dated a man with arguably zero body fat, a mixture of hard steel and pliable skin.

He countered her move by stripping her of her top and bra. But it wasn't until he took her right breast deep into his mouth that she relinquished important ground, incapable of doing anything but closing her eyes and relishing the delicious sensations rippling through her.

He cupped both breasts in his hands, licking and sucking and squeezing. Laney wriggled so her softness pressed more insistently against his hardness. She wanted him more than she wanted to press her advantage. Rather than counter him move for move, she surrendered, for the moment conceding that he might be the better ruler of her body.

And as he stripped her of the last piece of clothing, she was proven very, very right.

LANEY TASTED like ripe Texas peaches generously topped with fresh cream. And Carter's desire to swallow her whole inflated with each kiss and every lick.

He had suspected she'd just showered when she'd opened the door in her robe, but what he was sampling had nothing to do with soap and everything to do with the delectable woman in his arms.

Jesus, she was more beautiful without clothes. Something he didn't come across every day. Lingerie could go a long way toward hiding a woman's flaws. A bra could compensate for small breasts or support saggy ones. But not when it came to Laney. Her snow-white tits sat full and pert, her rosy pink nipples puckered, just begging for the attention he was giving them.

She shifted restlessly against his pulsing erection. He reluctantly ceased ravishing her generous chest and grasped her bare hips, hoisting her to sit back on the counter in front of him. He allowed his gaze to roam over every sweet inch of her. Every soft curve, every shallow hollow. She leaned against her elbows, watching him watch her through heavily lidded eyes. If he could bottle and sell the way he felt in that one moment, he'd be a millionaire a thousand times over.

In fact, he knew a moment of hesitation. Laney was almost too perfect. While he refused to accept that he was socially or mentally lower than her, when you put her brains and beauty together into that phenomenally sexy package…well, she was surely too good for the likes of him.

"Not having second thoughts, are you, Marine?" she whispered, her pink tongue flicking out to slide across her full, kissed red lips.

Was he ever. Not because he didn't want her, but because in that one moment he wanted her too much.

She spread her thighs, boldly baring herself to his gaze.

Carter groaned at the sight of the springy white-blond curls there. If he'd had any doubt as to the genuine color of her hair, he didn't anymore. There was no way this color came out of a bottle.

He couldn't help himself. He had to touch her. Had to see if she tasted as good as she looked.

He slid his fingers down her smooth legs, parting her knees even farther. The rounded mound that was the focus of his attention split slightly, the fleshy outer lips swollen, the inner the same deep pink color as her nipples.

He set his back teeth to keep from taking her right then. Burying himself so deep inside her he was afraid he'd never want to come out.

Instead, with more control than he knew he possessed, he followed the line of her slit with the pads of his thumbs, then opened the protective soft tissue, revealing the tight pearl at the apex. He leaned in and ran his tongue over it.

Laney gasped, her entire body shivering.

Carter fastened his lips around the engorged flesh and suckled it much as he would if he were licking the juice from an oyster.

Laney cried out just as he thrust two fingers deep inside her dripping channel, more to feel her muscles tighten and convulse around him than to draw out the sensations.

Before she could recover, Carter had sheathed himself with a condom he'd freed from his back jeans pocket and parted her farther, positioning the engorged head of his erection against her. He looked at her, giving her one last chance to refuse him.

Instead, she bore down against him, forcing entrance

even as she dropped her head back, her muscles instantly contracting around him again.

Carter was helpless and followed quickly after her.

THE NEXT FEW DAYS, the very air around Laney seemed to be charged with electricity. Everything crackled and popped. Her body hummed, her mind wandered, taking her back to the night before and the white-hot sex she'd had with Carter Southard.

In her entire life, she couldn't remember a time when she felt so aware of herself as a woman. So uninhibited. She'd hungrily taken and unselfishly given, utterly insatiable even after they'd moved their activities to her bedroom.

She must have finally fallen asleep somewhere around three in the morning. She had slept through the 5:00 a.m. phone call from her personal trainer. She didn't wake up until after nine when, finally, the ringing phone caught her attention. It had been Violet from the office, informing her of her lateness.

Of course, Carter had been long gone, having let himself out at some point. She hadn't bothered looking for a note. Didn't need to look for one. There was no way he could have been unmoved by what they'd shared. So she never entertained the thought that she might not see him again.

But now it was Friday afternoon, two days since she'd seen Carter. She was amazed at how quickly the time went by and wondered if she should call him.

She glanced at the file on the corner of her desk. It contained the documents Carter's JAG attorney had faxed over late last night. She'd found them waiting for her when she got in.

She opened the file and read the reason for Carter's suspension: "Subject is reportedly demonstrating extreme symptoms of post-traumatic stress disorder and in his doctor's opinion is close to a psychotic breakdown."

Laney tapped her pencil on her desk. The notation didn't seem at all in line with what she knew about Carter. He showed no signs of PTSD as far as she could tell. Something must be going on for him to be suspended at a time when the military was stretched thin and given that his overall record was impeccable.

Of course, it would be just her luck to fall for a guy who was a closet schizophrenic.

The intercom buzzed. Laney absently reached out to press the button without taking her gaze away from the file in front of her. "What is it, Violet?"

"You wanted me to remind you to visit the Mac-Gregor kid?"

Laney frowned and shifted her watch around her wrist so she could read the face. "Thanks, Violet."

"No problem."

She closed Carter's file and collected the items she needed for her visit to the county jail.

CARTER PACED the sidewalk for the third time, beginning to build up a sweat in the afternoon sun. He knew there was a reason he hated cities. All that damn concrete absorbing the heat like a charcoal briquette and then passing it back to whatever idiot happened to be standing on top of it.

In this case, it was him.

He stopped and looked at the church in front of him. He'd parked his bike a couple of blocks away instead of in the church parking lot. He'd thought the walk would do him good and had hoped that not having access to easy escape would compel him to go inside, rather than back to his bike like the half-dozen other times he'd come here.

Instead, he was being cooked to well done on the damn sidewalk.

"Can I help you?"

Carter turned toward a young man in Marine khakis. He was apparently going inside for the group meeting of PTSD-R-Us and had caught Carter loitering outside.

The kid couldn't be any older than twenty-two, and looked even younger when he grinned, despite the buzz cut and the size of his guns.

"Hey, I'm Matt Starkweather."

Carter eyed the hand the Marine held out. He didn't dare not take it.

"And you are?" the guy asked when he didn't say anything.

"I'm…late for an appointment," he said, pulling his hand back and walking quickly away.

God damn it all to hell. He wouldn't stand a chance

of getting back into the Marines if he didn't attend the group meeting being held in that church. Then why in the hell was he having such a hard time going inside?

Why? Because he didn't have a problem, that's why.

"We'll be here same time tomorrow," Starkweather called out behind him.

Carter threw him a look over his shoulder and grumbled something that may have sounded like a thanks. And then he practically ran to his bike, feeling as if the devil were on his heels.

If it weren't for Laney, he wouldn't have tried to come. But damn fool that he was, he'd gotten up yesterday morning feeling like a new man and had decided it was long past time he did a little work on the old one.

The problem was, the old one was fighting him all the way.

He didn't need help. That's what he'd told all those damn military shrinks over in Afghanistan. And nothing had changed since then. They should be putting him back on the front line where he could do the most good. Being mothballed here in the States wasn't helping anyone. Least of all him.

He got onto his bike and revved the motor, feeling worse than he had since he had been forced onto that transport to come back here.

And the only one who seemed able to make him feel better was Laney.

He pointed his bike in the direction of her office.

8

LANEY STARED at the kid across from her. She couldn't imagine how anyone could think him responsible for the crime he was charged with. But given the evidence against him, she was worried she might not be able to prove his innocence.

He was all of nineteen years old, a UT sophomore majoring in aeronautics. His record was clean outside a couple of minor incidents when he was fourteen involving graffiti and petty theft. Nothing that would indicate him remotely capable of murder one in the armed robbery of a convenience store where there was only sixty-five dollars in the till.

"Devon, you have to tell me who could have done this."

Devon blinked big blue eyes at her. "I have no idea, Laney."

The MacGregors went way back with her family. Laney had even babysat the boy across from her, along with his older sister, a couple of times when she was a teen. Although she hadn't needed to work, it was considered a rite of passage for kids her age. Babysitting was a way to get out of the house and out from under your parents' thumb so you could do what you wanted.

Of course, she'd never felt the need to get away from her father, but she had found she enjoyed babysitting. It was a form of role-playing. Stepping into someone else's life for a few hours, playing mom to their kids, housekeeper to their home. And after the night was through, you got to return to your own life.

And the kids she'd minded had always been good. Including Devon and his sister.

Which was why she hadn't hesitated to take on his case.

She tucked away her notepad. "You do realize that the trial begins a week from Monday?" she asked.

He dropped his chin to his chest. "Yes." He looked back up at her. "But how am I supposed to tell you something I have no way of knowing? All I know is that I did not rob that store that night and kill that guy."

"Then someone is setting you up, Devon. And it's possible you may know who."

He shook his head. "There's no one."

"Fine. Give it some more thought. If anything occurs to you, call my office."

"I will."

She was being threatened, so someone out there was afraid she would find out the truth. But what truth? Or were they afraid she'd get Devon off and have the light shone in another direction? Possibly theirs.

She needed to find out who was behind the threats

before an innocent kid went to jail for a crime he didn't commit.

And before her stalker slashed more than her tires.

She motioned the guard to be let out of the meeting room after saying goodbye to Devon. The door opened and then closed after her as she headed down the hall, pushing her notepad into her purse.

"Oh, hi, Laney."

She looked up to see Devon's sister. "Hi, Darcy. You here to visit Devon?"

The younger woman smiled. "What? Do you think I might know somebody else in here?"

Laney laughed. "You never know." Then it occurred to her that while Devon might not have a clue who was trying to set him up, his sister might. "Wait a minute, Darcy. Do you mind if I talk to you for a bit?"

"Sure. But I don't know how long they'll hold Devon."

"I'll be brief." She put her case down on the hall floor. "Do you have any idea who might want to set up Devon?"

"No. But his girlfriend might."

Girlfriend? Devon had told her he didn't have a girlfriend. Or friends, period, for that matter, outside a few kids at the university.

"Do you happen to have her contact information?"

"Sure."

Laney handed Darcy her pad and watched as she wrote a name and number down. "That's her cell. Or was. I haven't talked to her since Devon's arrest, but I assume that's the number she still uses."

Laney accepted the pad back. "Thanks, Darcy."

"Don't mention it."

"GET READY for a night out. Dress casual. Pick you up at nine."

Laney returned to her office to find the note on her desk. It was unsigned, but she didn't have to wonder who it was from. No one else would dare be as confident to leave her such a message and expect her to honor it.

No one but Carter Southard.

Now she was at her penthouse, rating the contents of her walk-in closet.

She really needed this respite in the middle of the chaotic sea she was navigating at work. The police didn't have any clues about who might have vandalized her car or sent her the notes. Her defense options for Devon's trial were limited to questioning every piece of evidence the prosecution was going to present, hoping to chip away at it and create that all-important shadow of doubt. She'd spent the afternoon with the defense team, lining up charts and photos and following up with witnesses to make sure everything—at least from an or-ganizational standpoint—would go smoothly. Junior at-torneys Dave Matthews and Matt Johnson would be cocounsels, along with senior partner Harold Reasoner.

Normally, she would be spending the night going over her opening statement, editing it, reworking it. Sleep would be the last thing on her agenda, much less any thought of fun. But when she'd read the note, and remembered her night with Carter, she knew that a fresh perspective was exactly what she needed at this point.

At least that's what she told herself. If the thought of seeing Carter made her want to leave the real world behind for just a few precious hours, she wasn't admitting it.

She stood before her open closet door. Casual. He'd said to be casual. The word could mean anything. There were at least three categories of casual. There was the "clean out the garage" variety, where old jeans, T-shirt and tennis shoes were the name of the game. The "let's go out for pizza" casual. And "dressy casual."

Okay, she could rule out the first one. Even Carter wouldn't take her to clean out his garage at nine o'clock on a Friday night.

But he had said "a night out" which could mean comfortable shoes for a walk through the downtown district.

Oh, what was she worried about? He'd be there in five minutes. She could find out exactly where he planned to take her and decide if what she had on was too dressy or not.

She dumped the pile of discarded clothes onto the floor and then closed the closet doors. She hadn't tried on more than two outfits for a night out in a long time. Especially not for a casual one.

Then why did her stomach feel as if the bottom had been cut out of it? And why did every inch of her skin tingle as if Carter had just blown his hot breath against it?

The intercom rang.

"Mr. Southard would like you to meet him at the curb, Ms. Cartwright."

"Thanks, Roger."

Damn. So much for her plan to change clothes if need be. Looked like she was stuck with what she had on—a gauzy white skirt, short tan cowboy boots and a white, scoop-necked top. Just to be on the safe side, she grabbed a light tan jacket and hurried to meet him.

"Evening, Ms. Cartwright," the doorman said.

"Hello, Roger. Where…"

She spotted Carter leaning against his motorcycle by the curb. A shiver of awareness drifted over her at the sight of him. His booted feet were crossed at the ankles, and a crisp white T-shirt pulled tight over his wide chest. His arms were crossed in front of him, emphasizing the width of his triceps and calling attention to his USMC tattoo. He wore a brown leather vest over his T-shirt and a matching cowboy hat. Sunglasses blocked his expression as he watched her come through the door.

"Something tells me I might not be dressed appropriately," she said, twisting her lips wryly.

"You worry too much about the unimportant. You're dressed just fine."

She gestured toward the bike. "Not for riding that."

"Why not?"

A challenge. He was challenging her. She looked down at her skirt. Given the slightly translucent quality of the fabric, it fell in several layers to just below her knees. She'd never ridden on a bike before, let alone in a skirt. But her father liked to joke that she was born on the back of a horse, and she'd spent a great deal of time in the stables on her father's estate while growing up. Surely the two couldn't be all that different.

Carter threw his right leg over the seat and started the engine. The loud roar evened out to a strong purr as he patted the seat behind him.

Fine.

Laney bunched the front of her skirt up to the top of her thighs, acutely aware he was watching her every move, and then straddled the bike behind him, scooting up close and personal.

"Mmm, am I doing it right?" she whispered into his ear, finding something very appealing about sitting so close to him. He smelled of laundry detergent and limes.

He handed her a black helmet that came to just over her ears and strapped under her chin. "You're doing it just perfect, darlin'."

The Harley leaped forward. Laney grabbed him around the waist to keep from falling off. She caught his naughty grin in the rearview mirror and knew instantly that he'd done that on purpose. She scooted closer so that her crotch rested against the back of his jeans. His grin melted into a suggestive smile.

The engine humming beneath Laney was oddly relaxing. The open air around her was freeing. The man between her thighs was hot. The engine also helped drown out the sounds of other vehicles around them. In fact, the world seemed to fade away, leaving just her, Carter and the bike.

For a moment, she wished that he didn't have anything planned other than a nice, long ride out of town. She wanted to see what the summer sky looked like from the back of the bike when darkness began to fall and the stars dotted the night.

She flattened her hands against his waist and slid them around until they rested low on his hard abs. She felt his quick intake of breath and smiled, her cheek resting against his shoulder. The rich scent of leather and cotton teased her senses as she watched the city streets quickly give way to the suburbs and then the wide, open plains.

Mmm, yes. In that one instant she wanted for nothing.

Unfortunately, Carter apparently did have a destination in mind. The bike slowed and he pulled off the road. Laney reluctantly lifted her chin and found they were at a place they had passed a good twenty minutes ago.

"You could have kept going," she said into Carter's ear.

"And miss what I have in mind? Not a chance."

Laney climbed off the bike, immediately missing the vibration. Carter pushed the Harley up onto its stand and climbed off. He took his hat off, ran his fingers through his hair and grinned at her.

"You ready?"

"Ready for what?"

He nodded toward the honky-tonk next door.

She smiled back at him. "I was born ready."

MAGGIE'S BOOT-SCOOTIN' Saloon was not a place Ms. Laney Cartwright would have ever entered on her own steam. Still, even in her designer duds, and obviously out of her element, she was up for the challenge he'd presented her with.

Of course, if he was having trouble answering *why* he'd felt compelled to challenge her, well, that was between him and the dance floor.

Truth was, he'd been struggling with his fierce reaction to their lovemaking the other night. Despite his experience, he was sure that his memory of her satiny smooth skin, the sound of her soft sighs, the perfect sex had to be an illusion, something conjured up by a subconscious that had been searching for the same but had never found it. There was no way it was real. It couldn't be. Because stuff like that didn't exist. And even if it did, it never happened to him.

With his hand low on her back, he led Laney toward the long bar at the far end of the large saloon, watching her look around in fascination. The place was already packed to overflowing with some people seated and enjoying dinner from the limited menu of fried items, others jumping on the dance floor, blocking a clear view of the band that filled the large area with heart-pulsing country and western music.

"What'll you have?" the barmaid asked him. Her tight T-shirt had Maggie's written across it.

Carter looked at Laney.

She shrugged. "Order for me."

He placed a request for two bottles of beer and then leaned against the bar.

Laney sparkled like a polished diamond among the rough rocks around her. Carter didn't come to places like this much himself, but he'd been curious to see how Laney might react in unfamiliar territory.

Their beers were delivered and Carter paid for them, handing Laney hers. She thanked him and took a long sip, licking her lips in a way that made his groin tighten.

The song ended and the band slid into a slow ballad, the lights going low. The dance floor filled with couples.

Laney put her bottle on the bar. "So, cowboy, were you planning on asking me to dance? Or did we just come here to watch?"

9

LANEY'S HEAD was cloudy and she felt unsteady on her feet. But she'd only had a sip of beer, so she couldn't be drunk. At least not on beer. But as Carter skillfully led her around the dance floor in a boot-dragging two-step, his beer bottle hanging from his hooked index finger over her left shoulder, she was afraid that if she were given a Breathalyzer test, she'd be way over the legal limit for what any hot-blooded woman could take while in the arms of a hot man.

Oh, she knew how to dance. While she'd never been to a place like Maggie's, a good Texas girl didn't pass the age of seven without knowing how to two-step. But in the venues where she usually danced, the couples looked more as if they were doing a Viennese waltz, not what the people around her were doing.

What she and Carter were doing.

Every time he got the chance, he brushed the top of his hard thigh between her legs. The first time she'd gasped and nearly stumbled, the electricity joining her to him nearly knocking her off balance. The second time wasn't any better. But then she fell into the easy, naughty rhythm he set, doing a bit of tantalizing of her own by grazing the tips of her breasts against his chest just so, rubbing her nose against the line of his jaw like that, until they weren't so much two people but one.

Laney's eyelids drifted closed, and again she experienced that strange feeling that the world had fallen away, leaving just the small bit of earth they stood on. She surrendered to the beat of the music. To the feel of Carter against her. To the yearnings of her own heart.

"You keep moving against me like that, Ms. Cartwright, I'm not sure what I'll do," Carter whispered into her ear.

She shivered from boot to earring, thinking that whatever he had in mind, she'd welcome it wholeheartedly. "I could say the same of you, Mr. Southard."

They danced through this set and into the next, their beer forgotten as they gave themselves over to the music and their growing desire, bodies shimmying and shaking and brushing up against each other in a primitive rite as old as time.

The overhead lights were turned on and off and final call for alcohol made. Laney was genuinely surprised they'd spent the whole night there. It felt as if they'd just arrived.

"Let's get out of here," Carter said, grasping her hand and leading her toward the door.

Laney was only too happy to oblige.

TOO FAST...

The two words ran around and around Carter's mind

as he rode back toward the city, Laney wrapped around him from behind. Even though he couldn't look into her face, he had the distinct feeling that he was drowning in her big, blue eyes.

Christ, what was going on? He'd meant to have a simple fling. Sleep with her and move on. But with every moment that passed, he wanted to spend another day with her. Couldn't seem to shake her from his mind, couldn't stop his body from wanting hers.

He pulled off an exit ramp just short of the turnoff for the city. Laney shifted.

"Where are we going?"

He didn't answer her.

"Are you taking me to your place?"

Oh, hell no. The last place he would ever take her was to his place.

Then again, maybe it was exactly the place he should take her. But he wasn't ready for that. Not yet. Baring that much of his life made him feel sick to his stomach.

Instead, he pulled off into the parking lot of an old roadhouse bar. There were other bikes and beat-up pickup trucks in front. He'd never been to this particular bar before, but he'd spent his fair share of time in others just like it.

"What's this?" Laney asked as he got off the bike to stand next to her.

"I thought we might stop for a nightcap."

He didn't miss her frown, despite her attempt to cover it up. "I thought we had enough at the saloon."

He grinned and led her to the door. It opened, spitting out two guys staggering their way into the night. Carter caught it and motioned for her to enter. She did so. And the reservation he'd expected to see at the saloon came out clearly now.

The clientele here weren't dressed in their Sunday best. Most of them wore the same clothes they'd probably worked in that day, filling the interior of the establishment with the smell of unwashed bodies and beer. He even detected the stench of vomit, and the bleach-based cleaner the owner had probably used to try to cover it.

Three quarters of the bar's patrons were male and more than halfway toward their next hangover. Carter pulled out a stool for Laney at the long, battle-scarred bar and then sat next to her. The stocky bartender asked him what they wanted.

"Give us two shots of Wild Turkey with draft chasers."

When the bartender walked away, Laney leaned closer to him. "Don't all places stop serving liquor at the same time?"

Carter grinned at her. "They're supposed to."

"Couldn't he lose his license?"

"Sure. If anyone reported him." He nodded toward the clientele. Those who didn't have their chins resting against the top of their glasses were openly appreciating Laney's presence. "I think that's the last thing on any of these guys' minds."

The bartender served them and then slid over a bowl

of cheap peanuts sitting in front of another customer who paid him no mind. In the corner, the jukebox blared a Hank Williams classic that somehow held a different kind of meaning in a place like this. Rather than inspiring patrons to dance, it stirred them to order another drink.

"God," Laney said quietly, "I haven't been here five minutes and I'm already feeling sorry for myself."

Carter raised his shot glass and she did the same. "To real life."

She searched his face. "To a more upbeat song."

Laney shuddered as she swallowed the bourbon. He pushed the glass of beer toward her and she grasped it with both hands, taking a long pull from the foamy depths.

She coughed into her hand. "So…come here often?"

Carter dropped his head and grinned. "Not here. No. But to a place like this."

She squinted at him. Down the bar to his right sat a young couple, likely married. They'd both obviously drunk more than they should have and were beginning to argue. The man accused her of flirting with a guy at one of the two pool tables. She accused him of being more like a father than a husband, offering up her wrist as proof that he had no shackles on her.

Laney somehow managed to shut the argument out as she continued looking at him.

"Why?"

The simple word was enough to knock Carter back on his boot heels.

"Why not?" he said back.

The people here were more like him than the people who ran in her circles. The beer was cheap, the surroundings unassuming; the jukebox had a good selection of oldies, and the kitchen could even rustle up a bowl of chili or nachos or a burger for you if you didn't feel like going anywhere else to eat.

The wife of the arguing couple stormed off in the direction of the restrooms, staggering through the smattering of tables and their occupants toward the hall at the far end of the room.

Carter finished his beer and put in an order for another round, shots included.

He didn't miss Laney's frown. It was the first he'd seen from her. And although it was what he'd been angling for all night, now that he had it, he wanted to wipe it away and replace it with one of her beautiful smiles.

"Excuse me for a moment, won't you?" she asked.

He watched as she followed the path of the angry wife, stopping in front of the jukebox to feed a dollar into the machine and making a couple of selections before continuing on.

It didn't take a sober man to know that she didn't fit in here.

She didn't fit with him.

And the sooner they both woke up to that fact, the better.

LANEY CAREFULLY MANEUVERED her way around a suspicious puddle outside the men's room and continued down the dim hallway to the door to the ladies'. This had to be one of the most god-awful places she'd ever been to. If it were true that every face told a story, then the stories in this place spoke of hardship and loneliness. Not that she didn't know people who were struggling and lonely. She'd just never seen them look as bad.

She pushed open the door, only to find something blocking it.

She heard a string of curse words and then, "Can't you see the damn thing is occupied?"

A man's hand curved around the edge and opened the door a little wider. Laney caught an eyeful of the drunken wife sitting with her pants off on the single bathroom sink, the man her husband had accused her of flirting with filling the space between her thighs.

He grinned at Laney. "Maybe she wants to make this a threesome."

The woman lit into him the same way she had to her husband not two minutes ago.

"Excuse me," Laney said, quickly making her way back down the hall and through the bar, not stopping until she was standing outside, drawing in a lungful of air.

Carter joined her. "Everything all right?"

"I think I've had about enough of the real world that I can take just now." She tried for a smile but failed as someone nearby retched. "If it's all the same to you, I'd like to call it a night."

Within moments, she was on the back of Carter's bike. She held on to him tightly, but for different reasons than she had earlier. She remembered the file the JAG attorney had faxed over to her. The brief rendering of a man she didn't know. A man different from the Carter Southard she'd met. But he wasn't different, was he? He was the same man. He was just letting her see a different part of himself.

They arrived back at her place quicker than she would have thought possible. After her experience, she'd expected it to take hours to return to her familiar world. Instead, it was right outside her back door, so to speak. She had just chosen not to see it.

"Are you all right?" Carter asked.

She swallowed hard as she stared up at her apartment building. "Fine. I must have had a little too much to drink, is all."

They both knew that she hadn't, but thankfully he didn't push the issue.

"Well, then, I'd better get going."

Laney looked at him in surprise. It was then that she realized he'd done what he had on purpose. That just as she'd been angling for a reaction from him at Raphael's, he'd been trying to provoke one from her tonight.

And, to her horror, he'd succeeded.

"Oh, no," she said. "There's no way you're leaving this bad taste in my mouth." She reached up and pushed his hat back off his head, forcing him to catch it as she thrust her fingers into the soft depths of his hair. Then she kissed him hard. "You're not going anywhere but upstairs with me."

She took his keys from him and tossed them to the doorman as they went inside. "See to the bike for me, won't you, Roger?"

She ignored Roger's bewildered expression as she pulled Carter into the elevator and pressed the button for the penthouse.

10

LANEY KNELT on the mattress in front of Carter, who stood next to the bed. She'd stripped out of her clothes and now took her time taking off his. He'd barely said two words since they'd come in, his handsome face drawn into the long lines she'd seen on too many of the faces at the bar he'd taken her to.

How close was he to being one of those men? Outside of the Marines, what did he do? She'd never asked him.

And she wasn't about to now, either. She wanted, needed to speak to him in a way that didn't require words. Was compelled to communicate what she was feeling.

She reached up, smoothing her fingertips over the strong planes of his face, over his cheeks, up to his forehead. So handsome. She pushed his thick hair back over and over again and then pressed her mouth against his, kissing him lingeringly.

It was somehow important for him to know that while she'd been knocked off balance by the glimpse he'd given her into his life, she was able to take a step back and see what had passed between them in an objective light.

She dipped her tongue between his lips, tasting Wild Turkey and beer.

Objective? Who was she kidding? What was happening had nothing to do with objectivity. Because if she were thinking with her head, she'd admit that she and the hot Marine had virtually nothing in common outside their combustible desire for each other. And that to take things any further, to tempt fate and feed her fear that she was falling for him might very well be the dumbest thing she'd ever done.

Carter had been impassive to her advances, watching her through half-lidded eyes as she kissed him. But as she scooted closer to him on her knees, snaking her hands under his arms and around his waist, pressing her bare breasts against his chest, feeling his arousal against her lower belly, she knew that he wouldn't be able to resist her for long. Hoped he wouldn't.

He groaned low in his throat and cupped her face in his hands, deepening their kiss. Laney knew a relief so complete she nearly melted to the mattress in a puddle of need.

Carter nudged her back. Laney walked on her knees and he knelt on the bed in front of her, moving until they were in the middle. He kissed her fiercely, entangling his fingers in her hair, the side of his hand resting against her neck. Heat rushed over Laney, her heart beating an unsteady rhythm in her chest.

What was it about this one man that made her want to reach out to him? Was it merely the sex? But she knew that couldn't be the only reason. She was no amateur when it came to dating. She'd slept with men before. Had even experienced some fantastic orgasms. But all of them paled in comparison to the sensations Carter inspired in her. He seemed able to reach deeper, demanding something within her she hadn't known existed.

He was her opposite in so many ways.

Yet they fit as completely as a love letter in an envelope.

Carter slid his hands down her neck and over her shoulders, bringing her closer so that her breasts brushed against his chest. Laney's mouth dropped open and he kissed her upper lip and then her lower until she came back to him, the thrum of her pulse growing louder in her ears. He cupped her right breast, running the pad of his callused thumb over her nipple and then back again. Tendrils of red-hot heat unfurled across her stomach, pooling in the apex of her thighs.

He moved his hands around to her back, pressing his fingers into her flesh and then driving them down until he reached the crease of her bottom. He filled his palms with her, his fingertips dipping into her crevice from behind. Laney curved her arms under his and held tight to his shoulders, relishing the languid need gathering deep in her belly.

There was no need to rush. No urgency. Time didn't exist. She was aware only of the flow of blood through her veins and the hands of the man touching her.

Carter sat back on his heels and wrapped her legs around his hips, pulling her flush against his hard arousal. She wasn't sure when he'd sheathed himself, only knew that he had. And in one, slow stroke, he filled her to overflowing.

Laney gasped, feeling as if every molecule of air had been forced from her body, leaving nothing but trembling desire in its wake.

Carter grasped her bottom, pushing her up and then down his rock-hard length. Laney dropped her head back. He nuzzled her neck as his every stroke seemed to go deeper, and deeper still.

She'd felt chaotic the first time they'd had sex, but this time…now…a throbbing, consuming heat claimed her inside and out. It was as if she were burning alive. And she didn't want to put out the fire; she wanted to feed it.

She rubbed her hands down the muscular lines of his back again and again, the rasp of her nipples against the crisp hair on his chest fanning the flames further. She kissed him, her mouth bowing open as he thrust inside her, then she kissed him again, looking deep into his eyes, seeing in them the intensity of emotion crowding her own body.

She couldn't take it…every move emerged a sweet torture. Laney crossed her ankles behind his back and braced her hands against his shoulders, allowing him to set the rhythm, giving herself over to him to do what he would.

Yes…no…the words swirled in her head. Yes, yes, please…no, no, don't ever stop…

One long stroke that made her catch her breath, then

another, and Laney climaxed, exploding into a million shiny pieces, somehow managing to hold on as Carter came, as well, his groan filling her ear along with his hot breath.

THE FOLLOWING AFTERNOON, Carter sat on his back porch with a bottle of lemonade, Blue lying on the ground at his feet, panting. This morning he'd woken up next to Laney, thinking himself in a dream. It couldn't possibly be real. Everything was white, soft, beautiful. Especially the woman lying asleep next to him, her milky hip bare where the sheet had fallen partially off during the night.

He'd hated to wake her. Hated to wake up himself. But a mechanism from the battlefield kicked in—a sort of survival technique that would protect him against an oncoming attack.

The problem was that when he stroked her satiny skin, and her blue eyes blinked open and she smiled, the dream had become even more exquisite instead of dissipating.

"Good morning," she said, stretching her arm across his waist and kissing his chest, her white-blond hair an angelic tangle of curls around her face.

He'd remembered she'd said something about meeting her father for brunch, so he'd reminded her then. Anything to stop the ache that had begun to grow deep in his gut the night before. To stop himself from giving in to the need to make love to her again.

Laney had seemed to tune in to his diversionary

tactic, but hadn't said anything. Instead, she'd made them both eggs for breakfast. And he found out that she had more than a few things on her mind.

"By the way, I heard from your JAG attorney," she'd said casually.

He'd squinted at her. She must have gotten the information yesterday at the latest, and was just now saying something.

"I'm sorry," she'd said, putting down her toast and brushing her hands together. "I meant to tell you last night, but I completely forgot. Forgive me?"

The way she'd smiled at him with her neat, white teeth made him think he'd forgive anything.

And that was an even bigger problem.

It wasn't so long ago that he'd sworn he wouldn't allow another woman to hurt him. Since JoEllen Atchison had accused him of attempted rape. He hadn't been allowed to defend himself and had wound up in jail without a prayer of getting out.

Until an angel in the shape of Laney Cartwright sprung him.

Now...

Well, now he was afraid he was coming to care for Laney in a way that transcended anything he'd experienced. No matter what the differences between them, perhaps even because of them.

There was so much she didn't know about the world. So much she'd been protected from.

He remembered her reaction to having her tires

slashed. And her pale face when she'd rushed out of the bar last night.

Carter cringed. He'd been trying to make a point. A point that was moot considering where they were now.

And where were they?

Old Blue looked up at him and rolled his long tongue along his moist chops, giving a small whine. If he didn't know better, Carter would say that hound had heard his question and was saying, "Beats the hell out of me, buster."

Time. He needed to give himself some time to think about what was happening between him and the lady lawyer. Problem was, time was his greatest enemy. He had too damn much of it on his hands now that the Marines had kicked his no-good ass out.

"I understand you've been given a list of criteria you need to meet before the Corps will consider your reinstatement?" Laney had asked him at breakfast.

He'd nodded and avoided meeting her gaze.

Oh, he'd been given a list, all right. And at the top was going to that damn group meeting. Something he had no intention of doing.

Laney had laid her hand with its short, red nails against his arm. "You have to do it, Carter," she'd said as if he'd mouthed his thoughts aloud. "Unless…"

"Unless what?"

She'd removed her hand and sat up a little straighter. "Unless you decide you'd rather take your life in another direction."

Another direction? There was nothing else he'd ever

considered doing outside the military. His father had been a Marine, and he was a Marine. It was as complicated and as a simple as that.

And if the Corps refused to reinstate him?

Suddenly Carter felt sick.

"Come on, Blue," he said to the dog. "Let's go for a walk."

The old hound lifted his head but didn't get up.

"Fine. I'll go for a walk by myself, then."

He had to do something, anything, to keep himself from calling Laney.

Time. He needed time.

If only there wasn't so damn much of it to fill.

11

AGAIN, TWO DAYS HAD PASSED and there had been no contact from Carter. And no matter what Laney did, she couldn't help worrying that she might never see him again.

It was late Monday morning. There was one week left before the MacGregor trial began. And she couldn't seem to keep her mind on anything other than the phone—wishing it would ring, and when it did, hoping it was Carter.

"Laney?" her associate Dave Matthews asked across the conference table that was serving as the war room for the trial.

"Hmm?" She glanced away from the telephone extension in the room. "Oh, yes. I think we should go with the new time line. It's much clearer than the old one."

And with that, Matt and Dave began tossing other ideas around, leaving her to sit back in her chair and review her notes. Written in large letters was "Meet Tiffany at 12:30, coffee shop." Laney checked her watch. It was nearly noon already.

She rubbed her forehead, marveling at how slowly

time seemed to go by minute by minute, yet zoomed by in batches when she wasn't paying attention.

"Why don't we break for lunch?" she said. "We can meet back here, say, in an hour and a half?"

She hadn't told either one of her colleagues about the existence of a girlfriend in the case. She wanted to feel things out first. See if Devon had still been seeing Tiffany when he was arrested before his lawyers all skipped down an avenue that might be a dead end.

She'd called the number Devon's sister had given her and requested the meeting.

"Yeah, I know who you are," Tiffany had said when she'd introduced herself over the phone. "You're that lawyer bitch representing Devon."

"Laney will do, thank you," she'd said in response, trying to remember the last time she'd been called the B word. At least two years, she believed. After she'd successfully defended her first client and the prosecutor had glared at her smile. She hadn't realized he'd expected her to lose until that moment.

Anyway, Tiffany had agreed to meet her today, first suggesting a park in Irving, then grudgingly settling on the coffee shop in the west end.

Laney drove there, parked at the curb, then went inside. She was ten minutes early. And, so it seemed, was Tiffany.

Her hair color could be anything under the black dye job, and her pale skin was peppered with several piercings. She was wearing a short, short black skirt and a too-small tank top that left her stomach bare and high-lighted the additional navel piercing.

This was Devon's girlfriend? She would never have picked her out of a lineup of possibilities.

"It's the lawyer bitch."

Laney winced. It was one thing being called that over the phone. Another to your face. "Laney will do fine," she repeated, searching for any sign of human warmth in the young woman in front of her. She saw none. Tiffany's dark eyes were hard and inscrutable. Spite oozed from her every pore. And she looked as though she would like nothing better than to get Laney's tan suit dirty.

"Does D know you're here?" Tiffany asked.

Laney refused to let her lead the conversation. "I think you should be more curious about what I'm doing here."

"And that is?"

"I want you to tell me what you know about that night."

Tiffany laughed, revealing that the piercings weren't limited to her skin. Her tongue was spiked with what looked like a barbell. Laney shuddered.

"Well, then," Laney said, "maybe you'd like to tell me who would want to set Devon up."

Tiffany's lips firmed. "What makes you think he was set up?"

"Are you telling me he did it?"

"I'm not saying nothing."

"Why did you agree to meet me here then?"

"You tell me."

Laney was losing patience, fast. What was Devon doing going out with a girl like Tiffany? And had his sister Darcy met her? Or had she only been in contact via cell phone?

It didn't make any sense.

"Look, Tiffany, I'm not here to play cat and mouse. I was hoping you might be able to help me in Devon's defense."

"Ain't no way in hell I'm going anywhere near a courthouse again."

Again.

Laney didn't miss the word.

She squinted at the young woman whose future looked about as bright as her hair color.

"I'm not suggesting you do," she said. "But I would like to ask you a few questions. Like how long you and Devon have been dating. Are you still seeing each other now? Where were you on the night of the robbery—"

Tiffany held up a black-nailed hand. "Forget you. I'm out of here."

The girl started to walk away and Laney did something completely out of character. She grabbed her arm to stop her.

Tiffany looked as if she'd like nothing more than to hit her.

Laney was pretty sure her expression displayed the same thing.

"I'm going to ask you one last time, Tiffany. Who would want to set Devon up?"

The girl set her jaw.

"Or should I be asking why *you* would want to set him up?"

IT APPEARED more and more likely that Carter wouldn't be invited back into the Marines any time soon.

Which meant he would have to start searching out an alternative lifestyle.

The thought would have seemed unimaginable even three months ago. But now Carter sat at his kitchen table with a pad and pen, ready to accept that his military career had reached its end.

He stared at the blank page and then scratched his head. A thousand ideas presented themselves to him, each immediately rejected. Truth was, he'd never considered a life outside the military. Men in every generation of Southards had served, with his father it being a career. It was understood that he would follow in his father's footsteps, straight into killed-in-action if need be.

But what did he do when that option was taken away from him?

He pulled the manila envelope sitting on the corner of the table closer to him, opening the flap and sliding out the documentation there. The small packet represented the whole of his life. From his birth certificate and passport to his Special Ops certification and his suspension papers. He found the paper that he wanted and smoothed it out on top of the pad. It was a list of steps he was required to take before being reconsidered for reinstatement.

It was surprising to him that he was contemplating not taking those steps. But something in him had changed when he'd been wrongfully arrested. Actually, he suspected the change had begun long before that, dating back to the incident that had ended with his suspension in the first place.

He rubbed his face and then looked at his hands. They bore cuts and oil stains that he hadn't been able to scrub out after working on his property clearing dry brush that could easily catch fire in the summer heat, then doing some maintenance on his bike in the garage. He'd always been a good mechanic. He'd even worked a stint at a full-service garage when he was sixteen, up the road at Old Man Johnson's place. His father had been pleased with him when he'd come home with his first paycheck.

"A man should always be self-sufficient," he'd said, and then given him an awkward pat on the back.

Carter would like to say that their relationship was peppered with such exchanges, but the elder Southard had never been comfortable with displays of affection. And Carter seemed to have inherited the gene.

The long stretches of time when the elder Southard was shipped out on assignment and father and son hadn't seen each other were at least partly to blame. But not totally. Because during those stints, neighbors and the families of his father's army buddies had stepped in to take care of him until he was old enough to look after himself, so Carter had been exposed to lifestyles different from his own.

Still, he'd always felt like an outsider.

He'd been on his own since he'd landed that first job at Johnson's garage. The old guy had finally kicked the bucket sometime last year. He'd never been married and was childless, so the garage sat abandoned.

It was funny how quickly the land could reclaim a structure. Weeds grew up through cracks in the asphalt of the parking lot, and ivy was growing over the side of the building and its three bay doors. Even the blue lettering announcing Johnson's Car Garage seemed to have faded quickly in the strong Texan sun.

Every time Carter passed the property and the For Sale sign tacked to the door, he remembered the summer he'd worked there. But he'd certainly never thought of working there again.

Now, he pushed the paper outlining Marine requirements aside and picked up the pen, writing "Reopen Johnson's place" across the first page of the pad and underlining it several times. His skills might be a little rusty, but he could always hire somebody who could pick up the slack until he felt he was up to snuff.

An odd gust of wind blew in through the back door, bringing the afternoon heat with it. The paper he'd pushed aside shifted to rest on top of the pad, the words seeming to stare up at him.

He folded it and stuffed it back into the envelope, trying not to think about how one Ms. Laney Cartwright would react to seeing him wearing a work jumpsuit, covered in oil.

He winced. It was just as well that they were ending things the way they were.

SOMETIMES LANEY'S FATHER told her that he didn't know why she drove herself the way she did. Lord knew she didn't have to. Had she chosen to live a life of leisure, she certainly had the resources with which to do so. In fact, several of her girlfriends from high school and college led perfectly simple lives defined by the many social events they attended rather than a time clock. Those who weren't already married with kids, that is.

Oh, to only have a time clock.

She stared at her watch. Past nine. She'd been working for fourteen hours straight. And her body was letting her know it. She had a crick in her neck and her lower back nearly gave out as she finally rose from the exhibit and file-covered conference table.

She stepped out of the room and looked around the deserted hall. She'd sent Dave and Matt home a couple of hours ago, but had wanted to finish up a few things herself while they were still fresh in her mind. She blinked and flicked off the lights before going to her office. She glanced at her messages; replies could wait until tomorrow. Then she gathered her purse and brief-case and headed for the elevator. The lawyers had ordered in dinner but she'd eaten very little of it, so her stomach felt empty and odd. Still, she couldn't think of a thing she'd like to eat. An omelet, maybe, at home. Something light and packed full of protein this late.

Within fifteen minutes, she was greeting Roger the doorman and getting into the elevator to take her up to the penthouse. Her head felt good and fried. Maybe she would just take a shower and call it a night.

It took her a few moments to find the right key on her chain and finally she was opening the door to a place that usually brought her joy but now only gaped large and empty. White on white on white, the décor loomed cold and unwelcoming instead of plush and pristine as she'd intended. Not even switching on lights and having light from the setting sun streaming through the sheers at the balcony doors did much to change how she felt.

She was just tired, that's all, she told herself. She loved this apartment. It reflected every part of her. Was exactly the way she wanted it.

Why, then, did she feel ill at ease?

She put her purse and briefcase down on the foyer table and kicked off her shoes, shrugging out of her suit jacket as she padded across the thick white carpeting toward her bedroom and the master bath.

Then it became clear why she felt uncomfortable in her own home: someone had been there.

12

"COME, CARTER, I need you…"

Laney's plea had him springing into action. Where it usually took a half hour to reach downtown, he made it in half that time, displaying his impatience to the doorman, who appeared intent on protecting Laney himself.

Now he stood off to one side in her penthouse apartment, a silent dark shadow against the brightness of the place, watching as the police finished making notes.

The door finally closed behind them and Laney launched herself into his arms.

"Thank God, you're here," she whispered. "I couldn't think of anyone else to call. My father's away on business and…"

He wanted to tell her that no explanation was needed but couldn't form words as he folded her easily against his tense frame.

"What happened?" he asked, looking around, trying to discern what had compelled her to call him for help.

"There was a break-in…my bedroom…"

He gently set her aside and walked to the doorway of the room in question. Swatches of color littered the top of the made bed and the floor. He walked inside and lifted what looked like a pair of panties. Only they'd been slashed in two so they appeared to be nothing more than squares of red silk.

"Every undergarment, slip, stocking and nightgown I own," Laney said from behind him.

"Christ."

He stood for a long moment, staring at the carnage.

"And there was another note."

He turned to face her.

Her usually flawless white skin was ashy as she looked away.

"What did it say, Laney?" Carter swore he could feel every drop of his blood as it rushed through his veins.

Her blue eyes looked up to meet his gaze. "Strike Three, You're Out."

He stood silently for a few moments before moving.

"What are you doing?" she asked.

Carter felt he had to do something, anything to expel the anger filling him. He was snatching the scraps of silky material up one by one from her bed and the floor and dropping them into a nearby wastebasket.

"How in the hell did they get in here?" He thought of Roger the doorman and had half a mind to go down and punish him for the crime.

"The best that Don, the day doorman, can figure is that the intruder must have gained access through the garage when one of the residents drove in. It would be simple enough to leave the same way once they were done."

"And the door to your apartment?"

"The police say there are scratches consistent with those made by a lock-picking kit."

Carter didn't stop until every splash of color in the white bedroom was gone. Then he picked up the wastebasket and marched through the apartment to the kitchen, where he found a garbage bag, dumping the contents inside. He tied the bag off and placed it outside in the hall, giving the door's locking mechanism a good look before closing it again.

Laney stood rubbing her hands over her arms. She seemed tired and scared, yet somehow she still managed to smile.

"The police say they're just trying to scare me." She laughed without humor. "Yeah, well, I figure they're doing a pretty good job."

"Do they have any leads on the first two notes?"

She shook her head. "No. The detective in charge says he's arranged for patrol cars to come by every half hour or so to check on things, but until he has evidence of a more serious crime, there's not much else he can do."

"A more serious crime? Like when you're attacked?"

He didn't think it was possible, but she grew even paler. Damn.

She smiled again. "I know there's probably little chance that anything more will happen tonight, but I was hoping that you might stay with me until morning?"

Carter was moved by her soft question.

She laughed again. "Oh, well. So much for me trying to charm you with my independent-woman-of-means role."

Carter stepped across the room and tucked her to his chest again, relieved when she melted against him.

"You're stronger than any person I've ever met, Laney." He smoothed her hair back from her face and stared into her doubtful yet hopeful eyes. "Let's just say that whoever's doing this better hope they never meet you in a dark alley."

She shuddered. "Please don't mention alleys and dark places right now."

Carter silently cursed himself again, moving his hands down her long back, trying to ignore his immediate and powerful response to her nearness.

"Have you eaten yet?" he asked.

She rubbed her nose against the sleeve of his T-shirt. "You know, for a macho Marine, you're awfully concerned with feeding me."

"That's because I like my women strong."

She laughed, a more generous sound now.

He gripped her arms and held her away from him before his growing erection began to dictate his actions.

"Why don't you go change while I whip us up something to eat?"

There was a curious light in her eyes as she stared at him for a long moment. "Yes. Okay."

She turned to walk back to her bedroom, hesitating as she looked around, as if expecting to find her shredded undergarments still littering the place. Then she disappeared into the master bath.

Carter drew in a deep breath and let it out again.

So much for keeping his distance from her.

LANEY WOKE with a start around 4:00 a.m. She sprang upright in bed, her breathing filling her quiet, empty bedroom. In her dream, she'd been asleep in the same bed while a man in a black mask shredded her lingerie on top of her. Then, running out of material, had stood eyeing her.

Her hand immediately went to the other side of the bed. Empty.

To her relief, Carter had agreed to stay the night. He'd fed her the best omelet she'd ever had, and then tucked her into bed. If she was disappointed that he hadn't made any physical advances, she wasn't going to admit it. But she had been glad when he'd lain on top of the blankets and spooned with her, his front against her back, until she fell asleep.

But where was he now?

She stripped off the covers and moved her legs to hang over the side of the mattress, listening. There was nothing but the quiet hiss of the air-conditioning coming in from the overhead vent.

She started when she heard someone speak.

Carter?

Who would he be talking to at 4:00 a.m.?

She grabbed her robe and walked down the hall into the living room. There she found him, sprawled across her oversized sofa, one leg bent at the knee, his left arm crossed over his eyes. He was asleep.

Laney pulled her robe closer around her. What was he doing in here? Why had he left the bed and come to sleep on the couch? She swallowed hard, hurt more than she would have thought possible.

She'd hoped that his coming here so quickly last night meant that he still wanted her. That they still had something that could be worked out.

But watching him sleep alone on her couch, which looked small when it was large, made her feel oddly lonely.

He muttered in his sleep again and Laney jumped. Her nerves must still be on edge from last night, she reasoned. She leaned closer, trying to figure out what Carter was saying in short, vehement spurts.

"IED! Move!"

There was nothing unclear about that outburst.

Laney's heart pumped thickly in her chest as she connected his nightmare with the items she'd read in the psych report from his JAG attorney.

He was always so good with her. Together. Alert and clear. When she'd originally received his case material, she remembered thinking that it couldn't possibly be true. There was no indication that Carter suffered any residual effects from his service in Iraq and then Afghanistan.

Of course, she'd never had any personal contact with someone diagnosed with PTSD before, either.

"Carter?" she whispered, reaching out a hand to wake him.

He shouted something incoherent again, and she noted the sweat that dotted his upper lip and forehead.

"Carter?" she said a little louder.

He jackknifed into a sitting position, grabbing her wrist in his left hand while his right produced a gun she hadn't known he carried.

THE WAR ZONE slowly faded away into the shadows of Laney's apartment. Carter sucked in deep breaths, staring at where she stood in front of him, hands over her heart as if to protect it. From the gun he held. From him.

He let rip a long stream of curses as he realized he was holding his 9 mm on her. He laid the gun on the sofa and then dropped his head into his hands, gathering his wits about him.

He was there to protect Laney.

He had nearly been the one to harm her.

"I'm sorry," she said haltingly. "You were having a nightmare and I…"

He looked up at her abruptly. Was she really apologizing to him?

At that moment, his entire life was a nightmare.

"What are you doing with a gun?" she whispered.

He went to great lengths to disguise its presence, but he took his 9 mm with him everywhere. If not on his person, then in the seat compartment of his Harley. Always careful when he was carrying that she wouldn't accidentally bump it.

"What were you dreaming about?"

Carter got up quickly, grabbing the gun as an after-thought. "I've got to get out of here."

He put his boots on while leaning against the front door, trying not to notice the way Laney looked both sexy and vulnerable as she watched him.

He stood up and slid the gun into the back waist of his jeans. "You should be fine now. I'll make sure Roger knows you're alone."

She nodded, but didn't say anything.

He curled his fingers around the doorknob, then let it go, moving to stand in front of her. He thread his fingers through her tousled, short blond curls and kissed her deeply. Something, anything, to rid her beautiful face of the expression of fear and concern that he'd put there.

Then he walked out the door, not leaving until he heard her lock it after him.

13

A FEW HOURS LATER, Laney woke to an odd sound in the room. It wasn't possible someone else had broken in again so soon. Was it Carter? Had he come back? She wouldn't question how he had gotten in. If career Marine Carter wanted to get into a place, he'd get in, no questions asked. In fact, she wouldn't put it past him to force Roger to give him access to the building's master key.

There it was. The sound again. Almost like…

Panting.

She scooted across the bed and peered over the side. Stretched out on her white carpeting was the ugliest dog she'd ever seen. Her brows rose as the old hound raised red, droopy eyes to stare up at her and then licked his sagging chops, causing a line of slobber to drop onto her slippers.

Oh, yuck.

She spotted a note tucked under his plain brown leather collar. She carefully reached a hand out and took it.

This is Blue. I've left him to protect you. Just make sure he's taken outside to see to his business

at least three times, keep his food and water bowls
full and he won't be any trouble at all to you. But
a stranger would need to take care.
Carter

Laney smiled. He'd brought his dog over.

She sat up and Blue got up, too. They stayed like that
for a long moment, just looking at each other.

"Hi, Blue," she said, slowly extending her hand palm
down so he could get a sniff. "I'm Laney."

His wet nose nudged against her hand as if trying to
turn it over and he barked once, a loud, soulful sound.

Laney jumped. "My, whoever named you got it right,
didn't they?" She scratched one of his long ears. "I feel
like singing the blues myself, sometimes."

She carefully rose to her feet, deciding to leave her
drool-soaked slippers behind, and checked that Carter
had put two bowls in the corner of her kitchen, one containing water, the other dog food. Inside the pantry, she
found a mammoth bag of kibble. She closed the door
and leaned against it, watching as the old dog sauntered
over to his water bowl and slurped up a good portion,
getting even more on the tile around it.

Whatever Carter's sins, she suspected a heart of gold
beat in his wide chest. She'd spotted it when she first
laid eyes on him in that San Antonio jail. And despite
the frightening middle-of-the-night encounter, she knew
it for sure now.

Who else could love a butt-ugly hound like this one?

Blue gave a couple of short barks, as if reading her thoughts.

Laney crouched down to pet him heartily, murmuring her apologies. She smiled, not only because of Blue's welcoming response but because his presence meant that she would be seeing Carter.

"THAT BACKGROUND CHECK on Tiffany Mullins just came in," Violet said from the doorway of the war room sometime later.

Laney was bent over an enlarged photograph of the masked robber with Dave Matthews, diagramming differences between an unknown gunman and Devon Mac-Gregor. As she rose, her lower back let her know it wasn't happy. She pressed one hand against it and reached to take the report from Violet with her other.

"Thanks, Vi."

It had been hours since she'd showered and left her penthouse apartment to Blue, with instructions to the daytime doorman to arrange to have the old hound walked. She'd been hoping that Carter would call, or otherwise indicate when she might see him again, but it hadn't happened yet and it was well into midafternoon.

"What is it?" Dave asked.

Laney read the report once, then went back to the beginning to reread it. Out of curiosity, she'd asked Violet to run the background check through the private investigation firm the lawyers retained. While Laney had expected to find a few odd misdemeanors, what she was looking at far surpassed expectations.

"Seems Devon's girlfriend has a rap sheet as long as my desk," she said, looking at him. "And included in it is an arrest for armed robbery of a convenience store."

THE LAST THING Laney imagined finding when she returned home was Carter fixing dinner in her kitchen. Nothing special, he said. Just a couple of steaks and a salad. Since she'd never had anyone cook dinner for her, it might as well have been a holiday feast.

It was after seven and she was beyond tired. Yet somehow seeing Carter salting slabs of steak and washing greens made her feel loads better. She patted the old hound that lay next to the counter stools and leaned in to kiss Carter on the cheek.

He chuckled. "Somehow I suddenly feel like the little lady of the house."

While his usual humor was injected into the remark, so was a bit of uneasiness—similar to Laney's own surprise at her casual greeting. She'd meant the kiss as a thank-you, but somehow it seemed to reveal much more.

Or maybe she was reading more into it than there was. Sometimes that happened after a long day of thinking too much.

She slowly sat down on one of the stools and slipped her heels off, rubbing her left arch absently. She decided the correct response was her first one: to keep things light. "Ah, I figured you for the traditional type. Keeping women barefoot and pregnant after they get married."

"Oh?" He dried the greens with paper towels and she stopped herself from telling him about the salad spin drier stocked under the sink. It was much more fun watching him do it this way. Large, strong hands delicately patting moisture from the delicate greens provided an interesting counterpoint to her workday.

"Is that why I'm already married with two point two kids, then?" he asked.

She smiled, glad that he was taking her lead and keeping things light. She'd had enough of heavy for now. "Touché."

"And what about you?" He left the leaves to dry and came around the counter to sit next to her. He touched her knee. Laney jumped and then frowned, guessing she was still mentally at work. Had anyone there touched her that way, she'd have threatened a lawsuit.

"Whoa, easy," he said quietly.

She took a deep breath and relaxed, enjoying the way he smoothed his fingers down over her calf. He nudged her hand away and gripped her ankle, moving her foot until it sat on the stool between his jean-clad legs. Then his long fingers began properly massaging her toes.

"Mmm, that feels good." And it did. Decadently good. Not only was he skillfully chasing away her weariness, he created tiny sparks of awareness that raced up the back of her leg, making her want to draw a road map for him to follow under her skirt.

"So? Are you going to answer my question?" he asked.

Laney considered him from beneath lowered lids. "What question?" His attention moved from her toes to the length of her foot and back again. Laney's panties dampened. "Oh, right. Why don't I have a wife who's barefoot and pregnant with two point two children…"

He ran the tip of his index finger along her arch, tickling her.

"All right, all right, uncle," she said.

He exchanged one foot for the other while Blue watched their activities from his spot on the floor, his panting periodically broken when he licked his moist chops.

"I don't know," Laney said. "I guess I've been so consumed with my career that I've never really thought about the rest of it. Not like my friends. They're incessantly talking about marriage and their biological clocks and life plans…"

She drifted off, wondering if he would consider giving her a full-body massage.

"I can understand that," Carter said quietly.

"What? Ticking biological clocks?"

"No. Being consumed by your career."

Laney met his gaze, seeing the sober shadow in his eyes. She slowly removed her foot from his hands, remembering last night.

There were few things that could have compelled her to call a halt to one of the best foot massages she'd ever had, but the memory of having a gun pulled on her was definitely one of them.

She instantly missed his hands on her, but had to go through the door he'd just opened.

"Are you armed now?" she asked quietly.

Carter stared at her for a long moment, likely following her line of thought. She couldn't read his emotions. Was that something they taught in the military? How to fashion the perfect poker face? If so, she guessed Carter had passed that test with flying colors.

He got up and went back into the prep area across the counter to wash his hands. "No," he said in answer to her question.

Laney didn't know if she was relieved or disappointed. While having the firearm pointed at her had been terrifying, the fact that he was packing and wasn't afraid to use it appealed to her on a primal level.

She hadn't felt threatened. She'd been surprised. And a little scared. More for him and what he must have been dreaming than any real concern for her own well-being.

Still, while she'd been around guns for most of her life—her father was a collector and an avid gun fan—and she knew how to shoot one, she didn't own one. Something her father had suggested she might like to consider now that her personal space had been violated.

Laney got up, patted Blue, who lifted his head into the gesture, and then nudged Carter aside so she could wash up herself.

"Let me get that," she said when he reached for the greens.

They worked in companionable silence for a few moments, Laney ripping the greens and cutting tomatoes and onions, Carter testing the stovetop grill on the industrial-size stainless steel oven that she rarely used because cooking for one was both not much fun and inconvenient.

"Have you had a chance to go over the JAG report yet?" she asked as casually as if she'd just requested him to pass the salt.

She suspected he might not have heard her over the sizzle of the steaks and considered repeating her question. But when he turned, she knew he had not only heard, he was having a hard time responding.

"Their requirements don't look all that complicated," she said, tossing the salad with the light dressing of olive oil, red wine vinegar and Dijon mustard she'd mixed. She put the bowl on the counter between two place mats.

"That's because they're not being asked of you."

She took out a bottle of rosé from the refrigerator and opened it, conceding the point. She had no idea how it felt to be in his position. Her superiors couldn't suspend her or bring her up on a court martial.

Still, avoidance had never been a tactic she'd employed when facing any problem, much less one as big as the problem staring Carter straight in the face.

"Beer?" she asked.

"Thanks."

She took out a bottle from the fridge, popped the top and handed it to him. His fingers folded over hers and remained for a heartbeat before he released them. She couldn't help thinking the gesture was a silent plea for her to drop the subject.

She poured herself a glass of wine, surprised to find her hand trembling ever so slightly because she knew she couldn't retreat and pretend the problem didn't exist.

"You know, the papers your attorney sent over didn't give an exact reason why you were sent up for suspension."

She watched the back of Carter's shoulders stiffen as he tended the steaks. "The Corps prefers to keep everything in-house."

Laney shivered as she took the loaf of French bread he'd brought out of its paper bag and cut a few slices.

"Is the incident what you were dreaming about last night when…"

She wondered if there was another way to say, "When you pulled the gun on me?"

"Can you get me the plates from the microwave?" he asked instead of responding.

There were plates in the microwave? She popped open the door and saw two plain stoneware plates. She touched one, felt it was hot and got a towel to protect her hands as she took the plates out. He'd thought of everything. A man who looked after every detail. She'd known that was the case when it came to their time in the bedroom.

Then why was it so difficult for him to honor the Corps requirements for reinstatement?

Carter didn't blink as he held the plates without protection, placing a steak on top of each and then putting them on the place mats at the counter.

"Do you want to talk or eat?" he asked with a raised brow as he switched off the grill and turned to face her.

"We can do both."

He smiled, but somehow it didn't reach his beautiful eyes. "I think your friends would be shocked to see you talk with your mouth full."

"Well, good thing they're not here, then, isn't it?"

At the smell of the steaks, Blue invaded the kitchen. Carter put a couple of cubes of meat he must have reserved for the old hound into his food bowl.

Laney rounded the counter and sat down, waiting until Carter sat next to her before filling a small bowl with salad and handing it to him, then another for herself.

"So…" she prompted.

He chewed on a piece of steak for a moment. "You're not going to let me enjoy this prime piece of beef, are you?"

"That depends."

"On what?"

"On whether you stop the smart-ass diversionary tactics and start talking to me like I know the worth of a half dollar."

The corners of his eyes crinkled as he continued to eat. "And how much is that?"

Laney stared at him as she put a bite into her mouth. The beef melted against her tongue. "Oh my god. That's got to rate among the best steaks I've ever tasted," she said, cutting another piece.

"So can we eat now?"

She laughed. "Yes. But just so you know, I plan on returning to this conversation as soon as we finish."

"We'll see about that."

She nodded, swallowed another bite, and then reached for her wineglass. "Yes, we will."

_14_

SHOULD I STAY or should I go?

What was it about this one woman that knocked him off-kilter? Compelled him to do one thing when he should be doing another?

Carter lay in her bed sometime later, out of breath, his skin coated in sweat, curving Laney's soft body against his side. God, he couldn't seem to get enough of her. The instant he thought that this was it, this was the mark they could never possibly improve upon, he'd reach yet another level with the busty blonde, making him wonder what in the hell he'd been doing wrong all these years. Because this, what they shared, was what those corny romance novels were packed with. Sexy women, bare-chested men, red-hot passion. Like the book open on Laney's nightstand.

Maybe the romance novel had something to do with it.

He reached for the book with the red cover and the word Blaze stamped across it and stared at the picture of a half-naked man.

"You read this stuff?"

Laney shifted her head where it rested against his

chest, her curls teasing his left nipple. He took in her smile as she said, "Mmm-hmm. You may want to give them a try. They might give you a new idea or two."

Carter flipped the book open to the part where she'd left off. "And here I thought I was doing pretty good without any help."

She laughed low in her throat. "Trust me, you're doing just fine in that department."

He read the steamy passage in the book, his brows lifting higher at every other sentence.

"Holy shit," he said.

Laney took the book from him. "Enough reading. What's say we get back to real-time action?"

"More?"

She straddled him, her round, milky breasts bouncing as she found her spot and reached for the box of condoms on the table next to the novel. "Oh, much, much more, I think."

Carter grasped her lush hips, stretching his neck to contain his groan as she slid over his hard, sheathed length. "Remind me to buy you a box of those books, will you?"

She leaned in and kissed him lingeringly. "What are you going to do when you see my supply of other playground toys?"

Carter met her gaze. The woman was going to be the end of him. She truly was.

"WHAT MADE YOU want to be a Marine?"

Carter's eyes drifted open an hour later. He lay on

his stomach across the bed, about ready to drop off to sleep. Had Laney just asked the question she had? How could she possibly hold a thought in her head after their sack sessions?

The digital clock on the bedside table read after midnight. They'd been going at it since nine. And he was exhausted. Surely she had to be, too?

He shifted his head to look at her. She lay on her back on the other side of him, rubbing the arch of her foot absently against his calf. She stared at the ceiling, but her attention wasn't on the plaster there.

"Uh-oh. Is this the part where you try to continue our predinner conversation?" he asked.

She turned her head to smile at him. "You're quick."

"Not as quick as I'd like. If I had my choice, you would have completely forgotten about the topic."

"Ah, so that was your intention all along."

"Yes, and apparently I failed the mission."

She laughed quietly. "We were talking about why you became a Marine."

"Actually, you were talking about it. I was thinking about contributing." Carter rolled onto his back and drew in a deep breath.

Her hand touched his upper thigh. He could try distracting her with sex again. But, good Lord, he didn't think he had it in him.

Easier to respond to her blasted questions.

"I never wanted to be anything else," he answered honestly enough, staring at the ceiling himself.

She was quiet, but he could feel her gaze on his profile, the soft, idle stroking of her fingers against his thigh.

He should have known that wouldn't be enough. But he had hoped.

"Why?"

The question hated by men the world over. Right after, "What are you thinking?"

Carter swallowed hard, reminding himself that he did have a choice. But given his wrecked physical state, his options were limited. He couldn't imagine getting up to use the john, much less leaving to avoid her probing questions.

"My father was a Marine. As was his father before him."

"So it's a family business," Laney said.

He smiled. "Yes, I suppose you could say that."

"And your mom?"

Christ. "My mom left a long time ago. Remarried, had more kids and lives a nice, suburban life with a nice, boring husband down in Austin."

"How old were you when she left?"

Carter turned his head toward her. "What, did JAG give you an outline of questions to ask?"

She looked hurt and he immediately wanted to take his words back.

"Sorry," he said. "I guess I'm not very good at this."

"That's okay. Given your response, I'm proving I suck at it, too."

He stretched out and then brought her to lay her head

against his chest, his arm across the back of her creamy shoulders. "I was old enough to understand what was going on, young enough to be wounded for life."

"Did she try to gain custody?"

Carter scratched his eyebrow with the back of his thumbnail. "I guess she did. But my father refused to give it to her. Told her he'd drag her through court until I was eighteen and make everyone a miserable mess unless she let us alone." The images of their arguments had dulled with age, but not the biting content. "My father preferred to view her as leaving both of us."

"But surely you know that's not true."

He shrugged. Maybe he did. Maybe he didn't. At any rate, since his mother had moved three hours away, where her family had come from, he'd only seen her for a day every other weekend because his father refused to allow her to take him out of the county, even when he was away on assignment somewhere, and placed Carter with extended family members or friends. He remembered being upset that his mother hadn't fought his father. But as he grew older, he'd come to understand that you didn't fight with his father so much as ram up against an immovable force of nature. So maybe she'd understood that any legal claims she would have liked to have made would have accomplished little more than fueling bad feelings to worse.

Laney made a thoughtful sound. "So since then you've been punishing every woman who's crossed your path for your mother's sins."

Carter jerked to stare at her. "What?"

She met his gaze. "I heard the expression some-place—I don't remember where."

"Do you think I'm punishing you?"

She squinted at him, as if trying to work it out in her mind. "Not so much punishing as trying to keep me at arm's length. Sort of, 'You can come this far, but no farther.' Frankly, it's beginning to piss me off."

He chuckled softly. There was a certain fuzzy kind of logic to her words.

And a flattering aspect that touched him in ways that he was unprepared to acknowledge.

Had it really been just yesterday that he'd worked out it was best not to see her anymore? That to continue building on a relationship that held no future was in neither of their best interests?

Yet here he was, lying with her in his arms, not wanting to be anyplace else in the world.

"Is everything in your life so simple, Laney?" he asked quietly. "So ordered?"

He heard her swallow hard. "My life is no less a mess than anyone else's. No less conflicted than yours, I think."

Carter smoothed his hand down her silky back. "Then answer me this—would you be here right now, lying next to me, if someone wasn't posing a threat to you?"

THE QUESTION had been unfair. And moot.

Laney sat in her office the following morning thinking about last night. She was due in the war room in five minutes but she couldn't seem to motivate herself to reach for her coffee cup, much less devote her attention to the MacGregor case.

She understood that Carter's question was exactly what she'd accused him of—an attempt to keep her at arm's length. And she supposed it was what she deserved after giving in to the temptation to play pop psychologist.

But knowing that didn't make her hurt any less.

She hadn't answered his question. Hadn't had the heart to. She'd sensed that he'd already locked her out, shut down the conversation merely by posing the query. They'd lain silently for a while. Then Carter had gotten up to take his position on the couch, leaving Laney by herself in the big, lonely bed that smelled of him. To have him so near, yet so far away, had hurt the most.

So this was what it felt like to be falling in love. The never-ending longing, the soaring highs, the ceaseless hurt and doubt. She'd heard it said by many people, including her father, that she'd know when she met that one person meant for her. She hadn't believed it. Wanted proof and a checklist so she'd know exactly what to be on the lookout for. But it turned out that falling in love wasn't about putting your finger on the emotion and saying, "There! That's it." Instead, it was something you felt with everything that you were.

And she was falling for a guy who might not be able to return the favor.

She knew Carter felt the incredible connection beginning to form between them. Knew that when they made love there were no barriers, nothing separating them as they melded into a single entity. Knew that he held her both gently, as if afraid he might break her, and possessively, as if he might never let her go.

Could she, by sheer force of purpose, lock him out the way he had done to her? Could she turn her back on what she felt? Shut her feelings off?

She wrapped her arms around herself and shivered. She'd like to think that she couldn't. But in her highly analytical lawyer's mind, she had to acknowledge that even love was ultimately a choice. Perhaps not the person you chose to love. But how and when you expressed that love.

Or not.

"Laney?"

She blinked her secretary into focus. The older woman wore a concerned expression.

Laney gathered her files together, then realized her cheeks were damp. She turned slightly and wiped them with her fingers. "Tell the guys I'll be right there."

Violet approached the desk, then backtracked to pick up a box of tissues on the guest table. She held it out.

Laney smiled and took one. "Thanks."

"You're welcome. You know, if you want to talk about anything…" She put the box down on Laney's desk. "I know you and your father are very close, but there must be times when you need a female ear to bend."

Laney was grateful. "Thank you, Violet."

In the outer office, the phone lines were ringing off the hook. Violet finally seemed to hear them.

"Actually, Laney, I didn't come in to rustle you to the war room. I came to tell you that the media appears to have gotten wind of the threats that have been made against you in the MacGregor case. And they're storming the place now."

Laney swiveled toward the window. On the street below, three news vans nearly blocked the street as techs set up portable satellite equipment and reporters did sound checks and double-checked their hair. She was familiar with each of them. Had answered their questions dozens of times outside the courthouse during the course of other high-profile cases. But never had they come to the law offices.

"Why didn't you say anything about your tires being slashed or your apartment being broken into?" Violet had come to stand next to her.

"They know that?"

Violet stared at her. "At least when I told them I had no knowledge of the incidents, I was actually speaking the truth."

"I'm sorry, Vi. There's been so much going on with trial prep that I haven't had time to think, much less conduct my life in any sort of logical way."

Understatement of the year. Of course, she was leaving out Carter's involvement in her scattered mental and emotional state.

"Here." Violet handed her a pile of messages. "The

television reporters may be outside, but the print media are tying up the phone lines. I keep telling them you'll call back but they're determined not to take no for an answer."

Laney absently accepted the messages.

"They're all asking if the threats against you are proof that there's another person involved. Another suspect that establishes MacGregor's innocence."

15

CARTER CAUGHT WIND of the media blitz when he decided to take Laney to lunch. She'd said she'd be hitting the MacGregor case hard all day and then had a charity event to attend that night. She had chaired the event and was required to attend…with him, she hoped.

He had no intention of getting anywhere near that event, with or without a black tie. But he figured what he could do was feed her. Considering all that was going on, she probably wasn't looking after herself properly.

If his impromptu lunch plans also gave him a much-needed chance to see her, he wasn't going to admit it.

To say this morning had been awkward was an understatement. He'd awakened to Blue licking his face and Laney pulling on her suit jacket, showered and ready to leave for work. He'd been disappointed she hadn't gotten him up so they could at least catch breakfast together. But considering what had transpired the last time she woke him…well, he couldn't blame her for not wanting to do it again any time soon.

Then there was last night…

Carter parked his bike and took the bag he'd brought

out of the seat compartment. Sunglasses firmly in place, he approached the media vans. Apparently they were all doing live feeds for the twelve o'clock news. He stopped to listen to one of the spot reporters, a pretty brunette unaware of his presence as she spoke into the camera.

"An undisclosed source reports that accused murderer Devon MacGregor's attorney Laney Cartwright has received several threats warning her away from defending him. The trial gets under way on Monday. The nature of those threats are as yet unclear, but we understand that her residence was broken into yesterday and intimate articles of her clothing violently slashed."

Carter walked up to the front of the building. Surprisingly, he was immediately let up after identifying himself. Perhaps Laney had cleared him as a client? Seemed likely. All he knew was that he needed to reach her, make sure she was okay.

Who had leaked the information to the press? He suspected she wouldn't much like the personal nature of the violations to be out there for public consumption. But there was nothing he could do about that now. What he could do was offer to serve as a buffer if she decided that's what she wanted.

LANEY STOOD in the war room, determined to focus on the case and what needed to be done. Her cocounsels weren't as disciplined, however. They frequently drifted toward the windows where they could see the media gathered at the curb.

"Christ, is that CNN?" Matt said.

"CNN?" Dave replied, going to check. "Laney, CNN is here."

"On a local case? I don't think so."

"God, it's Anderson Cooper."

"Anderson Cooper?" That got even her attention.

Everything had turned surreal. One of the senior partners had called her into his office a short time ago. He'd said it was completely up to her how she chose to address the media, but she might want to take some time and consider what she said so as not to compromise the case. She'd agreed and proposed using the same "My client is innocent and I'm positive the evidence will prove that" approach in regards to the case…and offer a "No comment" on any questions that involved her personally.

First one television then another was pushed into the room by associates to supplement the flat screen already on the wall. Remotes were pressed, channels selected, and the room began filling up with the occupants of nearby offices and cubicles.

"You're famous," one of the junior attorneys said almost wistfully.

Laney's picture was flashed in the upper right-hand corner of a newscast, along with a frozen frame of the grainy image taken at the convenience store robbery and shooting, crimes that Devon MacGregor was accused of committing.

"It's not about me," she said quietly. "It's about the case."

While the vast majority of her colleagues focused on the scene offered by CNN, she was drawn to a shot that appeared to be of her apartment building. She approached the screen and everyone followed her movements as a young male reporter related the incidents surrounding the break-in.

She blinked in shock. "Where are they getting their information?"

She knew that when a case was big, certain desk sergeants and other inside police sources were known to sell information to the media for extra cash. Sometimes the prosecutor's office and even defense attorneys were known to leak information if they felt it might help their case. No judge-ordered media ban was capable of keeping everything out of the press.

But there was no media ban either on the MacGregor case…or her personal life.

Everyone turned to look at her.

"Your underwear?" one of the female associates said. "Oh, that's creepy."

Laney worked her mouth around a response, but found none forthcoming.

Thankfully Violet rushed into the room, Laney's intrepid rescuer in a yellow polyester suit.

"Ms. Cartwright, your twelve-thirty appointment has arrived."

Her appointment? She didn't have any appointments.

Still, she didn't object when Violet steered her from the room and toward the ladies'. A junior attorney was washing up inside. Violet waited until she left and then turned the lock in the door.

"Thanks," Laney said for the second time that day, already feeling better away from the spotlight.

"You're welcome."

"There isn't really a twelve-thirty, is there?" she asked as she went to a sink and patted her face with cool water.

Violet handed her a paper towel. "Nothing scheduled, but there is a certain someone waiting in your office."

"Press?"

"Do you really think I'd do that to you?"

Laney wasn't sure of anything at this point.

"But you'll find out soon enough. I just thought you should know that Harold Reasoner is downstairs now, planning on addressing the press."

"What?" Why was the senior partner doing that? And why hadn't he said anything when she spoke to him earlier?

"Mmm. My response exactly when his secretary called me. Seems he wants to warn the press of harassment laws." She snorted. "More like remind himself and everyone in Dallas that he's important."

"The coverage is wider than that. CNN is here."

"CNN?" Violet looked as if she was going to do her own share of looking out the window when they left the room.

Laney slowly patted her face, wishing she had her purse so she could touch up her makeup. She wanted to look as though none of this fazed her. Maybe it had been a mistake for her to think that she could just ignore the media, pray that they went away. Perhaps she should have addressed them the minute they pulled up to the curb.

She grimaced. Precious good that would have done since she had no plans to discuss the threats that had been made against her beyond saying they were a police matter.

"So who's in my office, then?" she asked.

She caught Violet's smile in the mirror as she stood patiently behind her. "Lunch."

CARTER NOTICED the paleness of Laney's skin as she came into the room. She probably hadn't slept well last night. Which made two of them. But he didn't have half the population of Dallas waiting outside with a microphone.

Her eyes registered surprise and then warmth when she met his gaze.

"Carter."

It was almost a sigh.

He knew in that one moment that he'd done the right thing in coming.

He handed her a cup of sweet tea and motioned for her to sit down at the table where he'd laid out a virtual barbecue buffet from his favorite rib shack on Highway 303. He tried to ignore his desire to get her out of that cold place and take her to his, protect her from the mess swirling around her. Instead, he focused on her.

"Looks like today is going to be even hotter than yesterday," he said, choosing the chair opposite her. "The hog complained the whole way over."

Laney might be within touching distancing physically, but she was a long way off from being there psychologically. She looked around the table as if incapable of identifying the objects there, her hand tightly gripping her cup.

"What?" she said, finally blinking.

Carter smiled around his mouthful of pulled pork sandwich. "The heat. I hear it's one of the hottest summers on record."

She squinted at him. "Are you really talking about the weather?"

He chuckled and pushed a paper plate of samplers toward her. There were barbecue short ribs, chicken and another pulled pork sandwich. "Eat."

She finally released the cup and sat back. "I couldn't possibly swallow a bite."

"Then talk to me about the weather."

Another squint and then she shook her head.

Carter washed down the bite with a swig from a water bottle. "I remember one summer when I was about thirteen. It was so hot, I actually tried to fry an egg on our front steps." He shook his head. "Oh, it fried all right. And then calcified. Caught hell from my father later, who wasn't amused by my little experiment."

"Maybe you should have sprayed oil on the steps first," Laney said.

There. There was the woman he wanted to pull out. "Good point. Maybe I should try it again today."

Without seeming to realize she was doing so, Laney scooted her chair closer to the table and fingered the ribs. "Just so you don't do it on my steps, be my guest."

Carter loved a woman who could eat without feeling self-conscious. Of course, he suspected that Laney still wasn't one hundred percent at the table, but since this wasn't his first meal with her, he knew she would have torn into that rib no matter what her state of mind.

"You don't have steps," he said.

"Yes, I do. Three of them. Leading straight up to the lobby."

"Those don't count. They're not your steps."

"They are too my steps. I walk over them every day when I go home."

He pointed at her with his free index finger. "That doesn't make them yours. If I should go try to fry an egg on them, it won't be you who cleans it up."

"Assuming, of course, that the doorman would let you do it in the first place."

"Bingo."

"So what you're saying, then," she continued, licking sauce from her finger before taking another bite of rib, "is that the number-one responsibility of a step owner is to clean them."

"Mmm. And sit on them. And repair any cracks on occasion so that nobody trips."

"Your steps must need a lot of attention."

Carter's chewing slowed as he grinned. "You have no idea." He pointed to the other sandwich on her plate. "You going to eat that?"

She raised her brows. "I was thinking about it."

He shrugged. "Good. Because this is the best damn barbecue in the state. Be a damn shame if you weren't enjoying it."

Laney seemed to look at the stripped rib she was eating—the third—as if she couldn't believe she'd demolished it.

She put down the bone and wiped her hands. "You…" she began.

Carter swiped his own napkin across his mouth. "Me…" he prompted.

"You're good, do you know that? Real good."

"Wasn't that in a movie somewhere?"

"Yes, I think it was. Something with De Niro in it."

"And that Crystal guy."

She nodded, popping a French fry into her mouth. *"Analyze This."*

"And *That.*"

She laughed, a sound that touched him in places he couldn't begin to draw a map to.

Someone knocked on the closed door. The secretary that had ushered Carter into the office peeked inside. "Sorry to interrupt, but Harold Reasoner is on Line One."

The color instantly drained from Laney's face again.

Carter touched Laney's hand when she moved to get up, presumably to take the call at her desk. "Tell Mr.

Reasoner that Ms. Cartwright is unavailable at the moment and that she'll talk to him as soon as she can."

Was it his imagination, or had the secretary flashed him a quick grin?

"It will be my pleasure," she said as she closed the door.

Laney looked at him in gratitude and then turned her hand over so that she was holding his.

"Come on," Carter said. "Let's get out of here."

16

LANEY KNEW that Carter's talents were many, but she would never have listed among them an ability to duck the attention of the press. He'd moved his bike to the underground parking garage, where she met him, and they pulled onto the street without a second glance from the reporters.

"They'd never look for you on the back of a hog," he'd said.

Laney hugged his back, shivering as the midday heat penetrated her skin and began warming her bones. She hadn't realized she was so cold.

She had that same sensation again of wanting him to never stop. To ride forever. Until there was no more road to follow. But this time it was for a different reason. She wanted to run away. What from, she couldn't exactly say. The story-hungry media was a given, but it was more than that. Sure, she had a difficult case. But she believed in her client's innocence. She was experiencing the usual fear that she might not succeed in her defense of him, that she might fail, but she had been through the process enough to put it down to pretrial nerves. She was a damn good attorney and would do everything in her power to prove Devon's innocence.

Then why this sense that she was missing something?

The motorcycle slowed under them, bringing the ride to an end all too soon. She lifted her cheek from where she'd pressed it against his back, realizing they were outside her apartment building. A television crew sat across the street, but as Carter had predicted, the reporters showed little interest in the classic Harley and its passenger.

The daytime doorman peered out and Carter gave him a thumbs-up. The garage door accessible only by residents slid open and he drove inside.

If Laney was disappointed that he'd brought her home, she wasn't about to share it. What had she expected? For him to read her mind and keep on riding? Or had she secretly hoped he would take her to his place?

"You okay?" he asked as she stood next to the bike and waited for him to get off.

"Huh? Oh, yes, yes. I'm fine." She looked over her shoulder to see the garage door close, completely concealing them from sight. "Thanks for this."

"No problem." He swept his leg over the motorcycle and then took the bag of take-out food from under his seat. "Now let's get this upstairs. It's a crime of the tallest order to let great barbecue like this go to waste."

CARTER DIDN'T OBJECT when Laney went to change out of her suit. And while he was surprised when he heard the shower switch on, he didn't let it deter him from setting out the food the same way he had in her office, adding to the mix a couple of beers from the fridge. When she came back out, he was just about to help himself to her pulled pork sandwich. She plucked it out from under his nose before he could take a bite.

"Go get your own, Marine. This is mine."

She looked miles away from the woman he'd encountered just a few blocks up. Color had returned to her face. Her hair was curlier after her shower (he guessed she must have worn a cap because she couldn't have blown it dry that fast) and the spark he was coming to know and love had returned to her lively blue eyes.

His breath froze briefly in his lungs at his casual use of the L word. Of course, he used it as part of an expression.

Oh, yeah? Then why was he reacting the way he was at the thought of it?

He took in Laney's soft tan slacks and white top. "Don't you own a pair of sweats, for God's sake?" he grumbled.

Her preference for clingy and light-colored materials that accentuated her every soft curve was enough to force a man's mind away from everything but sex.

"Sure," she said, claiming the stool next to him and taking a bite of the sandwich. "I wear them to work out all the time."

"But not to relax."

"God, no. Why would I do that?"

He shrugged and downed half his beer. "Everyone else in the western world does it."

She smiled at him around the French fry she'd just popped into her decadent mouth. "When I wear sweats, I feel I should be working out. They don't relax me at all." She openly eyed him. "Do you wear them?"

He grumbled something under his breath. She had him there. He didn't own a pair of sweats, either. But he sure as hell didn't call wearing designer duds relaxing. "You could at least put on an old pair of jeans or something."

"Here," she said, holding out the rest of her sandwich. "Apparently I've upset you. Let me offer this by way of a truce."

He accepted it, cut it into two pieces and handed her back half, which she readily took. They continued eating in silence for a few minutes. As Carter watched her face, he could tell the big, heavy wheels of her mind were turning. He could virtually hear the squeaking and nearly asked if she needed a little oil.

"So what do you make of the media onslaught?" she asked. "I mean, knowing everything that has happened so far?"

He shrugged. "I don't know. It could prove to be a good thing, right? You believe your client is innocent and these threats and attacks might be an attempt to divert attention from the real guilty party. That would help your case, wouldn't it?"

"You mean by publicizing the threats made against me, public opinion could swing to favor my client or at least raise doubt."

He nodded.

"Is it a good thing?" She chewed on the last of her fries. "I don't know. I'm not so sure." She sat back and sighed. "God, at this point the media's probably wondering if my office leaked the information."

"And did they?"

She blinked. "Not even a remote possibility. The first note aside, no one knew anything to leak."

"You didn't say anything to anyone?"

"No. There really wasn't time."

"The police, then."

She fell silent for a moment. "That seems the more likely source, but…"

He handed her a napkin. "But what?"

"But they believe MacGregor is guilty, so why leak something that might make him appear innocent?" She absently wiped her hands and then put the crumpled napkin on her empty plate. "Sure, not everyone at the DPD is political. Their own pockets are more important than a case that doesn't directly impact them, but…"

He watched her work through the possibilities. Laney was drop-dead gorgeous when she smiled at him suggestively. She was even more appealing when she was thinking about something. Her Kewpie doll mouth edged down at one corner, her blue, heavily lashed eyes squinted, her rounded chin cocked to one side.

God, he realized that he wanted to ravish her, the case and the media be damned.

"I don't know. I feel like I'm missing something. An important puzzle piece that might change everything."

"Change how?"

Her intense gaze nearly knocked the breath out of him.

"That's exactly what I don't know. And it's what scares me most."

Idle hands are the devil's playthings. So Carter busied his to keep from directing some of Laney's intensity back to him rather than her case. He gathered their empty plates and utensils together, stuffing them back into the bags in which they'd come, and then rose to throw them away.

"God! Is that the time?"

Carter looked at the microwave clock and then back at Laney, who was gaping at her watch. "I have a four o'clock appointment at my hairdresser's. And my dress has yet to be delivered."

Carter propped his hands against the counter across from her. "You aren't thinking about still going to that damn thing?"

"Of course I am. I chaired the event. My presence is required."

"Meaning that it couldn't possibly proceed without you."

"It could, but why should it?"

Carter glanced toward the windows. There was only the one media van now, but at the end of the workday the rest would certainly figure out that she was no longer in the office building and would head here, looking for footage for the six and ten o'clock newscasts.

"So you're ready to address the media, then. Have a statement prepared?"

He watched her as she followed his line of thinking, her face going pale again. "I can have something ready between then and now. Perhaps even use the coverage to help publicize the charity."

He grinned. "You're savvy, Laney. Very savvy. But have you really thought this through?"

She crossed her arms over her chest, drawing his attention to the way the clingy fabric stretched across her generous breasts. "What would you suggest?"

"I'd advise you to lay low. For at least today. Maybe tomorrow. Until the press realizes they're not going to get anything and move on to the next story."

She fell silent, apparently considering his suggestion. He guessed that she'd never had to lay low in her life. If she had appointments to get to, a charity event to attend, she would see to those responsibilities come hell or high water.

"What about your responsibility to yourself?" he asked, after voicing his thoughts. Carter pushed from the counter. "Look, Laney, the world will not end tonight if you don't go to that damn thing. But if you do go, you'll be throwing fuel onto the media fire rather than just letting it die a natural death. No matter what you say, what you do, they'll latch on to you like a pack of hungry wolves."

"Until something else comes along and they move on."

"Are you serious? All they need is five seconds of

current footage of you speaking into the camera, much less with your beautiful self decked out to the nines, and they'll crave even more. Especially now that the national media is interested. They'll be able to stretch their seconds into minutes into an hour, easy. Which means this thing doesn't end, it only intensifies."

"Which puts the focus on my client when the trial begins next week. A good thing, since I have every intention of proving his innocence."

Carter squinted at her. Was she serious? "Are you serious?"

"About his innocence?"

"No," he replied. "About your capacity to control the slant of the media. You have no idea how they'll run coverage on the trial. But I can guarantee you it will be in the direction that will grab the most attention. And that usually doesn't bode well for the character they're focused on. We've all watched murderers be turned into saints, saints into murderers for the sake of ratings."

She twisted her lips and wiped at an unseen crumb on the countertop. "What makes you such an expert?"

"I'm not. But you don't have to be one to understand that what I'm saying makes sense."

She fell silent. But he also didn't have to be a body language expert to understand that she was gearing up for a fight.

"Consider your client, Laney. Can you honestly tell me that you can live with him possibly being portrayed in a negative light—something you might have prevented just by canceling a few unimportant items on your calendar?"

"You can't say that I won't have success slanting the media the other way."

Carter took a deep breath. "No, I can't. But do you really want to take that chance?"

God, she was even more charming when she was angry. Just look at the way her plump lips pursed, her shoulders pulled back, her breasts jutted out just begging for attention.

Of course, he was relatively sure that she wouldn't welcome a kiss, much less his growing need for more. She'd likely just as soon sock him as caress him.

Then again, angry sex with the competitive Ms. Cartwright could prove interesting. Very interesting, indeed.

"I'm going to the charity event tonight, Carter." She rose from the stool and looked at her watch again. "And that's that."

He shrugged as if it were no concern of his. "Fine. Just don't get upset when I say I told you so."

He rounded the counter to stand in front of her.

"Now, tell me where I can get a tux at this late hour. Because I'm not letting you go anywhere tonight without me."

Her smile was one hundred percent pure Laney. "It's being delivered with my dress."

17

LANEY HATED TO ADMIT that Carter was right, but his predictions so far were proving to be on target. Every press van had moved from the law offices to stake out the front of her apartment building, and she'd been blinded by lights and flashbulbs as Carter accompanied her out to the limo she'd ordered a month ago. Upon his suggestion that they take his bike, she'd pointed out that even on the back of the hog, the two of them—him in a tux and her in a slinky, sequined dress—would surely catch media attention. And if it were all the same to him, she'd prefer any photos circulating in the press to be flattering, not make her look like a criminal on the lam.

Then again, better to look like a criminal on the lam than a deer caught in the headlights. She'd been unable to make out one single question in the rapid-fire onslaught of questions that met her on the front steps. She remembered saying something about the charity event, the fact that she was looking forward to proving her client's innocence when the trial got under way next week…but her tongue was glued to the back of her throat when they'd asked her about the threats against her.

"Well, that went according to plan," Carter had said casually in the back of the limo.

Now, an hour later at The Centre, she found herself staring at him as she had so often since he'd emerged from the penthouse guest room wearing the tux. She'd guessed at his measurements and was glad to see that the black fabric fit his muscular form to perfection. While he absently tugged at the starched collar of his shirt every now again, and straightened his bow tie, he looked amazingly relaxed for a man who had never attended a formal event of this nature. His dark brown hair looked handsomely disheveled, giving him a reckless playboy sort of appearance that was attracting the women in droves. Every time she left him to mingle and to see to event details, they descended on him like a flock of doves, preening and cooing, each trying to command his attention even as he looked for a mysterious someone just outside their circle. Then he'd meet Laney's gaze and she would realize that someone was her. And her stomach would pitch to the heels of her black stilettos.

What she hadn't anticipated, and neither had Carter, was that everyone she came across would be as interested as the press in learning the specifics of the threats she'd received.

Without the glare of media lights, she'd been able to smile and deliver the line she'd choked on in front of the cameras. "It's a police matter now, so you'll excuse me if I can't discuss it further." Then she'd move on to the next group of donors to avoid answering their questions.

"Who's the hottie?" her friend Betsy now asked, taking her arm and leading her away from the pack.

Laney accepted a fresh glass of champagne from a passing waiter, trying to hide her smile as her gaze sought out the man in question. "Why, I don't know to whom you could possibly be referring," she said.

"Sure you don't. The guy is pissing off every other bachelor in the place, as well as a few of the roving married ones, because all the women are following him around like a bunch of groupies."

Laney laughed. "Yes, well…"

She and Betsy went back to their first day at UT. Oh, she'd always known who Betsy Ewing was. From what she understood, Betsy's family liked to pretend they were the inspiration behind the wildly popular 1980s television series, a distinction Laney couldn't fathom wanting to encourage. But even she had indulged in wondering which one was J.R. and which was Bobby with friends at events such as the one tonight.

On the first day of college, she and Betsy had become fast friends. While they always obeyed the style laws passed down by generations of Southern ladies, they also shared an unquenchable desire to achieve professional success independent of their families' wealth. Laney had focused on law with a passion, while Betsy had gone the business route.

The two of them still met regularly for what they called late-night exhaustion sessions, where they checked into a posh suite at a downtown hotel, both of them too wound up to sleep. They ordered almost every item on the room service menu, watched movies on pay-per-view, and usually but not always slept in the following day.

There had never been a need for either of them to check their tongues at the door. Unfortunately, Laney had the unsettling feeling that was about to change.

Betsy looked at her closely. "Uh-oh. Don't tell me you're dating him."

Laney knew she shouldn't ask, but she needed to. "Why?"

"Oh, Laney. By all means, you can fuck a guy like him, but you can't possibly be insane enough to date one."

Laney felt as if Betsy had just poured a drink over her head. "Oh, and just what do you think you know about him?"

"What, do you think I just got out of high school yesterday? I know this guy. And hundreds more like him. Wannabe cowboys who can't tell the difference between a good shiraz and a cabernet."

"I can choose my own wine. And he's not a cowboy, he's a Marine."

Betsy paused with her glass halfway to her mouth. "Same thing."

Laney's cheeks burned. "I think you'd better lighten up on the champagne, Bets. You don't know what you're talking about."

"I know exactly what I'm talking about. Oh, don't get me wrong. Things are nice for the first couple of months. Great, really, because these guys...mmm. They're fantastic in bed. Then the passion starts to cool and you realize that the only thing you share in common is the bathroom you use."

"That's so crass!"

Betsy shrugged. "It is what it is, Laney. And it always has been. You can take a guy off the range, but you can't take the range out of the guy. It's just the way things are. How they've always been. I can name at least ten women we both know who have made the mistake and are spending the rest of their lives paying for it."

A pudgy man in a tuxedo at least two sizes two small walked by, nearly tripping over his own feet. Barton Fogarty had married into the Cantrell family, one of the wealthiest families in the whole of Texas, thirty years ago. And while his wife appeared to grow more brittle as a result of excessive dieting and plastic surgery, her husband had turned to drink to amuse himself while she was otherwise busy.

Betsy looked at her pointedly. "Exhibit A."

Laney rolled her eyes. "You can't possibly compare Queenie Cantrell's marriage to a ranch hand to Carter and me."

"Can't I?"

Laney's throat almost refused to swallow her champagne.

"Take my advice, Laney. Screw him as long as you like. Then dump him. But promise me you won't make any decisions beyond the next sack session. Please."

"God, I can't believe what a snob you are," Laney said under her breath.

Betsy's date came up and took her by the arm. Laney raised her brows as she realized it was Jason Gaston, a high-profile business attorney from old money that Laney herself had dated a couple of times.

Her friend's smile was nothing if not predatory. "You remember Jason, don't you, Laney?"

She managed to exchange a few pleasantries with him and then the couple walked off, likely to crow about what a great power couple they made and ponder the lifelong mistake Laney might be on the verge of making.

She looked for Carter's handsome face in the crowd, suddenly feeling sick to her stomach. She found him near the buffet table pulling at his collar even as he piled shrimp on a plate.

"SO, MR. SOUTHARD, what is it that occupies your time?" a certain Miss Texas U asked, batting lashes the length of his finger.

An hour into the event and Carter had been approached no fewer than a dozen times by what he was coming to think of as the Dallas Debutante Society. He'd stopped trying to remember names and instead labeled them in a way that differentiated one from the next. Miss Magnolia for her white-and-pink dress, Miss Stone for the diamonds dripping from her every limb, and now Miss UT, who looked as if she might break into a cheer any second, or jump behind the bleachers with him if he made the suggestion.

"I'm chairman of the very successful dot-com hoodoo," he said, offering up another in a long line of answers he'd given to each of the women even as he visually searched for the only woman in the room important to him...and the only woman who knew the truth about him and what he did.

And that's the way he intended to keep it.

"If you'll excuse me..." He almost called her Miss UT.

"Daisy."

"Of course, Daisy," he continued. "I see that my presence is being requested elsewhere."

The young brunette looked put out and made no secret of her curiosity as she craned her neck to see who he had come with.

Laney's blue eyes flashed at him warmly as he crossed the room. She took a long sip of champagne and his attention moved to her red, pouty lips.

"So, Mr. Southard, how does it feel to have every eye in the place on you tonight?" she asked when he reached her.

He gave her an open once-over that seemed to embolden her as she thrust a bare shoulder forward and tilted her head, sending him a look that could only be described as come-hither.

"I beg to differ, Ms. Cartwright," he said. "Every eye is on you and that shockingly sexy backless dress you have on."

Her laugh was low but full of spunk.

"You're proving quite popular tonight," she said after briefly greeting a couple passing by.

Carter put his hand in his jacket pocket to prevent himself from pulling at his too-tight collar yet again. He felt something and pulled it out to find two business cards, likely slipped there by the women he'd met.

"You have no idea," he grumbled, putting the cards on the tray of the first waiter that passed by.

"Discover any interesting prospects?" Laney asked.

"That depends." Damn, she was sexy. The most beautiful woman in the room.

"Oh? On what?"

He leaned in closer to her, wrapping his fingers around her bare upper arm. "On whether or not you plan on propositioning me," he whispered into her ear.

He felt her shiver and then she drew back to smile at him. "Let's say your place? In an hour?"

His place.

Carter grimaced and removed his hand.

After tonight's media circus, he knew that going back to her place wouldn't be an option. But neither was going to his, for more reasons than he cared to explain, given their present company.

"I was thinking something a little more…conducive to what I have in mind," he said instead.

"Oh. What is it, Mr. Southard? Are you hiding a wife at home?" she asked.

He chuckled. "Just an old hound dog that thinks my bed is his when I'm away."

"I think I've learned to live with a little dog slobber over the past couple of days."

Carter accepted a glass of bourbon from a passing waiter and sipped at the fiery liquid. "I'm thinking more along the lines of a hotel. Preferably one with a hot tub."

He had to give her credit for not voicing the disappointment that slipped across her face. "Sounds illicit."

"You have no idea."

Now, if he could only talk her into getting the hell out of there within the next five minutes, maybe he could get back to a place where he didn't feel like a damn penguin a thousand miles away from the nearest block of ice.

_18_

TWO HOURS LATER, Laney led Carter through what she said was one of her favorite places growing up: the horse stables on her father's estate.

Carter had been under no illusions when it came to her family's wealth. But he could never have imagined the expansive compound a half hour outside Dallas where she'd been raised. The house sat back nearly a quarter of a mile from the road, looking more like a sprawling three-story hotel than a single-family home. The garage alone was larger than most people's houses, and he counted at least seven bay doors that hid, he had little doubt, seven high-end cars.

He tried to imagine the long, black stretch limo that had brought them there pulling up outside his two-bedroom shack. Here, it was right at home, cruising up the long, circular drive and coming to a stop in front of double doors that looked large enough to drive a Mack truck through.

But rather than take him straight inside the house, she'd led him to the stables some way off to the right. The darkness cloaked much of the opulence of his surroundings, he was sure, but the estate was well lit, allowing him to take in the enormous stables and extensive landscaping.

Christ, his military pay over the course of a year probably wasn't enough to cover the upkeep of this place for a week.

He watched Laney walk ahead of him. She still wore her slinky black dress but had taken off her heels, letting the straps dangle from the index finger of her left hand as she moved like a sexy ghost through stables that, if he wasn't mistaken, were built of mahogany or some equally expensive wood.

Hell, the place was so top-shelf, he wondered how the horses dared drop a load on the pristine, straw-covered floor.

Laney placed her right hand on top of a carved stall door that bore a brass nameplate and turned to face him, her smile lighting her pretty face.

"Song, there's someone I'd like you to meet," she said.

The head of a black Arabian poked over the top of the door. The horse whinnied and then sat still as Laney stroked his long, shiny nose.

Carter leaned against the connecting wall. He'd taken off the blasted bow tie and stuffed it into his pocket the instant they'd climbed into the limo and then had undone a few of the top buttons of the scratchy shirt, but he was a long way from feeling comfortable, a condition not helped by their current surroundings.

"Is there something I should shake?" he asked with a raised brow.

Laney laughed softly. "I've had Song for ten years. My father named him that because he said that's what he bought him for—a song."

She quoted an amount that could probably buy the rights to one of Michael Jackson's albums.

Carter reached out and allowed the horse to smell his hand, then ran his palm over the horse's solid neck. He hadn't been around horses much other than the neighbor's broken-down beast who liked to graze in his overgrown backyard every now and again. But obviously Laney was right at home talking baby talk to the great stallion and feeding him sugar cubes she took from a nearby bag that hung on the wall.

"Does your father breed horses?" he asked.

"Dad? No. He did for a couple of years when I was younger, but horses were more my mother's passion than my father's." She absently patted the horse. "He sires out a couple of the stallions, like Song here, but that's the extent of his interest. And even then, the stable manager sees to the details."

She drew in a deep breath, bringing his attention to her long, elegant throat and the modest diamond-and-amethyst necklace she wore. "I love the smell of the stables."

Carter twisted his lips. "Depends on how recently they've been cleaned."

He got the feeling these stables were cleaned twice

a day by a manager and hands who likely lived on the premises.

"Come on," Laney said. "Let's go inside the main house so I can show you around."

"How many houses are there?"

"Not including staff accommodations? Four."

He'd been joking when he asked the question. So he didn't quite know what to do with the answer.

"Dad says it's important for guests to feel at home when they visit. So he makes sure they have their own houses, complete with working staff and transportation."

"Transportation meaning…"

"Cars."

Carter was suddenly all too aware that he didn't have his bike here. In fact, as good as he could figure it, he was stuck at the Cartwright mansion and completely at Laney's mercy when it came to getting back to town. He didn't think taxis responded to calls this far out. And as far as he could tell, the nearest neighbor was a mile up the road and their place looked about as welcoming as this one did. If he knocked on their door unannounced, he'd likely find a police cruiser summoned for his transportation.

It might just be worth escaping this parallel universe of lavish excess.

He was slightly grateful that Laney led him around to the back of the house instead of the front. He held the door she opened and then followed her inside what could be considered a mudroom but was the size of his living room. Raincoats neatly hung on hooks and various boots were lined up along the wall, with two benches to sit on. He noticed that she didn't even have to click on any light switches. It was as though a spotlight followed her wherever she stepped.

Welcome to the lives of the wealthy, he thought wryly.

She dropped her shoes in the hall and walked into a kitchen large enough to cater half the city.

"This was always my favorite room in the house," she said, washing her hands at the sink. He followed suit and accepted the towel she offered. "Are you hungry? I could probably rustle us up some leftovers. Or there are always sandwich fixings."

Rustle…fixings…Carter couldn't help his grin. Somewhere along the line someone had injected a dose of everyday Texas expressions into her life. He wondered who. Did she hang around the stables when she was a kid? Had the housekeeper or cook played a big role in her life?

"I could go for a sandwich," he said.

A stout, middle-aged woman in a maid's uniform appeared in the doorway, presumably from a back stairway or servants' quarters. She looked as if it were seven in the morning, rather than midnight, and she was clocking in for the day.

"Good evening, Miss Laney. Shall I prepare something for you?"

Laney greeted the woman warmly. "No, thank you, Gladys. We can take care of ourselves. Sorry to have woken you."

"No apologies necessary. Let me know if you need anything."

"We'll be fine. I'll see you in the morning."

Carter watched the woman disappear as silently as she'd appeared. He sat down at one of six stools positioned around a prep island as large as a car, running his hand over the dark, smooth granite. The room was brightly lit, displaying all its over-the-top glory. Was that a pizza oven in a small room off to his right? Laney opened a cabinet to reveal a series of switches, and experimented until just a couple of the soft lights in the ceiling shone on the island and above the sink. She smiled at him as she walked over to the refrigerator.

Damn. His face must have given away his uneasiness with his surroundings. But even the dimmed lighting couldn't hide the fact that he was in way over his head here. While this house might be Laney's home, he couldn't imagine ever taking a place like this for granted. Or remembering the times when his father had been stationed overseas and he'd faced bare cupboards.

He absently rubbed the back of his neck, surprised when Laney slid a plate in front of him holding one of the largest sandwiches he'd ever seen.

She laughed. "My father always says that if you're going to make a sandwich, there's no reason why you shouldn't make a good one."

She filled a couple of bowls with chips and pretzels and came to sit next to him, her sandwich a much more modest version of his own.

Damn, but she was beautiful.

He took a deep breath, feeling some of the tension seep from his muscles as he looked at her. What a fascinating creature she was, sitting there in bare feet, designer gown, a smear of mayonnaise at the side of her mouth as she took a bite of her sandwich.

Carter tilted her chin up with his fingers and wiped the mayo away with a swipe of his thumb.

"Drinks!" Laney said, appearing suddenly antsy. "I forgot to get us something to drink."

Carter squinted at her. So not all was well with the only child of the house, either. Interesting…

"Do you bring many guys home?" he asked, trying for casual as he took a bite of his sandwich.

Laney didn't answer right away. Instead, she asked him if beer was all right and he nodded.

"Actually, outside my senior year prom date, you're the first."

That got his attention. "Any specific reason?"

She shrugged. "I don't know… Until now it never struck me as odd. But when I was working toward getting my law degree, there seemed to be so little time to develop a strong enough relationship with a guy I would want to bring home."

Carter reminded himself that the only reason she'd brought him here was because of the press nipping at her heels.

"Besides, Dad and I are so close that when I came home, I did it for the express reason to spend time with him." She smiled. "Another person would have detracted from that."

"Ah, a daddy's girl."

She drew her shoulders back. "And proud of it."

They fell into an easy silence, and before Carter knew it, he'd polished off his sandwich along with half of hers and had drained his beer bottle.

"Good?" she asked.

"Great."

"Good."

Was it him, or did Laney suddenly seem uncomfortable?

Damn, he wished more than ever he had his bike here. Because this was exactly the point where he'd wish her a good-night and take off.

Instead, he felt like he was going to end up as that detraction.

"Where is your father?" he asked, looking around. Somehow he got the feeling that if Mr. Cartwright were here, he'd have made his presence known already.

Laney shifted on her stool. "He's out of town until tomorrow morning. Some trip up to Alaska to see about an invention that converts natural gas to hydrogen."

He nodded. "Of course."

"So…" she said.

"So."

"Um, it's after midnight. Shall I show you to your room?"

"I have a room?"

She laughed, and Carter realized that she was as uncomfortable about the sleeping arrangements as he was.

"Lead on," he said with a sweep of his arm after they'd cleaned up after themselves.

Laney did. Across a half acre of the first floor, up the sweeping staircase, and on to the second floor, which very much resembled the upscale hotel he'd compared the outside to.

She stopped in front of a door and then opened it, switching on a light. "This is one of the guest rooms that are always kept prepped."

He stepped inside, took in the king-size bed, the mammoth flat-screen TV, the fireplace.

He turned toward her. Was it his imagination, or had she just backed up a step?

"My room's in the east wing."

"Ah. Let me guess. A long way from this room."

She smiled and looked down at her feet. "I'm sorry… It's just that even at my age, this will always be my father's house…"

Carter stepped closer to her, cupping her face in his right hand. "It's all right. I can understand your need to respect him."

Her expression of relief was so profound that he couldn't help leaning in to kiss her.

Laney sighed against him, melting into his arms as he threaded his fingers in her hair, shaking the soft strands free of the pins holding them in place.

Moments later, they pulled apart, Carter's breathing

ragged. "I think you'd, um, better go before I have a change of heart."

She nodded and walked backward toward the door, nearly tripping over the hem of her dress. "All right. Um, I'll see you in the morning."

"Good night."

The door clicked closed and Carter turned back toward the bed. He was better off spending the night alone. In a place like this, he was afraid even a man like him could come down with a massive case of performance anxiety.

_19_

CARTER WOKE to the sun slanting in through the window. He jackknifed to a sitting position in the bed, squinting at his surroundings before picking up the clock on the nightstand.

Seven-thirty.

Damn.

After Laney had left him alone, he'd been convinced he wouldn't be able to sleep a wink, but he must have drifted off shortly after having the thought, just now awakening to an empty room.

He tossed the blankets to the other side of the bed and sat scrubbing his face with his hands, wondering how he'd gotten into such a mess. He…Laney… They weren't just from different classes, they lived on different planets.

He looked up to find a pile of clothing on the dresser. He got up and read the note on top. "In case you'd like a change of clothes, Mr. Carter," it read. He fingered through the choices of jeans and shirts, and noticed where a few pairs of casual shoes had also been left. All of them still bore price tags.

Christ, they kept clothes on hand?

He shook his head and walked into the connecting bathroom, catching a quick shower before putting on the tux from the night before, minus the jacket. He rolled up the shirtsleeves, then went in search of life.

He found it in the kitchen.

He'd suspected the night before that the darkness had prevented him from seeing the room and the estate as they really were, but he was still unprepared for the reality. Through the back windows, he saw land that stretched on forever, a series of lush, manicured paddocks, an Olympic-sized pool, what looked like a dirt bike track complete with death knolls and carefully positioned gates.

"Good morning!"

The sound of Laney's voice jarred him out of his thoughts. She got up from a long table to his right that overlooked a large deck. The man with her was no doubt her father, and he was looking at Carter with a mixture of wariness and amusement.

Laney was dressed in riding apparel, complete with boots, as was her father. Had they already been out?

Even as Laney kissed him on the cheek and took his arm, he couldn't help feeling put out. Why hadn't she woken him?

She led him toward the table. Her father wiped his mouth with his napkin and then stood.

"Daddy, I'd like you to meet Carter Southard. Carter, this is my father, Blake Cartwright."

"A pleasure, Mr. Cartwright," Carter said. "This is some place you've got here."

"It's Blake, please. And thank you."

"We were just having breakfast. Won't you join us?" Laney asked.

Carter wanted to say no, ask her to take him into town pronto, away from this strange existence back to a place that was more familiar, but he realized he couldn't. Unless he jumped on the back of one of the horses he could see being led into the stables, he was stuck for now.

"Thank you," he said, sitting next to Laney and across from the elder Cartwright.

Thankfully father and daughter appeared to have finished with their meal so Carter accepted a breakfast roll and a cup of black coffee and uneasily traded casual conversation on the weather and riding.

"Well, I think I'm going to grab a shower and get dressed," Laney said finally, getting to her feet again. Carter rose, as did her father, to acknowledge her departure. "Will you be ready to leave in twenty?" she asked Carter.

He wanted to ask if ten was out of the question. Or why she couldn't just take him right now.

Instead, he nodded. "Twenty minutes is fine."

Carter watched her leave, appreciating the way her riding pants fit her rounded bottom. Then he realized he was checking out her ass in the presence of her father. Not the smartest of moves.

"Come, Carter. Let's go out onto the deck," Blake Cartwright said.

He opened a door that had no handle as far as Carter could tell, then motioned for him to walk through. The two men stood side by side holding their coffee cups, looking out over the vast tract of land.

"Do you mind if I just cut through the bullshit and come straight to the point, Carter?"

He blinked at the older man, immediately respecting the way he did business.

"I wouldn't have it any other way."

Blake looked at him squarely. "Don't let your current surroundings fool you. If you hurt my little girl, I will come gunning for you, Mr. Southard. Military training or no."

Carter held his gaze for a long moment, and then finally nodded. "I would feel no differently if I had a daughter, Mr. Cartwright."

Blake stared at him and then seemed to come to the conclusion that he'd been understood. "Very good, then." He grinned. "Now, Laney tells me we share an interest in motorcycles. Why don't we take a walk down to the dirt bike track?"

EARLY THE FOLLOWING Monday morning, Laney sat in her office, barely aware that the sun had yet to rise outside her window. It was barely 6:00 a.m., but the office buzzed with activity. Or at least her end of it, as she and her cocounsel, assistants and paralegals prepared for the MacGregor trial, which would begin in just under three hours.

"Did you sleep last night?" Violet asked, bringing in a cup of coffee.

Laney gave her a long look.

"Right. Neither did I. I kept thinking I'd forgotten to copy the witness depositions, and then when I did finally fall asleep, I dreamed that I'd fed them to the shredder instead of the copy machine and there were no other copies anywhere to be had."

Laney smiled. "I dreamed I was strapped to a table and being administered a lethal injection."

Violet raised her hands. "Okay, on the creepiness scale, you win."

"Small comfort."

Laney leaned her head against her hand and sipped the hot coffee, allowing the strong liquid to surge through her veins, feeding her much-needed caffeine.

"Has the process delivery receipt come back yet on Tiffany Mullins?" she asked.

Violet narrowed her eyes. "I put it on your desk."

Laney moved papers around and came up with it. "So you did."

Thankfully, Violet didn't say what she was obviously thinking as she collected a pile of folders from the out-box, some of which were the original copies of depositions featured in her dream.

"Let me know if you need anything," Violet said.

"I will. Thanks."

Okay, so maybe her sleepless night had more to do with Carter than with pretrial jitters. She'd rewritten her opening statement no fewer than five times over the past few hours. About as many times as she'd found her hand reaching for the phone, yearning to call Carter.

She hadn't seen him since she'd driven back to her apartment the other morning after they spent the night at her father's house. She'd chattered about inane topics all during the drive, feeling suddenly awkward in his company for reasons she couldn't quite pinpoint. Or, rather, feeling suddenly uncomfortable with his reaction to her.

He'd sat back and stared out the window, contributing little to the conversation. And the more silent he became, the more she'd talked.

Truth was, she'd felt uncomfortable when she'd viewed the Cartwright estate through his eyes. It had always been home to her, but for a few brief, unwanted moments it had looked like a horrible example of excess, especially in these difficult economic times.

How must he have viewed her in those surroundings? How must he have judged her father?

Of course, she understood that the family money had been earned through the hard work of her great-grandfather and grandfather, then multiplied by her father, but how much did one family need?

Laney shook off the uneasy feelings. Never, ever, had she experienced anything like it. So when Carter had said goodbye to her in the garage, climbed onto the back of his Harley and driven away, she didn't try to stop him. She was almost relieved he was going.

And she'd been haunted by the image and the memory ever since. Along with a dull achy need that refused to go away, no matter how busy she kept herself.

She picked up the process server receipt. She'd requested and had been granted a Subpoena to Appear to one antagonistic Ms. Tiffany Mullins. Her cocounsel Dave Matthews had questioned the move. One of the first rules in the defense attorney handbook was never to ask a witness a question that you didn't already know the answer to.

At this point in the case, after suffering through three threats and conflicting information, Laney decided she just wanted answers.

Besides, she didn't expect Tiffany would get anywhere near the courthouse. Girls like her didn't earn the rap sheet they did by obeying the law.

No. Laney's intentions were to scare a few birds out of the bushes and see what happened. She glanced at her watch. Problem was, time was running out and the birds appeared to be clinging to the bush.

CARTER SAT in a coffee shop just up the street from Laney's offices. While he didn't expect her to recognize his bike, he wasn't taking any chances and had parked it a block over. Far enough to keep her from knowing he was watching out for her. Close enough to intervene if someone did try to pull something.

"More coffee, sweetheart?" a pretty, young wait-ress asked.

He pushed the cup in her direction and continued to stare out the window.

He hadn't meant to be as cold as he was the other day. Laney hadn't deserved that. But his emotions had been too raw. She may have come from a place where every-thing was put on the table, but he'd been raised that emotions were best kept to yourself. Where talking was thought to be overrated and it was what a man did that defined him, not what he said.

He grimaced as he sipped his coffee. He bet that Laney and her father talked about everything under the sun.

He remembered Blake Cartwright's words to him.

Hurt my little girl, and I'll come gunning for you.

It was then that Carter understood what he had to do. He had to end things with Laney before they went too far. Before he ended up hurting her more than she would be already.

Before he ended up hurting himself more, even though that seemed impossible given his own pain, which was like a hunting knife to the chest.

He cleared his throat and pressed both hands against his coffee cup.

There was no future for them. His world was foreign to her. Her world was another planet, inhabited by aliens who could drop a hundred grand on a bike track in the backyard that was barely used just because they woke up with the idea one morning, but had yet to actually ride on it.

Impossible. That's what any thought of a future relationship with Laney seemed like to him.

And in case he needed proof, all he had to do was remember the details of his own parents' failed marriage.

Oh, his mother's family wasn't anywhere near as wealthy as the Cartwrights. But just enough to make his father feel like less of a man. Just enough to cause love to turn to bitterness.

Christ, his father would love this. Like father, like son. He'd ended up making the exact same mistake as his dad.

Well, almost. By stopping it now, at least he wouldn't be hurting any children.

A vision of a young boy with his mom's pale blond hair and his dad's hunger for adventure riding over that hundred-thousand-dollar track filled his mind.

He rubbed his closed eyelids with the pads of his index fingers. Now he was seeing things that would never be.

But the fact that he'd even thought about children with Laney was momentous. Because he'd never considered them before beyond a niggling fear that the condom might have broken and he'd impregnated someone he'd never had any intention of marrying.

Yet with Laney...

He shoved his coffee cup aside, causing liquid to spill over the side and the cup to clatter against the saucer. He really needed to stop this adolescent bullshit. He wasn't some damn kid wet behind the ears. He was a thirty-year-old man who certainly knew when to climb off a ride that wasn't fun anymore.

But what was a man to do when all he could think about was that damn ride?

There was movement in front of the office building.

Carter focused on a motorcycle that had just pulled up to the curb. Not a Harley like his, but one of those newfangled racing bikes, yellow, with the driver dressed all in black, including a helmet with a mirrored visor. But it wasn't the driver who caught his attention; it was his passenger. A girl of about eighteen or nineteen, wearing a short black leather skirt and a neon-green belly tank, got off the back of the bike. She pulled the large bag hanging behind her around to her front, then turned away from the lobby of the building. Hunching over slightly, she took something out of the bag, seeming to check it.

Carter realized it was a gun.

He took out a twenty-dollar bill and flicked it to the table.

"Hey, mister! Don't you want your change?" the waitress called after him.

Carter ignored her. He was too busy cursing himself for being so far away from the building. Too far away to stop the young woman packing heat from entering. Too far away to stop her from doing whatever it was she planned to do.

20

LANEY PACKED the last of the exhibits in a large, vinyl carrying case. This was it. Everything was ready to go. Even now, her client, Devon MacGregor, was being transferred to the courthouse lockup. And whether she was prepared or not, in little more than an hour the trial would begin.

She stood near her office window, hands on hips, and let out a long sigh. Down on the curb she spotted a motorcycle. Her heart skipped a beat. Until she realized that it wasn't Carter.

She watched one of the lobby guards come out of the building and head in the biker's direction. The rider took off in a squeal of tires and a loud roar she could hear even at this height.

"All set?" Dave asked, collecting the carrying case from her desk.

Laney turned from the window. "All set. All we have left to do now is pray."

"I thought that's what we do when the case goes to the jury."

She smiled. "I tend to do it through the entire process." She put her briefcase and purse on her desk. "I figure it can't hurt."

"Good point. Meet you there?"

She nodded. "See you there."

She watched Dave leave. Violet followed after him toward the elevators, loading him down with even more case materials.

Laney plucked her suit jacket from the back of her chair and turned toward the window again as she shrugged into it. She didn't know what she was looking for, but she couldn't help herself from looking nonetheless.

"Stay right where you are, lawyer bitch."

Laney slowed her movements, making out the figure of the young woman in the glass. She was pointing something at her as she closed the door to the office. Laney had little doubt that something was a gun.

She hadn't anticipated the gun.

But the girl's appearance was exactly what she'd hoped for.

She slowly shifted to face her, holding her hands slightly up in the air. "Hi, Tiffany," she said as calmly as she could. "You're late."

The girl looked over her shoulder at the closed door and then back again. "What are you talking about?"

Laney pulled out her chair. "Why don't we sit down—"

"Look who thinks she's calling the shots!" Tiffany waved the gun. "See this here? This tells me I'm the one in charge."

"I didn't mean to imply otherwise."

"Sit down. And if there's any kind of silent alarm or something, don't you dare touch it. Not if you don't want to see blood all over that pretty white suit you're wearing."

"I wouldn't dream of it."

"Why did you say I'm late?"

Laney shrugged as she carefully took her seat. There was no silent alarm button. This wasn't a bank office, it was a law firm. And this was the first time to her knowledge that any of the lawyers had had a gun pointed at them in their own office.

She cleared her throat. While this wasn't going down quite as she'd expected, it didn't mean it was a lost cause. So long as she kept her wits about her.

She said as calmly as possible, "I expected to see you twenty minutes after the subpoena was served."

The girl's eyes narrowed, the gun shaking along with her hand. Laney realized she was more at risk of an accidental shooting than a purposeful one. Not exactly the mark of a girl who was used to pulling guns on people.

Then again, hadn't she learned to stop indulging in basic psychology with Carter?

Hopefully this wouldn't end up as horribly wrong as that had.

"So all this was some sort of ploy to force me out of hiding?"

"No, Tiffany. This was all some sort of ploy to get you to admit that Devon didn't rob that convenience store or kill that clerk. You did."

The girl laughed, a hysterical sound that set Laney's teeth on edge. The door swung quickly open behind Tiffany, catching her side and sending her reeling. But not before the gun she held discharged, sending a bullet whizzing in Laney's direction.

Laney dove for the floor, unsure if she'd been hit. She didn't hurt anywhere. That was a good sign, wasn't it? She glanced up to see that the bullet had hit the glass wall, leaving a tiny hole and a starburst of lines ringing it.

She crawled to peek around the desk. Carter stood over the girl and twisted the gun easily from her hand.

She'd never been so glad to see anyone in her life.

HALF AN HOUR LATER at the courthouse, Laney stood outside the basement holding cells rubbing her arms. Despite the weather report that predicted today to be one of the hottest on record, she couldn't seem to warm up.

"Are you sure you're okay?" Carter asked her.

Carter.

She didn't have to ask. Although it had felt as if he'd abandoned her, he'd been watching after her all along. She understood now that he was that kind of guy.

She also understood that despite his concern for her, he had effectively locked her out.

She nodded, although she felt anything but okay. "Thanks to you, I'm fine." She smiled without humor. "The next time I accuse someone of murder, remind me not to do it when they're holding a gun."

Carter reached out and touched the side of her face. Amazing how she immediately warmed under his fingertips. And how the small gesture inspired hope that not all was lost.

A buzzer sounded and the metal security door swung open. "You're clear to enter, Ms. Cartwright," an armed guard said.

She turned to look at Carter. Would he still be there when she finished what she had to do? She didn't know. And the prospect of his leaving frightened her more than the coming meeting.

"Ma'am?" the guard prompted.

Laney had no choice but to turn away from Carter and go talk to her client before the trial began in fifteen minutes.

She was led into a meeting room. Devon tried to stand, his hand and ankle shackles clattering. She didn't tell him not to bother. She waited until the door was closed behind her and remained standing.

"I'm going to request a dismissal," she said.

Devon blinked at her. "What?"

Laney approached the table and sat down opposite him, her movements measured to delay her response. "I'm going to request a dismissal on the grounds that the real perpetrator has been arrested."

Devon slumped back into his seat. "What?" he said again. Laney got the impression that he wasn't so much asking her the question but himself.

"Yes." Laney opened her briefcase and pretended

she needed to refer to her notes. "A Ms. Tiffany Mullins was taken into custody a short while ago."

"But that's impossible."

Laney put her hands on top of the pad. "She's already admitted to writing me threatening notes, slashing my tires and breaking into my home."

As a criminal defense attorney, Laney was used to playing her cards close to her chest. But this time one wrong card, and her entire plan would collapse.

"Is something the matter, Devon?" she asked. "I understand that Tiffany is your girlfriend—something I had to find out from someone else, I feel compelled to point out. But surely you knew her past."

"What's her past got to do with the present?"

Laney tilted her head. "Are you saying she didn't commit the robbery and shoot the clerk?"

Devon's mouth audibly snapped shut.

Throughout the course of the case, Laney had always felt she was missing something. A puzzle piece that floated just beyond her reach. And despite the bullet aimed in her direction a short time ago, she'd finally been able to grasp the bit of mystery and examine it until it made perfect sense.

When she'd met Tiffany, she'd suspected the girl had been behind the threatening notes and actions demanding that Laney drop Devon's case. But seeing that she was his girlfriend, it didn't make sense that she would want one of the best defense attorneys to leave her boyfriend hanging.

The simple explanation was that she had wanted him to hang for a crime she committed. But Laney didn't like simple. It was too neat.

Instead, she'd figured out that Tiffany had been following orders. Orders made by the boyfriend who sat across from Laney now.

She began to get up.

"Wait! Where are you going?" Devon demanded.

"To present my request to the judge in his quarters."

"But…Tiffany didn't do it."

It was a start, but not exactly what she was looking for. And seeing as the clock was ticking, she didn't have much time to get what she needed.

"So if Tiffany didn't do it, Devon, who did?"

"Whatever I say to you doesn't go beyond this room, right?"

"Attorney-client privilege."

"Tiffany didn't do it because I did it."

Bingo.

"So the threats…"

"Were supposed to throw a shadow of reasonable doubt on my case."

Just as she'd suspected. "So your idea was to convince the public that someone out there, someone who might be the real shooter, was responsible for the threats."

"Yes."

He looked all too pleased with himself. Which made what she had to say next less difficult.

She began to get up again. "Then it's my advice to you, as your attorney, that you take the prosecutor's plea deal."

"What?"

"You're guilty. Plead it."

The look on his face was one of absolute shock.

"That's my advice to you, Devon."

His mouth worked around words she couldn't make out. Then he said, "You can't do that. You have to represent me. You can be disbarred if you don't."

Laney remembered the fear she'd felt when she'd discovered her slashed tires...her ransacked apartment... when Tiffany had held the gun on her only this morning. Just so a bored kid of means could get his rocks off robbing a convenience store and shooting the clerk.

She pressed her hands against the table and leaned toward him. "Do you really want to stick with your not-guilty plea? Do you want me to represent you in a drawn-out trial, Devon? If you do, I will. But rest assured, the little stunt you tried to play on me? It will be nothing in comparison to what I can do to you."

"But you're my attorney. You're supposed to represent me no matter what."

She straightened to a standing position and crossed her arms. "Trust me, Devon, I will. But mark my words, you will still go down for this. An innocent man was murdered. Do you really expect me to overlook that?"

She shook her head and then checked her watch.

"You have five minutes to make up your mind, Devon. My advice is that you take the plea deal."

Then she left the room.

"I think you should have been a homicide detective instead of an attorney," Carter said after the court business was done.

Devon had ultimately taken her advice and would be serving a twenty-five-year-to-life sentence for armed robbery and second-degree murder.

She and Carter had gone to a diner afterward and sat across from each other, Dallas rushing by outside the large, picture window. While they were talking about the morning's events, something even larger loomed between them. Something that neither of them dared bring up. Something neither one of them could ignore.

"What, and throw away my law degree?" Laney said.

He considered her over the rim of his coffee cup as he drank, his eyes full of emotion.

Laney had to look away. "Not that that will be worth much after this morning is over. A senior partner has requested my presence in his office immediately."

Carter's cup clanked against his saucer as he put it down. "Shouldn't you be getting back to work, then?"

Her heart expanded in her chest. She didn't want this moment to end. She yearned to draw out this brief respite from reality as long as she could.

"What, so I can rush my resignation?" She shook her head. "I'll do it when I'm good and ready."

She supposed she couldn't really blame Harold Reasoner. Devon was his godson and the only child of his best friend. It was natural that he would want to protect Devon.

She wondered if his view would change if he knew what she did.

Then again, she suspected it wouldn't. If Devon had been found guilty as a result of trial, the firm would have lobbied heavily for him to serve his sentence at a mental facility rather than in prison, and an appeal would have been filed immediately.

This way, a bit of justice had been served. And Devon would probably still end up in a mental facility, although it would take some fancy legal maneuvering. But his father had the kind of money that could make it happen.

She shifted uncomfortably in her chair, coming closer to the something that hovered between her and Carter than she was prepared to admit.

"You're leaving the firm?" Carter asked quietly.

Laney looked down and nodded.

"What will you do?"

She shrugged. "I honestly don't know."

She took a deep breath and then exhaled, feeling better than she had in a long, long time when it came to her career. Even a week ago, uttering those words would have sent the fear of God through her. Now…well, now she'd been given a different glimpse of her future. And she needed to pursue it. At least where it pertained to her work life.

As for her personal life…

"And you?" she asked quietly. "Are you going to meet the Corps requirements and petition to be reinstated?"

Carter looked out the window. "I don't know."

Laney's cell phone vibrated in her jacket pocket. She didn't want to answer it. Didn't want to let the outside world back in just yet.

She slipped it out and reluctantly eyed the display. Violet. It was the fifth time in as many minutes that her secretary had tried to get through to her.

"I really should be getting back," she said softly.

Carter nodded, and then squinted at her as if through a cloud of smoke.

Laney took his hand before he could get up. She wanted to say something, anything, to get him to agree to meet her later. To try to work things out between them.

Instead, she whispered, "Thank you."

Carter looked as if he'd wanted her to say something different. Perhaps the words she'd been considering. "Just so everything worked out okay."

She smiled a watery smile. "Yes. I guess it has, hasn't it? On both sides."

If only she could convince her heart of the same.

21

IT HAD BEEN a long time since Carter had made this drive. And he wasn't all that clear why he was doing it now. But at some point over the past month since he'd left Laney standing outside that Dallas coffee shop, he'd begun questioning the decisions he'd made in his life so far. And one of the biggest was his decision to allow his estrangement from his mother to go on.

His old pickup truck ate up the road between Dallas and Austin. It was September now, and the heat wave might have let up, but it was still hotter than hell. He reached over and patted Blue where he sat with his head out the window, blessing those cars behind them with the gobs of slobber the wind knocked free from his sagging jowls. Taking the truck rather than his bike allowed him to bring Blue along. The old dog seemed to appreciate the gesture. The neighbor's five-year-old kid had discovered that his blunt-edged scissors cut more than colored construction paper, and Blue had the bald spots to prove it.

Oh, Carter knew that the estrangement from his mother was all his doing. She still wrote him a letter once a month, called on holidays and his birthday, and kept up on his goings-on. Without fail, she continued to hold up her mother end of the bargain.

But as a son he'd dropped the ball a long time ago. And now it was time he picked the blasted thing back up.

He grudgingly admitted that a lot had changed in his view of the world since he'd met Laney. For a man as set in his ways as he'd believed himself to be, she'd easily taken his stubborn chin in her soft, white hands and turned his head from here to there, showing him different landscapes, making him see beyond his narrow view.

And there wasn't a day, an hour, a minute, a second that went by that he didn't remember what it was like to have her in his life. Not a moment passed when he didn't ache for her in a way that was shocking in its intensity.

He thought of calling her up. Showing up on her doorstep—which wouldn't be too difficult because every now and again he found his bike leading him to her apartment building, where he'd sit for a time watching for her, even if she no longer needed looking after.

"One of man's greatest flaws is thinking he can conquer a problem by hitting it with the same ole hammer."

Carter rubbed his chin, remembering group leader Gary Nussom's words yesterday at the biweekly meetings he'd begun attending. Like him, Gary was a Marine, now retired. But no matter the twenty years Nussom had on him, he openly admitted to nightmares and nightly sweats and waking up filled with a bloodlust that left him shaking.

Who needed drugs, he'd asked, when war could screw up your mind far more than a drink, a puff, a snort or a needle? And the damage was permanent. You could use some tools to help deal with it, but it would always be there. To the very day you died.

Carter never thought himself the kind of guy to get into this sort of shit. And he certainly hadn't participated to the extent that Nussom would have liked for the first couple of weeks. But gradually he was coming to understand that he wasn't alone. And they weren't alone. And by accepting that, he was beginning to open up in a way that he never could as a true blood, Devil Dog Marine.

While in the beginning he might have convinced himself that he was just going through the motions, attending the meetings so he might earn his way back into the Corps, it didn't take him long to understand that he didn't want to go back. Maybe at some point in the future, but not now.

The Corps had been right in suspending him. He'd been in no mental shape to be out there on the front lines where he imagined enemies everywhere. And he had no idea when that might change.

So he'd gone ahead and used the money he'd saved up while stationed away from home and bought Old Man Johnson's closed-up auto repair shop. No sooner had he pried the boards off the windows than he began getting business from Johnson's old customers, some looking for an oil change, others a tire rotation. Most of the vehicles needed repairs that might have been ignored a year ago, with the owners trading them in for new models. But in the current economic mess, repairs seemed to be the name of the game.

Business already, and he hadn't officially opened his doors yet. Three weeks in, and he was interviewing mechanics. One of the neighborhood teenagers hanging around the place was helping out without pay—something Carter was going to change when he got back with a nice, fat check. Some customers made cracks about Naomi being a girl, but Ni had proven herself gifted when it came to a car engine, and Carter had no intention of letting her go anywhere.

Still, no matter what he did to occupy his time—be it fixing up the shop and repairing cars, renovating his father's old shack of a house or attending group meetings—he couldn't seem to escape one small fact: he missed Laney like hell.

What was the saying? Time heals all wounds? He snorted. Right.

Then there was another one. Absence makes the heart grow fonder. Now *that* he could relate to. Only fondness didn't come close to describing his almost crippling need for her.

So you've been punishing every woman who's crossed your path for your mother's sins.

Laney's words, spoken while she was spooned against his body in all her nude glory, had haunted him ever since she'd said them.

Could she be right? Was that why he never let a woman closer than arm's length? Oh, he could have sex with them. But anything beyond that was forbidden territory. Even with her.

Especially with her.

He punched at the truck's radio station buttons, searching out a song that didn't have to do with crying into somebody else's beer, tractors or unfaithful ex-lovers, and then shut off the radio altogether, earning him a look from Blue.

"What?" he asked the old hound. "Did I interrupt your slobber session?"

Blue licked his chops and went back to pole watching.

The whole class thing, he knew it was all just so much superficial bullshit. While he admitted discomfort at the wealth her father displayed, the problem lay not with her father, but with himself.

And that was the real reason he was heading down to see his mother, wasn't it? To figure out how much his own father had screwed his head up. And get his mother's perspective so he could help screw it back the other way so it would finally be straight.

His expectations were high. But he had to try. Because one thing he knew beyond a shadow of a doubt was that he was going to do all he could to get Laney back. He'd just prefer to do it as a better man. And he wasn't talking about money, either.

Although it had been years since he'd visited, Carter knew the way to his mother's house as if he'd been driving there all his life. In a way, he had. Emotionally. Her whereabouts had been one constant in his ever-changing world. And while he had never turned to her, somehow he had always known he could.

He pulled up in the driveway of the medium-sized house in an older Austin subdivision, noting the green lawn and the colorful flowers and the Welcome sign on a homemade wreath on the door. He'd called her yesterday to tell her he was coming. She hadn't hesitated when she told him she'd be waiting.

He shut off the truck engine, listening to the sounds around him—children playing basketball, a lawn mower, birds. Then he slowly got out, holding the door open for Blue to jump down. He was halfway up the walk when the front door opened and there stood his mother, smiling at him as if he'd just seen her yesterday...as if she'd been waiting for this moment for a long, long time and now it was finally here.

HAD FOUR WEEKS PASSED since she'd last seen Carter? Laney wondered with no small amount of surprise as she stood in front of her office window looking out. Gone were the neat downtown streets, replaced by those of the more sparsely populated, industrial south side of town. She smiled. While the new view didn't have quite the cachet of her former office, neither did it have the isolation or the pressures from her superiors.

As she'd suspected, senior partner Harold Reasoner had a large bone to pick with her over how she'd handled the MacGregor case. She'd been prepared, so that the instant he made a veiled threat to terminate her association with the firm, she'd quit on the spot.

It had taken her a week to pass on her active case files, clear the clients who wanted to follow her to her new solo practice and make the needed arrangements for her new business address.

Of course, having Violet along for the ride helped immensely.

"There is no way you're leaving me here all alone," she'd told Laney matter-of-factly when Laney shared the news of her departure.

The office of Laney Cartwright, Attorney-at-Law, consisted of three rooms. A small lobby, Violet's office and then her own. It was nowhere near as posh as her former surroundings, but that's just how she wanted it. She had no intention of catering strictly to those who could afford her previous firm's exorbitant fees. While she wouldn't turn them away, either, she wanted to open her doors to a wider variety of clients, many of which would be sent her way via the Dallas Public Defenders Office, with whom she'd contracted to handle a minimum number of criminal cases.

She didn't fool herself into thinking that clients from a lower-income group would be any more honest than Devon MacGregor had been. But she'd handle that aspect when the time came, with no one above her telling her which cases she had to take or pass on.

And the first client she'd signed up was Tiffany Mullins.

"Where do you want this?" Violet asked, struggling with a plant nearly as tall as she was.

"Not another one." Laney hurried across the room to help her put it down near the dozen other plants and floral arrangements she'd been receiving steadily since announcing the opening of her new office. She looked for a card. "Who's this one from?"

"You're not going to believe it, but I think Reasoner sent it." Violet frowned in obvious distaste. "Probably had his secretary pick it out."

Laney read the congratulatory wishes and then put the card on her desk along with the others. "Huh."

Violet leaned against the doorjamb. "Never hurts to keep the lines of communication open. Especially since you're going to be sitting in as consultant on a couple of the cases you left behind."

"Right," Laney said, wondering at how incestuous the legal profession was.

Of course, she'd already seen many of her former coworkers at a recent symphony charity event, so she needed no reminders of how tight the Dallas business community was. Still, there were some people she didn't care if she ever saw again. And that thought would never have crossed her mind before…

Before Carter.

Violet went back to her own office, leaving Laney alone with her thoughts. Which was never a good idea. Because the more time she had to think, the more her thoughts turned to Carter.

Okay, so maybe her heart did lurch in hope every time a delivery came. Was it too much to hope that he might send her something?

Then again, for all she knew, he was back in the Marines and stationed halfway across the world.

She refused to allow herself to call his JAG attorney to check up on him. But with every day that passed, her resolve eroded just a little bit more.

"So call him."

Not her words, but her father's—at lunch earlier that day.

"What?" she'd said, sitting across from him at Raphael's and forking poached salmon she had no intention of eating.

"I said call him." Her father's eyes had a knowing glint in them as he'd sipped his water. "You've been awful company all month. Ever since you stopped seeing the Marine."

"Carter," she corrected.

"So call him."

Could it really be that simple?

Could she just pick up the phone and rid her heart of the ache that threatened to swallow it and her whole?

"Look, Laney," her father had said, "I'm just going to say this once, and then we never have to talk about it again if you don't want to. But it's obvious you love the guy."

Her eyes had burned with unshed tears, rendering her speechless.

"Have you told him how you feel?"

Of course, she hadn't. It had all happened too soon to sort everything out. Too fast for her to get her feet under her. To figure out what she wanted.

And then the decision had been taken out of her hands and she'd let it go.

"That doesn't mean you can't grab it back," her father had said.

A slow smile spread across Laney's face.

Grab it back, indeed.

She reached for the phone, dialing a number she knew by heart, and suspected she always would.

22

ON THE DRIVE back to Dallas three days later, Carter felt as if someone had taken him by the shoulders, dunked him in a giant tub of soapy water and then hauled him out to dry in the fresh Texas sunshine. Group therapy was partially to credit for his new take on life. His three-day visit with his mother and extended family was also responsible. Both had laid the foundation for his response to Laney's phone call.

His cell phone had rung the first day of his Austin visit as he'd stood at the kitchen door of his mother's house, watching her spray his niece and two nephews with a hose in a plastic pool. They'd even splashed Blue, who had run around like a puppy rather than the old hound he was. It had been an hour before dinner, and she had invited him to stay. An hour before, he had been welcomed by his half brothers and half sister with open arms as if he'd been away on assignment rather than by choice. His mother and he had had a four-hour conversation about all they had missed, and all they intended to make up for.

Seeing Laney's name on his cell phone display had made his throat feel tight. He'd answered on the third ring.

"Carter?"

The knots in his stomach had unfurled as if coaxed open by her sweet voice. "Hello, Laney."

He'd heard the clutch of her throat, her nervousness reflecting his. "I was wondering how you were doing."

He'd watched as his mother dried her hands on a towel and headed back in his direction. "I'm fine. And you?"

"Fine. Fine."

A long pause made him want to be next to her instead of halfway across the state. "Look, Laney, I'm out of town now—"

"Are you back in the Corps?" she asked with obvious alarm.

"No, no. Just down in Austin for a few days. Can I call you when I get back?"

He could almost see her smiling. "Yes. I'd like that."

He'd hung up immediately, but not before his mother caught him on the phone.

He was coming to learn that there was such a thing as mother's radar. Mary Manson had the ability to pluck items from his brain the moment he thought them.

It wasn't that his father had been any less observant. He guessed there were just some things men weren't as well equipped to deal with as women. Or maybe women were just more willing to give them a try.

His mother had instantly homed in on the fact he'd been talking to a woman. Not any woman, but one that meant a great deal to him.

So as he helped her prepare a dinner that would

include the entire family, keeping an eye on the playing children in the back, he'd told her about him and Laney. He'd weathered looks of pain and encouragement, and then when he was done, she'd taken the basket of bread he'd sliced from his hands and urged him to face her. He'd stared down into a face that looked so much like his own it almost hurt to think how long he'd gone without enjoying it.

"Don't close yourself off to Laney, Carter. Don't ever let something small like class prevent you from loving the person you want. Your dad did that with me."

He'd glimpsed the pain there, the pain she must have felt so many years before when his father had pushed her out of their lives.

"I never stopped loving your father, Carter. Love, true love, is something that never fades, never goes away." He'd wanted to hand her a tissue or a paper towel to wipe the tears about to spill from her bright eyes. But she refused to release him from her gaze. "Make the decisions you have to, but remember that the way you feel now, you will feel always. It's what you do with those feelings that can mean the difference between happiness and a lifetime of pain."

"But you went on to create another life," he'd said quietly.

"Yes, yes, I did. But only when I knew there was no hope left in returning to the one I'd made with your father. With you." She'd looked down and then quickly back up, as if afraid to break the connection. "I've gone on to love again. And am happier than any one woman has a right to be. But that first love…it's always there. And it was only with your father's passing that I was truly set free to love fully again."

She touched the side of his face and smiled.

"You're so much like your father, Carter."

He'd grimaced.

"No, no. It's a good thing. A very good thing. You're strong and loyal and have this incredible capacity for love." She'd swallowed hard. "Don't let fear rob you of happiness. Like fear robbed your father and me of ours."

Fear. Was that ultimately what was holding him back from giving his all to Laney? Fear of what would happen if he completely surrendered to his feelings for her? Fear of getting hurt? Of being rejected? Rejected by her and the society she belonged to?

Of one day waking up and finding the passion gone and Laney gone with it?

He was on the outskirts of Dallas now. Despite it being dinnertime on Sunday, the traffic was heavy and he turned up the radio to drown out the sound of a pair of motorcycles passing to his left. He gave a little salute to the two riders and then listened as Blue threw his head back in the passenger's seat and issued a low and long howl, singing along with Clint Black.

"I hear you, brother," he said to the old hound, patting him heartily on the back. "I hear you."

He had yet to call Laney back. Was even beginning to wonder if it was the right thing to do, despite his visit with his mother. He had so much to work out, to absorb. Maybe he'd wait a little while before inviting her into the chaos.

The thought incited a sharp pain to rip across his chest. He ignored it as he exited the highway and set his direction for the final stretch toward home.

The instant he pulled up into the gravel driveway of his small house, he knew something was off. The front door was open and music drifted out, country and western. He shut off the truck engine and opened the door, taken aback when Blue rushed over him and jumped out first, running to the front steps in a way he hadn't done before.

One of his neighbors? It seemed the most likely guess. Julia Jackson had cleaned up a bit once or twice before when he was stationed in the Middle East and due for leave. Then there was Naomi, who was a resourceful kid and had some trouble at home with a drunken stepfather. Could she have needed a place to stay and crashed here?

Either way, it wouldn't be difficult to gain access. Since he didn't own much worth taking, he often didn't lock the back door, figuring a broken window would be more costly to replace than anything a burglar might take.

He climbed out of the truck and walked up to the steps, opening the screen door to let Blue in before entering himself. Someone was singing softly. A female somebody.

Carter tossed his overnight bag to the living room floor and walked toward the kitchen, where the sounds were coming from. He stopped there in the doorway, his breath stolen straight from his body.

There at the ancient stove stood none other than an angel in blue.

Laney.

A million thoughts rushed through his mind as he took in the back of the simple linen tank dress she wore, her feet bare against tile that had been mopped, her short blond hair curling every which way as she hummed the parts of the Carrie Underwood song she didn't know the words to that played on the transistor radio in the window.

He'd never brought her here, but he figured it wouldn't have been difficult for her to find out where he lived. It was probably listed on the papers his JAG attorney had forwarded to her.

What she was doing there was another matter entirely.

Blue half galloped, half lumbered his way to press his wet nose against the back of her knee. Carter watched as she gasped and then crouched down to pat the old hound, who was as happy to see her as Carter was.

"Hey, Blue. How are you doing, boy?"

Carter felt as if his heart had grown to the size of a summer watermelon even as he noted that the hound was no kind of watchdog.

Seeming to realize that if Blue was there, then his owner had likely also returned, Laney slowly stood up and turned to face Carter.

The watermelon pitched to Carter's booted feet. Christ, she was even more beautiful than he remembered. But it was more than the sum of her physical characteristics. It was in the way she looked at him, as if the sun rose and set on him.

Her elegant throat worked around a swallow. "Um, I hope you don't mind. I just thought I'd come over and make dinner for you." She gestured toward the stove. "You've fed me so often that I figured it was time I returned the favor."

Was she afraid that he'd be angry with her? He suspected she was. But damned if he could do anything about it. His boots seemed cemented to the floor.

"How did you know I would be coming back tonight?" he asked.

She smiled and tucked an errant curl behind a perfectly formed shell of an ear. "I didn't. That's why there's already two days' worth of dinners in the refrigerator."

She seemed uneasy with the confession and bit her plump bottom lip.

That this self-assured, confident woman could be so nervous touched Carter beyond words. But even as the observation crossed his mind, he watched as Laney reacted to his lack of response. Her round shoulders pulled back slightly and her chin went up just a bit.

"Are you telling me I'm not welcome?"

Carter grinned and shook his head. Oh, she was more than welcome. She was the answer to all of his prayers.

Before he was consciously aware of wanting to make the move, he'd crossed the room and hauled Laney into his arms, holding her as close as he dared, pressing his hands over her soft back, into her silken curls. And when he kissed her, he did so with an honesty that not even he could mask.

Her low moan spoke volumes as she returned his needy attention, curving her leg around his knee and rubbing her calf against his restlessly even as she thrust her fingers into the back of his hair.

"God, this past month has been hell without you," she whispered against his mouth as he kissed her again. "I feel as if I've spent my entire life trying to live up to a list of expectations. Expectations from my father, from my friends, from myself..." She kissed him long and hard. "And then you came into my life and I felt that bridle of expectations cut into my soul."

He couldn't seem to get enough of her, and predicted that he never would.

"I love you, Carter. I'm not afraid to say that anymore. I love you."

He kissed her more deeply, drinking in her sweet essence and the warm shadow in her eyes.

"Laney, sweet Laney. I love you so damn much it hurts to breathe."

He stared at her, his heart pounding in his chest.

Then she smiled and pressed her nose against his. "So now what do we do?"

"We ride this road and see where it takes us."

If he'd once feared that road might dead-end or run out, he wasn't anymore. So long as he had her along for the ride, he suspected they could circle the globe twice and still find something new and exciting to see.

A burning smell eclipsed the scent of her hair even as Blue let rip a howling bark.

"But first," he suggested, "it would be a good idea if we didn't let the place burn down around our ears."

"The garlic bread!" Laney stepped out of his embrace and then turned around to open the oven door. She attempted to take the bread out with her hands and then grabbed a towel instead, tossing the half-blackened loaf to the counter.

Carter took in the bubbling tomato sauce in one pan and the boiling pasta in another on the stovetop. She was making him spaghetti.

He spotted a pie in the window next to the radio. She turned off the stovetop burners and followed his gaze.

"Blueberry pie. I'd like to take credit, but the truth is a couple of your neighbors brought it over an hour or so ago."

"Did they, now?" Word that Carter had a woman at his place would have made the grapevine by now and he'd be hit with even more offerings, his other neighbors looking for a juicy tidbit or two about Laney and him.

"You've been staying here?" he asked.

Laney's chin came up again. "Yes, I have. I waited until late the first night and, well, decided I should just sleep over rather than drive back into town."

Carter couldn't believe Laney had stayed the night in his place, or that she looked at home doing it.

All his fears of how she might judge him if she saw

his place exited on an exhale. He'd been stupid to think she'd be so shallow.

"I know you were reluctant about bringing me here," she said quietly, seeming to read his mind in that way he was coming to think any woman close to him could. "And I won't pretend to understand why, beyond your house being modest. But the truth is, I've enjoyed being surrounded by your things."

"My things, huh?" he asked, advancing on her.

Laney leaned her back against the sink. "Uh-huh."

"And just how many of my things are you talking about?"

Her smile aimed sunshine into every shadowy corner of his soul. "Oh, everything."

He cocked a brow. "Everything?"

"Mmm."

He laced her arms over his shoulders and then lifted her so that her legs hugged his hips, her feet crossing behind his back.

"Well, okay," she said, restlessly licking her lips as she stared hungrily at his mouth. "Maybe not everything."

He kissed her and turned to walk toward his closed bedroom door.

"But there is one thing I did change. I hope you don't mind."

Carter barely heard her as he turned the knob and kicked the door open.

There in the middle of his bedroom sat a king-size bed covered with a multicolored quilt and dozens of pillows.

He looked at her.

She shrugged. "That twin bed just wasn't going to do."

"No," he admitted, wondering what other kinds of changes were in store for him. And for the first time looking forward to every last one of them.

Blue's nails clicked against the floor as he followed them. Carter blocked him with his boot and then nudged him back out.

"Your food's in the other room, boy," he said and closed the door. He gazed down at the woman in his arms. "This meal's all mine."

* * * * *

MIDNIGHT RESOLUTIONS

BY

KATHLEEN O'REILLY

First published in Great Britain 2010
Harlequin Mills & Boon Limited,
Eton House, 18-24 Paradise Road, Richmond, Surrey TW9 1SR

© Kathleen Panov 2010

ISBN: 978 0 263 88151 6

14-1210

Harlequin Mills & Boon policy is to use papers that are natural, renewable and recyclable products and made from wood grown in sustainable forests. The logging and manufacturing processes conform to the legal environmental regulations of the country of origin.

Printed and bound in Spain
by Litografia Rosés S.A., Barcelona

First published in 2001, **Kathleen O'Reilly** is an award-winning author of more than twenty romances, with more books on the way. Reviewers have been lavish in their praise, applauding her "biting humor," "amazing storytelling" and "sparkling characters." She lives in New York with her husband, two children and one indestructible goldfish. Please contact the author at kathleenoreilly@earthlink.net or by mail at PO Box 312, Nyack, NY 10960, USA.

Dear Reader,

A while back I noticed a trend in my stories. Unexpected love, unexpected places. My editor suggested a trilogy, and the Blaze® senior editor came up with a grand title for it: WHERE YOU LEAST EXPECT IT.

In the first book, *Hot Under Pressure*, the characters meet on a crazy airplane flight. For *Midnight Resolutions* I focused on New Year's Eve.

When I came up with the idea of a magical kiss on New Year's, I knew I wanted to create two characters who needed to start over. It was only a matter of figuring out the why. With Ian and Rose, I found those two people. There was Ian, who knew what he needed to do, and was already on his journey. And then there was Rose, who didn't have a clue...until she started to fall in love.

I hope you enjoy the story, and I hope your 2011 is bright, joyous and full of new beginnings.

Look for the next WHERE YOU LEAST EXPECT IT book soon. There's this lake, and this hero who wants to be left alone...

Best wishes for the New Year!

Kathleen O'Reilly

_1_

NEW YEAR'S EVE IN TIMES SQUARE. Ian Cumberland was done dwelling on last year's miseries. Tonight was about new resolutions, new hopes, new opportunities. Cheerfully he stuffed his hands in his pockets and inhaled the crisp, seventeen-degree air. It was nearly midnight, and he was primed for the winds of change to blast open new doors. The neon carnival that was Times Square had seemed the ideal location—apparently it was also the ideal place for another two million huddled masses. They were huddled because those winds of change were blowing from the north at approximately thirty-five miles per hour. And not that he wanted to complain, but okay, those winds were freaking cold.

Noisemakers and plastic horns bleated in the air, riding over the upbeat tempo of the latest and greatest boy-band—greatest, that is, until they hit puberty or got involved in the latest sex scandal, whichever came first. No—no negativity. Not tonight.

Determined to make this work, Ian gave his senses free rein, marveling at all the tiny details he'd overlooked before. Ear-blasting sounds, a kaleidoscope of brilliant colors and a melting pot of smells. He took a deep breath of New York air—a million divergent perfumes, roasted chestnuts and strangely enough, honeysuckle.

Over the past year, he'd divided his life into two distinct periods. Prelayoff and postlayoff. Prelayoff ended precisely at 4:30 p.m. on February seventeenth. Then, Ian didn't have the time to waste twelve hours standing around Times Square waiting for a giant multicolored orb to fall from the sky. Postlayoff, he still didn't have the time, but now he had the will.

New Year's at Times Square had been on his list of life to-dos since he was ten, waiting to be checked off. Prelayoff, he didn't worry much about getting to Times Square. Postlayoff, he realized that life was not cooperative and orderly, and when you got the chance to have a once-in-a-lifetime moment, you just did it.

The night's crowd was packed shoulder to shoulder. It was impossible to move, nearly impossible to breathe, and he found himself sharing the uncomfortably close personal space of a large group of awestruck foreigners who didn't understand the common English vernacular: "You're standing on my foot. Please move."

As he took in the trolling lights and squinty-eyed police and happy, perky people, Ian waited patiently for something miraculous, something life-altering, something hopeful. But all he got was a trampled foot and a deafening horn in his ear.

Still he waited, colder, sober, and now thinking that perhaps he'd been a little wiser prelayoff when he had avoided Times Square like the plague.

Hell. On what planet had he actually thought this was a good idea? It didn't matter that it was New Year's Eve, Times Square, nearly midnight. In the end, he wasn't an investment banker anymore; he was an employment counselor, and a lunatic one at that.

Beckett had told him it was stupid. Told him that nobody froze their ass off in New York in January when they could stay home and have a decent party, guzzle champagne and watch the ball drop from the confines of a well-insulated apartment. And of course, it was at that moment that Ian had looked his best friend square in the eye and launched into his winds of change spiel: new beginnings, living life—doing it right.

And there, crushed amidst two million other cockeyed optimists, he felt a killer wind shoot through him, the truth dawning with frigid clarity.

Ian was a sap. Time to pack in the New Year, accept what he had and trudge onward. Life was what it was, and nothing—not even a few mind-shattering hours in the center of the universe—was going to change it.

Feeling all sorts of foolish, he turned, starting toward the relative tranquility of the subway, because somewhere out there, his sanity and his friends were waiting. Before he managed another step, a pull at his arm knocked him off balance. Ian whirled, prepared to tell the jerkwad—foreign relations be damned—to quit touching him. But then he stopped—

Stared.

Gawked, actually.

Gorgeous.

She was honeysuckle in the flesh. She looked like it, smelled like it and damn, he wanted to know if she tasted like it, as well. His body shocked to life, filled, throbbed.

Hello, winds of change.

Watercolor-blue eyes were panicked and filled with worry. Warm, tawny hair streaked with gold spilled from her knitted cap.

"Have you seen my phone? I can't find my phone. Help me find my phone. Oh, God. I lost my phone."

Her voice was soft and tense against the noise of the crowd. She was searching for her phone. *Help her.*

"Where'd you lose it?" he asked, raising the volume, noticing the beefy tourist sizing her up with beady eyes.

"On the ground. I dropped it and I really need to find it. I shouldn't be here. It's a complete zoo. Why did I come here?"

To meet me, thought Ian, a stupid, romantic thought, right up there with his winds of change spiel. Ian grinned, a foolish, romantic grin, but he couldn't help himself. "We'll find it," he offered, and bent to the ground. She hesitated, her eyes wisely fearful, but then she bent, too, testing the restraint of millions of drunken partygoers, probably taking her life in her own hands, yet still trusting him.

At ground level it was like being underwater, swimming against the tide of directionally challenged fish. The dim light was diffused by shifting legs and restless feet and a continuous swirl of coats. Her hands grabbed for the edge of his sleeve, her eyes terrified. "You okay?" he asked, and she nodded once, but still he worried.

"We'll find it," he assured her again, keeping one hand tied to hers. With the other, he searched for what had to be the most important phone in the world.

"I can't believe I lost it," she chattered, the words tumbling out in a panic. "I can't believe I screwed up. I'm not careless. I can't be careless. I won't be careless." A clumsy set of legs bumped into her, and she jumped, flying closer to him.

"Don't get crazy. It's got to be here somewhere," he soothed, heroically gathering her closer, trying to find her phone, trying to keep her from being flattened, all the while warning himself that just because a beautiful woman stumbled into his arms, it did not mean the winds of change had finally blown his way.

Blindly he groped the rough asphalt. His hand got stomped on twice, but apparently the gods actually owed Ian something good this year and apparently Frank Capra wasn't dead in spirit—because at that moment Ian's fingers latched on to plastic. Rectangular, sturdy, magical plastic.

"Got it," he yelled, quickly pulling her upright before they were both trampled to death—which never happened in Frank Capra movies.

The flashing neon signs lit up the jittery alarm in her eyes, and he pulled her to him, instinct more than reason. "It's okay. It's here," he said, feeling the tremors run through her, absorbing them into himself. "It's a phone," he murmured, whispering against her hair. "It's only a phone. Don't cry."

"Don't like the crowd," she muttered, her face buried in his shoulder.

"You picked the wrong place to figure that out." He was relieved to hear her awkward laugh, and decided that holding a beautiful crowd-o-phobic was worth a layoff, worth being labeled a sap.

In the end, Ian had been right. New hopes. New opportunities, and they all smelled like honeysuckle.

He stroked the back of her woolen coat, feeling the slow ease of her shivering. It didn't take her long, and he knew the exact moment when she stiffened, her chin lifted and the fear had passed. "I'm not crying. I don't cry," she told him, her voice a lot firmer than before.

Then she gazed at him—her eyes dry, and more focused than before. "I'm not crying," she repeated. "Thank you. This was stupid. I'm sorry. I don't like being stupid."

Her profile seemed so fragile, so oddly out of place in the chaos of the crowd, the lights and the noise. Her face was thin, delicate, a medieval maiden out of a fairy tale. Yet there were hollow shadows in her eyes, shadows that didn't belong with such beauty. It took more than a lost phone to cast shadows like that. Gently he tracked her cheek, pretending to wipe at nonexistent tears, only wanting to touch the golden rose of her skin.

"You're not being stupid. Everything's fine now. Everything's perfect now," he said, watching as the control eased back into her face.

"Thank you for finding my phone."

He casually shrugged off her gratitude, knowing the night was young, the year was young. What was a job, anyway? What was financial security? Totally oversold. In the big scheme of life, could anything compare to that world-by-the-tail feeling of her dreamy eyes looking at him as if he was a hero—and not just any hero, but *her hero?*

"It's nothing. You're okay now?" he asked, leaning in to be heard over the crowd. Oh, yeah, right.

"Sorry. I never fall apart," she answered, her head close to his, so close he could make out the carefully concealed freckles on her nose.

"Don't apologize. I fall apart on a regular basis."

She glanced at him oddly. "I was joking," he told her, and cursed himself for being a blockhead. There was something in her face, in her moon-kissed gaze, that held him fast. Hidden behind the composure, he could see a child's curiosity peering out.

Her mouth curved up, a pink Cupid's bow that touched him somewhere near his heart.

Right then, one of the tourists jammed her into him, and she started at the movement, until he pulled her close again, fast adjusting to the heady feel of her in his arms.

"I shouldn't have come here tonight. I thought I could do this."

"I know, a bunch of idiots who think New Year's Eve is a night for new dreams. What a bunch of dorks. I should have been home guzzling champagne instead of freezing my... Never mind." Once again he felt her muffled giggle and decided he didn't mind being a blockhead, didn't mind being a fool. To hear her hesitant laugh, to fit those lush curves to his body, to have her hair brush against his face.

After a moment, she raised her head and carefully studied him. "You ever do this before?"

"Nope. You?"

"Never again," she answered firmly.

Apparently God was still watching, Frank was still filming and the winds of change were definitely on the move because suddenly, miraculously, the crowd began to count.

Thirty-three. Thirty-two. Thirty-one.

Her eyes glowed bright, the muted blue heating to liquid, trapping him there. Her hands locked to his lapel, as if she'd never let go. The air began to arc between them, almost visible, coiling and floating like warm breath in the chilled night.

New life. New love. New year.

Nineteen. Eighteen. Seventeen.

Totally entranced, Ian slid his right hand behind her neck, twining it in her hair with a lingering sigh. Her lips touched his even before he asked, even before he begged. Soft, sweet, and tasting like a new beginning.

When the crowd jostled her closer, Ian didn't complain, his left hand riding under her coat, finding the glorious skin of her back, the inviting curve of her waist. Around them, the world blew by, showers of confetti, bursts of cold wind and the joyous shouts of millions of not-quite-sober partiers. Ian ignored them all, because in the midst of these millions, it was only he and this woman, and the rest of their life.

Her generous mouth opened, her tongue merged with his, coaxing, seducing. Oh, yes, he was so seduced, no coaxing necessary. His nerves fired, pulsing with life, pulsing with ideas that were older than time. He would take her home. He would make love to her. He would marry her. It was the Frank Capra way.

Impulsive arms locked around his neck, burying her fingers in his hair. He could feel the insistent touch of her restless hands. Against his greedy mouth, she moaned. Music. Bells. Chimes. Somewhere he'd died and was kissing an angel.

His hand slipped lower, pressing her against him, soft to hard. Her hips curled into him, her thigh rocking between his. His eyes crossed. Nope. No angel. They didn't have moves like that in heaven.

An irritant vibrated against his leg—not his cock, nor his pulse, which were both buzzing in their own overjoyed condition. She broke away, her breathing heavy, then lifted the phone, the exact phone he'd found for her only moments before. Which, if he had not found, she would not be talking into. No, they would still be kissing. Man, he was such a stupid dweeb.

Next to them, one of the tourists shot him a look of male approval, but Ian ignored it, trying to restart his brain. Here was the inspiration he'd been seeking.

As she talked, her gaze scanned the length of his cashmere coat. For the first time, he could see that elusive recognition flicker in her eyes—seeing him as a man who was worthy—financially viable. Possibly insecure, but there it was. Maybe the male code had some unwritten law saying it was cowardly to trade on his past life, but did geeky Clark Kent ever want to throw open his jacket, exposing the all-powerful *S*? Hell, yeah.

The shouts of the crowd fell away. Only her words touched his ears. She was talking, trying to reconnect with her date. Date? No!

Ian wanted to yell at her to hang up because this was kismet, karma, and the entire outcome of his postlayoff life rested upon this one moment—no pressure. Instead, he kept his mouth shut, a confident grin plastered on his face as if this didn't mean a damn thing.

When she looked at Ian again, the soft blue eyes were so lonely and sad. He wondered if she had sensed the pull, too. Ian had never felt it before, never met a woman who stepped out of his dreams and into his arms. It should have been fate.

"I'm over here," she said into the phone, waving a graceful hand in the air for someone other than Ian. *Other than Ian.* He wanted to stop her because she couldn't be with someone else. This was a new year. New opportunities. New loves...

"I have to go. He's my date," she apologized, dashing the final vestiges of his hope to the ground much like last year's sodden confetti.

"No surprise there," answered Ian, his voice faux cheerful. "Have a good year." *Have a nice life.*

One heartbeat later, her expression turned to the well-mannered smile given to a stranger on the street. Without another word, she politely asked her beefy neighbor to move out of the way, and then she moved out of Ian's life.

All before he'd even gotten her name.

The winds of change blew cold and heartless, and Ian stomped on Hans's foot, hard—international-incident hard—and Ian was gratified when the giant oaf muttered something in another language that probably involved mothers and copulation, not that he cared. Tourism was overrated anyway.

As he made his way home, Ian looked back at the ball that was glittering like a fallen star, making outrageous promises it wasn't going to keep.

Happy New Year.

In a crowd of two million, Ian had never felt so alone.

Damn.

2

ROSE HILDEBRANDE WANTED TO wind back the clock to last year, when Remy wasn't sipping his champagne and discussing in elaborate detail his latest performance in the operating room.

Rose wanted to return to that unforgettable instant when the stranger had been kissing her with such desperate need, as if he couldn't get enough of her. As if with one kiss, he had found something golden and fleeting inside her. Romance—that was what they called it.

The people, the crowds, the fear. Everything had been a black, paralyzing blur—except for the feel of that strong body holding her tight. Not to punish, no, it was protection.

On a normal day, Rose knew exactly when she wanted to be touched, when people expected it and how she was supposed to react. That blood-pounding, swept-away sensation should have terrified her. But it was tempered by something new. Something almost…warm.

Quickly she shook off the weakness. Control. Always in control.

Now, sitting in the lobby of the Four Seasons with New York's crème de la crème, her blood was neatly congealing back to its more reserved state. Her date for the night, world-renown pediatric cardiology surgeon Dr. Remy Sinclair, was cheerfully describing his day. The rest of the universe was planning a celebration, and Remy was slaving over the operating table, saving the lives of small children. Heroic, handsome, charming and rich. The man had zero flaws.

So, why was Rose merely nodding at suitable intervals with a polite bob of her head, while her mind clicked back to that dazzling feeling inspired by one exquisitely hard, hungry mouth? No, she thought, pushing the dazzle aside. More hocus-pocus that had no basis in anything real.

Idly, she shuttered her lashes, an indication of perhaps not actually listening, but a sincere pretense of it.

It was a look she'd perfected by the age of six, when Rose had been primped, painted, powdered and coiffed, and then ordered to skip down the charm school runway with bubbly poise and a lollipop smile. Her parents had had big dreams for her—beauty pageants, charm school, marrying well. Rose Hildebrande's heart-shaped little face was their ticket to a better life, and Rose had quickly learned to fall in line. There was no little girl better at perfection, a concrete diamond mined from the worst of hell.

The suffocating blackness filled her, but she took a long, purging breath. This was safe. This was good, and Remy was everything she had always dreamed of. He was a fourth-generation Sinclair, heir to the Sinclair fortune, in case being a heart surgeon wasn't secure enough. And there was something princely about him—a chiseled profile, the Roman nose. His dark hair was carelessly brushed back from his face. The dove-gray suit was tailored perfectly to show sculpted shoulders and a tapered torso.

Best of all, the man was on the wrong side of thirty and trolling for a wife. A beautiful blonde to hang up on his wall along with his summa cum laude diploma from Columbia, his medical license from the State of New York and the live-action photo of the impala he'd seen on his last safari in Tanzania.

"Have you thought about the auction?" she asked, shifting the conversation from surgery toward a more stomach-surviving topic. She had promised the countess she'd deliver, and it was a promise Rose intended to keep. Sylvia was her boss and her friend; Rose owed her a lot more than a charity auction.

"Yes, I've thought. The answer is no."

"Please," she asked, not blaming him for saying no, but still determined to change his mind. It was demeaning, it was embarrassing, but truly, there was no more perfect bachelor in the entire tri-state region.

"No." Those princelike eyes were firm, but Rose was undeterred.

"Think of the puppies, those little fluff balls that need a good home. You can't be that heartless."

"I'm a heart surgeon. I replace hearts on a daily basis. I don't fear heartlessness like ordinary mortals without a god complex."

They were more alike than he would ever suspect. He saw her as the ideal, the perfect woman, and she never let him see behind the flawless mask to the person that was missing both a heart and a soul. Very rarely did she dwell on that loss, except on a starry night like this one. When a sexy stranger had appeared like magic, a Prince Charming coming to sweep her away to someplace quiet and glorious and decadently warm. Oh, yeah, right, next thing you know, you're flossing your teeth with a diamond-studded tiara perched on your head. Rose lifted a hand to her hair, just to check. All clear. No, if Rose wanted her happy ending, she was going to have to work for it.

"Would you do it for me?" she asked in her best, most earnest voice. This was only their fourth date, so really it was too soon to ask things from him. Still… Their relationship was a battle plan, carefully executed, plotted, and to date, proceeding exactly on schedule, with the countess cheering on from the sideline. Very few people saw similarities between relationships and battle, but Rose had read and memorized *The Art of War.* Those similarities were all Rose had ever known.

"You're going to make me, aren't you?" he said, affectionate resignation in his voice. It was why she liked him so much. He never asked anything of her, never told her what to say or what to wear, all she had to do was sit prettily at his side and listen. Piece of cake.

"Make you? Me?" She fluttered her lashes and he laughed.

"You can say all the heartless jokes you want, but I'm on to you."

"Do you always get your way?"

"Yes. You should have figured that out by now."

She waited, fingers crossed under the table, until finally he nodded, and she remembered to breathe. "I'll do it."

Rose was so excited she nearly kissed him, except for the hot hunger that still lingered on her lips. She wanted to keep that taste there, just for a little longer.

"You're sure? I mean, if you *really* don't want to…"

"You'd let me off the hook that easily?"

"Not really, but I'm trying to show some pretense of sensitivity. Humor me, here." Because she owed him, she endured three more blow-by-blow surgical descriptions without even a visible quiver of nausea.

Before he moved to number four, he glanced down at his watch. "It's late. You look tired."

A secret peek at her watch said it was nearly one, and all Rose wanted to do was go home and fall into bed. Alone.

She'd had exactly zero lovers. When you were groomed for matrimony as a blood sport, virginity was highly prized, right up there with a clean complexion and a coming-out dress. Her parents hadn't had the money for white satin and richelieu lace, so the Hildebrandes had over-compensated with endless lectures on virtue and a lifetime supply of Neutrogena. Rose—being a bright girl and not one to rebel—had taken the hint.

Now she yawned, not exactly faked. "I'm exhausted, and with your day—honestly, I don't know how you do it."

"Good drugs," he answered with an easy laugh.

And the stamina of a camel. Mentally, she slapped herself, feeling tired, punchy, and the bubbles in her blood were starting to die down. A master of efficiency, he helped her into her coat, always the gentleman, and she took a last sweep of the patrons in the lobby. Everything was so beautiful here, the polished marble, the gleaming silver, the people with their gentle laughter and placid faces. The six years of charm school had been so similar to this. Every day, the candle-glow lights and high-gloss perfection had been a safe haven for her, a few peaceful hours away from home. There, here, Rose had survived and thrived, grown hard and strong.

Her chin lifted, perfectly parallel to the ground, and she pivoted smoothly, slow and elegant, and the entire room watched her leave.

As they made their way out the doors, her heel caught on the step and when her foot moved on the shoe stayed behind. Remy—happy, smiling, gloriously rich Remy—swooped down and brandished it with a romantic flourish. "You did this on purpose?" he asked, as if she could be that clever.

He bent down, dark hair gleaming in the light, and placed the shoe on her foot. It should have been enchanting.

"Do you believe in fairy tales, Remy?" she asked curiously. If you lived within the invulnerability of the castle walls, did the myth of ever-after seem a big con on the rest of the world?

"Do you think this night is magic?" he countered, rising to his feet, and she saw a flash of something in his eyes. Something that she'd seen when she kissed the stranger. Hope. On New Year's, everyone wanted to believe.

"I think people deserve one night of magic," she answered, almost the truth.

It was his cue, his moment, and Remy was not stupid. He leaned closer and took her mouth, and Rose was too determined to pull back. Remy was a lot more viable than a fairy tale. He was everything she'd worked for, and his kiss was every bit as accomplished as it should be. So where was the triumph? No triumph, only the persistent taste of a hot hunger that even a fourth-generation Sinclair couldn't ease.

Patiently she waited for the thrill of victory, the absoluteness of her control. Perhaps she hadn't won the war, but this battle belonged to her. So why did she feel the same as before, the same as yesterday, the same as she'd felt all her life—

Numb.

As his hand moved purposefully toward her waist, Rose realized the hot hunger wasn't going to return. It couldn't be forced, it couldn't be tricked.

Damn.

Deliberately, her hand covered his, and she raised her head, gave him her nicest smile—a pretend smile designed to make people believe she had a heart.

"I can't."

"Too quick?" he asked.

"Yes," she told him, regret in her voice. "I'm sorry, Remy."

And she was, disappointed in herself, in her trickster mind. Sometimes she saw monsters where there were none, and sometimes she felt nothing when she should be pulsing with life.

"Soon," she promised. "I'm still not there, yet."

Remy thought her heart was involved elsewhere, that Rose was pining for a man who was desperately unworthy of her affections. A failed love affair had been Sylvia's idea, but Rose had approved because it solved a lot more problems than it created.

"I can wait," he said gallantly, not wanting to imagine a woman would be stupid enough to turn him down forever. Someday, Rose wouldn't turn him down, but not tonight.

"Can I see you home?"

"I'll manage. It's not far." Another big fat lie.

He took her hand, as if she were a princess, and kissed it once. If she were being honest with herself, she'd stop playing this game and get on with the life that she had planned. Instead, she stood there watching him go, a worried smile on her face.

After Remy had left, Rose hoofed it on aching feet to the number six train, which would take her to the Bronx. The Bronx was home, but not for too much longer. Rose had big goals for her life. She was grown, a woman fully formed, and stronger than her parents had ever guessed that Little Mary Poofster could be.

Rose wouldn't live on false hopes and broken dreams. She didn't have to worry about whether fairy tales or magic truly existed because they didn't; all she had to do was foster the illusion. Rose had long ago mastered the art of the illusion. Money was security, money was real, money made you invulnerable to whatever the Fates chose to throw your way.

After she got off at her stop, she walked past the pet store boxed between the bodega and the OTB site. It was an odd place for animals, and she liked to stand outside the glass, watching the puppies from a safe distance.

The puppies always fascinated her, confined to a small pen that they didn't seem to mind. Five tiny black fur balls with twinkling brown eyes that saw only the best in the world. They always looked carefree and content and safe behind that store window. The Hildebrandes never had a pet. Not even a fish. And

Rose hadn't missed them. Dogs were smelly and loud and dirty and could rip a hole in pink satin, quick as you could say boo.

But she liked watching from behind the window, and she wondered what they thought while they played behind the pane. Sometimes she'd put her hand on the glass and leave it there, waiting to see if they'd come to her, but they never did. Animals didn't like her, knowing things that people never would.

Tonight, there were no puppies, only a big black monster dog with huge jaws, but tired eyes. He was curled up on the hay, with absolutely no faith that tonight was the start of something new. Lazily he opened an eye, squinted at her, and Rose squinted back. She placed her hand to the window, because from behind the glass, there was nothing he could do to her.

The dog growled.

Rose quivered, her hand falling to her side.

However, she did defiantly stare him down, until he realized she was no threat and shut his eyes, prepared to sleep once again.

Yup, animals knew things that people never would.

Before she climbed the steps to her building, Rose looked one last time at the lights of the skyline, the late-night partygoers making their way home, shouts of happiness ringing in the air, as if all was right with the world.

For a second, for one heart-stopping second, she had felt that way, too. Rose pressed a finger to her lips, remembering his kiss.

Somewhere he was out there. Was he alone? Was he thinking about her?

My prosperous Prince Charming.

The words whispered inside her, seductive and golden and warm. Quickly Rose shushed them away.

She turned and went inside.

It was New Year's Eve, and all she wanted to do was be alone, let down her hair and slip into a pair of cushy polka-dot socks. Bright lights and a polished world might put stars in her eyes, but it sure was hell on the feet.

3

THE HOME OF COUNT ANTON Simonov and his lovely, Brooklyn-born wife, Sylvia, was a stately twelve-room penthouse with soaring painted ceilings, a bank of windows overlooking Central Park and frame after gilt frame of stony-faced Old Masters. In the count's private offices was a set of ornate cabinets that displayed his most treasured possessions—glass shelves full of Imperial eggs, handcrafted by Fabergé.

Every morning, a truckload of fresh flowers was brought in, all in white, because Sylvia adored white. As Sylvia's personal assistant, it was Rose's job to ensure that the flowers were properly placed, dead petals properly plucked, and that there were no nasty chrysanthemum's in the bunch. According to Sylvia, "Mums look cheap, and if I wanted cheap, I'd have Anton spring for 36 double Ds and dye my hair platinum."

To Rose, Sylvia was a living, breathing, teetering, stiletto-wearing hero. Nearly thirty years ago, Sylvia had risen from the ranks, trading in on her beauty and her wildly successful fund-raising abilities to snag one of New York's wealthiest bachelors—who happened to be a Russian count to boot.

Rose had been doing a fine job working at a shipping insurance office in Pittsburgh, but there were always whispers that trailed after her. What the heck was *she* doing in an insurance office? Oh, her name wasn't famous and her face wasn't one they'd seen before, but her profile was too striking, her posture too straight, her walk a little too prissy for the shipping business. The curse of expectations never met.

When she spotted the profile on Countess Sylvia Simonov, a

plan emerged. For two weeks, she had taken the 4:37 a.m. bus from Pittsburgh to Manhattan to volunteer at the Simonov food pantry. Not only was she helping feed the hungry, but in less than ten days, she had convinced Countess Sylvia Simonov that Rose was a charity organizer extraordinaire.

For the past three years, Rose had been in the Simonov employ, where the smell of peace and prosperity filled the air. It'd taken her twenty-seven years, but she had finally found a place where she fit. Here, under Sylvia's nurturing eye, she was given on-the-job training on how to belong in the upper echelon, as well as steady exposure to Manhattan's most desirable bachelors. Best of all, Sylvia and Anton were the poster people for how affluence can positively affect your life.

With Sylvia's energetic influence, Rose had watched and learned how to achieve the life she wanted.

Today, January 1 in the Simonov household, Rose's happy gaze touched on polished wood, perfumed satin and, most appealing of all, contentment. *Dorothy, you're not in Kansas anymore. Attention World: Dorothy is now arriving at the Plaza.*

A stack of engraved envelopes landed on Dorothy's desk, reminding her that Rose was actually paid to do more than daydream. Impatiently, Sylvia tapped a scarlet nail on the blotter.

"Rose. Thank-you notes for the Christmas gifts. Be a darling. Linda kept a running list with three categories: mine, Anton's, ours. Here's what I need. For mine and ours, write a personal, funny message, and let your gushing know no bounds. Sound like me if at all possible, preferably without the accent. For Anton's list, especially the blue bloods, be impersonal, cold and stodgy. They really seem to go for that."

At fifty-five, Sylvia was an odd contradiction of humility and beauty in an approachable, yet elegant package. Her dark hair never looked meticulously coiffed, but Rose knew the truth. The stylist was there every morning before Anton woke up in order to make the "high-glossed, natural softness" a fait accompli. Anton affectionately called it Sylvia's bedroom hair. Sylvia would then shoot a conspiratorial wink at Rose. Rose never winked back, but sometimes she wanted to.

Daintily Sylvia stroked a black brow back into place. "Do you know the best cure for hot flashes? Believe it or not, Cristal. Seriously. But the next morning, oh, my God, the hangover is killer. Speaking of hot flashes, how'd the date go with Dr. Sinclair? Do I need the caterers and printers on speed dial, eagerly awaiting my call?"

Four dates and Sylvia was ready to post the banns. Unfortunately, Rose moved tortoiselike to Sylvia's hare, not wanting to go too fast, not wanting to go too slow, which usually stalled things to not going anywhere at all.

"It was nice," Rose answered vaguely.

"Yessss?" prompted Sylvia, who braced her hands on the filigreed wood, causing fingerprints aplenty. "Tell. Spill."

Spilling wasn't easy for Rose. She wasn't impulsive or impromptu, she was meticulous and well rehearsed. Being around Sylvia, though, she had learned to relax. Sylvia was…a friend. "I froze. I shouldn't have clammed up. I should have been forthright, open. Instead, I'm with world's most perfect man, and I find flaws. I think my standards are wonky." She ended the whine with a perky smile, which never seemed to fool Sylvia.

"You're too hard on yourself, Rose. A woman like you? Your poise, your face, those boobs. If I weren't on the Forbes list, I'd have to hate you. Lighten up. It's early yet. Give yourself a little time. Not everyone can move at light speed like moi."

And in case life affirmations were required, Sylvia waltzed to the piano, her sheer leopard print caftan billowing around her. Delicately she plucked a white magnolia from the crystal vase and inhaled, beaming at Rose with a "yes, your life could be this grand," gleam.

Then she squinted, stared.

"Why are you pale? You're missing the usual glow. And those circles. You either need another brand of concealer, or else something's keeping you up."

"It's nothing," answered Rose, but Sylvia waggled a creamy white flower in her direction.

"Let me be the judge of nothing."

Carefully Rose made neat stacks of the envelopes on the

blotter, then dabbed at the smudged glass with the edge of her blazer, and finally adjusted the tiny silver desk calendar, all of which made her feel better, but did nothing to stop Sylvia's tapping foot.

Of all the topics that Rose would love to discuss with Sylvia, this wasn't one. Although, maybe if she talked about it, maybe if she put it out there, it would be no big. After all, it *was* no big, not big at all. The countess's shoe clicked on the marble like a ticking time bomb.

Frantically, Rose scanned her desk, but there was absolutely nothing else to straighten. Because she was not a coward nor intimidated by the idea of confessing meaningless minutiae, Rose crossed her legs and lifted her chin in her best "it was nothing" attitude.

"I kissed someone last night."

"Remy?"

"Another him," Rose admitted.

Now looking completely intrigued, the countess raised her eyebrows, but didn't speak. Rose was on her own. Grudgingly she owned up to the truth.

"I met someone. Times Square. It was a total fluke. I dropped my phone. He helped me out. He was… I don't know, but…"

"And you kissed this flukey someone?" the countess asked, cutting to the heart of the matter.

"Yes."

"At midnight?"

Evenly, Rose met her eyes, showing no fear at all and nodded.

"I see."

"What do you see?"

"New Year's Eve. Times Square. Midnight. Stranger. Handsome, I presume."

"Certainly, but it wasn't the handsome that bothered me."

The countess flew to the desk. "Bothered you? Grab the police sort of 'bothered you'?"

Rose shuffled the envelopes. "No. Worse."

"Are you going to make me play twenty questions, Rose?"

There was an empty pit in her stomach when she looked up. The countess was a friend, the mother Rose had always known existed, but confiding never came easy to her. This time, however, the temptation to talk was strong, to understand, to purge.

"You had a plan, you executed, you got exactly what you wanted. Along the way, did you ever get sidetracked? Did you ever think you weren't in control? That life wasn't going to cooperate with what you wanted? Or is that part of it? A test of strength to see if you can overcome getting sidetracked?"

That nefarious possibility crept up on her, making Rose nervous. When you needed your life to be plotted, planned and perfectly implemented, the idea of bigger forces being at work was a disaster.

No, the bigger force was self-will and determination. Rose had to stay focused. Think Sun Tzu, think tough. Think…*magic*.

No.

Yes.

Maybe?

All muddled inside, she looked to the countess for advice, not even concerned that she was frowning, which wasn't her best look.

"You believe in fate, an invisible nudge that is pushing you toward that perfect someone?"

"No." *Probably not.*

Sylvia tapped a finger to her head. "And that is the correct answer, young grasshopper. Never forget. As women we can't sit back and let the world whip us around, gusting this way and that, all because we're too spineless to design our own destinies. Take this place. Do you think this is destiny? Hell, no. I adore Anton, there is no other man for me, but…"

"But what if we have a soul mate?" The words were clearly audible, yet Rose's gaze flicked worriedly around the room, because there was no way that she had said that.

"Right, and there are three crones sitting around a pot, cackling like constipated hens. The hard truth is that they all live on the thirty-second floor of Central Park West, not somewhere in the wilds of a Shakespeare fable, missy."

Relieved, Rose nodded once. "You're right. When you're right, you're right."

The countess patted her hand. "Don't get caught up in the

fantasy, Rose. A kiss can linger, sticking in your brain like yesterday's chewing gum. Are you going to see him again?"

"I can't. I don't even know his name."

"Problem solved!" Sylvia popped away from the desk, and spread her arms wide.

"It's a billion to one shot I'd even run into him a second time," Rose reasoned. Manhattan was huge, it was impossible to find someone unless they, for example, wanted to be found, or put an ad in missed connections. Why, if she didn't read missed connections then she'd never know. On the face of it, the odds against her ever meeting him again were boggling.

"Not just a billion to one," the countess corrected, "a gazillion. But, let's walk down the primrose path. Let's say you do run into him. Then you let him take you home, screw his brains out and promptly get him right out of your head. Unless he's royalty. And then, dear Rose, you have my permission to marry him. But there's no screwing with royalty. At least not at first. Women must appear to be patient, passive and never, ever, eager beavers. You have to think about these things. Sex has repercussions. Consequences."

Rose didn't want to think about sex; she'd spent all last night *not* thinking about sex, and frankly, all that not thinking about sex was making her dizzy. Finally she snapped back to the present. "I'm pretty sure he's not royalty. Maybe finance."

Sylvia's mouth tightened into a disapproving moue.

"He looked like he was still doing okay," Rose added, wanting to defend him.

Still, Sylvia appeared doubtful. "I can see you've got your mind preoccupied here. It's written all over your little dreamy face."

Hearing that, Rose removed all traces of dreamy from her face, and Sylvia continued.

"If you do have a chance encounter, go ahead, work him out of your system, and then come back and we'll start in immediately on Plan B."

"The bachelor auction?"

"Of course. You're going to win the bid, you're going to bed him, and it will turn out to be the best night of your life." Sylvia strolled over to her flowers, then looked up and shot Rose a wink. "But do not forget. If there's any sex to be had with this Prince Charming, you have to share every sordid detail. And leave nothing out."

Rose held up a solemn hand. "I promise."

FOR IAN, BEING A RUTGERS men's basketball fan was a testament to his unwavering loyalty. Win, lose or pulverized, the three friends were always there. It had started during college. He, Beckett and Phoebe had hung out at the games between exams. After graduation, after all the life choices had been made, they moved from the student section into the moderately snazzy mezzanine where the alumni presided, secure in their life choices and their employment decisions.

On the first day of the New Year, Ian was no longer secure in his employment decisions, but the Rutgers team was sucking like a vacuum and the arena was empty, so hey, he kept his head high.

After grabbing a soda and springing for an order of nachos, Ian jogged up the concrete steps to his spot. There was the standard ritual of unspoken greeting. Phoebe waved a red cup, slightly rumpled in jeans and a Knights sweatshirt. Beckett merely grunted.

All social obligations aside, Ian checked the score. Down by ten already. Okay, not a good night at the RAC, but the Knights could come back, never say die.

However, by the second period, the Knights were still losing, and no one was talking. Worse, Beckett was pale, unshaven and crabby. Now, crabby wasn't that unusual—Beckett put the mud in curmudgeon—but Beckett always shaved. Precise grooming was one of those boarding school rules that Beckett conformed to without even realizing it. Since boarding school was a sensitive topic, Ian chose to keep his mouth shut. "Bad hangover?" he asked instead.

"Yeah."

"Sorry about last night. I couldn't go to your place and smile and be all friendly."

Phoebe leaned in, peering around Beckett. "Don't worry

about it, Ian. How was Times Square? Nightmare on Forty-Second Street, sardined in until you are intimately acquainted with people of questionable hygiene whom you never want to see again?"

"More or less. But I'm glad I went. You have to do it in order to say you've done it, unless you lie, and what's the satisfaction in that? Think about it. On December 31, it's the most perfect place in the world to be—and we live here. Why not take advantage? You ever stop to wonder about how many things we don't do?"

Beckett didn't look convinced; of course, Beckett never looked convinced. "There's a reason why we don't go to Times Square, Ian. You can watch it on TV."

TV. As if all life's problems could be solved on a twenty-seven-inch screen. "But you miss all the excitement," Ian pointed out, knowing it would do no good, but needing to try anyway. Life involved spontaneous kisses and meeting the woman of your dreams, having her visit you in your dreams. Of course, it would be nice if the evening ended a little better—not that he was going to think it was a sign.

"I'll live without the excitement, thank you," Beckett answered, completely unenthused.

Choosing to abandon the impossible, Ian turned his attention to Phoebe. "Sorry about Dexter." Dexter had been Phoebe's latest.

"Eh," she answered with a shrug.

"Don't worry. You'll meet somebody new."

"Yes, I could meet someone new. Possibly. Or the world could end first, destroying all male civilization as we know it, leaving me the sole survivor, and alone I must discover the path to mono-sexual reproduction without any knowledge of biology at all. I'm thinking that's the more likely scenario."

Beckett snorted. "You could do it."

Phoebe quirked a brow over her lenses. "Meet someone new?"

"The asexual reproduction thing. You're really smart."

"Bite me," she replied with very little heart, and then frowned in Ian's direction. "Why are you so happy? It sounded like last night was a bust."

For a second he considered keeping his secret, but too few

charmed things had happened to him. Right now, he needed to share the miraculousness of the kiss, cement it in his head and probably ride it out for the rest of the year.

"I kissed this woman. In Times Square. It was absolute magic, the best time of my life, topping graduation, my first bonus check, the day I bought my first place."

Phoebe looked worried. "You kissed a stranger?" she asked. "Really?"

"Like you've never done it," Beckett argued, both of them completely missing the profound significance of the moment.

"Not in Times Square. I think that's creepy."

Ian laughed, because he didn't expect the rest of the world to understand. "It wasn't creepy. It was like an old movie. She was there and then poof, she was gone. It's a sign. A bubbling glass of Dom Pérignon, a rainbow after the storm, a golden unicorn."

"I'm concerned about you, Ian. You shouldn't be talking about unicorns with a serious face."

"It's only an expression, Beckett. You know, when you feel as if all around you the world is full and bursting, and you need to soak it in."

Okay, that was laying it on too thick, but if a man couldn't have big dreams on January 1, then there was no hope for him at all.

"Missing the firm, aren't you?" Beckett asked, not fooled by Ian's never-say-die smile.

Ian met his eyes, man to man. "Hell, yeah."

Phoebe looked at them, confused. Honest to God, females had no idea the pressure that society put on men. It wasn't smart, and eventually, some poor sap could break under the strain.

Right then, a roar went up as the Scarlet Knights took the ball on a streaking run, layup, net, followed almost immediately by a steal and a three-pointer. Phoebe shot up from her seat, fist-bumped Beckett, and then sat down, adjusting her glasses. "What was her name?"

Details, details. Ian coughed. "I don't know her name. We didn't have a lot of time, and then she had to go find her date." Even to his own ears, it sounded weak.

"She kissed you, and she had a date? Ballsy," murmured Phoebe.

"She didn't like the guy," explained Ian, because he knew it wasn't ballsiness on her part, more the inescapable truth that for one perfect night, two souls were brought together, merging into one incandescent flame that was bigger than either of them.... He sighed. Maybe she'd been drinking too much. No. He wasn't going to be put off. If the Scarlet Knights could win—

The visiting team got a steal, three-points, followed by a foul.

Ian buried his head in his hands.

"Why don't you try and find her?" asked Beckett. "Put an ad on missed connections. What if she's The One? You can't miss out on that."

Ian glanced over at Phoebe, noticed the way her face softened.

"You should," she told him. "Women would eat it up. Trust me, as a woman, I'm almost seduced."

"It doesn't take much, does it?" drawled Beckett, who usually didn't take this many shots at Phoebe.

"Don't be an ass," Phoebe fired back.

"I'm not. You're the one who's talking about the destruction of the entire male species."

"It was a joke, Beckett."

"I'm sorry, when it comes to you and men, sometimes it's hard to tell."

"What does that mean?"

Beckett swore and fixed his eyes on the court, and the three of them watched the game, or at least Ian pretended to watch the game. He was still dwelling on the mystery woman of last night, trying to figure out if the ideal of a dream was better than charging in, throwing the dice, only to watch the Big Bad Wolf blow down the house he'd made out of happy straw.

The doubt, the insecurity, the mixed metaphors, they were all postlayoff, because prelayoff, he would have gambled all night and not panicked about losing his house at all.

At the half, when the Scarlet Knights were down by twenty-six and all hope had left the building, Phoebe turned to him, scarfing his last nacho. "Seriously. We'll help you write the ad. Maybe she's searching for you, too."

Ian looked at the scoreboard, saw his future and worried. "So she meets me and she asks what I do for a living, then what am I supposed to say?"

In his mind, there were certain advantages to staying virtual strangers. Okay, there would be no sex, but on the bright side, he wouldn't have to explain the prelayoff, postlayoff stages of his life. In the battle between his libido and his pride, pride trumped all. Although after a few days, that might be subject to change.

"All you have to tell her is that you help people find employment. Ian, it's very noble. You should be proud of it."

Phoebe talked in that faux-sincere voice, as if being an employment counselor was on par with working with millions of dollars at an investment bank. Not even in Phoebe's noncompetitive universe were the two on the same scale. Pointedly, Ian stared at the emptying stands.

This wasn't a conversation Ian wanted to have, not now, not ever. Instead, he wanted to dwell on the happy memory of last night. On her honeysuckle lips and the burst of electricity that was still humming inside him. To have her, splayed out below him, above him, truly he wasn't picky. Just to see the warm invitation in her eyes, that ripe mouth parted and plump breasts rising, falling, tips begging to be teased…

"You should find her. Place the ad." Beckett's voice cut through his fantasies. *Thanks, dude.*

Ian weighed the options, the thought of her underneath him, surrounding him, damp thighs glistening, waiting… For him.

In the end, libido ruled. "I'll do it."

_4_

ROSE'S APARTMENT WAS a far cry from the Simonov decadence, but it was neat, tidy and for now it was home. Her frown was automatic when she walked in the door, her eyes critical.

It never felt right. It didn't matter if the slipcover for the sofa was hand-sewn, or that the coffee table was a steamer trunk covered in a designer print. She could hear that growling voice in her head telling her that it wasn't straight, or that it looked cheap. Automatically she pulled at the fabric until the pleats hung at a precise ninety degrees. When she noticed the stain on the sofa, she attacked it with spot remover until the light beige fabric was restored to perfection. Yes, there was a certain cathartic satisfaction in having a clean home, but she hated that it was *that* voice that was responsible. Frustrated, she threw the rag in the trash and decided to concentrate on the things that made her happy.

Her pride and joy was a darling little writing secretary that she had discovered at a thrift store on Staten Island, buried between a nonworking television set and an overgrown stuffed rabbit named Helen. The desk was a solid wood Queen Anne with lots of hidden components, delicate carved legs and a dropfront lid. After changing into her pajamas, she grabbed the thank-you cards from her bag and settled down to work.

By the time it was midnight, she wasn't tired—she was buzzing. Not caffeine. Careful excitement, the kind that almost made her squirm in her chair. Sylvia had given her the green light to proceed. Not that she was going to proceed, but...*what if?* Dangerous words. Rose rolled her eyes, told herself to get a life and picked up the pen.

One after another she went through the list of gifts, writing like a fiend, channeling her inner Sylvia, knocking out thank-yous. There were notes for bottles of wine, for autographed baseball gloves—Anton was a fan—and for an antique jade vase from the Kremlin. Jeez, did the Simonov household really need another vase, another set of crystal glasses, another set of mono-grammed cuff links? *Cuff links?*

She backtracked over the list, just in case she'd read wrong. Why was Anton getting cuff links?

Rose studied the maid's tidy handwriting and flipped the paper over to find the name of the gift-giver on the following page.

Rose swore, loud and completely improperly.

Blair Rapaport? Hussy, with a capital *HO*.

By the age of twenty-one, Blair had written a tell-all book on her breast augmentation surgery and had financially exploited seven sex-tape scandals—and the clock of misdeeds was still ticking. On the last television interview, her parents defended her, saying that drunken voice-mail messages over the Internet was "all part of growing up."

So why was Blair giving a Christmas present to Anton? Rose checked the list again. Cuff links? Seriously? Did Blair even know what cuff links were?

This couldn't end well. Rose looked at Helen, who remained stubbornly silent.

No, Rose. Keep out. This was none of her business. There was probably an easy explanation…actually there was no easy expla-nation that wouldn't end with Sylvia pitching a fit, and Rose didn't like it when Sylvia pitched a fit.

She didn't like it when *anyone* pitched a fit.

Opting to do nothing except her job, Rose inked a bland note. Although, maybe, if Blair was smart enough to read between the lines, she'd notice the overuse of the word *we*. And the "such a grown-up gift from such a young girl." That was a definite dig.

Rose reread the card and in the end, tore it up into tiny pieces and dumped it in the trash. Blair was getting no thank-you card from the Simonovs, and if Rose had her way, she'd get a bitch-slap instead. Well, probably not an actual bitch-slap, but if Rose were inclined, if she were *truly* channeling Sylvia, she could do it. She curled her fingers in a fist, wound it up and slammed it down on the desk—killing her hand.

Okay, no bitch-slaps for now, but tomorrow was another day.

By the time she'd finished the list, it was 2:00 a.m. and she was no closer to wanting to sleep. She could hear her computer calling her, a languid come-hither hand inviting her to only peek and see if maybe…

What would it hurt? Honestly. And how would she know otherwise? A gazillion to one. Not a chance in the world.

Tiny goose bumps appeared on her arms. Not fear.

Even though she was alone, she looked both ways before hitting the keys. Navigating Craigslist, she arrowed in on Missed Connections, scanning, scanning, scanning…

Who knew that so many strangers hooked up on New Year's Eve? There were four pages of—

Oh.

My life started on the first second of the New Year…

Magic.

Rose jumped out of her chair, knocking over the pile of thank-you cards, and then immediately picked them up.

He was looking for her. His name was Ian. Her feet slowly touched the ground. Ian was not Dr. Remy Sinclair. He was a stranger in Times Square who had really good shoes and an expensive coat. That coat was a triple-word score, spelled *A-R-M-A-N-I.*

Rose knew that justification of a wrong was a dangerous game, but she wanted to play. Her loins ached to play, and her loins had never ached before.

Under her parents' eagle eyes, she hadn't dared stray, and after Child Services had removed her to a group home at age fourteen, the environment hadn't been conducive to activities of a sexual nature.

However, at fifteen, on a cold December night, she'd learned to explore. Quietly, hidden under the blankets of her bunk so her roommates couldn't hear…

Those dark silent moments were instructive to Rose. She wanted to learn about pleasure, to create it, to control it, to deny it. Pleasure led to impulsiveness, which led to mistakes. Mistakes were not tolerated.

On those dark nights, with the scratchy wool on her thighs and her hand between her legs, there were never any fantasies for Rose. Men didn't arouse her with their arrogance and their games. Rose knew the prison-warden side of the alpha male—the rules, the constraints, the dominance.

Rose hated it.

But last night when her hand had crept beneath the covers, she had seen him, felt him, remembered his mouth on hers, trailing down her neck, teasing one breast then the other, sliding farther...

Rose stopped that line of thought and fanned herself, surprised by the heat on a cold January night.

Ian—she rolled his name off her tongue—turned her on with something else. Her fingers slipped between her legs, beneath her panties, and she found herself wet, aroused.

Odd, yet fun. Curious, she pleasured herself, conjuring his face, remembering his mouth. Her finger stroked faster, her body flushed, and for tonight, she could imagine a man's hands on her, feel his gentle caress, sure, easy, hungry yet restrained. Her breathing staggered, and this time she didn't see the dark of the ceiling. Instead, she saw deep brown eyes burning with a light she couldn't understand. She tasted the heat of his mouth on hers. A tiny moan escaped from her throat. Pleasure. Stealthy and sly. The pleasure teased her, beckoned to her, testing her control. Warily her lashes drifted shut, and she surrendered to the fantasy, finding her rhythm, sensing the orgasm chasing after her.

The first flutters of pressure increased, building more, and her heart began to race at the challenge to cut it off before it took control of her.

In the end, it was no challenge at all. Here, no man would follow her, and Rose closed off her mind, banishing the twinkling eyes, blocking the feel of that devouring mouth. Here, no one followed but Rose. The warmth pooled over her, and there was only a second—never more than one gossamer second—that her muscles contracted and her body flooded with pleasure. Deliberately, Rose shut the pleasure down.

Here was her secret place, the quiet blanket in the dark where the blustering voices had never entered, where only Rose could hide. She'd been quick and careful and silent because little ladies didn't touch themselves and little ladies were not to be touched, and Rose needed to be the world's most perfect little lady.

In the blink of an eye, her cheeks had cooled, her heart had calmed and Rose had smoothed the silk pajamas. Gracefully she took her seat and typed out an appropriate response on the keyboard. When she was finished, she allowed herself one tiny punch into the air, all while keeping her feet firmly on the ground.

His name was Ian.

THIS WAS WRONG. BECKETT never trusted sex, it was too full of complications and emotions, but he trudged after Phoebe, ignoring the eight thousand logical and rational reasons that this would be a mistake. He'd been in her long and empty apartment many times before, but not like this. Not with his cock painfully full, and images of her plastered in his head.

Foolishly he followed her over scuffed, golden oak floors, followed her into the dark recesses of her bedroom. She had five seasons of *Family Guy* on her dresser for late-night watching. He kept rolling over that mundane fact in his mind, but when she began to strip off her clothes, suddenly he was obsessed.

He wanted to touch her. Badly. His blood burned with it, but his brain—the part that was still functioning—held him back.

The sweater came off, exposing a sheer bra and the dark nipples underneath. The air smelled of pine cleaner, burned soup and Beckett's lust. His breathing grew ragged as he watched her shed her shoes, her jeans. The glasses were removed, dropped on the nightstand near the bed.

Through the window, the Upper East Side slept quietly in their beds, a ship's horn bleating, a truck honking and somewhere a siren screamed.

Beckett didn't care. Tonight, the entire East River could burn and he wouldn't budge from this place.

In his mind, he'd never considered a naked Phoebe. Yet there she was. The half-opened slats of the blinds pushed light into the darkness of her bedroom, her skin flashing gold, then shadows as she moved.

She walked forward, bare feet padding on the thick rug, and from the living room he could hear the crazed cackle of her parrot, scolding him. Still, his eyes didn't stray. She was…not exactly beautiful, but something that fascinated him even more. The long, lean curve of her that ran from the high breast to the arch of her hips. His gaze drifted lower to the sleek muscles of her thighs. The dark shadow between.

When they were a whisper apart, Phoebe raised her head and stared, and those normally shielded, practical gray eyes were blurred with confusion. Beckett hated confusion, but his mind wasn't thinking, or more likely, he didn't want his mind to think. Furious, with her, with himself.

Complications and emotions. He could feel them swirling in the air, smelled it, stronger and more potent than the musky scent of desire. If they did this, they could never go back.

Complications and emotions.

There was a clanging in his brain. A bell. A foghorn.

A phone.

"Do you want me to answer that?"

NO! "You should," he stammered. "Get that. Now."

"Whatever you want, whatever you say," she muttered. "Get the phone, Phoebe. I'll get the phone, Phoebe." As she walked, he watched the miraculous perfection that was her bare ass, until she selfishly wrapped herself in the duvet covers and picked up her phone. *"WHAT?"*

He nearly laughed, but then she would glare, so he kept quiet. Beckett needed the break. He was nervous and desperate—never a good combination. Fate had thrown a kink in their plans. Why the kink? Was fate trying to tell him that this was a bad idea? It hadn't seemed like a bad idea earlier.

"Who wrote you?" Phoebe was talking into the phone. Without her glasses, she looked so different, so unsure. Okay, this *was* a bad idea. The duvet cover slipped, his eyes tracked the movement…

"Why didn't she tell you her name?" Phoebe glanced at him, mouthed the word, *Ian.*

She was talking to Ian. Naked. She was naked, talking to Ian. Beckett tried to follow the conversation but *naked* kept getting in the way. He turned, futzed with the *Family Guy* DVDs on the dresser, doggedly studying the nefarious face of Stewie, knowing that behind every innocent expression lurked the mind of evil. Beckett looked at her reflection in the mirror, now doggedly studying the V between her breasts, and felt his tongue start to swell.

Her eyes met his, but she wasn't wearing her glasses. She wouldn't notice. Her brows furrowed. She noticed. Quickly he refocused on Stewie, because somewhere in the world, the Fates were laughing.

And if he didn't get it, her parrot started cackling, as well.

She put her glasses on, her eyes magnified, the confusion magnified, his guilt magnified. Damn it.

No, he was above all this. Carefully he moved toward the bed, step by step, inch by inch, and then balanced precariously on the very edge. "What he's saying?" he whispered.

Phoebe hit the mute button. "She e-mailed."

"She didn't give her name?" he asked, his mind resuming function.

"No name, no number, but he still set up the date. Jane Doe agreed." Her voice was brisk, businesslike, as if nothing had ever happened. As if she wasn't sitting there bare....

"No good," he cut in. "What if some other strange woman saw the listing and decided that Ian sounds like an easy mark? Or worse yet, what if he shows up and she's a serial killer, or like, a cow?"

Phoebe glared, and he sighed with relief. Okay, this felt normal. This felt right. She unmuted the phone. "Ian, listen. What if some other strange woman saw the listing and decided you sounded like an easy mark? Or worse yet, what if you show up, and she's a serial killer, or umm…mean?" There was a pause. "No. I'm not channeling Beckett, thank you very much. I'm just concerned."

Beckett beamed at her. Silently she shot him the finger.

"No, I don't think she's trying to protect herself. *You're* not a serial killer."

She sighed, bosom heaving. Beckett sighed, too, then looked away. "No, you couldn't be a serial killer, Ian."

Beckett snickered.

"I'm not trying to mother you. I give you my word." She stared at Beckett pointedly. "Yes, if you wanted a brutal evisceration of reality, you would have called Beckett."

Insulted, he stood up and went back to studying the DVD. Mostly.

"I'll try to be positive. How about this? It's a huge sign and you're right to be over the moon." Ew. Beckett frowned. Really, she needed to come up with better lines than that.

"Yes, I firmly believe it's the same hottie who kissed you and the two of you are going to live happily ever after."

"No. I'm not just saying that to make you feel better."

"Ian," she warned.

"You're not needy. Okay, you're needy. Good night, Ian."

With a click she hung up, and they were back to being alone. Beckett held the DVD to his chest like a shield. "I have to go. Can I borrow this?"

"Do you want to find out about Ian, about his date, about how excited he is?" She sounded ticked; he knew she'd be ticked, and it was better this way. Safer. No complications. No emotions. If only she'd get...dressed. Until then, he was screwed. Metaphorically, not literally. If he meant literally, he wouldn't be having this stupid conversation with his brain.

Manning up, he met Phoebe's eyes squarely, prepared to set things straight between them. "He's screwed. It won't be the same chick, or if it is, he'll get punked on some reality prank show. Life doesn't work out that good. Nothing works out the way you want it to." He held up the DVD. "Mind if I borrow this?"

Okay, he'd settled nothing, but she wasn't looking at him all soft and confused anymore. Now she looked pissed. "Just go, Beckett."

She was proving his point. Beckett ran for the door, clutching the DVD, her parrot's crazed cackle echoing behind him.

5

THE MANHATTAN OFFICE for Employment Displacement. It was the tenth floor of a worn midtown building with an elevator that sometimes went wonky. All around the three-room office were signs of encouragement, pictures of eagles soaring in the sky, posters that proclaimed: "Yes, you can." Yet inside the reception area were also the faces of the employmentally displaced, and it was hard to reconcile them with the pictures of soaring eagles when all they wanted was to find work and pay the rent.

For all the wisecracks Ian made at the eagles' expense, he did his part. Jeans and goofy T-shirts were the uniform here. His boss, Sal D'Amato, said it made people feel less out of touch. Privately, Ian thought that a T-shirt that said, "Practice Safe Lunch—Use a Condiment," didn't do squat, but he kept an encouraging smile on his face and his prelayoff wardrobe stored in his closet. "Interview clothes," that's what Ian called them now.

Although, tonight "interview clothes" would morph into "date clothes," because tonight he had a date, and not just any date. This was the date of a lifetime. With a woman whose face had been embossed on his brain, in his dreams. He could remember her smell, the silken touch of her skin, even the feel of her fingers pressing against his neck. He looked at the eagles, wings outspread, images frozen in time, and he gave them an encouraging smile. *Tough luck, dude. Tonight, it's my turn to fly.*

Alas, today he had to actually work like a turkey before he could fly.

The hiring project of the day was Mitchell Unger, an unemployed ad man, forty-nine, with a family of three to worry about.

Adding to his misery, the oldest boy would be starting college soon, and Mitch was starting to sweat not only food and rent, but tuition, as well.

At precisely 9:13 a.m., Ian started on the phones—because true New Yorkers took precisely thirteen minutes to get down to business. The first three calls went straight to voice mail, the next number had been disconnected, company number five believed that marketing was overrated, company six had just hired someone new, but on lucky call seven, Ian finally hit pay dirt and the negotiations began.

Without any remorse in her cold, cold heart, Mary offered the lowest of the low. Mail room. Ian jumped all over it, because any opening was progress of the very best kind.

"What about this? You pay him the mail room salary, but throw him some creative work. Think of the cost savings alone. Imagine the visual. Your managers sitting around a table, and you're pitching Mitchell's ideas, and they're all looking at you as if you're a goddess. This is your moment, Mary. Humbly you explain about Mitchell, explain how little he's costing the company and how much he's bringing to the table. And then the suits crack a smile—nay a broad-bowed grin that is going to crack the Botox right off their faces. Imagine it, Mary—suddenly you're the hero."

His hero wasn't completely buying it. "No, I don't write fiction. Come on, Mary. Give him a shot. I'll do anything."

And those were the magic words she'd been waiting to hear. Ian wondered if he ought to feel cheap, pimping out his investment skills in exchange for work, a habit that was marginally illegal since he wasn't employed by a licensed broker, at least not presently. On the other hand, it was for the greater good, the ultimate sacrifice, and best of all, his skills stayed razor-sharp.

"Altriva? The dog food company. You heard something?" Ian hunched over the keyboard, fingers flying as if they were born to soar. "Maybe. Give me a second." He scanned the numbers, catching the six-month-long uptick. "You know this is going to cost you, right?"

Mary knew.

"I don't come cheap. But the Portland Scientific recommendation panned out, right? The numbers are solid. Liabilities are low. Recently a lot of insider trading, all buys, but I don't see any clues in the news. It's definitely trending up. The P/E looks sweeter than my mom's apple pie, and they have new management. Go ahead, buy. You have my blessing." Sensing victory within his grasp, Ian strolled back over to his desk and kicked up his feet. "I'll send Mitchell over for an interview today. Clear the schedule, Mary. You're going to love him."

After he rang off with Mary, Ian punched in Mitchell's number. "Mitch, my man, it's Ian. You need to turn off the daytime talk shows and break out the suit. Interview at Scholstein, Harden, today at four. It's a junior position. Sorry about that, dude, but I have great faith in your abilities to turn a silk purse into something even silkier. After all, you *are* in advertising."

For the next five minutes, Mitch cooed and oohed, expressing his undying gratitude until, embarrassed by the compliments and accolades, Ian made up an excuse and hung up.

The gratitude always hit him between the eyes. When Ian was in banking, his clients were smug, taking their ten percent returns with a clipped nod and a bottle of aged scotch at Christmas. At the employment office, this gratitude felt off. Ian didn't deserve it. Honestly, there were no miracles working here, none at all. Not like in finance, where miracles occurred by the trillion on a daily basis.

Thinking of his prelayoff life was not a good way to start today. Automatically his hands reached for the polished rock that sat on his desk, tossing it up and down like a baseball. When Ian was seven, he had wanted to be an astronaut. His father had sat by his bedside and solemnly told him the stone was a moon rock. After that, every single night he had slept with the tiny fragment of the galaxy under his pillow. By the age of nine, he wanted to be a basketball player, and his father had said that it was a piece of foundation from Madison Square Garden. However, by the age of nine, Ian was smarter and wiser, and called his dad a big, fricking liar. His father had gazed at him, man to man, and told him the rock's initial place of residence didn't matter. The most important thing, according to his father, was to think about the rock's final destination. A rock could be moved from place to place, but where it ended up was a lot more important than where it started.

Being a cocky nine-year-old, Ian had rolled his eyes and drawn out *Da-ad* to a long two syllables. But when his father wasn't watching, Ian took the stone and casually tossed it in the air before tucking it in his pocket.

Ian felt his dad's smile, rather than saw it, and to this day, Ian found myriad uses for his stone. Maybe this wasn't his final destination, but for now, for today, the victories were starting to smell sweet.

One file on his desk was not smelling so sweet. There were no victories for Hilda Prigsley. For four months, he'd beaten every bush in town—and a few out of town—but sadly, in New York, very few individuals saw the wisdom of taking on an over-fifty teapot-shaped immigrant from the UK. She typed well over one hundred words per minute, one-twenty-two to be exact, but unfortunately believed that computers were the handiwork of the devil. Ian had tried his damnedest to find her something, but positions for a portly Mary Poppins weren't as plentiful as some might think.

Once a week Miss Prigsley stopped in the office, bringing him a tinful of handmade English biscuits. Ian always called them cookies, because then she would correct him in her proper English way, and he would pretend that he'd forgotten, and she would giggle and smile and he felt as if he'd just charmed his grandmother. If he could only figure out a way to market a sentimental lexicologist, she would be *so* employed, but reluctantly he pushed her file aside and focused on the nonlexicologist extraordinaires.

By the end of the afternoon, Ian had found two more positions. One for a budding young medical assistant, Deirdre Synder, and one for Mortimer Haswell, a fifty-eight year old mortgage broker who wasn't happy about a secretarial job and came down to the office to whine in person.

After a few seconds of polite listening, Ian paused for dramatic effect and then held up his stone. He looked Mort in his basset-esque eyes and asked, "Do you know where this came from?"

Mort shook his shaggy gray head.

"This stone is from my first job. Recycling. Now, if you've ever worked recycling in this state, you know it's not a pretty job. It's not elegant. It's not one of those run-out-and-brag-to-all-your-friends job. But I did it. Dirty, crappy and I smelled like bad fish until I went to sleep with that smell on my pillow. I stuck my hands in things better left unidentified, and my friend, in garbage, ignorance is the only thing keeping you sane. After my first month, when I was one refuse load away from quitting, I found this stone, winking up at me like a talisman. For seven years I shoveled trash, saving up for college. And let me tell you, on the bright, shiny day I graduated from Harvard, this little stone was tucked under my mortarboard. It was my lucky charm. You gotta see the big picture, Mort. It's not where you start, it's where you end up."

Mort's unibrow furrowed deeper into his forehead. "I don't know, Ian. I can't type."

Ian was used to the objections and nodded sympathetically. "Yes, you can, Mort. You can do anything you want. Go in there. Make yourself indispensable. You'll be fine, wait and see. Within a year—tops—you'll be back in finance where you belong."

It took a little more convincing, but eventually Mort left—almost satisfied. Ian picked up his polished rock and put it in the drawer. Wasn't going to need any props tonight. Tonight was all about the shimmer and shine.

When five o'clock rolled around, he watched as the civil servants left before pulling out his suit and studying it with a critical eye. The lapels didn't have quite the spiffy stiffness that Wall Street required. Some wayward lint had wormed its way under the cuffs, and even an untutored nose could detect the faint aroma of mothballs. Okay, lots of work to be done here.

For the next thirty minutes, Ian toiled away at mothball-scent-removal. Using a combination of high-dollar cologne, an emergency container of Febreze and a twist of lemon, he finally transformed mothballs into something resembling the elusive, yet highly potent, scent of success.

When the cuffs were straight, the collar was angled exactly

right and the shoes were shined, Ian admired the finished product in the men's room mirror. This was the Ian Cumberland of yesteryear, maybe a little skinnier. His chin rose, his smile got slightly harder and his eyes sparkled with that familiar devil-may-care glint. Yeah, that was it. *Absolutely perfect.*

Watch out, world.

Ian Cumberland was back.

THE RESTAURANT WAS IN the financial district, on the thirty-second floor of the Liberty Towers. The view was spectacular—the lights from the tankers on the Hudson, the skyscrapers across the way, the Statue of Liberty in the New York Harbor—but it was nothing compared to her.

She was standing by the window, waiting, and his breath caught, held.

He'd never seen a woman whose face was so exquisitely formed. Would it always be like that? Did the curators at the Louvre ever stop gawking at the Mona Lisa?

Up to now, Ian had always made fun of the pretentious types who had season tickets to the symphony, idling their time in pursuit of cultural beauty. He never quite "got" that. Growing up in Scranton warped a man's artistic perspective. But this woman's perfection stopped his heart.

She turned, smiled, and he wiped the goofy gobsmackery off his face before she saw. Tonight he was the investment banker, a confident man who was never caught being gob-smacked at all.

"Ian Cumberland, at your service for the rest of your life." He meant it as a joke, but his voice sounded serious. Serious and gob-smacked. He tried to get the devil-may-care look back. Failed.

"Rose," she answered. "Rose Hildebrande." Her smile was shy, blushing, and he thought Rose was the exact perfect name.

He took her elbow, twirled her, admiring the flair of her little black dress, the way it crossed over the straining perfection of her breasts, the way it set off the long line of her legs. Sexy, simple. *Hot as hell.*

"You know, all the guys in there are going to want to kill me."

Her cheeks flushed, her lashes lowered. "Sorry," she told him, a bit of hesitation in her voice.

And now he'd scared her. *Dude, get on your game.*

"No, I'm the one with the apologies. You look lovely," he told her, leading her inside, seeing the eyes follow them, follow her. *Yeah, eat it up, New York. Tonight, forever, she's mine.*

The evening had been meticulously planned, perfectly arranged, each step designed to turn her glorious head. Ian figured that tonight he had one shot to seal the deal. One shot for him to recover his prelayoff charm; it could be done.

The maître d' greeted him by name, leading him to the designated table, the prime spot at the apex of the windows, where all of New York awaited her pleasure. She looked at the table, stared up at the vent and then—so delicately that only a man attuned to her every smallest movement would notice—shivered.

"Is there a problem?" he asked, praying to God there was no problem; he'd given the maître d' an extra C-note for that table, and he knew the man wouldn't give it back.

"No," she answered, but there was a tiny quiver in her voice.

"If you want to sit somewhere else, honestly, it's no big. You get cold?"

Her soft blue eyes filled with anxiety. "I'm sorry to be such a pain. My internal thermostat is crazy. I'm hot, then cold. Do you mind?"

"Of course not," he said, and then gave the ever-efficient maître d' a commanding nod. "What else do you have?"

"A small table in the back, sir," he responded, a stodgy whiff of England in his accent. "By the kitchen. Unless you'd like to wait at the bar."

"I don't mind the kitchen," she told him, then pitched her voice low. "It will probably be warmer anyway."

"Tonight, whatever you want," answered Ian gallantly.

After they were seated, she balanced her chin on her palm, eyes wide and liquid. She had ridiculously long lashes, shuttering against the golden sheen of her cheeks. "I'm the world's biggest idiot."

"Nonsense," he answered, because he would fight her for that title. Probably win.

"So, Ian. Do you come here often? It's gorgeous. I love all the flowers." She sniffed the heavy perfume of the nearby vase of lilies, her glorious breasts filling, creamy skin beckoning to him.

Ian leaned close, ignoring the flowers, his hungry gaze following the line of silken skin, his fingers itching to touch. She noticed, and her mouth twitched with humor. Charmed, Ian shrugged, just as any good investment banker would. "Busted. Sorry. I'm not usually such a carnal-vore. Actually, really, I usually am, and it's been a long…" *Shut up, Ian.* Quickly he changed the subject. "My building's around the corner," he explained, forcibly removing his eyes from her chest. "We take a lot of clients here."

"Clients? What sort of clients?" she asked innocently, leading him into the very subject he really should avoid. But why should he be so determined to avoid it? If he was truly a courageous man, he would be honest. Let her evaluate him on his own merits, charm and roguish good looks, rather than his bank account.

Ian hesitated for only a second. "I'm an investment banker," he lied, opting not to be evaluated on his own merits, charm and roguish good looks. Immediately he glanced around, waiting for lightning to strike. None did. Ian smiled, relieved.

"Still on your feet, I see. No pesky recession to strike you down?" There was respect in her eyes, and Ian knew he'd answered correctly. He loved that flare in a woman's face, more powerful than a beknighting sword to the shoulder, more satisfactory than when the tellers at the bank had greeted him by name. He exhaled, his chest swelling with pride, completely undeserved.

"I survived, but it's been tough. A total bloodbath, but they like me. I do a good job for the firm. What about you?" he asked, getting the subject away from him. He didn't want to talk about his prelayoff job; he didn't want to talk about his postlayoff life. That pretty much limited the conversation to her, which was fine with him; he wanted to know everything about her, every secret, every dream…every inch underneath her dress.

"I'm a personal assistant. Not as glamorous as you."

"Still, I bet it's a cool job."

"Someday I'm going to do more."

"Like what?" he asked, reading the uncertainty in her face. He saw it all the time in his world. People adrift, not sure which way to move, frozen into doing nothing.

She shrugged, a small lift to an elegant shoulder. "I'm not sure. Nothing feels right. How did you know that banking was for you?"

"I've wanted to be in banking for…pretty much forever. Dad didn't make much money, and I wanted more. Greedy, I guess."

"I call that ambition."

"See, this is why I like you. With spin like that, you should consider a career in advertising." Automatically his brain shifted to job-finding mode—there was an agency in Park Slope, small, boutique and… *Stop it, Ian.*

Rose glanced toward the doorway where a waiter appeared carrying a large porcelain vase of two dozen perfect white roses. Handpicked by Ian only two hours before. Every woman's eye was drawn to the bouquet, longing to be the one, and Ian's smile got a little more cocky. The man started toward the window.

Walked closer to the table by the window.

Walked even closer to the table by the window.

Finally, with a continental bow, the waiter presented the two dozen perfect white roses to the elderly woman seated at what used to be Ian's table. Her husband, a white-haired man with silver glasses—and most likely, a fat bank account—beamed, as if he'd given her the world. The wife blushed. Ian seethed. Quietly, unobtrusively, so no one would notice.

"Is something wrong?" asked Rose.

Ian blanked his face. "No. He looks like a VP that I once worked with. Really didn't like him. Always took credit for the slog he didn't do. You know the type—they haunt every office of every industry in America."

"Of course," she said, but she was watching the couple, her heart in her eyes. "It's fascinating. He still orders her flowers. Why?"

"Maybe there's no reason." Not every gift needed an occasion; sometimes it was just because.

"I don't think so. There's always a reason, even if they don't realize there's a reason. People don't give without expecting in return."

"Wow, beautiful and cynical, too." He'd assumed that men paid homage to her, built temples and monuments, wrote odes and symphonies. But contrary to her hard words, her gaze was firmly glued to the sight of those white roses and the contented smile on the other woman's face.

So it was flowers that were her raison d'être? One more piece of data to put in the Rose file. *Bring flowers for no apparent reason.*

Eventually she looked away, her eyes more firmly entrenched in the here and now. "In the long run, pretty isn't the big whoop that everyone thinks it is. There are levels in the world. Pretty will get you invitations, five dollars off on your laundry and maybe a free pass on a parking ticket, but that's as far as it goes. But the man at the top, the one who sits fifty stories above the masses, that's the pinnacle. He lives life on his terms, and no one tells him what to do."

Ian felt a cold knot in his gut, and wondered if she had guessed at his sorry truth. "You're talking about money, aren't you?"

She nodded once. "Sure. Money, power, control."

Something flashed in her face—pain? And then the moment was gone, the shutters in place. The impassive Mona Lisa was back and the light began to dawn. This wasn't about him. This was about her. "He did a number on you, huh?"

"Who?" she asked sharply.

"I have no idea."

Immediately the wistful dreams reappeared like magic. "I'm not sure what's bothering me tonight."

"Don't want to talk about it? I'm a good listener, and I know absolutely nothing about you."

"Not much to say. Personal assistant. Moved from nowhere to New York. I manage."

With a pile of men trailing after her with their tongues hanging out. Like Ian. "So what happened with your date?"

She didn't pretend she didn't understand or play coy, and he admired her for that. He liked that. She might sell herself short on brains, but she could read people well. Including him. Politely he dabbed at his mouth, in case his tongue was hanging out, as well.

"His name is Remy. It was our fourth date. He's very nice. He's perfect."

"How perfect?" asked Ian, now surreptitiously checking for hidden cameras, in case this was reality TV at its worst.

"He's a heart surgeon. Pediatric. Saving small children is a line on his resume. Good-looking. Family money."

"Cheats on his taxes?"

Sadly she shook her head.

"Undisclosed porn addiction."

Rose looked at him and laughed. "I don't think so."

"Wow. I don't see anything wrong there."

"I know," she told him unhappily.

"Rose? Why are you here?"

"Do you believe in it?" she asked him, her face serious and nervous.

"What's 'it'?"

"Fate."

He could invent something really romantic and magical, something to make her sigh, but she'd probably heard all that before. Instead Ian went with the unremarkable truth. "In the past, I didn't. I mean, I wanted to, but it never went my way, so it was a lot better for my mental health to think it wasn't out there."

"Why not?"

There were a lot of ways to answer that question. Ian chose the least incriminating. "There was this kid in third grade, Kevin Trevaskis, and his parents were a total pain because every year he stayed up waiting for Santa Claus and he never got any presents. But he still believed in this great concept of goodness, even though nothing ever came his way, either. I always felt sorry for that kid. At least, if your parents perpetuate the Santa Claus myth, you have those formative years to hang your hat on, but Kevin didn't even have that. It was sad."

"You didn't tell him the truth?"

Now that he thought about it, it was becoming completely obvious that Ian had issues with truth, even as a young child. Yet now was not the time to dwell on past—and possibly present—indiscretions.

"Who am I to take away his hope? And before New Year's I'd been thinking about Kevin, thinking maybe he had it right. What if we were the ones who had it all wrong? I went down to Times Square, drinking the enchanting elixir, because for one day, for one second in time, I wanted to believe in that hope, too. I wondered if I'd been missing out. Then I saw you, and I knew. Kevin *was* right."

Rose turned a little pale, her eyes wide. Definitely fear.

"Why is that a bad thing?" he asked, not wanting to be insulted, but worried that once again, this was not going to end well, especially in light of Dr. Pediatric Perfection.

"Destiny implies an absence of choice. It means that my decisions, my choices, my words don't matter. Somebody somewhere is playing chess, and I'm the pawn."

Relieved, Ian exhaled slowly. "You don't have strings. You just follow the open doors and see if you like where it leads."

"Doors aren't good. Doors can be shut."

"Doors can be opened."

"But you're an idealist," she pointed out. He'd never thought of himself as an idealist before, and she was wrong, but he liked that she saw him that way.

"So you don't think this…is fate?"

"I've thought a lot about it since that night. I'm not a big romantic. But you make me want to believe in something nice."

When he looked at her, he could see the ghost of Kevin Trevaskis. Hope and fear battling it out. Ian's feelings were much more defined. Rose made him believe in a better road ahead, in soul mates bound by a single kiss—and then, of course, getting her naked, not specifically in that order. Prudently, Ian shook off the lust and then deflected the conversation to her.

"How come you've never married?" He couldn't wrap his head around the fact that she'd stayed single, sexy and beautiful for this long.

Again she fiddled with the silverware, hesitating. Eventually she decided to trust him. Rose looked up, her eyes not so hard, now almost wistful. "I keep thinking that something better is out there. Like I'm missing out. You ever run up to the crosstown bus stop just as the driver's pulling away, and you know that was your bus, but you can't see the number, so you stand there for a minute, not sure if you need to start walking. That's the way I feel about the men in my life. That I've just missed the bus, but I don't know if I should start walking or wait for the next bus."

Self-consciously, she pushed at her hair, the long strands falling, covering her eyes. Hiding.

Ian didn't say much, watched, wondered, until the waiter appeared at their table in all his tuxedoed splendor and presented the wine list to Ian. "Would you care for wine, Mr. Lawrence?"

"It's Cumberland, not Lawrence, and I've already—" Ian stopped and watched the wine steward moving toward the table by the window. His table. His wine. Champagne, actually. Dom Pérignon, four hundred a pop. Ian managed a weak smile for the waiter. "Give me a minute to decide," he said. The waiter left silently, efficiently, most likely having a really good night, unlike Ian.

Frustrated, he gazed up at the magnificently painted ceiling where all the angels were watching, pointing, laughing.

He should have told Rose the truth.

"Quite an evening they're having."

Ian looked over at the other table, where the older woman sat laughing then leaned over to plant a shaky kiss on her husband's lips. Ian heaved a regretful sigh. "Yeah."

Resigned to his fate, he gestured, and the waiter reappeared. "You've decided, sir?"

"I'll have what they're having."

6

IT WAS SOMEWHERE BETWEEN dinner and dessert that Rose found herself getting drawn into the land of Prince Charmings and magic wands. She'd never seen a real magic wand, only a twelve-inch ruler that hurt like hell on her knuckles. The memory was always there, ground into her marrow, but tonight, it didn't make her sit up straighter. When the waiter clattered the silver lid, she didn't jump in her seat.

It was Ian. He had such a nice face. The way his eyes watched the world with a light all his own, not afraid of what he would see. Hope, that's what he'd said, and when she looked into those sparkling eyes, she wanted to see it, too.

There was something else in his expression, something more basic that made her nerves tingle and stir. He wanted her. Sometimes it flared in his face, the way his gaze skimmed over her, her mouth, her breasts. But there were no innuendos, no sly remarks, no expectation that Rose would play the game. It was desire without strings, and she could feel an answering prickle on her skin. The longer she was with him, the more she relaxed, the more her body opened up. Tingled. *Desired?*

She was forgetting her training, forgetting her lines.

When he quietly listened to her rant for over ten minutes about the cost of living in the city, there was a staggering moment when she imagined his hands cupping her shoulders, sliding the dress down her skin. When she sent back the chocolate torte because they'd forgotten to take off the raspberry sauce—an extra one hundred and twenty calories—Ian smiled indulgently, and Rose felt a hard pulse between her thighs. Her face flushed, and she crossed her legs tightly.

She tried to summon an enthralled, sophisticated air, wide-eyed, pursed mouth and a fawning hand to his shoulder, but all she was managing was inching her chair toward him, absorbing his scent, and a trampy hand to her own cleavage. When she realized what she was doing, she sat up straight, her back glued to the chair.

Yet the exquisite allure remained. Over coffee, she slipped off her shoes. Like a child hypnotized in a toy store, her impudent foot glided over the polished mahogany floor, flirting closer to his chair.

Her mother's voice echoed in her brain. A woman who made fast moves was a slut and a whore. Yet closer and closer her foot moved. Nearly there, a toe's breadth away, when a shadow fell over the table.

"Ian? Ian Cumberland?"

Shocked, *shocked,* Rose pulled her foot home and into her chair, curling it up under her in case the appendage decided to roam again.

The man was alone. Mid-thirties. A high-dollar business type with a narrow-lapelled suit that looked custom, no tie, and sharp blue eyes that oozed over her, assessed her, appraised her. His wolfish smirk said that she passed.

Ian stood, they clasped hands, one firm shake to test who would flinch first.

"I was wondering about you the other day." The man's smile blasted Rose with his well-practiced charm. "I can see you're doing fine."

"Rose, this is Michael O'Leary, aptly named for his voracious appreciation of the female sex."

"You were always jealous." Michael covered his heart. "But now I think I'm the jealous one. Rose. *Rose.* You should leave this loser."

Her smile was open yet satisfied, a slow, subtle curl to the mouth, exposing a flash of dimple on her right side. "I'm happy where I am." *Happy.* She rolled the word in her mind, enjoyed it.

"Where did you land?" Michael asked Ian, and Ian grinned, that carefree smile that so impressed her. He didn't care what people thought, merely content to be who he was.

"I'm at Caldecott Capital. You've probably never heard of them. European. Small. Very—" he waggled his fingers "—private."

"Congratulations. I knew you'd do fine. We'll have to do

lunch. Call me." He gave Rose a last, slow once-over. "So fine. If he mistreats you, you call me, too."

As he walked away, he flipped his card on the table with the casual confidence of a man used to having women call. Rose took his card, and once the cutthroat Michael O'Leary was out of sight, she tore it into little pieces.

"He's not that awful," defended Ian, which only made Rose like Ian more, because he wasn't critical or judgmental. He accepted everyone—flaws and all.

"Maybe he's not that awful, but that much ego in one room makes it hard to breathe. You're different. You've done so well, but you don't have to throw it around." It was a standard compliment, usually offered to men who needed to feel humble in their quest for billions. This time, it was sincere.

Instead of appreciating the compliment, Ian only seemed to grow more uncomfortable. "I don't deserve that," he said, the true definition of humble, which only impressed her further. Even Sylvia was going to be impressed with Ian. Rose couldn't wait to introduce them. Finally, she'd found a possibility.

"I think you deserve it. You're the exception."

He winced, placed his napkin on the table. "Rose, I need to tell you something," Ian began, his voice serious.

She didn't like the regret in his eyes, didn't like not knowing what to expect. She liked to know what to expect. Always. Underneath the table, Rose slid her feet back into her shoes, not wanting to have this conversation barefoot. "What?" she asked, now fully prepared.

For a few eternal seconds, he fiddled with his napkin, folding it into neat, orderly triangles, an odd trick for a man who didn't appear to be neat and orderly. Then his eyes lifted, met hers squarely. "I'm not an investment banker. To be fair, at one time I was, about ten months ago. I lost my job. But I got a new one. I'm an employment counselor. I find people work. It's not pediatric surgery, it's not well-paying, though the city benefits are nice. I have trouble reconciling my personal belief that some people are not meant to work with our mission statement of 'we find jobs for all.' But that's personal, and not germane to the fact that I lied to you. I'm not rolling in the dough. I used to, albeit not necessarily roll, but maybe wash, or loofah, or something, but it was definitely better than now—although I'm not starving, either. I'm getting by fine. I have trouble admitting this, I'm not proud of my current profession—on a lot of days I don't even like it. But it's what I do, and you should know that. You should know the truth."

His gaze never wavered, never blinked, never backed down, not once.

Rose took a moment, slipping words on her tongue, words that she'd practiced over and over again. Something earnest, where she told him that she didn't tolerate dishonesty, which was a nicer way of saying financial struggles were not in her plan and hell would freeze first.

She'd seen hell, she reminded herself. She'd lived it. She wasn't going back. Yet none of those warnings moved her as much as the defensive vulnerability in his eyes, that defiant bravado that said: "Go ahead. Get it over with so that I can move on with my life."

Oh, God.

She'd never possessed that bravado. Not once.

All her carefully practiced words disappeared, and her cool, polite smile faded like an old memory.

"I live in the Bronx," she confessed in a voice so low he had to ask her to repeat it.

"A three-story walk-up that's two blocks from the waste disposal plant. I hate the Bronx. I told myself I should move to Jersey and be done with it, but I'm too much of a snob to live there, so I end up calling myself all sorts of stupid. Did you know there are three hundred and seventeen synonyms for stupid? Over twenty-five hundred if you count hyphenated words."

"I bet I could come up with more synonyms for poor." He was so rueful and so endearing, so tempting.

A smile cracked across her face as something cracked in her heart. "Poverty can be overcome. Stupid is forever."

"I like you, Rose Hildebrande."

Of all the compliments that Rose had received in her lifetime, this was the first that made her grin—an honest, true grin created from happiness, not a wildly pleased facial gesture designed to foster the male ego.

"I like you, too, Ian Cumberland," she answered, and she stared into his eyes and breathing began anew. The night began anew, no expectations, no performances.

Slowly she talked, about different things. He wanted her opinion on which *Star Wars* movie was the best and they argued—*argued*—over the original versus *The Empire Strikes Back*. Rose had never argued in her life. It had been over twenty years since the word *no* had passed her lips.

Over the second cup of coffee, he wanted to know the best way to fix the world, and Rose, who had decisive, yet carefully closeted opinions on the world economy, found herself comparing and contrasting the philosophy of world aid against fostering economic independence. She was firmly on the side of independence, no shocker there, but Ian was a remarkably bulletproof marshmallow, telling her that fishermen couldn't fish unless somebody bought the pole.

By the third cup of coffee, she was captivated by the expressions on his face. Surprise, horror, shock, desire, everything shown through his eyes. The horror made her laugh, the surprise made her goggle, and the desire made her...hot.

A lurid image flared in her mind, that indulgent smile flashing in the dark, a tangle of bare limbs, those lean, extra-attentive hands tracing over the full curves of her breasts, pressing between her thighs. Inch by wayward inch, her hips moved, curled upward in the chair, like a flower seeking the sun.

Pleasure beckoned once again. Tempting her to see whether this bubbling magic truly existed. If her virginity was the price she paid, so be it. Her parents were out of her life. Rose was in control.

Tonight she wanted to invite him to her secret place. Just one night, that was all. For one night, she wanted to believe in so much. The goodness of Santa Claus, the ideal of true happiness, and most importantly of all, in giving herself up to fate.

The wispy voice in her head bothered her, with its weakness and excuses. Sun Tzu would not approve. But wouldn't this be the ultimate test?

The ancient Chinese general had said that a ruler must know if his army can obey an order to advance or retreat. If he didn't, misfortune would fall and the battle was lost. Therefore, if Rose didn't know if her mind could outwill her own body—if her own orders would be obeyed—then wasn't she setting herself up for failure?

Wasn't she *required* to find out?

Her foot slid across the floor, finding Ian's ankle, causing him to jump with a start. That single jump, natural and completely without guile, cemented her decision.

Tonight was a test, nothing more. Tomorrow morning she would walk away, completely in control.

IAN KEPT WAITING FOR the other shoe to drop. For the fickle finger of fortune to deliver another debilitating blow, but by they time they were at his apartment, the only shoe that dropped was hers. Along with the other one. Along with the dress, along with the bra, along with the stockings, along with the black silk panties.

Ian froze, fully clothed, one of his shoes clutched helplessly in his hand. Undressing further would require movement. Mental capacity. Right now, he was incapable of both.

The dropping of a shoe had never been such a brain-sucking event.

Rose stood before him, a pocket-size goddess, nude skin glistening in the night-lights of New York. He reached out to touch her, fully convinced that she couldn't be real, and his hand fell to his side, because he didn't want to know. He wanted to stay in the dream. But she took hold of his fingertips, skimmed them over a full breast, a taut nipple. His lungs refused to breathe.

"Will you kiss me?" Her voice shook on the words, and underneath his hand, he felt her heart beat. Too strong for a dream.

Still playing in this happy dream, he inched closer, until their bodies were a whisper apart. His hand slid upward, to cup her neck. There he found soft skin that was too warm for a dream. His head lowered, still terrified that he was going to wake up, but then their lips met and lingered.

Rose breathed against his mouth. A tiny sigh that was too audible for a dream. Not quite so terrified, Ian shifted closer still, burying his hand in the perfumed silk of her hair, the scent of honeysuckle following in its wake.

Please God, do not let me wake up. This is too good. Too real.

Slowly, warily, he kissed her, as if his future depended on this one moment, this one meeting of lips. Her warm breath stirred his senses, echoed by the soft rise and fall of her breasts. Naked breasts burned into his skin.

Not a dream. Not a dream. Not a dream.

Very real fingers slid up his chest, clenched his shoulder. Then the distance between them was gone, Ian was gone. The kiss turned, fast and deep.

Desperately he touched her, explored her, memorized her. A wise god would not grant a moment like this to a desolate man. With each pleasured sound she made, his hopes soared even higher. *Not a dream.* His mouth stayed on hers, sampling, feasting, savoring, not letting up for a second. Now that he had tasted her, now that he had tasted this happiness, nobody was taking it away.

He laughed softly when she tugged frantically at the buttons on his shirt, his fly. It was an odd dance—lips fused, his clothes falling ungracefully, all accompanied by a staggering shuffle toward the bed. In the end, they only made it as far as the couch before Ian fell on her. An ungainly flop. Thankfully, Rose—perfect Rose—giggled, finding a sensitive spot below his ear, above his ear—*hell, yeah*—in his ear. Every place this woman touched, his skin heated then burned. Already his cock was pulsing, prodding, arrowing between her thighs, but there were other things to be done first. There would be time. By now he had persuaded himself that he had all the time in the world.

Reverently his palm shaped her breast, testing the full curve, the plump weight of it. One pink nipple rose under his finger-tips, and he took the peak deep in his mouth, his tongue abrading the flesh. Her body shifted underneath him, her hips arching up to his, and suddenly he was the most powerful man alive. Oh, hell, yeah.

Her hands pulled at his hair, then harder, and pain had never felt so damned good.

Wanting more, his finger slid between her legs, between her lips, the passage warm, moist, heaven. Her muscles tightened, clenching, and he thrust his finger again, her body beneath him. His cock tightened, pulled, but he wanted to please her; he needed to wait. Ian bent his head, finding her mouth, settling in, matching the rhythm of his hand.

When he broke the kiss, he heard the sound low in her throat. One, single sultry moan that broke through the night. A sound that made up for an entire year of heartbreak.

"I can't think," she whispered. "Can't…think."

For Ian, that was it. No more time. His hand located the condom, sheathed, and with one ragged thrust, he was inside her.

Her eyes flared open, melted blue swimming with fear. *Fear?*

"Rose?" he whispered, because she still wasn't moving. "You've done this before, haven't you?"

"Yes," she told him, but her face looked unusually pale. A liar's shade of pale—or a virgin's.

"Oh, jeez. Uh, listen—" he started, but she stopped him with a kiss. It was no ordinary kiss; it was full-bodied, her mouth soft and welcoming, her arms locked around his neck and her nipples were conducting ten thousand volts against his chest.

Ian thrust once.

Rose arched her hips, pulling him deeper inside her, and Ian thrust again. Her face was buried in her shoulder, but he heard a small gasp of pleasure.

Ian stilled at the sound. The tiny sound that ripped through his heart. He wanted to stay here like this, waiting, hoping, praying that this…this very best second of his life would not end. That would be worse than ten thousand pink slips. Frankly, death would be easier. Gently he pushed the tawny silk of her hair away from her face. He needed to see her eyes. Needed to see the fear gone. Needed to know that she was okay.

She sighed, a long, shuddering nonending sigh, and then, with the strong grace a dancer would covet, her legs slid over his hips and locked around him like a vise. Her lashes fluttered up to reveal diamond-bright seduction, glinting brighter than gold.

Oh, thank you. Thank you, thank you, thank you.

At heart, Ian wasn't a man to let opportunity go to waste. This time, he tempered his motions. A slow, gentle glide rather than a sharper thrust, taking the chance to savor the magnificent details of making love to one Rose Hildebrande. Apparently, one Rose Hildebrande was an opportunist, as well. Her hips pushed upward then pivoted, causing all oxygen to leave his brain. He gasped. Pleasure, tremors of pleasure, remained.

"You can't move like that. I will die. You don't know how good this feels. If you move like that—"

She did it again.

Ian rose up on his elbows, glaring, as much as a man could glare in midcoitus. There was something wrong here. He was supposed to be gentle because she was supposed to be a virginal lamb. "You did that on purpose," he accused, not completely upset.

Proudly Rose beamed at him, more foxlike than lamb. "I did."

"Why?"

"If you attack when your opponent least expects it, he is most vulnerable. And," she added slyly, "he likes it better."

"Did you read that in *Cosmo?*"

"The Art of War."

He laughed at her joke, and swept a hand down the curve of her spine.

"Let's forget a moment about what you think I like better. Honey, this one's for you. What do you want?"

Nervously she licked her lips. "Anything?"

There were few words that energized a man's sexual imagination like the word *anything*. But Rose was a virgin, he reminded himself. Inexperienced in the carnal arts. To her, *anything* implied a back massage, or a kiss on the neck, or maybe, if he was lucky, a little muff-diving would be involved.

"Anything," he assured her.

"I want to be in charge."

In charge? Ian rose up on his arms and studied the Cinderella-blue eyes, the cupid's-bow mouth—his gaze slipped lower—and those *Penthouse* breasts. "How in charge?"

She hesitated, her teeth worrying her lower lip, and Ian's

mind raced ahead to handcuffs and *Penthouse* breasts in black leather. Holy shit. Rose was no lamb. He was the lamb.

"Go ahead," he urged, praying no pain was involved.

"I want to be on top," she whispered, and he breathed a sigh of relief.

Gently he touched his mouth to hers. "I have been thoughtless, pig-brained and, for lack of a better word, a total nudge for not noticing sooner. If you want—no, if you *need*—to sit on top of me, showing no sexual mercy at all, it would be selfish of me to refuse."

Rose tilted her head, mulling the possibilities. "I would like that, I think." Her eyes held an audacious glint that might have scared a lesser man. Ian found himself…curious.

Curious he might be, but he was now prudent, as well. He took her hand and led her to the larger confines of his bed. "It will be safer here," he said, before pulling her down on top of him, deciding that being the sacrificial lamb had a lot of perks he'd never realized before.

"I get to be in charge?" she whispered, her voice husky with possibility.

Heroically, Ian restrained himself from jumping her. "Whatever you want. My body is a mere tool to be used and abused."

All humor died when Rose settled herself over his thigh, seeming intent on both pleasure and torture, all at the same time. Her sex brushed close to his cock, sliding, riding, but not quite there. Completely intentional. Completely shameless. His body bucked, but she stilled him with a surprisingly firm touch. Then, with bold eyes, her hands stole over her breasts, teasing her nipples to hard peaks, and against his thigh he could feel her wet, wetter… *Oh*…

His cock jumped, searching for that moist heat, but she wasn't done. Her lips feathered his chest, her teeth scraping with exquisite purpose over his nipples.

"Rose…honey…sweetheart…" His voice strained, and she froze. She looked at him with wide, innocent eyes, then slowly, her mouth curved into a smile, the eyes no longer innocent. Her body shifted, rose. Then, inch by heated inch, she lowered herself, filling her, surrounding him. Killing him.

She watched him, aware, curious, as gently she began to move. Slow, languid strokes, her body gliding over his, up and down. Her fingers teased his chest, dancing, caressing, and she leaned down, taking his mouth in a long, open-mouthed kiss. He reached for her, craving more, but she pulled away.

Okay.

"You want?" she taunted, her hands settling on her breasts, and her body arched, hips riding him faster now.

I want.

Quickly she moved, and his hips pistoned up and down, matching her rhythm, until he was at the point of breaking, but he didn't touch her. No, Rose needed this; he would not deny her. Her gaze locked with his, sapphire-bright, until he was drowning in the blue of her eyes. His body pulled, his balls tight. Her smile was the devil. Her muscles clenched him, and she stopped. He thought she was going to come, but then the lashes fluttered open again, and there was something driving her. Something that he couldn't understand. Helpless, he caught her hips in his hand and thrust inside her, higher and higher. Rose gasped, her body clamping down on his cock, and he needed one…more…

He was ready to move, ready to drive in there one last time, but then she pushed down on him, until he was buried deep, too deep. Her body froze, tensed, and before his eyes, she shattered.

Too much. Too much.

His cock pulsed once before his body shuddered, finding its own release. She collapsed on him, her body slick, her breathing shallow. Carefully he stroked the length of her spine, wondering what she kept locked up inside her—and wanting to know. He wanted to know everything about her.

Ian lifted his weak head and pressed a kiss to the shoulder of a Valkyrie. "Now I have truly lived. Jessica Alba? She's dead to me."

Against his chest, he felt her mouth curve up in smile. "Jessica Alba?"

"I was young. Impressionable. A gullible fool." He shifted their positions, liking the way her body curved into his. Fate. "Rose? This was your first time?"

"You weren't supposed to know. I screwed up."

"No," he said, stroking her hair. "You were perfect. Better than perfect, actually. Quite…inventive at the end. So, how did you know all that?"

She stirred, tilting her head, and Ian found himself distracted by the erotic shelf where her shoulder met her neck. Rose slid upward on him, arousing him even more.

"Know what?" she asked.

"The way you were, um, touching yourself. You didn't read that in *The Art of War*, did you?"

"Not *The Art of War. Cosmo.*"

Then her mouth took his. The kiss started slow, but not for long. Her tongue glided between his lips, in and out, in a movement lovingly copied by her hand on his cock. But now Ian was clued into her tricks and he tumbled her beneath him. "You're mine, my pretty, all mine."

And for the next hour, while the city of New York burned and beamed, Ian poured himself into Rose, heart and soul. At least for tonight, he was king of the world and she would be his queen.

ROSE AWOKE TO THE unfamiliar sensation of an unfamiliar bed, an unfamiliar ceiling. Through the window she would see the lights of New York, not the diffuse lights of the Bronx. She could feel the warm heat of his body calling to her. Just like last night.

Last night.

He lay on the bed, his hair tousled with sleep, his hands outstretched, reaching for something that he'd never have. Ian Cumberland was a beautiful man in sleep, and last night had been a shock. She'd never known that her knees could buckle under the lightest touch of a hand. That her heart could weaken with the taste of a kiss. That her mind could go thoughtless from the pleasure of a man. His heart had been so strong, pumping wildly against her own.

Stronger than her own.

Rose had told herself that this was a test of strength and will. One night, and then she'd be able to walk away.

If she was as strong as she told herself she was, all she had to do was leave now and not look back. If she wanted to be in control of her life, her destiny, all she had to do was walk away. She wasn't that little girl who was forced to obey. She wasn't that young teenager in the military-style barracks eating peas off a green plastic plate. No, Rose Hildebrande had dreams.

Quietly she pulled on her clothes, tried to smooth her hair. Could she make it to the bathroom without waking him? Of course, Rose was an expert sneak, silent as a shadow.

When she eased the bathroom door closed, a small night-light clicked on, and Rose blinked at the reality she had created.

The mirror reflected so many things, bad things, and Rose felt her hands tighten before she forced them to relax. Who was that person staring back at her? The hair was in tangles, her makeup smudged, and the eyes were too vulnerable. Even in the feeble light, the faded bruises of her soul were too exposed. Still, she made herself look, made herself study the imperfections that were there, planning how to fix them. Battles were not won by making mistakes, only by eliminating them. Eventually the weakness dimmed from her eyes, resolve in its place. Then she began to work in earnest.

In less than ten minutes, her makeup was repaired to a flawless pale gold and her clothes were neatly in order. But she needed to escape.

Last night she'd forgotten everything, woozy with the force of his smile, weak with his kiss. It wasn't a mistake she would repeat. Her eyes searched in the mirror, her chin lifted. No one was better at being a stone than Rose. She knew what she had to do.

Break the woks, sink the boats, burn the bridge. Every army in every language had some equivalent of the actions that would make retreat impossible. All Rose had to do was light the match.

She reached into her trusty makeup bag and brought out True Love Shimmer, a subtle pink lipstick with flashes of gold. Efficiently she scrawled out the words *Please don't call* on his mirror.

The lure of Ian Cumberland was strong, but she'd worked too

hard to rebuild herself, and she wouldn't be broken down again. She liked this Rose Hildebrande. The strong one that made her own way. He would find someone new; the world was full of women who didn't mind being torn apart.

But Rose knew better.

7

IAN WOKE SLOWLY, COUNTING the beeps of the sanitation trucks outside. Normally it annoyed him. Today he didn't mind. Unless of course, last night had been a dream. Happily, the scent of honeysuckle hung heavy in the air. The glorious musk of sex wafted from the sheets. Ian reached out one arm, searching, finding…

Searching…

Finding…

Searching, searching, searching…

He threw the duvet aside and looked.

Rose was gone. Ian rubbed his eyes because he was sure that he hadn't dreamed last night. The dinner, the dessert, the quiet pillow talk, and yes, hallelujah, the sex. A man did not hallucinate wild, unrestrained sex like that. Well, some men might, but not Ian. Postlayoff, he wasn't that vain. To be truthful, last night exceeded prelayoff fantasies, as well. It had been…whoa. Now he was making himself dizzy again.

Quickly he sat. "Rose?" he called, but by now he knew she wasn't there. Her essence was gone from the room. That quiet glow that followed around her like a moonstruck shadow. Silence remained, except for his lonely sigh.

One more time, this time with feeling.

Gathering all his energy, Ian stood up, stretched and stared at his bed—the rumpled covers, the shallow dent where she had slept. He should have the whole thing bronzed and framed above the mantel, cherishing the accomplishment, the very pinnacle of his happiness. But then people would think he was shallow. Rose would think he was desperate. There was truth in that, but he could hide the desperation from her. After all, he'd already told her about his job situation. And still, she'd stayed. And still she'd made love to him.

No, the crazy-talk needed to stop. Ian had to quit reliving last night and get on with today. After he got to work, then he would call her. He was practicing what he would say, grabbing a towel for the shower, when he stopped, frozen in the doorway to the bathroom. There he saw the words. *Her words.*

Ian blinked twice, because he knew he was reading them wrong, the letters scrabbled up in a mishmash that had to be wrong.

His hand went to the sink, held there.

Please don't call.

The room grew so quiet, so insanely quiet, three words sing-songing round and round in his head.

Briskly he wiped at the mirror, keeping his mind carefully blank, but the lipstick only smeared, leaving his hand stained with pink. Ian pressed at the glass harder, but Rose Hildebrande must use the world's most indelible lipstick, because the words wouldn't go away. A towel didn't work. Glass cleaner didn't work. Finally he shoved his fist into the glass.

Much better.

Blood streaked over his knuckles, down his fingers and into the sink. Finally the pain started to settle in, his hand, his heart, the hole in his gut. Ian hadn't expected to be sucker punched again. But here he was, his hand wrapped in a towel and one fucked-up mirror. But at least he didn't have to look at those words anymore.

After a long, cold shower, Ian got dressed and bandaged an old T-shirt around his hand. The buzzer sounded, and his first thought—his first pathetic thought—was that Rose had changed her mind. That she'd somehow realized the utter betrayal of her actions and come back, begging forgiveness.

He ran, *ran,* to the button next to the wall and jabbed it twice before pain took over and he realized that he'd have to stop using his right hand for a while. "What?"

"It's Phoebe. Buzz me up."

Two minutes later she was upstairs, tossing off her coat,

wiping the sleet from her shoulders and the fog from her glasses. Then she scanned the room, for what, he didn't know. "Is she here?" she whispered, dramatically loud.

"No one's here, Phoebe."

She noticed the bloodstained shirt on his hand. "Your hand is bleeding. Getting crazy with the Ginsu knives again?"

"Yeah. Why did you come?"

"Are you kidding? I have to get the dish on last night. Was it awesome?"

A bell sounded in his head, louder than the pounding pulse in his forehead, harsher than the throbbing from his hand. "I don't know what you're talking about."

"Don't get all innocent and noncomprehending here. Hello, Mystery Date?"

"Can we not talk about this?" Ian glared. Phoebe didn't get it and plopped on the couch instead, the same stuffed leather couch where he'd had Rose underneath him....

Honestly, Ian had to work on his glare.

She leaned forward, her eyes curious, but Ian didn't want company. Not even Phoebe.

"Go away. I can't do this right now."

But at least she finally got it. "I'm sorry," she said. "I don't understand. You were my great white hope for happy endings, 'cause I knew I wasn't getting any." Her eyes turned sad, and she looked at his hand. "Do you have a bandage or something? You need clotting here. Serious clotting." Gingerly she unwrapped the cloth, saw the scarlet streaks of blood and pulled a darker face. "Ian. What the hell? Come on." She grabbed him by the arm and led him into the bathroom, not saying much until she saw the mirror and was hit with the full extent of Ian's idiocy. "Oh. Dude. We should go to a clinic."

He didn't like the pity in her eyes. Another time, he might have soaked it up, but today he felt stupid and raw. "Phoebe, it's not a big deal."

"It's a big deal," she insisted. "You put your hand through a mirror."

"Into, not through. The proper preposition is important. There's a Duane Reade around the corner. I'll buy a roll of gauze. I'll be fine. No clinic."

Phoebe blew out a breath, stared at him, stared at the mirror. Apparently she began to put two and two together. "Ian, what happened?" she asked gently.

His gaze cut toward the wall, and he shrugged. "It was an accident. As I said, not a big deal."

"No. Not the hand. What happened with Mystery Date?"

Yeah, good question. What the hell had happened? Ian called forth his cocky investment banker's smile. "Her name was Rose. No sparks. Nothing was there."

Her eyes narrowed, not quite calling him a liar, but he could see the suspicion. "After all that—the anxiety, the public kissing, the great moment of time when your lips met—and there were no sparks? I don't get it. Your face had sparks aplenty. I could have charged a lightbulb with your—your—" her hand gestured somewhere in his pelvic region "—that energy. Your feet did not touch the ground. You were sparky."

Another time he might have laughed, but right now, Ian didn't want to be sparky. He didn't want to rehash last night with Phoebe. He wanted to be numb and pain-free, and get on with the rest of his life. Obviously he needed to think up an even bigger lie. "She was really boring. Very little personality. I was shocked," he said flatly, adding a sad shake of his head for effect.

Phoebe cocked her head, but she seemed to go along with it. "Okay. That's your story, we'll stick with it." She tapped him on the shoulder. "You're better off without her. Men get so hinky around gorgeous women. Here's a test for you. If you knew that her personality had been deficient ahead of time, would you still have taken her to dinner?"

In a heartbeat, he thought, before he told his heart to shut up. "Not a chance."

"Speaking for average-looking women everywhere, my hopes are restored. You're a good man, Ian Cumberland."

And a total patsy for a great pair of tits and wistful blue eyes.

"See, everything works out in the end."

"Got that right," Ian told her, putting an extra shot of cheer in his voice. "Now, go to work. I'll talk to you at the game tonight. Wait— Why *are* you here? Just because you were curious? I mean, couldn't it have waited?"

Casually she shrugged. "Probably. I just needed to see a friend. And hey, I saw a friend." As she walked out the door, she waved. "Take care of the hand."

Ian's smile was full of bullshit, and if Phoebe had had a full load of caffeine, she would have noticed. But he was glad she wasn't fully aware. That was one inquisition he didn't want to have.

THE MORNING'S WEATHER WAS cold and miserable, much like Rose's general attitude toward life at the moment. She slid into her sturdy wool coat, pulled the wool cap over her ears and headed out into the sleeting rain. On the way to the station, she made the route down one block, over two and past Rudy and Thom's Paradise of Pets.

She stopped under the awning, out of the sleet, and huddled close. The puppies were out this morning, yipping and tumbling over each other, and she almost smiled. In the pen to the side, the big monster watched her carefully, but she didn't look at him, she fixed her eyes firmly on the cute and cuddly ones. Puppies that couldn't hurt a fly.

"You want to see one?"

The man stepped out from the door, a rough-looking gentleman with a large dragon tattoo on his arm, a flannel shirt that needed ironing and what she hoped was a tomato stain on his jeans. God, please don't let it be blood. Carefully, Rose kept her eyes off the tattoo.

"No. I just come to watch them."

"You like dogs? They need a home."

"I can't have dogs. Building regs," lied Rose.

The gentleman shrugged meaty shoulders. "You should move."

"Someday. You know how it is," she said, her gaze drawn back to the one puppy who was careening over another.

The man nodded once, scratching behind his ear, just like the fur ball in the window. "Yeah. I do."

"My boss is holding a benefit for the humane society," she said, because she didn't want him to think she was a dog-hater.

"Does he want to hold one for Rudy and Thom's, too?"

"It wouldn't have the same impact."

"You should have the dogs there."

"It's a dinner and auction," Rose explained, shuddering at the idea of dogs and food and crystal and pristine white tablecloths.

"Still, the dogs are the stars."

No, she thought to herself. The bachelors were the stars. Those little puppies were cute and fluffy, but they couldn't provide either security or shelter. Puppies were a decoration, much like her. "I'll think about it," she promised.

Her part said, all expectations met, she turned to go, but then stopped. Firmly Rose pushed her hair from her eyes, and gave one curt nod toward his jeans. "White vinegar. It'll take that right out. Nontoxic, too."

A few minutes later, she made the transition from the unkempt Bronx to the rarified Upper West Side. She hung her coat and cap in the closet, then checked her hair in the mirror until the waves looked perfect.

The cream-colored serenity of the living room always calmed her. With three windows that looked down upon the city, it was like a fairy tale, she thought, humming to herself. Outside, the world was cold and sleeting, but here, it was a perfectly moderated, perfectly humidified seventy-two degrees. Here, it was so easy to forget about last night. Forget about bare skin and bared souls, primitive emotions laid out for the world to see, to examine, to judge. Rose stopped her humming, frowned and picked at the flowers. This morning, the delicate aromas didn't help.

Last night, there had been so many mistakes. If she hadn't slept with him, there would have been no fear. If there had been no fear, there would have been no bitchery. Writing kiss-off messages in the mirror? She'd never done anything like that before. Oh, yeah, she'd dreamed about doing it lots. She'd seen it on television, where the kick-ass heroines told the world to take a hike. But not Rose. Never Princess Rose. Sometimes, when her dates went sleep-inducingly bad, when she smiled like an angel, her mind had schemed the worst sort of rejections, but not once had she ever delivered one. Not Rose.

Until Ian. No man had stripped her bare so fast without her even suspecting. It had been a long time since she'd felt that powerless, that loss of control. Her leg began to shake. Even in the perfectly humidified seventy-two degrees, she began to shiver.

Music filtered through the hidden speakers in the room, something classical and soothing. But she wasn't soothed. Restlessly, she grabbed a rag and wiped down the spotless piano, rubbing and buffing to remove marks that weren't there.

The only marks were on her skin. A hickey on her breast, a bruise on her thigh. Rose threw down the rag and swore. No matter how busy she kept herself, her mind was determined to remember, and her body wasn't ever going to forget.

All that tautly muscled male strength constrained under her thighs. Ultimate possession. Ultimate control. Ultimate power. Ian hadn't minded. He had let her lead willingly…. She snickered and corrected herself. No. *Enthusiastically.* He let her lead enthusiastically, his smile so disarming, unabashed sin.

No wonder she'd resorted to bitchery. The man was lethal. Surrounded by his trappings, the classic restaurant, the crystal and champagne, he was no threat to her. But without them, when they disappeared…

The damned flutters started all over again.

Rose ran for the security of the cream-colored love seat, covered her face with a frilly throw pillow, and screamed her most silent scream.

"You know, if you're trying to exercise the neck muscles, there are much better ways. Morning, Rose."

Sylvia. Rose shot up, ceased fluttering and giggled in the manner of a woman who had been caught doing facial exercises instead of fantasizing about a man's—

"You're exactly right. You should teach me."

"You're too young to worry about your looks. He called, didn't he? I see it in the overheated gleam of your eyes."

Overheated gleam? Rose stopped overheating and frowned.

"No. He didn't call. I wasn't exercising. That was a silent scream of frustration. He didn't call. There was no call."

"So now you're disappointed, aren't you? Why do we women do it to ourselves? Build up the impossible with hearts and flowers and then we get crushed when it doesn't fly into our lap with little pink wings and a cupid's arrow." She snapped her fingers. "You know what you need? A new dress. Something sexy and adorable—currently available for twenty-percent off at Saks. I love being frugal. Anton gets such a charge out of it. And we'll get shoes. White, with killer heels. You have to try the Louboutin shoes, darling. I know you've resisted, but they're the perfect pick-me-up—or pick-you-up, as the case may be."

When it came to fashion, Sylvia was beyond generous, but Rose didn't want her employer buying her clothes simply because she was depressed. Sabotaging a man's dreams, being the kick-ass heroine of her fantasies, wasn't what it was cracked up to be, and the last thing she wanted was to go shopping. But when Sylvia was determined to shop? Rose knew the stubborn gleam in Sylvia's eyes. Sometimes it was easier to give in; Rose was a professional at giving in.

An hour later, Sylvia was dragging her through Saks, holding up dress after dress, clicking her tongue, and then shaking her head with a regretful sigh. "The Kellehers' party is Friday night. Are you going with the doc?"

"He didn't ask," explained Rose.

"And why not?" Sylvia looked indignant at the thought.

"Because my heart is involved elsewhere and it's not like he's going to stage a full-frontal assault while I'm supposedly pining for someone else." Rose bit down on her tongue, because that was rude and mouthy and something that she wouldn't have said if she'd had more than three hours of sleep. And if she didn't have his marks on her body. And if she hadn't spent the night losing her virginity to a man she could never see again.

Sylvia didn't even notice. "With the right dress, you bet he would. For instance, something innocent, classy, sexy. Not black. That's too vampy for you. You need princess. Think Cinderella. Blue? It would show off your eyes."

Rose was prepared to argue. She hated Cinderella blue, but
then Sylvia's head snapped, her eyes narrowed—a hunter
spotting the prey. With what was best termed a war cry, the
Countess of Simonov dived for the rack, ripping the white dress
from an unsuspecting teenager's hands.

The girl looked as though she wanted to fight over the spoils,
but Rose touched her arm and slipped her a twenty. "You don't
want to do that," she warned. "Last time there was blood."

For a moment the girl studied Sylvia, probably seeing the
scary echoes of a Brighton Beach catfight and then swallowed.
Quick fingers snatched the twenty from Rose and off she ran.

Sylvia beamed at Rose proudly. "Now, see? That efficiency
and attention to organizational detail is what I pay you for."

Next up was the fitting. Mutely Rose stood while Sylvia held
up the lacy fabric, oohing and ahhing, and then calling over the
sales assistants, commanding them to ooh and ahh, as well. "It's
perfect. We should have a tiara."

Rose felt the beginnings of a headache. "No."

"You're right. Subtle, subtle, subtle. Nothing showy for you,
my darling. You don't need accessories."

Once she was alone in the fitting room, Rose studied herself
in the full-length mirror, discarded the blue and reverently pulled
out the white concoction from the pile. Her parents had dressed
her in something similar for the Dream Princess U.S.A. pageant,
but that cheaply sewn rayon had nothing on the gossamer layers
that floated around her now. The silvery beading almost disappeared until the light caught it just so. It had been the only
pageant they could ever afford, and cheap fabric and thrift-shop
shoes hadn't been able to compete with the other girls.

Rose had lost.

Cinderella, she thought with a frown.

After the dress came the bag, even the requisite white,
princess-length coat. Rose objected, but Sylvia was in a mood.
"Do not argue, missy. You have to be perfect. Absolutely perfect.
After you're married, after Dr. Sinclair snatches you up, then you
can pay me back with a six-figure contribution to the charity of
my choice. Until then? Let your fairy godmother get a little

crazy." She snapped her fingers, a flash in her eyes. "Let's go find some shoes. Something tall, a killer spike."

This time, Rose didn't even pretend to protest, allowing Sylvia to go wild. They ended up with a Christian Louboutin pair that Rose thought was mildly trampy, but Sylvia disagreed. "Trampy? You think? More courtesan. Those were the days, weren't they? Gorgeous clothes, men falling all over themselves to scramble into their beds, and those dresses. Good lord, to have such cleavage. I'm so glad Anton isn't a boob-man. If I thought he was straying toward double-wide Winnebagos, I'd have to worry, and I hate to worry. Or I'd have to castrate him."

Sylvia looked absolutely unconcerned about the possibility, and Rose kept her head low, the worry out of her eyes. Blair Rapaport had cleavage aplenty. Artificially augmented cleavage. Rose should say something. Like: "Blair is giving your husband cufflinks."

Yeah, sure. That's what she should do. Today, of all days, when every time she opened her mouth thoughtless words flew out in abundance. Maybe she should, but she didn't have any concrete proof of wrongdoing. It wasn't her business, and she wasn't going to worry Sylvia about nothing. No. For Sylvia, she would do something more, and as a plus, distract herself from the pit of shame in her gut. "Is Anton going to the Kellehers' party?" she asked, oh, so innocently.

"He'll be there. He bought me a new set of diamonds just for the occasion. I love my Russian count, I do, I do."

Sylvia radiated happiness, so blissfully sure of her Russian count, and Rose hid her frown. Hopefully Sylvia wouldn't have to castrate him.

8

WHEN IAN GOT TO WORK, everyone asked about his hand. He joked about learning to juggle with knives. No one seemed to notice that his laughter sounded forced. On his desk, three files were waiting for him: Sarah Cooper, an investment analyst; Charles Dowd, former VP of financial products; and Harley McFadden, cook. None sounded appealing, or easy. But he had a job, people needed this, and dammit, he would not let a minor disappointment spill out and ruin it for everybody else.

Sadly, he managed to ruin it anyway. He called Albany, talked to some manager in the state's office of labor, and got so furious with the tight-assed twit, he ended by hanging up. Strike one. Next he phoned personnel at Municipal Life and got a "I really don't have time for this." Ian told the man he was a heartless bastard who had no business working in HR. Strike two. And the best part of his morning was when his own mother called his cell, Ian put her on hold and then forgot her. It took him ten minutes of solid compliments and shameless bribery in order to make things right.

He needed to clear his head. He needed to find something positive. He needed to take positive steps. Encouraged, he dialed his old boss—keeping the foot in the door was always a plus. For a few minutes he hedged, making polite conversation, asking about the wife and kids.

"We miss you around here, Ian. I'm glad you found something."

"That's what I was thinking about. I miss the bank. What's the situation there?"

"We're dead now, but I'll keep my ears open. You were good. I'd love to have you back."

"Thank you, sir," Ian answered, feeling better. After he hung up, he took a deep breath and promptly spilled coffee all over his desk. Apparently his desk contained no blotting material, because he was still rifling in the drawers when Beckett called.

"What?" he yelled, possibly more rude than he intended.

"Oh, touchy. Want to have lunch?"

Ian mopped at the dark liquid, swearing ripely.

"Is that a no?"

"Coffee spill. I'm overcaffeinated."

"Yeah, you and Phoebe."

"What do you need, Beckett?"

"Hello, lunch? You could tell me about last night."

"I already told Phoebe."

"I didn't talk to her. Don't assume that I talk to her all the time. I see her at the basketball games. And I don't even like to talk to her."

"Beckett?"

"What?"

"I don't want to have lunch. I don't want to go over last night."

"Well, what if I wanted to go over last night? Does it always have to be about you?"

"Look, I appreciate the concern, but it's not a big deal."

"This is about me. *I* want to talk."

"I don't."

"What the hell is wrong with you? I'm having a crisis of logic and reason, and you get all pissy."

"What crisis?"

"It's not a crisis. That makes it sound bigger than it is. It's just an…issue."

Ian abandoned his cut-rate cleaning efforts and sat. "What kind of issue?"

"I have this thing, and I want it, but it's not a healthy thing, and I think if I actually had sex with this thing, I could do some permanent damage."

"What thing are you considering have sex with, Beckett?"

"It's a woman."

"A woman is not a thing. It doesn't matter if you actually believe it or not, but you can never say those words aloud."

"Trust me, it's better if I think of her as a thing. Objectify. Tits. Ass. Nothing more."

"What sort of permanent damage could she do?"

"Bad. The bad sort of damage."

Ian glanced at his hand. "Is this because she's not interested?"

"I think she's interested, but I think it's an irrational interest. Like when you're at a party and everyone's drinking, and you start asking stupid questions, and then people sit there, contemplating the stupid questions because it was one of those things you only think about when you're drunk."

Only Beckett could be emotionally stupider than Ian, which cheered him up even more. "Did this start when she was drunk?"

"No. She was sober."

"Were you?"

"Unfortunately. It would be easier if I was aroused under the influence."

Yeah, men were suckers for sex. "Do you want to make love to her?"

"I think I want to have sex with her."

"Then, if she wants to, you do it." *Go ahead, run with the scissors, play out in traffic, use the dynamite with the Acme label.*

"And what about the consequences?" asked Beckett in a voice that said he wasn't going to pay attention at all.

"Wear a condom. You'll be okay," Ian lied.

"You're sure?"

"Absolutely."

IT WAS FRIDAY NIGHT, THE FIRST Friday of the New Year, and the ballrooms of the St. Regis were decorated in seasonal splendor. Pine boughs and berries hung from wave after wave of arched ceilings that belonged to a grand age long past. A towering Christmas tree filled the main hall, decked with shimmering pearl garlands and fat velvet bows. Crystal stars caught the candlelight, reflecting it back with a holiday wink.

The ballroom bustled with elegant men in distinguished

tuxedos, and beautiful women who shone and sparkled with color and jewels. From every corner, from every crevice, laughter and good cheer spilled forth.

Rose smiled, a slight smile, because she knew this place. Her fairy tale, her wonderland, the place that had always kept her safe. A deferential two steps separated her from Anton and Sylvia, because she didn't want to be in the spotlight anymore. She didn't mind, it was never the attention, only the light that called to her. As the band struck up a lively tune, the count turned and gave her a wink. Dressed in black formal tails, Anton was tall and handsome, every bit the aristocrat. Next to him, Sylvia stood, surveying the room, stunning in maroon silk and an elaborate choker of diamonds.

For a long second, Rose closed her eyes, inhaling deeply, searching for that elusive scent: happiness, joy, life as it should be lived. Her eyes opened as she reached for the old familiarity that always comforted her.

The frilly dresses, the bubbling smiles, it all took her back. When the Hildebrandes had dropped her off at Little Princess School of Charm, her parents had been so...*parental* when other people were around, as if they loved her. To Rose, those dreamlike days were tiny moments that she had clung to like a security blanket.

But tonight, it all seemed off. The knot in her stomach, the nerves dancing on her skin. Feeling. *Guilt.*

"Rose, you're looking so gorgeous. The shoes are exactly perfect." Sylvia nudged her husband in the ribs. "Anton, tell her she looks gorgeous."

The count took Rose's hand, lifting them both to his lips. "A work of art." Then he turned to his wife, eyes warm and amused. "But when your hand begins to dabble, perfection follows like a shadow."

Rose spied the emerald cuff links on his arm and her stomach tightened even more. He never had, as far as she knew, worn the monogrammed present from Blair, making her worries seem silly.

Straying? Anton? It should have been laughable. When he was with Sylvia, he didn't seem bored, or itchy or roving. He was a man in love. No reason to worry. None. Okay, so maybe she trusted Anton. But Blair? That was another problem entirely. A problem that Rose intended to handle tonight.

The three of them walked the room, Sylvia air-kissing the world and directing traffic, Rose planting a quiet self-satisfied smile on her face, and Anton laughing at the appropriate intervals.

Under Sylvia's watchful eye, everything was easy. After several years of working for Sylvia, Rose had gone to a lot of these events, and she was familiar with the drill. Sylvia was the current and Rose followed in her powerful wake. Rose knew the crowd; she knew the names, their position on the social register, their birthdays, the favored wine and the amount of the last contribution to Sylvia's charities. It should have been a habit by now, nothing more than a paycheck and a job, but for Rose it had always been a sleepy dream.

Not anything like the charged dream that haunted her; a mouth at her breast, her body arched into him.

Please don't call.

Instantly her spine stiffened, her back rigid, her chin pointing up. Once again, she was in control.

"There!" Sylvia bent low, shoved a glass into her hand. "Twelve o'clock. Leaning against the marble pillar. He looks lonely. Go!" whispered Sylvia, giving her a hard push.

Rose frowned over her shoulder, but she obeyed. On paper, there was a lot to like about Remy Sinclair. The gossip rags tried their best to paint him with the scandal-brush. Club sightings, the woman of the month, but nothing really juicy. There were no arrests, no public fights, no drunk and disorderlies. He knew the line, and never stepped across it. Controlled and content and rich. Remy Sinclair was perfect. All she had to do was toss aside her lifelong behavior of poised female restraint and hook him like an Upper West Side, diamond-bellied trout. Easy.

Rose took a sip of her champagne. Then another. Lifelong behaviors were tougher to shake than one might suspect.

Except with Ian, her brain reminded her, and she promptly reminded her brain to keep its nose out of her business. Tonight, she had a diamond-bellied trout to hook.

Automatically her shoulders squared and her smile was a picture of radiance. "Excuse me, is this wall taken?" she asked, gliding up beside him.

He grasped her hand, raised it to his lips, and her smile widened. "If I had known you were going to be here, we could have come together."

"Surprises are so much more exciting," she lied smoothly.

"Are you searching for new bachelors to torture?"

"Excuse me?"

His grin was almost innocent. "For the auction."

Her heart started again. "Tonight is all about fun."

"Then why the sad face?"

Quickly she adjusted. "No sad face. In this place? Impossible."

"Even sad, you still look beautiful. That dress suits you. Sexy. Vulnerable. Aloof."

"Exactly what every woman wants to be."

"Really?" he asked, and she noticed where his eyes landed— on the Sinclair matriarch who stood there, amusing her subjects. "Have dinner with me tomorrow?"

"I have to work," she told him, not exactly untrue. "The benefit's less than a month away. I think I'm going to have dogs there."

He laughed. "My mother will love that."

Rose glanced at his mother, noticed the look in their direction and smiled politely.

"She approves of you," he said, not a surprise. Everyone approved of Rose. Her smile tightened. "Dinner on Monday, then?"

"You're much more persistent tonight."

"Blame it on the dress," he answered. "If I were really persistent, I'd take you out for a drink later. I know the perfect place." There was an unusual heat in his eyes, and she didn't think it was all because of the dress.

"Dinner on Monday."

"I'm crushed," he mused.

She cocked her head and studied him. Tonight, everyone seemed to have their battles to wage. "But you'll survive." *And speaking of survival.* Rose turned and scanned the room. "Have you seen Blair Rapaport?"

"How could I see any woman but you?"

"Seriously."

"Seriously." He lifted his glass, watched her. "Why Blair?

You don't seem—how can I say this and be polite—suited for each other."

Rose smiled vaguely. "No reason."

Remy studied her, intrigued. "You look like there's a reason. But I'm too well behaved to pry."

No, he was too well behaved for everything. He was, quite simply, the perfect man. Except… No, she corrected herself. No exceptions. None, none, none.

So, why was she in such a hurry to leave? Because she had a job to do, nothing more.

Politely she nodded at him. "It was wonderful talking. Monday. Looking forward to it," and then she was off, leaving Remy Sinclair behind. As she moved across the room, there was a new, more confident spring in her usual, elegant glide. Almost jaunty. Heads turned. She pretended not to notice. Sylvia would approve.

She had a date, and it was all of her own finagling. Happily she allowed herself a self-satisfied smile. She searched through ballrooms and salons, finally coming across a tiny reception area. Dim, candles flickering, a smaller Christmas tree casting the room with silvery lights. Much more intimate. Much more private. Blair Rapaport would have to die.

Quickly she spotted the count leaning against the dark wooden bar with Blair close by. Too close by. The long black dress was cut insanely low. Trampy. Definitely trampy, thought Rose, wishing she had the cahones to pull it off. Maybe she didn't have the daring fashion sense, but she could recognize the fawning little touches on the arm, the wide-eyed, "oh, big boy, the better to eat you with" expression. Truly, Rose did it so much better. Subtlety? Hello?

Then there was Anton. The idiot. What the heck was he thinking? Where was Sylvia? Oh, God, this was a mess. What was Rose thinking? She reversed course, racing out, fully prepared to drag Sylvia back toward her husband and let the woman see the goings-on that were possibly going on right under her nose.

In the main ballroom, Rose spotted Sylvia, chatting, laughing, looking gloriously content with her life, and now, the dragging-Sylvia plan didn't sound so appealing anymore. Rose had nothing but dire suspicions, a pair of insanely inappropriate monogrammed cuff links and a deep distrust of women with more cleavage than her.

Rose would handle this herself, no Sylvia-involvement necessary. Her parents had thought she couldn't do anything right. They were wrong. Dead wrong.

It was a new year, a new life. Rose had been with a man, she'd rolled in the sheets—barnyard immorality at its finest—and she'd survived with no scarlet *A* or a screeching lecture from her mother. Why was she still jumping at shadows that couldn't hurt her anymore? Her parents had long been removed from her life. It wasn't about them. This was about her.

One night, but she had walked away, strong and sure. All this week she'd seen the changes. Her claws were sharper, her aim was more sure.

She'd taken the test and passed.

With steely resolve, Rose took a deep breath to elongate and strengthen her spine. Then she walked, no, she *marched* directly to the other room. Sylvia Simonov had taken care of Rose. Tonight, Rose was going to return the favor, and for Blair Rapaport, payback was a bitch.

Her mind seethed with all those unused comeback lines, those dramatic scenarios never played, all those imagined put-downs that she'd never said. When she spied a tray of champagne, Rose politely stopped the passing young waiter, snagged a crystal glass and drank. Bubbles tickled her brain. In fact, for Sylvia, she would go to hell and back, kicking ass and taking names. As the young man waited patiently, Rose downed another glass, mainly because she knew it was a good idea. When she was done, the man smiled at her, impeccably politely, completely nonjudgmental. Rose nodded once, rubbing the pad of her velvet gloves to polish a tiny print until the crystal was restored to its proper sparkle. Then she handed him the glass. "Thank you," she added. "It's a very lovely party. You're doing a fabulous job."

Now, on to the carnage of war.

With bold steps she approached the couple, as if she had just as much right to occupy this darkened corner as anyone else.

"Anton. There you are. Have you seen Sylvia?"

"Sylvia? The last time I saw her, she was gossiping with her friends like little chickens. Some time ago, I lost patience and abandoned her for a glass of well-deserved champagne."

Rose looked pointedly at Blair. Held out a hand. "Rose Hildebrande."

"Blair," said the other woman, sizing up Rose, dismissing her. Rose was in no mood to be dismissed, and her smile became a little thinner, not that anyone would notice.

"So, are you enjoying the evening? It's a great cause. Sylvia is a huge champion for literacy. Do you have a cause? Homeless, food pantries, protecting the sanctity of home and marriage and supporting the very foundation of this civilization as we know it?"

Blair threw back her head and laughed. A move designed to draw a man's eyes to her throat, her neck and even lower to the double-wides with the For Rent sign nestled snugly in between.

Oh, cattiness. Rose grinned to herself.

"I'm too young for a cause," Blair replied. "That's for old people." *Like you.*

Under the velvet gloves, Rose's hands tightened into fists. "You're selling yourself short," lectured Rose. "All you need is a little grit and something to believe in. People always think they can't do anything, that they can't make a difference. But you have money, connections and time. You have the world at your fingertips. Why don't you use it?"

This time it was Anton who laughed. "My darling wife has been spreading the propaganda."

At that, Rose nearly popped him one. *Propaganda?* "If more people listened to your darling wife, this planet would be a better place. That's all Sylvia wants. To take care of people and see that no one's forgotten. Speaking of, the auction is starting soon. You and *your wife* should talk. I bet she'd adore that emerald necklace. Maybe an early Valentine's Day present, hmm?"

"You think I should?" he asked, his face worried as if he'd been derelict. Not guilt, but not so innocent, either.

"Trust me, she'll love it," Rose told him, giving him a hard nudge toward the other room, where his wife was waiting. If the count stayed here any longer, Rose couldn't be held responsible for her actions. She'd had two glasses of champagne and was loaded for bear.

"She told you to tell me, didn't she?" Anton asked, stubbornly not moving.

"Sylvia? Subtle and secretive?" Rose threw back her head and laughed. Okay, her white dress had cleavage, but it hinted discreetly. It did not bellow.

Finally Anton seemed to get with the program. "What was I thinking?" He placed his glass on the bar, where it was efficiently whisked away, and then nodded to them both. "Ladies. It pains my heart to leave such beautiful companionship, but when the countess beckons? What can I say, I am her slave."

And he was going to remain that way if Rose had anything to do with it, which she did.

After he left, Rose stuck around, fiddling with her gloves, stalling for time, waiting to hear the prime MO of one Blair The Ho Rapaport.

"Love the shoes," said Blair, unleashing her claws right from the get-go. "Cinderella's got a wild side."

Rose reached for a glass, took a sip and eyed her prey over the rim. "Cinderella can kick your skinny ass."

She shoots, she scores, the crowd goes wild....

"Go back to your mommy, little girl. The pigtails and the bows, the cute Mary Janes? You don't belong. You're the hired help, nothing more."

Rose ignored the sting from the dig, but slammed down her glass a tad more forcibly than she intended. "What do you want from him?"

"It's a bet. One night. If I can seduce him, I win," Blair answered, not even bothering to lie.

"What do you win? Miss Congeniality? Miss My Vagina Can Swallow Idaho?"

Apparently, back-alley insults were the only thing that struck a nerve. This time, Blair looked at her, annoyed. *At last.* "What is your deal? Why do you care?"

"These are people. You can't just rip them up and then throw them away." Her own words tripped through the anger, through the champagne, falling flat on her conscience. *Please don't call,* blazed in her brain. Oh, God.

Blair watched her with cold eyes and a bitchy smile, and Rose desperately fumbled for something to say. Sadly, all those dramatic scenarios, all those imagined put-downs disappeared along with her judgment.

Blair merely rolled her eyes. It seemed fitting, and Rose found her tongue.

"Leave Anton alone. He's happy. He loves her. She loves him. Go find…someone else to toy with."

"Rose, sweet little Rose, I don't like to lose."

Rose got up in her face, not so sweet. Not so nice. "You're going down, sister," she blurted and then immediately wanted to slap herself. She'd been on a roll. Clever, witty…kick-ass, and then—blah. That was the best she could come up with?

Blair laughed, and blew her a kiss. "Going down? Yeah, I think I am."

Rose watched her walk, that sultry little side-to-side, and seethed quietly. She didn't know who made her angrier. Blair or herself.

After a minute she called Sylvia, choosing to avoid a physical meeting because Sylvia would sense she was ticked. The physical signs were all there. Heaving bosom, shaking hands and the look of death in her eyes. Sylvia would want to know why.

"Sylvia. I've got a headache. A real pain in the… Anyway, it's a big pain. I'm heading out."

"Sorry about the head. Go home, relax. Did you talk to Remy? I saw you two chatting. A little back-and-forth, a little this and that, before you know it, a little hootch and cootch, but not too soon. Always be the little lady. You make such a great little lady."

"A date on Monday," Rose answered, buffing her nails.

"Oh, my little girl is growing up. I knew it. I have remarkable instincts when it comes to matters of the human heart. Speaking of. Anton's asking about the necklace, Rose. Look at you, setting it all up. Every day…oh… It makes me proud. Monday night. We'll have to shop. I fully expect you to knock his socks off."

Rose smiled wearily. Sometimes Sylvia exhausted her. "No

more than the socks. I have standards and morals and most of all, a strategy."

Yeah, she had a strategy, to mend a bridge that she had burned.

Yeah, now there's some socks you want to knock off. You go back there and you'll be doing a lot more than mending bridges.

So, she argued with herself. She wasn't a precious virgin anymore, she didn't have anything to lose. It was only sex. Now that she was an experienced woman, Rose could walk this line. Not that he'd talk to her anyway. Heck, he might not even let her in the door, so why was she worried?

And if he did let her in, if things got a little steamy, so what?

She'd already proven that she could handle it. Sex wouldn't change anything.

She'd started something with her life and it was working. Finally. Finally she was where she wanted to be, she had her target in her sights, and she was proud of what she had accomplished.

Her eyes surveyed the ballroom, reveling in all the beautiful things, all the beautiful worlds.

Ian Cumberland was merely another beautiful thing that she wanted.

And one she intended to have.

9

IAN STARED BLINDLY at the television. He hated television. The buzzer sounded and he so badly wanted to ignore it. Tonight he didn't need Phoebe or Beckett babysitting him. Not when he felt like this. Tonight, he wanted to sit and watch mundane blather and get slowly, blindly drunk. He was even prepared; the bottle of Scotch nestled snugly into the cushion of his sofa as if it was his long-lost friend. He hated Scotch.

Annoyingly, the buzzer blared again, and Ian shot a loving look at the bottle. Not yet, but soon, my pretty.

"What?" he bellowed into the speaker.

"It's Rose. Can I come up?"

Well, well, so she had decided to revisit the scene of the crime, to find out how badly he'd been damaged. Ian took a long swig of Scotch and jabbed the button with his good hand. See, he was already learning.

He opened the door with an elegant bow, mainly mocking; he hoped she got the point. "After you."

Instead of entering, she stood nervously in the open doorway. Apparently tonight's attire for genteel bloodletting was cocktail wear with long white gloves and a matching white coat. She looked young, innocent, ready for her first winter cotillion. Wow. You really couldn't judge a book by *that* cover.

"What do you want?" he snapped, noticing her wince. Ignored it. He propped the door open with his foot in case he did something painful, like wanting to keep her there.

"I'm sorry," she said, sidestepping his body, moving farther into the room, invading his domain. The honeysuckle smell trailed after her. Not that. Anything but that. He'd spent two nights trying to get honeysuckle out of his brain. Now it was back.

Stubbornly, Ian refused to shut the door. He was not, *not,* going to fall for this again. "Okay. You can leave now."

"I had a really nice time with you."

Realizing she wasn't going to leave, Ian slammed the door, loud, enjoying her jump mainly because now he was really pissed. "By nice time, I guess you mean great sex, a couple of orgasms and a really good laugh."

"I can't see you." Her eyes kept dodging his, staring at the floor, the wall, the bottle of Scotch in his hand.

"Funny. I can see you. Why are you here?"

At that, she raised her head, lifted her chin. "Because I'm not very smart."

"That makes two of us." Then Ian laughed, one of those loud, awkward laughs, made by people who have things to lose. Already she was messing with his head, and dammit, his head didn't need this. He held out his Scotch. "Want some? It helps."

Gingerly Rose took the bottle. Without hesitation she took a long swig and then coughed. Yeah, too cheap for her blood and her virginal white dress. She'd probably lied about the virgin thing, too. Another act. *So why the hell was she here?*

He didn't need this pretense, he didn't want her to ease her conscience. He didn't need to have his body poised, his skin warmed, as if… Dammit. Ian shut off his brain. "You've apologized. You can go."

"I want to stay." She wet her lips, his gaze tracked her tongue. Ian had another long drink, then proudly shook his head. See, he could reject her.

"Oh, no. Maybe I look like a masochist, but no." He stalked back toward the door, because the awareness was still there, hounding him. Even now, he remembered being inside her, and the rotting smell of honeysuckle was killing his brain.

Rose didn't follow. Instead she stood in the middle of his apartment, her hands wrapped around her stomach, and he stared at her gloved hands. A stripper's gloves.

Oh, damn.

"Why can't we do this?" she asked, not getting the whole rejection thing.

"Do what?"

"Sex. Why can't we do sex?"

At the word *sex*, Ian could only stare, slack-jawed, engines starting to fire. Obviously forgetting that last crash landing. "You're fucking kidding me," he said, mainly to himself.

"No. There are things I won't give up. I assumed you wanted something more than sex, and that was arrogant and conceited and unfair."

Now she'd done it. He stopped worrying about the door and collapsed on his couch. "So you're willing to fuck me?"

"Yes." Nervously she remained a statue, not moving.

He didn't like that look on her face. Fear and vulnerability, as though she was putting herself on the line. Ian scrubbed his eyes, wiping it away. "Why?"

"Because I want you. And I like the sex."

"And that's all," he asked, still thinking, still hoping, still wanting to believe. She stood there like a debutante, those sexy gloves, little white shoes and that glorious face that even now was still feasting on his heart.

"Yes."

There were men who would jump at the chance. Men who took sex wherever they could. And if his mirror hadn't accidentally bumped into his hand, if he hadn't spent last night dreaming of her—again—if his life weren't postlayoff and not getting any better, he would put his pride behind him, screw her once and then say adios, washing his hands of her. But here he sat, actually…considering it.

It was official. This was the worst moment of his life. Okay. Fine. Yeah, he would do it. But she wanted to wring him dry? Oh, no, honey. Two could play that game. He leaned back into the cushions, and took another drink of alcohol, the burn much nicer than the burn in his gut. "Strip," he ordered, grinning to the entire world. See, he could be a bastard.

Rose blinked, completely missing his proud moment. "What do you mean?"

"Show me what you got. You want sex? Get naked." He shrugged, negligently crossing his legs, and waited to see how low she would go.

Quickly she shot up and headed for the door, her spine looking ready to crack. Apparently the mighty Rose had more pride than he did. Her hand grasped the door, but then she hesitated… turned…and came back.

Her hair formed a curtain, but he could tell when her chin lifted. Ian froze. Forgot to breathe.

Her little beaded purse dropped to the floor like an anvil, and Ian didn't want to get turned on. This was humiliation. This was about revenge. His body shouldn't care.

She took off her coat, folding it neatly before laying it over the back of the chair. That tidy gesture tweaked him, as if she could keep herself unmoved and dignified. Carefully she removed her shoes, tucked them next to her coat.

Then those gloved hands moved to the back of her dress, pulling the zipper and slowly the fabric fell away. Why couldn't she look like a slut? Goddammit. Underneath the top was a white satin bra, creamy flesh spilling out. Okay, enough with the innocent act.

Guilt kept rising in his throat, but then she met his gaze, pushed her hair out of the way—her eyes were blank, emotionless. This was nothing to her. *Nothing.*

Ian had another swig, but the alcohol wasn't working anymore. A hole was rotting in his gut and it wasn't from Scotch. The fancy dress slid to the floor, and now she was clad only in shimmering stockings and white lace and stripper gloves. Like a five-star, top-dollar debutante. Ian fisted his cut-up hand, pain radiating out, and he reminded himself that this was the same woman who had written a kiss-off on his mirror, the one who had robbed him of pride. No guilt necessary.

Uncomfortably Ian shifted against the cushions. However, when she remembered the gloves and peeled them back, he knew enough to leer in a completely soulless manner. The gloves dropped to the floor.

Next, she unclasped the bra, and he was happy to notice her

bare hands were shaking. The scrap of satin panties followed, and then she stood there, clad only in stockings, taking it.

It wasn't fair. An angel's face, wide empty blue eyes, but the body… He knew those breasts, intimately. The fullness, the hard peaks burning into his chest. One night, and he wasn't sure he'd ever forget. Again, his fingers curled, and this time he welcomed the pain. All those sleek, fair curves sliding into long legs, and a tiny shadow of gold between.

His cock jerked in ignorant bliss. A man's cock had no pride, no morals, no conscience. None, at all. At the moment, Ian envied that piece of his body that didn't care. Silently he waited for her to do something. Say something. Try and seduce him. Yell and scream. She did neither. Rose merely stood, as if she wasn't sure what to do, either.

Fine. Somebody had to put this goat-rodeo on track. "Turn around. Bend over," he ordered, and he saw the fury snap in her eyes.

Finally, he could breathe again.

She almost obeyed him anyway; then her feet poised to turn, or to run. Ian should have been celebrating, but he heard something break from her throat. Not a laugh, not a sob. Choking. Hastily she grabbed her coat, wrapped it around her and then gathered her clothes.

"Thank you," she said quietly. A lot of dignity from someone who had just been deliberately dehumanized. This time, the guilt exploded like a bomb, empty blue-eyed shrapnel embedding itself deeply in his heart. But he told himself he didn't deserve to feel like a heel. *Stupid shit.*

"What are you thanking me for?"

"I needed this. Sometimes the price is too high. I needed to see you as a son of a bitch. I burned my bridges, and now you have, too. We're done."

His hand began to throb, his conscience hurt even worse. Ian had never been that guy. Never. "Rose. Wait."

"No. Thank you." She headed for the door, her stocking feet skimming the floor. Quiet, elegant. Beaten.

"I'm sorry," he said.

That seemed to stop her. Whether it was his words or the self-loathing in his voice, he didn't know. For a long time, an eternity, she remained at the door. She didn't look at him, and he was glad. Right now, he didn't want to see her face, he didn't want to see her hurt.

"You decimated me that night," he continued. "I don't think you know what you did." Ian put the accusation out there. Partially as an excuse, and partially because he *wanted* her to know. In his world, you didn't go around ripping people's hearts—like what he'd just done to her.

"Yes, I know," she admitted quietly, and he was glad. Glad he heard the ring of guilt in her voice, as well.

"Why did you do that to me?" he asked.

She opened the door, but Ian was faster and he shut it, blocking her exit. This was too important. "Why did you do that to me?" he repeated. There was no reason that could justify it, but he wanted to hear it anyway.

When she moved her head, her hair fell over her face, hiding her from him. Dammit. *Hiding her.* He needed to see her eyes. He needed to know if they were blank and expressionless, as well. "I can't do this."

"Do what?" he yelled. He realized he was yelling and lowered his voice, trying to maintain sanity, calm, reason. "We had a date. We had great sex. I didn't ask you for anything."

Rose dug a hand through her scalp, lifting the curtain of her hair, and now he could see the tears. Oh, God. Tears. He was a bastard. He didn't want to be a bastard. He'd never been that guy, either.

"I won't give up. My life is my own. I choose. I decide. I rule. No one takes that away from me. Never."

Ian stared, confused. Where had this come from? Now he was determined to understand. "Rose?" He took her hand, put her on the chair—not the sofa—then sat across from her, safely away, where he couldn't do any more harm. Silently she huddled in her cotillion-white coat, her hair in her face, not saying a word, not moving.

"Talk to me, Rose. Please."

Carefully she sniffed, and lifted her head. Tears swam in her eyes before she wiped them away. As he watched, her hands twisted in her lap. "It'll take a long time."

Ian leaned back. "I've got all night."

WHEN SHE SPOKE, SHE WANTED to keep her voice carefully void of emotion, but the trace of the mountains crept in, the piece she'd worked so hard to scrub out.

"I grew up in the shadow of the Appalachians, poorer than dirt, but there it wasn't that uncommon. You didn't see money, didn't see fancy cars. Not like here. My dad, he was a big, quiet man, and he didn't talk much. He didn't know much but his job. Every day he worked in the mines, and Mom kept the house, puttering around, making pies and watching her shows."

Her smile was dreamy, because this was the life she'd made up. The family she'd made up. Those long hours, sitting on the floor in the dark, she'd had a lot of time to think about what kind of family she'd pick if she could.

"The mine was dangerous and Mama always prayed every morning when he left. Seemed like she was always praying about something. Not that they ever did any good. I could have told her that."

That part was true. Her mother had been a devout woman, and as far as Rose knew, she still was. But her mama's heart was as black as the soot from the mines and no amount of praying changed that. It took a few years before Rose realized that not every kid had to walk with a book on her head, or got her knuckles rapped smartly when her smile wasn't just so.

"I was the princess. That's why they called me Rose, or at least that's what Mama always said. Everywhere I went, people would ooh and ahh, and tell me that I was going to have a great life because I was so pretty. Mama liked to dress me in pink and white, and put bows in my hair. At first I thought it was dumb, but then it just began to seem normal 'cause I didn't know anything else."

Rose sniffed and looked down at her hands where slowly and methodically, she was pulling at the skin around her nails. Her mother used to hate that. Her mother wasn't in her life, so why should she care anymore? But it didn't matter. She folded her hands and stopped.

"Three years running, I was the lead in the high school play. Couldn't sing, sounded like a wounded dog, but nobody seemed to mind. Mama was smart, though, and strict. She told me to be careful of the boys because they were gonna want things, and I needed to hold out because I was destined for something big. Something better than a coal miner and a waitressing job. So I kept my eye out for something better, and as soon as I turned eighteen, I headed for New York. Determined to make it big, determined that I wouldn't be poor anymore."

There was no way to dress it up, no way to make it more appealing. Oh, hell. He thought she was a heartless bitch. What difference did vain or stupid make? But they did, she whispered. What he thought was frighteningly important. She raised her eyes to his and met them, firmly, evenly, no backing down. "I won't be poor again."

"Is that all?"

"What do you mean?" she asked, and heard her voice break nervously.

He looked into her, looked through her, and he knew. She could hear the words in her head: *Tell him. Trust him.*

Instead, she smiled automatically because she didn't want him to worry.

"After I moved to the city I got a job as a secretary, because I've always been good at details and organization. You should see my makeup drawer. Labeled, expiration dates, what works with what." She was starting to ramble, the accent getting thicker, and her leg started to shake. With her right hand, she latched on to her thigh and held. The shaking went away.

When she spoke again, there was no more trace of the mountains at all. "I won't go back to that life. It was hell."

"Why was it hell, Rose?"

Rose rubbed her hands on her knees, felt the current run through her again. She lifted her head and fixed her shoulders, looking Ian right in the eye, because this was the one moment that she held above all. That time in her life when she came into her own. "I want pretty things. I want soft music. I want laughing and joy and people who aren't afraid."

"Not everybody's afraid," he said gently, as if he didn't think she was the hardest bitch alive.

"Not everybody likes to be poor," she reminded him, because he shouldn't like her. He should hate her.

"Come here," he said, his voice so gentle, so tender.

Automatically she walked to him, started to take off her coat, but he stopped her, held the material together. "This isn't what you want?" she asked.

"Yes. But it's not what I'm going to do. I'm sorry for what I did. I'm very, very sorry." He talked to her, slow and careful, as if she was an idiot. She hated that tone.

"I don't want you to feel sorry for me. Lots of people were born poor. Lots of people get over it."

He trailed the back of his hand on her cheek. "Can we start over?"

Rose shook her head; it wasn't that simple. "You can never start over. Everything builds on the foundation you've already got."

"Then go out to dinner with me. Tomorrow." He looked at his watch. "Tonight."

He still didn't seem to understand what she had said. Why couldn't people listen to her? Before, when he thought she was some model of perfection, he had listened, but now he was only hearing what he chose to hear. "We can't do that."

"Why not?"

"I'm not that girl anymore. I'm a lot smarter now. I know what I want out of this life and I'm going to get it. I won't be that girl."

"I don't want you to be," he said, staring at her as though she was the princess.

Rose pulled away and began to pace around the room. "Yes, you do. Maybe you don't want me to be stupid and a big lump of clay, but you don't like my dreams."

"What dreams?"

"I want money, Ian. I don't want that stress in my life." She wetted dry lips, because when she talked about this with Sylvia, they laughed about it, and Sylvia understood. Rose didn't think Ian was going to be that easy. "I'm going to have the life that everyone always told me I could have, but I wasn't strong enough to latch on to it. I'm strong enough now. I told you I was a personal assistant, but I didn't tell you everything. I work for Sylvia and Anton Simonov. What I want, it's there. It's close. I just need to be patient and not so eager to jump at everything that looks good."

"And I look good?" he asked harshly.

Rose flushed, embarrassed. "It wasn't meant to insult you."

"Thanks. I feel better."

"I'm sorry."

He held up a hand. "No. Ignore me."

"I could never do that," she said. It was the truth, but she had said it to make him feel better. All it did was make him swear under his breath. So she waited.

"You want money?" he asked. "You want to marry well?"

"I can do it." And she could. People expected it from her, and she was tired of people being disappointed.

For the first time he looked at her, into her, and she let him see those pieces of her that she hid. They weren't nearly as pretty as the rest. Men didn't like women who could stare into the darkest parts of the world and be honest about it. They would call her a gold digger or a whore. But if a man sought money, he was ambitious. Everybody wanted money. Everybody needed money, but nobody liked to say it, and Rose was getting tired of tiptoeing around reality.

Ian stuck his hands in his pockets, and she didn't like the way he watched her. Then she told herself to grow up. For way too long, she'd worried what everyone thought of her. Everybody had bad in them, even Ian. She'd just had a first-class demonstration. But even knowing that, she still desired him. That thought cheered her up.

"So what do you want from me?" he asked.

This was trickier, and she knew that she was walking a mine-field, but tonight she'd already walked through one and survived. "I liked the sex. I like being with you."

"For how long, Rose? After you're married?"

That shocked her. "No."

Slowly he shook his head. "I can't do this."

Of all the scenarios she'd run through in her mind, she'd never considered him saying no. She knew that men loved sex, and when men were offered it without strings, no wasn't a part of the vocabulary. Sylvia had told her so, and Sylvia knew all.

Silently Rose met his eyes, wishing he were a little weaker. But if he was, she didn't think she would want him so badly. Her heart clutched, because there were few things Rose wanted badly, but now there was nothing left to do. She gathered her clothes a little closer to her chest, hiding the wound she was leaving behind. All she had to do was turn around and leave.

Leave him?

What the hell was she thinking? How long had she worked for Sylvia, and in that time hadn't she learned anything?

Furiously Rose stamped her foot. Not once, because the first time wasn't that great. But the second time? That one was good. "Why the hell not?" she demanded.

"I think too much of myself," he said. "When you decide you want *me,* I'll be here. But I'm worth more than you think I am, Rose."

He believed she thought he was worthless? Oh, heck. She was messing it up again. "That's not what I'm saying." Sweet heaven, she was offering him free milk along with the cow. Why wasn't he jumping?

"That's exactly what you're saying."

"Ian…"

He stood up, walked to the door, and Rose stared after him, confused. He wasn't supposed to do this. "What do you want me to do?" she asked. Yes, her voice sounded weak and helpless, but she wasn't leaving. She wasn't moving from this spot until she was ready.

"I want a chance. There's this thing between us. It's magic and good and it's supposed to be. And okay, I didn't realize exactly what was going on in your head, but now I know more, and sure, not everything is simple, but it can be okay. But you have to trust me. I'm the good guy here. And yes, I screwed up earlier. God, did I screw up. And okay, that was me, too, but I was pissed, and you did bad, too. But you didn't screw up, Rose. Truly. Trust me."

Trust me. Her whole body screamed to collapse, to fall in on itself, because those were the two deadliest words in the world. "No. You haven't earned it."

It was a little white lie, because she could never trust him, but she didn't say that. This way, if he thought there was hope, she could keep him in her life. It was a rare occasion when she could pat herself on the back. Mentally, she did.

"I can earn it. You have to let me."

She didn't like the easy confidence in his voice. He thought this would be a walk in the park. Oh, well, she wasn't about to disillusion him, not when she was getting her way.

He put a hand to her face, so extraordinarily gentle, as if she would break. Not anymore. No one could break her anymore. Shyly she met his eyes, nearly blinked at the things she glimpsed there. Magic. The most dangerous sort of magic. Her eyes closed, shutting it out, and then, because she couldn't wait any longer, she pressed her mouth to his.

His lips were so tender, so careful, so…affably romantic. Honestly, Rose was getting tired of this damned princess bit. She liked when he saw her as flesh, as blood, as heart. Boldly she dropped the coat, rubbed like a cat in heat and tore at the buttons on his shirt. Tonight she wanted to fly again, and he was the one who gave her wings.

"Rose," he said, and there was desperation in his voice. Her smile was all power and the promise of the sex. Truly, the man didn't stand a chance.

IT WAS A LONG TIME LATER, and Ian thought Rose had fallen asleep. Worn herself out would be the more appropriate description. Her head was pillowed on his chest, one thigh buried between his. Every now and again her hands clutched at him, holding him there, as if he was planning to leave. Yeah, right. In sleep, she was closer than she'd ever been awake. Or when they made love.

Once again, Rose had been the dominant, needing to take charge. At first, Ian was nervous and tried to be gentle, but that didn't help. When he had rolled Rose underneath him, she grew still, lifeless. He asked her if she was okay. Rose had smiled and said yes, but he wasn't fooled; he was learning the Stepford look. A few minutes later, they rolled again, and like magic, wicked Rose was back, pulling him deeper inside her, her thighs tight, almost painful. Ian had felt odd, as if he was taking advantage. But when she was there, her body so open and willing, icy-blue eyes burning into him, burning him... All he could do was comply.

The lights from the building next door filtered through the window, and he watched the pale beams stroke across her bare skin.

What was her truth? He'd heard some tonight, but not enough. Her eyes were too blank when she talked. She was too quick to jump, too quick to please. She bore scars somewhere. He'd wanted to ask, but one step at a time.

Ian was in this for the long haul. Rose Hildebrande was his fate, and he knew it. It wasn't going to be an easy fate, but slowly Ian was realizing that life wasn't about easy. Life was about good.

The silvery light passed over her again, and she clenched her hands, stilled. That absolute stillness, like stone. It lasted for a bit too long, but then her chest filled and she stroked a line down his torso.

"You're awake," she whispered, and one of her hands slid down his body. Found his cock. Lingered. Ian took his right hand and placed it over hers. It was the first time in his life he'd ever reined in a woman's touch on his cock, but someone had to keep their head. Unfortunately, it would be him.

Her hand moved up, traced over the outline of his bandage. "What happened?"

He considered the truth, decided that was a big no. "I was running with scissors."

Rose looked up and met his eyes. Hers were cool and unbelieving. "Dangerous."

Ian tried to smile, but this was too new, and he had no idea what to say, what to do, how to touch her, how to make a joke. "I know. I have trouble with authority."

The magical fingers moved around his hand, glided up and down over him, and his blood throbbed and settled low. Slowly, very methodically, Ian felt himself being seduced. "I bet you have trouble with authority, too," he told her, his jaw tight.

One bewitched finger slid over his seam, and Ian closed his eyes, giving in to the pleasure because it was easy. Too easy. Eventually that voice in his head—some called it a conscience—was nagging too loud to be ignored. Very methodically, yet very firmly, Ian removed her hand. His body would forgive him later. Maybe.

He looked down at her, hair tousled, eyes sleepy and aroused, the curve of her breasts…

Damn.

"I'll be back," he mumbled, and tore out for his closet. There, he shrugged into a pair of old jeans and found her a T-shirt and sweats. He needed her covered, awake, with preferably twelve, maybe fourteen inches of space between them. Then, and only then, would she be safe.

When he walked into the room, suitably clothed, he saw the light dim from her eyes, and he hated that he did that. But what was he supposed to do? Wearily, he ran a hand through his hair and Rose laughed. He liked to hear her laugh, liked that moment when her face grew soft and warm. He was fast learning there weren't enough of those.

"What?" he asked.

Rose leaned back into the pillows, the covers falling away, in what was a very planned, very well-executed, very effective attack on his virtue. "You look like you're about twelve," she told him, her plump mouth curved enough to be dangerous.

Because he wasn't that easy, Ian kept his gaze glued to the white wall behind her.

"Mrs. Robinson, you're trying to seduce me, aren't you?" Then he tossed her the sweats and shirt, where they magically landed across her bare torso. Ian told himself he was happy. "I'll go find breakfast." It sounded like a good plan until he remembered his refrigerator and its usual complete absence of food. "I'll go hunt for breakfast," he corrected, and then turned his back, listening to the soft rustling sounds of Rose getting dressed.

He was such a stupid shit.

A few minutes later, his head was buried deep in the cabinet, where he salvaged a lone can of green beans, expiration date, 2004.

Rose came up behind him, not touching, but he could feel her, smell her. Honeysuckle was back. Ian smiled, and held up the can proudly. Those sharp eyes locked on the label, and without a word, Rose tossed it in the trash, ignoring the very real possibility that green beans had a shelf life that extended well into the next millennium. Apocalypse provisions, that's what he was talking about.

However, Rose had other ideas. She stood, hands on her very cute, sweats-covered hips, and contemplated his cabinets. "I could help you with that. I'm a master organizer," she said, and immediately started opening doors, frowning soon after. Cinderella in gray fleece, his Rutgers T-shirt clinging with carnal purpose. Very sexy.

Eventually she turned and raised a critical brow.

Still very sexy, but he wasn't so inclined to jump her.

"I don't believe in a lot of clutter in the kitchen," he answered by way of explanation.

"I've got this great system. I can take your spices, sort by alphabetical order and the date they need to be replaced. We can branch out into—" she glanced toward the lone can of beans "—food."

"I don't have spices. I don't cook much. I don't think the oven's ever been turned on." Ian leaned back against the counter, giving her his best Oliver Twist look, something he'd mastered postlayoff.

"Why didn't you ever have a girlfriend, a fiancée, a wife?"

"I don't know. There were some, but nothing ever felt right. It was like there was some voice in my ear, whispering for me to wait."

"Commitment phobic. That's what I call it."

"Yeah." *Or fate.* Ian frowned, wondering what the Fates actually thought of him. At midnight, January 1, when they had planted a beautiful, sexy woman into his life, he had assumed that meant that Ian Cumberland was back, hitting the fast lane, shifting gears. Instead, he'd been pulled into the life of a beautiful, sexy, slightly lust-crazed woman who had more issues than he did. Rose Hildebrande was a double-edged sword, a sword that knew how to draw blood, he thought with a glance toward his hand. Lots of blood. Honestly, Ian wasn't big on blood loss.

When she looked at him with those big pools of pale blue, he got dizzy and confused, and honestly, Ian wasn't big on dizzy and confused, either.

Ian blinked, realizing he needed to feed her before she thought he couldn't afford that, either. "I'll run out, get some orange juice—and food, too. Breakfast of champions."

"Please don't. You don't need to go out of your way," she replied cheerfully, and Ian wanted to shoot himself for saying the wrong thing. Everything he did or said seemed to hit some pre-programmed response in her. He had faced automated phone systems that were easier to get past. But she was lucky, because his automated phone system skills were now legendary. Mentally, he cracked his knuckles.

"Would you sing for me?" he asked, testing his new strategy: diversion.

"Uh, no," she said with horror—not, he was pleased to note, one of her five most popular preprogrammed responses.

Okay. Diversion is good. "Oh, come on. It can't be that bad." Ian used his coaxing voice, the one that had gotten past stifled bureaucrats, surly secretaries and main desk attendants with a mild Napoleonic complex. Rose was no match for the master.

"It's that bad," she told him, holding her own against the master. "Trust me."

"Come on, you've seen the dark secrets of my kitchen. I think I'm entitled. I think I've earned it," he said, testing out his second theory: outlogic-ing her own logic.

Her eyes narrowed, but she nodded. She cleared her throat, then gave him one last chance to change his mind. "You're sure."

Ian waved a go-ahead hand, watching with fascination as she launched into a glass-cracking chorus from "Everything's Coming up Roses." Fascination turned to sainted martyrdom as she hit notes that made his eardrums curl up in a fetal position, but Ian kept a rapt smile on his face. After she was finished, Rose looked at him smugly, waiting for his reaction.

"Wow. Just, wow."

"At least you don't lie and tell me it sounds like the angels. My mother thought I could hit it big on Broadway, and she made me practice that song over and over, until the pageant director set her straight. Mama cried for a week."

As he listened to her talk, Ian smiled, much easier this time. A pageant director? One more little piece of her life. Maybe it wasn't deep emotional insight, but they were talking and she wasn't jumping him—it was progress.

A few minutes later, when she started on the cabinets, Rose reached across him, her breasts brushing his back, not even on purpose. Didn't matter, his nerves popped awake and Ian jerked, thwacking his head on the empty cabinets.

Deep into organizing the empty recesses of his life, Rose didn't even notice. Definitely progress.

Discreetly Ian turned away, shoving his hard-on from the locked and upright position, into something less…obvious. "I'll go get breakfast. Bagels?" he asked, eyeing her ass as she rummaged through the cabinets.

Rose didn't look up, didn't see the lust in his eyes. "Bagels would be fine."

AFTER IAN LEFT, ROSE stood there, alone in his apartment, clad in his clothes. All morning, he'd worked so hard to make her feel comfortable. Instead, all he was doing was messing with her head. The T-shirt was like some ancient device of torture. Sure, it was clean and freshly laundered, but there was some intrinsic mark that he'd left behind, and it made her itchy, nervous…weak. She almost pulled the thing off, weighing that option against the white cocktail dress from last night. Reluctantly she stayed in his shirt, feeling the material stroking her breasts.

It wasn't the physical that worried her. It was the feeling of intimacy, the very intimacy that she wanted to avoid, because Ian was sneaky, nearly as sneaky as she was. Look at how fast he'd gotten her into his clothes?

And when had "just sex" transformed into breakfast and the sharing of clothes? Rose wasn't a clothes sharer. Heck, she'd never worn a man's clothes. They were big, bulky…comfortable.

Right as she was telling herself that she was being freaked for nothing, her cell phone rang—Sylvia—and Rose punched the button.

"Rose? Are you feeling better?"

Rose pulled at the T-shirt, trying to find that place where it didn't touch her nipples. There was none. "Oh, yeah. Loads. I don't know what happened last night." *Yes, she did. Sultry McSlut invaded her body and rode the F train to O-town. Over and over again.*

"I was worried about you, but now you're fine, so tell me… Remy? The date?"

Rose glanced toward the apartment door, feeling oddly disloyal, then making a face at herself for feeling oddly disloyal. This was the arrangement. Signed, sealed, cleared. No disloyalty when everyone was honest. Mostly honest. "I'm looking forward to it," she answered, noticing the bedspread was close to falling off. Rose bent, straightened the covers, smelled sex, Ian, sex and Ian. Abruptly she sat on the edge, getting the flutters down below.

"You don't sound very excited about this, Rose."

Excited? Rose stared at that bed with longing, a slow and insidious longing, a dangerous undertow pulling at her. "You'd be surprised at how excited I am." Before Sylvia could go any further and drag something out of her, Rose switched to a safer subject. "How was Anton? Did he get you the necklace?"

"Wasn't that delish? We spent most of the night in the sauna, making out like teenagers. Walter nearly walked in on us. I think I gave the man a heart attack, but sometimes…"

"I know," said Rose with an understanding nod. "Listen, I have to go. Do you need anything today?"

"No, be free. Take the day off. Get a facial. Or a pedicure. Something fun. I'll see you tomorrow."

"Sunday?" Rose frowned.

"Yes, Sunday, silly. Got the food drive to get started on. Can't let the grass grow under our feet, now, can we? People are hungry in this city, and they need to be fed, *muy pronto*. Unless… Oh, listen to me. Can you believe I'm such a Marie Antoinette. You'll be screaming, 'off with her head' before I realize. Do you want Sunday off? We can do everything on Monday. Truly."

"I'll be there on Sunday," promised Rose. "For today, a facial sounds divine. I think I'm going to call right now. I'll see you first thing in the morning. Bye." Rose rushed the words, disconnecting the call before Sylvia wanted to delve more into Rose's state of mind, which was currently as tone-deaf as her singing.

With phone in hand, Rose considered the insane impulse to sprawl on the bed, roll in the covers and replay last night. No, not the sex, which was great, but the torrential aftermath, when she had been curled next to Ian, feeling safe, sheltered, protected, letting him take charge of her life. She had felt his chest, his heart, and the light of the day was so preferable to sleep.

Trust me.

In the light of today, which, she realized, was yesterday's tomorrow, "trust me" didn't seem so impossible. Ian hadn't barked, or yelled, or snapped, or criticized…except for last night. And she'd deserved that.

Stop. It.

Rose would not make excuses for him. He was who he was, and she was going to follow the path that she'd decided on. Not Ian. Not fate. But Rose alone. She could sleep with him. He hadn't asked to marry her, to love her, to do anything but go out to dinner. Yet it was the dinner that terrified her.

When terrified, Rose called back those skills that served her best. Beauty and organization and an unnatural talent for cleaning. Beauty wasn't going to do beans for her, organization needed things—and Ian certainly didn't go overboard with the material possessions—so there was only one thing left to do. Rose headed for the bathroom, because when you needed to clear your head and tackle the world, the harsh smells of ammonia and bleach could work miracles.

Armed with paper towels and spray cleaner, she walked through the threshold then stopped, and stared. The mirror, or what was left of the mirror, stared back. Rose took a step closer, found her reflection crisscrossed with jagged cracks and gaping holes.

"Rose?"

It was Ian. Ian was looking for her, but Rose couldn't move from her spot, and that was where he found her.

This bathroom was really too small for two people. Terribly small. Her arms started to itch, the soft cotton scratching like wool.

He raised his hand—helpless, not violent. Rose flinched anyway, and Ian saw.

"It bothered me," he was telling her. She heard him speak, but the words fell on her ear with a distant echo. "I don't usually hit things. I've never hit people. Ever, except this one kid…"

Trust me.

Rose glanced at the mirror, and she could feel the sweat on her neck, beading there, but no one would ever know. Ladies did not sweat. She needed to move, but if she moved back one step, they would be touching. She made herself move back. Made herself touch him. Gently, she kissed his cheek.

"I know. You're a good and decent man, and we all have our moments. Sylvia called. I have to go into work. I'll do breakfast another time."

"Rose?"

The vulnerability was there in his eyes, the concerns and the worry. She didn't want to talk. She didn't want to hear explanations, or defenses, or excuses. She handed him the bottle of cleaner, because ammonia and bleach weren't going to help. She only needed to leave. "I had a lovely time," she told him, painstakingly polite.

"Later, we can have dinner. Go for a walk. There's a club…"

Her laugh was particularly happy. She was good at that laugh. Most people couldn't tell. His eyes narrowed. Ian could tell. Rose took one more step away, and then she managed to lift her face, meet his gaze evenly and decided to outline the situation very clearly, so that he would understand. It wasn't something that she'd ever done with her mother, and she'd always regretted that she hadn't been brave enough. Not anymore.

"No dinner. No walks. No clubs. We're having sex. You agreed. I'll see you later. Probably not tonight. Maybe tomorrow. I'm not sure."

With that, she left.

10

IT WAS A COOL, CRISP Saturday afternoon, and Ian pulled up a bar stool, ordered a beer and objectively considered his current miserable condition. This was supposed to be his good year. And yes, some things were great, some things were awesome, but the way Rose had watched him before she left? Like he was Jack Nicholson wielding an axe? How could it get worse?

"What's up with you?" Beckett asked, sitting down. He took a sip from Ian's beer, reached into the bowl of peanuts and got cracking.

"That's my beer," Ian reminded him. Now people were stealing his beer. Things were getting worse.

"So, what's wrong? You sounded really ragged on the phone." Beckett popped a nut in his mouth and munched happily, looking cheerful and unconcerned. Unaccountable rage suddenly built up inside him, almost all currently directed at Beckett. That's what friends were for.

Earlier, when Ian had invited Beckett to the bar, he had wanted to confide, ask his advice, rag about his situation, and maybe, in the end, come up with a plan. But now he realized that this was Beckett he was talking to. Beckett would tell him that life sucks, the world was a dank cesspool of misery and corruption, and Ian should wise up and follow along like the rest of the lemmings. Not exactly the sort of optimism that Ian wanted to hear.

"I'm excellent. How's your crisis?" asked Ian instead, sounding more smug than he had any right to be. Feeling guilty, he ordered Beckett his own beer. By the time Ian was finished, Beckett would need it.

"What crisis?"

"The female thing," Ian reminded him.

Comprehension dawned on Beckett's face, and misery followed. "Still there."

"Sucks." Idly, Ian cracked a few peanuts, leaving the husks in his wake.

"Yeah." The beer arrived, but Beckett only stared into the amber liquid, and then sighed. "I remember what you said, and I've ended up on her doorstep a few times, but then…jeez. Sex is a big step. There are all sorts of complications. And emotions. And complicated emotions. If I hadn't seen her naked—"

"You've seen her naked, but you haven't had sex?" Ian popped a peanut in his mouth. Beckett's misery felt more cathartic than he expected.

"I can't have sex."

Ian gaped. Beckett looked up, noticed and backtracked. "I mean, I could, but I didn't. I *chose* not to. I should have just done it. Got it over with, but sex is… I don't know. It's this huge abyss. And you look into the abyss and it's dark, and you don't know what lies down there, and you could get sucked in and never return. An abyss is a scary-ass thing."

"I know," agreed Ian.

"Ian?"

"Yes."

"After you have sex with someone, are you intrinsically bound to that person, and does it alter your relationship forever, never to be forgotten until the advent of some form of memory-erasing device?"

Generously, Ian shoved the bowl of peanuts in Beckett's direction. It was the least he could do. "Yes."

Beckett ignored them. "Yes, you are intrinsically bound to that person, or yes, it alters the relationship forever, or yes, they have invented some form of memory-erasing device?"

"Yes, yes, no," Ian answered, cheerfully watching as Beckett thwacked his head against the bar.

"I thought that's what you were saying. I can't do this."

Ian slapped him on the back, not to induce pain, but to actually help. "Yes, you can, Beckett. Some things are worth it."

It was true. Rose was worth it. It was going to be hell. A dark abyss that would suck him inside, but he was already intrinsically bound to her. He had been bound to her even before the sex. After the sex, seriously, who was he kidding? Somewhere, somehow, the Fates were laughing at one previously cocky, self-assured Ian Cumberland. He looked up, mentally shot them all the finger and felt better than he had in days.

Alas, Beckett still remained miserable. "I don't know if it *is* worth it," he said. "It's the abyss. You don't know what's in the abyss."

Ian sighed, feeling old and wise and resigned. "But if you want to fall into it, then it's worth it."

"I'm not convinced," Beckett argued, still struggling with the inevitability of his destiny.

Hearing the doubts in his voice, Ian pushed Beckett's beer mug toward him. Destiny was best confronted with a cold beer, an overflowing bowl of peanuts and a good friend who understood.

Patiently he watched as Beckett drank, waiting until Beckett was done.

"You're convinced, but you're nervous," Ian rationalized with slow words, because Beckett had a Spocklike engineering brain, and the subjective caused him problems. "You don't know what to do, but you know what you *want* to do, and that's what you're going to do. You can't fight it."

It was a brilliant piece of philosophy, suitable for framing. In the face of such brilliance, Beckett didn't say a word, sipping at his beer and cracking peanuts.

For some time they sat in the bar, watching the Tar Heels stomp all over whoever the heck they were playing. Destiny. Truly, it was a game-changer.

Eventually Beckett finished his beer and stood, looking if not happier, at least more courageous. "You're going to be at the game tonight?" he asked, when the bartender slipped over the tab.

"Odds look good," answered Ian.

Beckett picked up the tab, glanced over it, put it back down. "I owe you a beer."

"You owe me fourteen," Ian reminded him.

"They won't let me buy you fourteen at the arena. I respect the law. I'll buy you one," he said, and tossed his jacket over his shoulder.

"Beckett."

"What?"

"Thanks."

"Dude, you've lost a million-dollar job and now you're thanking me for one beer? It's weak, man. I feel like I'm losing you to…estrogen."

Ian laughed, his spirits restored. Nothing like wallowing in the abyss and coming out alive. "Beckett?" he said, deciding to be even more generous.

"What?"

"Forget about the beers. I'm good."

SATURDAY-NIGHT BASKETBALL games drew a crowd at the RAC, lots of action and lots of cheers. Rose hadn't called, but Ian had known that she wouldn't. He would wait, be patient and let her lead the way, since that seemed to be her most favored state. In the interim, he was looking forward to Beckett, Phoebe and plastic nachos. Life didn't get any better than this.

But when he got to his seat, Phoebe wasn't there. "Where is she?"

Beckett looked at him, oddly guilty. "I don't know. I haven't talk to her. Do I look like her keeper? I'm not her keeper."

"Just asking," muttered Ian.

"I don't know why she isn't here. Why don't you call?"

Ian stared. "Why don't you call? First you steal the beer, now you want me picking up all the phone charges, too."

"I thought you were okay with the beer. You told me you were okay with the beer. If you're not okay with the beer, it's your problem, because I don't want to owe you anymore, and you said I didn't, so I'm not."

Ian considered arguing further, then decided that Beckett was acting irrational, and dialed Phoebe instead.

"What?"

"Phoebe? It's Ian. Where are you?"

"I'm at home," she snapped. *Good God, was nobody happy today?*

"Why aren't you here?" he asked in his nicest, friendliest voice.

"At the basketball game?" she answered, the words dripping with sarcasm, missing his nice, friendly voice.

Ian abandoned all pretence of civility. "No, I'm at frigging Tiffany & Co. What the hell is wrong with everybody? You know, I have a reason to be in a crappy mood. But am I in a crappy mood? No, I'm the Mr. Cheerful of this crowd, but nobody appreciates it. Why don't you appreciate it?"

"I don't want to be there, Ian," she told him, still not appreciating it.

"And why the heck not? Who died and made you princess of the universe? You're supposed to be here. I need you."

"Beckett doesn't."

"Beckett's a jackass. Why are we talking about Beckett? I want to talk about me."

Beckett grabbed the phone, muted it. "Is she talking about me? What'd she say?"

Ian glared, unmuted the phone. "Phoebe. Get your ass down here. Now. I need more nachos. I want a beer, maybe fourteen, and I don't expect to be treated like somebody's backwash."

He heard her sigh. California could have heard her sigh. "Fine. I'll be there in twenty."

"Make it ten," he snapped.

After he put away his phone, Beckett was watching the game, lock-jawed. "She's coming?"

"Man, I don't know what her problem is. Probably got dumped."

Beckett grunted, started in on Ian's nachos.

Twenty-two minutes later, Phoebe arrived.

"You're late," Beckett told her.

Phoebe stayed silent.

"You having a hard week, too?" asked Ian, feeling a little guilty because he shouldn't have been so mad with Phoebe. She looked pale and there were circles under her eyes, and Phoebe didn't pull off pale well. Not like Rose who pulled off everything well.

Instead of thinking of Rose, Ian stuffed another nacho in his mouth.

"Who's the guy?" Ian asked when Phoebe didn't answer.

"Nobody," she said. "There's no guy."

"Okay, so if there's no guy, then what's wrong? Problems at work?" Phoebe was a manager of IT at an insurance company. There were always problems at work, but usually they didn't bother her like this.

"Work's fine."

"Family?" asked Ian, running out of options here.

"Family's good."

"You're not going to tell us?"

"There are certain things that I'd like to keep private."

"Absolutely," agreed Ian, because private was code for PMS.

"I didn't want to come tonight," continued Phoebe, because she was going to talk more about private. Sometimes women were difficult. "I was looking forward to staying home and watching TiVo by myself. Alone. No company."

"I think we got that," said Beckett.

Her eyes narrowed to slits. "You have no right to be pissy with me, mister. None. I am the victim, and you are the...non-victim, and I get to be pissy. Do you understand? I have earned that right."

Now it was Ian who was studiously watching basketball. Phoebe was on a tear. Ian kept silent. Beckett? Not so smart.

"I am as much a victim of this as you are. Just because I don't look as depressed as you do doesn't mean I'm not disappointed. You have to be careful with the abyss."

Abyss? Ian crunched into the chip, missed, bit his tongue instead. His stomach began to curl and twine and finally, when it was knotted into a tight mass of nerves, the nausea kicked in.

No. He was leaping to conclusions. No leaping. Absolutely no leaping here.

"Are you calling me an abyss? And I'm not depressed. This isn't my depressed face. This is my relieved face. I knew exactly what you knew. Afterward we'd be stuck with a big, stinkin' pile of awkward, and I'm too smart for that."

Unable to keep the evil conclusions at bay any longer, Ian leaped up from his seat. "Oh, no. This is not going to happen."

Beckett and Phoebe looked up at him, confused, which was so much better than...

"I will not allow this to happen."

Phoebe grabbed his plate of nachos and stole one, crunching defiantly. "Who died you and made you princess of the universe?"

Ian noticed the irate glare from the people behind them and wisely sat. He took his nachos and leaned low. "Listen. This is not smart. I need both of you right now. I will remind you—since everybody keeps forgetting—I'm having a hard time of it. Now, I've tried not to whine and burden everybody with my problems, because you know I don't want to be Whiny Guy, but if I can't whine, I at least need to have the comforting knowledge that nobody is going to dare whine to me."

They didn't look convinced. Beckett looked stubborn, Phoebe looked mad. Ian tried a new approach. A happier approach. "We're the Three Musketeers. We have stuck through everything together. We drink, do the wenching thing—except for Phoebe, who does the male-wenching thing. And we do this because it's bonding. Ten years we've been together. *Ten years.* A full decade, and now, you guys are flirting with disaster. Did Athos and Aramis ever do the deed? I think not. They were too smart. They understood the rare gift that is friendship. You can't just toss that away."

"Uh, Ian," Beckett interrupted, "Athos and Aramis are guys."

"Don't be so close-minded. It's not the gender—it's the complications."

Beckett wasn't done. "You told me that if I knew what I wanted to do, then that's what I was going to do, and I couldn't fight it. I want to do this."

And *now* Beckett makes his decision? Ian glanced at Phoebe, and, noticing the gooey look in her eyes, felt his stomach loop even tighter.

"You want to do this?" she asked Beckett.

This was a mistake. A recipe for disaster. Over the arena

speakers, organ music began to play. Right now Ian craved continuity, and everywhere around him, continuity was going on strike. Desperately he tried one last time. "I'm not going to pick between you two. You split up, I'm not taking sides. You guys will be dead to me. Do you understand? Dead to me."

They ignored him, caught in the wonderglow that was ill-advised lust.

Idiots.

Ian stood up. "Leaving now. Going home. Can't watch mistakes being made."

Nobody was even listening.

ON SATURDAY, ROSE SPENT most of the day at the Empire Hotel, arranging details with the caterers. After that, she met with the florist, explaining in precise terms exactly how the table arrangements needed to look. She checked in with all the heroic bachelors who were donating their time for ungrateful animals that would never throw them a bone, or probably do something cowardly like run away at the least sign of conflict because they were afraid of being mistreated by people, even by people with sparkling eyes that saw the best in the world.

Rose settled in her hard-backed chair, stared into Helen the Rabbit's judgmental blue, yet still-sightless eyes and sighed like a baby. She wanted to see Ian. She was still in his T-shirt and sweats, prowling through her tiny apartment, getting used to the cushy softness of the cotton, getting used to the idea that she didn't need to suck in her gut, because frankly, in these baggy pants, nobody could tell if she was gutless or not.

It was in that gutless moment that she realized that she was wearing the perfect excuse. Reluctantly she doffed her own clothes, pulling on the usual black woolen pants and a coordinated knubby sweater and then left for the laundry room, where at 9:00 p.m., she was laundering Ian's clothes, using extra fabric softener to make them lavender fresh and not smelling anything at all like Powder Puff Rose. Fine, she would be a powder puff, but at least she was a well-bred powder puff.

Two hours later, she was at his apartment, his clothes neatly folded in her hand. When he opened the door, Rose shoved the pile at him. "I brought your clothes. I cleaned them."

He was smiling at her, and it was nearly as nice as wearing his clothes.

"I should go," she said and turned. Ian caught her arm.

"You don't have to. I'm glad you came back. Sit down. Want a drink? Orange juice. Bagel? I bought food." He sounded nervous, but a good nervous. They both stood there, not moving. Ian tucked his hands in his jean pockets and rocked back on his heels. Rose felt her palms start to sweat. Ladies should not perspire.

"It's late. I should have called, but there was laundry," she babbled, still not moving.

Ian broke the not-moving thing first. He walked to the sofa and then, in a bold commitment to relaxing in his own apartment, sat.

Oh, God.

Rose rubbed her damp palms on her woolen slacks, found them itchy and took the opposite end of the sofa. "How was your evening?"

"Really miserable. You would not believe." He stopped, winced. "Sorry. It was great."

And now he was the one who was on Rose Alert. Great. "What was miserable about it?" she asked, being polite and actually curious, as well. Her night hadn't been that great, either.

"You don't care. Honestly, I don't expect you to care. It's stupid and it's pointless, and I shouldn't complain. Two people decide to get together—it should be a time for joy and happiness and little birds singing, and instead, I start twisting up into knots…."

Rose frowned at that, because it didn't bode well for the future of this relationship, which was based only on sex, of course.

"They're going to have sex. I know it."

She stared, even more curious. "Who?"

"Beckett, Phoebe. My two best friends."

"You have best friends," she murmured.

"You don't?"

"The countess."

"But you work for her?"

"Yeah, but I spend a lot of time working for her, so it's convenient having her for a best friend, as well." Over the years, Rose had discovered that women didn't like being around her. She was too quiet, too pretty, too reserved, too everything. Sylvia was too everything, too, but she understood. And sometimes Rose suspected that Sylvia knew more than she let on. Amazing, improbable, yet most likely true.

"So, you think Beckett and Phoebe are, even as we speak, having sex?" she asked.

"Probably," he said, looking miserable.

"Why shouldn't they, um, get involved?"

Ian stared at her blankly, and then shot up from his seat. Rose's hand twitched, but it was a small movement, actually more of a tremor, and Ian didn't notice.

"You think it can work?"

"You don't think it can?" she asked, because this was a game. Guess the reasons a relationship is doomed for failure. Reason number one: Party A is a basket case who jumps at shadows and has a fondness for the smell of bleach.

"It probably could work," he answered, but he didn't sound optimistic, and she missed that undertone of optimism in his voice. She liked that about Ian. He was a glass half-full person. Rose, on the other hand, was a "Glass, what glass? I don't see any glass," sort of person.

"Maybe it can," she encouraged.

Ian went back to his end of the couch and collapsed. "They're doomed. It's Beckett. He's all black, white, death, taxes and we're all going to fall into the abyss."

Instantly Rose knew she would get along with Beckett.

"And Phoebe?"

"She's sensitive. Sometimes she gets in over her head, and we sort of take care of her."

"Does she have problems?"

"Phoebe? Are you kidding? She's got a great job, managing about a hundred software developers. Truthfully, she runs the place." Ian stopped. "We really don't take care of her. It's more the other way around. She's the stable one."

"You're not?" asked Rose carefully, because Ian struck her as very stable. Relatively stable. More stable than her.

"I used to be." He looked at her. "I shouldn't have said that, should I?"

"I think you still are," she told him, and meant it.

"I usually am. But now…"

"I hurt you," Rose whispered, uncomfortable with that bit of truth. Being on the blunt-force edge of a lot of pain, she went far out of her way not to do the same to others. Ian was a first.

"I shouldn't have hurt you. I'm sorry."

"No, you shouldn't. But you did."

She moved to sit next to him and took his hand. It was a bold action that flew in the face of her sex-only manifesto. Gently, Ian squeezed her hand. Rose inched closer, wanting to kiss him, wanting to lean in and nibble along his jaw, where the evening's stubble ran wild and free. It called to her, that lean line of his jaw, beckoning, tempting.

Gently, he moved her head, pushing it firmly to his shoulder. "I think we should talk."

"All night?" she asked, hearing a bit of peevishness in her voice. It wasn't an attractive sound. Talking was right up there with clothes-sharing and trust. She needed a set of rules for this relationship. He was supposed to fall in line.

"Not all night. Maybe for a while."

"I'm not a good talker," she explained.

"I think you'll do fine."

"I don't know about this."

"Rose? Trust me."

His dark eyes looked uncomfortably sure of her, as if *she* was going to fall in line. Quietly she nodded, letting him think what he would.

It was only talking after all. How dangerous was that?

Deep inside, she knew the answer to that question, but right now, it was a risk she wanted to take.

BECKETT RIPPED OFF HER jacket, and Phoebe wanted to yell at him for being so careless. But he was already attacking her sweater and then the bra, swearing until, finally, he had his hands on bare, naked Phoebe flesh. For a second, he stilled, eyes on her chest, hands poised on her breasts, an expression on his face she'd never seen before. Like a chocoholic diving into a hot fudge sundae, or looking up at the sun on the first day of spring. Heaven.

Phoebe smiled.

"Hey," she whispered.

A dark flush ran up his cheeks, an adorable dark flush. How did he manage to be studly, arrogant, rash-mouthed and adorable all at the same time? Tomorrow, she would ponder. Tonight was about great sex.

"Sorry. Lost myself. Does this feel weird?" he asked. His hands were still latched on her breasts, like a man lost, confused and frozen at the cantaloupe bin, testing produce. At this rate, they would never leave the bin, let alone check out, and in a flash of clarity Phoebe knew exactly why they'd spent ten years apart.

Throwing caution to the wind, she grabbed his sweater, yanking it over his head, exposing one bare-chested Beckett. Oh, gawd. Phoebe's mouth went Sahara dry. Yes, she'd seen him shirt-less before, but not with Phoebe-lust burning in his eyes, not with all that power-pack musculature heaving and miles of golden skin happily within touching distance. And all this could be hers…

Like ice cream. Better than ice cream. Breathlessly, Phoebe slid her hands over the glorious firmament of his chest, over the wide breadth of shoulders. Under her touch, she could see the play of emotions on his face. Confusion. Pleasure.

Fear.

"Kiss me," she ordered, because she didn't want a discussion, a debate or a logical twelve-point analysis on why this was wrong. She wanted to feel those curmudgeonly lips hard against hers. She wanted to feel the slide of that bitter tongue mating with hers, and most of all, she wanted to be filled with that primal piece of Beckett that was currently burning against her thigh.

Her lady parts began to purr with eager anticipation.

Tentatively, gently, his hands cupped her face. Next he took off her glasses, and then they were kissing. Phoebe and Beckett were kissing. She waited for the universe to collapse upon itself.

She waited for God to hit them with lightning. It felt wicked. It felt right.

Phoebe sighed, pushing closer.

Beckett swore, lifted his head. "Oh, God."

His brain-freeze was back. It was there in the panicked green eyes that were selfishly denying her pleasure—long overdue. *Well-deserved* pleasure. "What now?"

"It shouldn't feel this good."

"It can and will feel this good." *If we stop quibbling about it.*

"I don't know," he said, and then his gaze locked on her naked breasts. Stayed locked.

Because she was a vile, malicious person, she took her finger, wet it and then hypnotically traced first one nipple, then the other, praying tarty and tawdry would work.

The sound that broke from his throat most resembled a wounded animal. A wounded animal that badly wanted sex. That, Phoebe understood.

She flashed him a smile—slow and sinful—the sort men understood.

It was all the inducement he needed. Beckett jumped her, and together they crashed to the bed in a tangled heap. Frantically, he kissed her, her body quivering, his hands running over her, hot and greedy. Her fingers locked in his hair, her legs fused tight around his waist. She was not leaving this. Not now. Not ever. It was more than she'd ever imagined, had ever fantasized. *Beckett.*

Her mouth was going to be numb tomorrow, and she knew there would be bruises, but oh, it was a small price to pay for *this*....

His hands grabbed her fly, unzipping, pushing, down to her panties, and then, *oh, yes,* he cupped her. She shot upright, all that frustration bubbling inside her, building, pressing, until...

"Phoebe," he gasped, lifting his head. No, there would be no doubts, no chance to back out now. She would kill him if he did. Because she was such a good friend and it would be really wrong—as well as sexually unsatisfying—to kill him, Phoebe brought his lips to hers, whispering promises, wicked promises against his mouth. There was only one man she'd ever said these things to, only one man she ever would. This man.

He groaned, but he didn't pull away. "I can't survive this," he told her, furiously pressing kisses on her mouth, her neck, her breasts. Phoebe arched, pushing that ravishing mouth closer, sensations shooting from her breasts to her thighs, down to her toes. She wasn't going to survive it, either. And she didn't care.

Like a total wench, she ground herself into him, hips pressing, thrusting, feeling the thick hard piece of cock that belonged to Beckett. *Beckett.* She'd had dreams, fantasies, but oh, heaven… Her heart thudded, pounded. Louder. Louder.

Phoebe froze at the sound of the door. Beckett stopped, swore, his green eyes marvelously frantic. "Leave it. It's not important."

The ticking frog clock on the wall said midnight. People didn't knock on doors at midnight when it wasn't important.

A woman's voice called out. "Con Ed. Anybody there? We're evacuating the building. We think there's a gas leak." Now there were other sounds in the hallway. A flurry of agitated voices, clomping footsteps on the stairs. People were leaving.

Beckett shook his head. "It's nothing."

Oh. This was torture. Beckett was nearly naked. She was topless, unzipped, dazzled with the idea of having sex with the man currently lodged between her thighs. Alas, Phoebe knew how this was going to end. She paid her taxes, she didn't cheat at Monopoly, and she had only lied to her parents once, and that was when she'd blamed the olive oil spill on her baby sister. Deep in her heart of hearts, Phoebe wasn't a rule-breaker. "It's a gas leak, Beckett. We need to go."

"It's probably a fake." He sniffed. "All I smell is the scent of a desperate man who's one minute from having carnal relations with his best friend and moving to the next level—which is impossible to return from—but willing to go for it, because damn, you have a dirty, dirty mouth, and my head is going to explode if I'm not inside you."

The door pounding started again. "Hey. I know you're in there, and look, I'm not happy to be bashing doors at midnight. I got a warm bed at home, too, and a husband who's going to *still* expect breakfast on the table at 7:00 a.m. I might be out saving the city from a gas disaster, but does he care? No. So, please, whoever you are, stop pretending you're not there. I have a job to do and I'm going to do it. So get up, and get your ass out here before I get really nasty and start kicking down doors. City doesn't like us to do that, 'cause doors are crazy expensive."

Phoebe gave him her best managerial we-must-be-responsible-citizens look.

Beckett, understanding the look and what it meant, rolled over and groaned. "I stared into the abyss, I was ready. I was totally in the moment."

Phoebe pulled on her sweater and rushed to the door, tapping her foot as Beckett hopped to her, one shoe half-on.

"I'm waiting, folks. Zip it up, throw on some shoes and coats—it's cold as a mother outside. We need to get moving because I've got another fifty apartments in this building, and I'm feeling my PMS starting. You do not want to be around for that."

Beckett picked up his coat and flung open the door. On the other side was a short, squinty-eyed woman in a blue Con Ed uniform, requisite white hard hat with Charlene scrawled on it in black marker. In the hallway, Phoebe's neighbors were starting to swarm out. Mrs. Garretson in a pink housecoat, the cute little waiter who worked at the corner pub and always called her Chicky. Phoebe yanked her coat tighter and tried to look like this was an ordinary night. Beckett? Not so much.

He glared, visually condemning Charlene to the worst of public utility perditions. Phoebe knew exactly how he felt, but she wasn't stupid enough to mess with Con Ed, especially since the woman looked as if she ate small children for breakfast.

However, Mr. Well-Adjusted liked to live dangerously, especially around monopolistic enterprises that provided his heat and electricity. Frankly, it was part of his charm. "I was in the abyss, lady. I stared it in the face, and I would have done it."

The woman rolled her eyes at Phoebe. "They look into the abyss and they're so proud. They think they deserve a medal of honor."

"You have no idea, lady."

Charlene turned, stabbed a stubby finger into Beckett's chest and got in his face, not an easy task for a woman half his size. Half his size, but twice the attitude and willing to shut off all the heat for Manhattan without a second thought. Beckett was doomed.

"Try being a woman, pal. Try dressing up in three inches of itchy black spandex that leaves your ass bare, and then stare into the face of a one-eyed love snake and swallow it whole. That, my ignorant friend, is true courage."

With that, Charlene gave them one last glare of disgust before pounding her radio on the next apartment.

Beckett glanced at Phoebe and shook his head, leading them toward the stairwell. "I think she ruined me for life."

"Don't be such a baby," she told him, and locked her arm in his, trudging behind Mrs. Garretson, making sure she didn't fall. The woman seemed a little wobbly; she liked her wine with Letterman.

A few minutes later, they were all outside, huddled, most everyone in pajamas. Beckett stroked his chin. It was a good chin, begat from elitist *Mayflower* genes, with a slight "screw you" jut to it. Phoebe loved all the complexities of that chin.

"You have three inches of itchy black spandex?" he asked, a slo-mo gaze skimming over her, causing a shiver in the very best sort of way, in the very best sort of places.

"Doesn't everybody?" she asked, making a mental note to buy some.

Expectantly he looked at her, as if there were favors left to be discussed, as if their sexual relationship were to be some sort of equal partnership. Ha. Phoebe had taken women studies. Aced it.

Militantly, she crossed her hands over her chest. "You want me to stare into the face of the one-eyed love snake?"

The elitist *Mayflower* chin tucked into his chest, and Beckett had the grace to appear ashamed. "Maybe."

Pleased, Phoebe kept her smile to herself. No way was she letting him see the full extent of her heart in one night. She had suffered a long, long time, and honestly, if he suffered and had some doubts, in the end it would only make him a better person. "There are very orderly steps in relationships. First, you jump in the abyss and earn your medal of honor. After that, we'll talk about moving to the next level."

Soberly he nodded. "I knew that."

THE APARTMENT WAS DIM, full of shadows, and outside, the city was bustling. Inside, Rose could hear the sound of his heart. Peace and contentment. It was something she hadn't felt in a long, long time.

Ian's hands stroked her hair, and every now and again, his lips would press there. A woman could stay like this for a long, long time.

"So, after you abandoned your lifelong dream to sing on Forty-Second Street, what did you want to do?" he asked.

"I'm a very good organizer and a cleaner," she explained, which wasn't exactly an answer, but people didn't usually expect more. No one ever expected Cinderella to be a rocket scientist. Nobody wondered why Snow White spent her days with little men and singing birds.

"Oh."

Anxiety filled her chest, a balloon sitting there, waiting for the pin. Obviously in Ian's world, Cinderella was a rocket scientist, too. "You think I should have a career goal. Some sort of worthy vocation?"

Happily, he laughed, and Rose felt the balloon deflate. "As someone who got busted up on that one, I think career goals are overrated. I think flexibility is the key."

"But you don't view organizing and cleaning as a viable career option?" she prodded, because there was judgment. He had tried to hide it, but it was there.

"I didn't say they weren't a viable career option."

"It's what you thought."

"Reading my thoughts?"

"Sometimes I can. I'm good at that, too."

"Don't take this the wrong way—"

Rose never let him finish. "You know, that's one of those lines," she snapped. "'Don't take this the wrong way' implies 'I'm going to take it the wrong way.' It's like 'no offense intended.' Of course it's going to offend. If it didn't, there'd be no reason to caveat it ahead of time. Bah. They should be banned from language."

"You're right," he said, and then remained silent. Her mother would have yelled at Rose for giving her sass.

She waited, but Ian sat there, his mouth firmly closed, until she was curious to know.

"Go ahead. Say it. What shouldn't I take the wrong way?"

"I shouldn't have said anything."

"You haven't said anything," she reminded him.

"I shouldn't have thought about saying anything."

In a lot of ways, her mother was a lot simpler to understand than Ian. "But you did think of saying something, and if you don't want to make me mad, you'll tell me."

"Do you get mad a lot?" he asked, and she realized that she had actually gotten mad at him just now. She'd yelled. Nearly. He hadn't yelled back. Yes, it pleased her that he didn't yell back, but it worried her, as well. Better the devil you know than the devil you don't.

The devil she didn't know was waiting for her answer. Rose shrugged. "I hardly ever get mad. I'm very much a powder puff." At that, Ian snickered, and she promptly whacked him on the arm. Hard. Very un-powder-puff. "That was sneaky and underhanded," she said, but there was admiration in her voice.

"It almost worked."

His easy smile nearly diverted her, but now she was on to his tricks. "Tell me what I'm going to get mad about."

"Why don't you want to do something? You know, for pay, punch a clock."

It was a question that she dwelled on long and hard, and never came up with an acceptable answer. Rose chose to punt. "I haven't really been trained in much. I can organize, clean, look pretty and sometimes cook. My meat loaf is truly awesome."

"There's a lot of opportunity for meat loaf makers. Don't underestimate yourself."

Sadly, her expectations, and the world's, as well, were high. It was her less-than-stellar results that were causing the difficulty. This time when she shrugged, her hair fell into her face. Rose left it there. "I'm a helper. I'm a follower. Number two on the org chart, never number one."

"Did you ever want to be number one?"

"No."

"I did," he said gently, pushing the hair from her face. "Come on, you can tell me. I bet as a kid, you dreamed of being number one. I mean, you learned Ethel Merman. Not some pansy-assed folksinger, or a delicate warbler, but Ethel Merman? That's shooting for the moon."

"Maybe I did. Sometimes. But in my town, you didn't see a lot. There was the banker, the three waitresses, Zinnia at Curl Up and Dye and a handful of schoolteachers. And the mines."

"And Ethel Merman."

"Dreams. Nothing more. Mama would make me sit, glued to those musicals for hours. All the long gowns, the sweeping music. I think she thought I'd pick up musical talent through sheer force of will. She was disappointed."

"I bet not. Mothers don't disappoint easily. It's a pregnancy hormonal thing. It's impossible."

People always thought the role of parents was to protect. Rose, who had no protection until CHS stepped in, was always surprised at how wrong people could be. Everyone wanted to see the best, but sometimes there was no best to see.

"Ian?"

"Rose?"

"Can we not talk about this? You wanted to talk, and by my calculations, we've been talking for about two hours."

"A hidden talent for timekeeping, as well?"

"I have more hidden talents."

"I live to uncover hidden talents."

It was the signal that she had been waiting for, and Rose pounced. Now she dared to touch him, to slide his shirt apart and revel in the feel of his body. This was no powder puff. Sure, he had a quicksilver smile, but this... Her fingers stroked the hard ridges of his chest, absorbing the strength and the restrained power. Truly, men had it made. "You have a very nice chest. Rangy and sinewy and very explorable. I could spend a long time with your chest."

He nipped at her neck, his hands gliding between her sweater, starting to explore, as well, but Rose was too impatient. Shamelessly, she pulled her sweater over her head, glad to be rid of the scratchy thing. His gaze settled on the black demi-bra, the fullness of her breasts. When he looked at her like that, hunger and heat, Rose felt her body swell, felt her nipples tighten, sharp with desire.

"You have a very nice chest, too. Personally, I think it's much better than mine."

She grinned, and without a speck of self-restraint, Rose tumbled into his lap and began to play in earnest.

Before this, Rose had very set rules about the displays of pleasure and restraint. With Ian, she didn't have to pretend because with him there was no Ever After, no tomorrow. Just this. There were few things as freeing as casting off the shackles of her own image. With Ian, her hands didn't have to be still or composed; she could touch, taste and in general, overindulge a sweet tooth she didn't even know she possessed. Happily Rose did.

Her mouth feasted on his, his heart racing under her hand. She did that. The hard length of his erection burned against the layers of her clothes, and the wool of her pants was creating an itch that urgently needed to be scratched. Rose shifted, sank onto him, sighing with the thick feel of him trapped between her legs. Because she could, her hips moved with a steady, succulent back-and-forth rhythm, and she delighted in the raw need in his face. Fascinated, she watched as he struggled for control and lost. Spurred on by her own success, her hands dived for his fly, teasing with soft whorls of hair that arrowed into his jeans.

"Rose, don't take this the wrong way."

Her hands froze. Nervously she licked her lips, and waited for it… Three. Two. One.

"It's a lot of fun being the ravage-ee, but sometimes—a lot of the time—I have an inclination to be the ravage-er. Would you let me?"

Not bothering to hide the hurt, Rose pulled away, because apparently she couldn't do sex right, either.

He caught her face in his hands and made her look at him, and she wished he were a little jerkier, because then, it would be so much easier to stick to the script. To pull her face into something pliant and serene. To nod at the approval internal. To keep everything locked inside. Those were the rules she knew. "I thought you would like that."

"Oh, sweetheart, I love that. But sometimes, you know, I want to be number one on the org chart, too."

Mutely she stared into his eyes, searching for some hint, some clue of what she was supposed to do. All she saw was painless concern.

"Trust me."

He waited on her, waited for her to decide, and she was torn between letting him take control and making a run for the door. For the past eight years, Rose had focused on molding her life as she wanted, but Ian… He knew exactly how to unravel her, how to get her to lose sight of everything: who she wanted to be, who she needed to be, who she could be.

Trust him.

Her insides screamed, telling her to run, but instead, she nodded slowly.

He didn't touch her; he studied her, looking very touchable and temptingly disordered with his shirt hanging loose, jeans soft and worn and that deceptive tenderness in his eyes. Rose tried to be patient, but it wasn't easy.

His hand reached out, stroked back her hair, gliding over her neck, her cheek, tracing over her mouth with the pad of his fingers. Rose took a nip, only because if he put it out there, she wasn't one to waste the moment.

Ian's response was a soft laugh. He bent his head, lips nuzzling her neck. The evening stubble that had tempted her earlier was warm and ticklish, and she tilted her head to one side to let him do more. She sighed, feeling the pleasure start to build inside her. The quiet current that kept tugging at her, pulling her low. He didn't rush her, didn't push, didn't force. Instead, his kiss warmed her, coaxed and tempted. Rose relaxed, giving over to the liquid sensation of being indulged.

For long minutes, they sat on the sofa, his mouth discovering nothing more than the silk of her neck, the line of her shoulders, the sensitive spot behind her ear. All the while, he murmured silly nothings that made her want to laugh, but she couldn't. Between her thighs, a hard pulse was beating, louder, more demanding.

Ian took her mouth, an easy kiss, slow, an exchange of breath, of sighs. With the tip of her tongue, she traced the seam of his mouth, teasing, and was inordinately satisfied when he groaned. For a second, the kiss turned, and he entered her mouth, thrusting in and out, a blatant foretaste of how this would end. The pulse at her center grew, thundered. Rose quivered, pressing closer, chest to chest, hard to soft. Ian to Rose.

She thought she had him when his hand slipped between her neck, underneath her hair, tangling there, pulling her to him. But he broke the kiss, struggling to breathe, and swore.

"I'm on to you now, Madam Satan."

Rose merely quirked a brow.

When he smiled, when he teased, when he coaxed, she could feel herself responding, feel her emotions romping inside her like an unsuspecting child, and she didn't know how to tamp them back down. Right now, she didn't know that she wanted to.

His eyes were sparkling in the dim light, lighthearted until they rested on her mouth, the edge of her bra. "You are so beautiful," he whispered, and there was something so painfully raw in his voice. She was used to men saying that, but it'd never stripped her bare before.

With one hand, he reached out, intently tracing the line between the black silk and white skin. Rose held her breath, forgot her requisite restraint, and silently pleaded with him to touch her. He met her eyes, held them, and before she suspected his plan, effortlessly picked her up in his arms.

For Rose, this was the pinnacle. The absolute, hands-down most powder-puff moment of her life, but, oh, mercy, it was worth it. She didn't want this sort of romance, this sort of seduction with Ian. For exactly this reason. The dull buzz in her brain, the heady thump in her heart, and the absolute certainty that he was going to take her well-planned, well-thought-out strategy and chuck it all to hell.

Her hands explored the strong sinews of his arms, and when

he laid her on the bed, she heard the thump, the booming sound of strategies being abandoned. Goals being ripped into shreds. Manifestos being torn asunder. Battles being lost.

"Rose," he whispered, and he bent over her, lowering the silk of her bra.

Her eyes shut because she couldn't bear to see his face, bear to see the pure desire in his eyes. It hurt, even while his mouth covered her breast and made her sigh. Sensation washed over her, drowning her, and Rose fisted her hands, curling them into the covers. Ian was in no hurry; he favored one breast then the other with his mouth, his tongue, conjuring a slow, sensuous coil that made her weak.

She felt his hands on her zipper, laying her naked in the worst sort of way. She was complicit. She was encouraging. Worse, she was begging.

The pants slid off, and she needed him to take her panties with them. Screw her and be done, but Ian wasn't close to being done. Reverently, *lovingly,* he kissed her belly, tarrying there, toying with her. His hand slid lower, playing between her thighs, and limply, her thighs fell open. She couldn't fight this. He stroked inside her, feeling the dampness there, finding her clit, and her body arched, taut and ready to explode.

With each stroke, each touch, her need grew. Need. Binding them together, knotting them tight. Rose bolted up, but with a gentle hand he pressed her back and put his mouth on her.

No.

His tongue was killing her, robbing her, and she buried her hands in his hair, pulling. But he didn't stop. It was exquisite. It was torture. "Please," she whispered. "Please."

That stopped him. He raised his head, watched her, and then he shifted closer, laying a soft hand on her face, wiping away a tear. He didn't ask, didn't demand an explanation, but instead pulled her into his body and held her. The tension was still inside her, the muscles cramped tight, her body screaming with frustration, with betrayal. Underneath her ear, his heart beat strong, steady. A victor's heart.

He was so sly, so tender, his eyes so dark and warm. *Trust me.*

When all is lost, when you believe that defeat is inevitable, you must choose your weapon wisely. You will have only one chance before you will be vanquished.

She had only one weapon to choose, and she would use it wisely. "I have a date on Monday night."

She could feel the precise strike to his body, the way his breath caught and held, the way he stiffened and then made himself relax. "Is this one of those, 'don't take this the wrong way' or 'no offense intended' sort of things?"

His voice was rough, raw, hurt.

Rose didn't like the sound of his hurt, but the claws of fear inside her were starting to loosen and ease, and she knew that her hard-fought control was back in hand. "I wanted you to know."

He rose above her, his dark hair tousled from the damage of her hands. There was fury in his eyes from the damage in her words. Exactly as she had intended.

"Leave." He got up, shrugged into his shirt and tossed her clothes at her. "Get out. I can't do this. I know you've got issues, and I'm sorry about that. But I can't do this. I can't keep taking this and pretending it doesn't open a vein. Go. Just go."

This time, she felt the precise strike to her own body, the way her breath caught and held, the way she stiffened and then made herself relax. "That would be best."

11

EFFICIENTLY, ROSE DRESSED, feeling his eyes on her, but she didn't meet them; she couldn't. She tried to sustain her poise, glide effortlessly across the room, composed and refined, but her feet were like lead. Her sweater was like thorns on her skin and the remains of her dinner were lodged in her throat.

When she got to the door, she tried to open it but her palms were damp and the handle twisted and slipped from her grasp. "Ian?"

"Don't say a word. You've done enough."

She rested her head against the door. Struggled to breathe. "I told you what I wanted. You didn't listen. No one listens to me."

"Fuck you," he said. It was fitting. It was what she had wanted; it was what every inch of her was screaming. Leave. Go, before it's too late.

But there was a piece of her that knew it was already too late.

Abandoning the safety of the door, the quick escape, Rose turned to face him, face many things. Her fingers wanted to stay locked on the door handle, but she licked her stone-dry lips, and forced her fingers free.

He stood in front of the window, the lights of New York at his back, and Rose met the anger in his eyes, because she could see the pain there, as well. "Would you ever hit me?"

The anger eased but the pain stayed behind. This time, she thought it wasn't pain for him, but for her. "No." Ian smiled, but it was a nervous smile, an oddly reassuring smile.

"Would you yell at me?"

"Probably," he answered, and she coveted the honesty of it. Yelling wasn't nearly so bad. It was the other things that leeched her of blood, flesh and heart.

"When I do something you don't like, what if I still want to do it? What if I want to ride you like a two-assed pony for the rest of my life? What are you going to do about that, huh? Are you going to tell me it's wrong?" Her words were quicker now, her hands fisted tightly at her side, but she was not going to run. Not anymore.

Outside the window, a light pulsed, on and off, matching the rhythm of her blood.

While she watched, his hands raised then fell. "Are you going to explain this?"

"No. Not yet. And you have to accept that. Can you?"

"Is this a game?"

"No."

"Then I can accept it. For now. I'll wait until you're ready. But you keep throwing these punches, Rose, and honest to God, you'd be surprised at how much blood they produce."

She'd never wanted to hurt anyone like this, never imagined that she could with so few words, and it didn't sit comfortably inside her. "I didn't realize."

"No one's told you before?"

"I've never done it before."

"I guess I'm the lucky one."

"I'm sorry."

"I'm sorry, too. I don't…" He met her eyes and shrugged. "I know it's not easy, but you can't keep throwing punches."

"Fair enough."

He nodded once. "Are you still going out on a date on Monday?"

"Don't push this, Ian. Don't push me." The words surprised her, but she was glad she had said them. She tilted her head, made her voice strong. "I'm going."

Surprisingly, he didn't argue. This was more courage, more confidence, all without the typical swagger. "Don't sleep with him. Can I ask that?"

"I wouldn't sleep with him anyway," she told him, because she never would have, but Ian wouldn't know that.

"Why?"

"Because he's not…" *You.* "We just started dating. I don't…" How to explain without giving away more than she was ready to? He had no idea what he was doing to her insides, giving her power with one hand, taking it away with the other. For now, she wanted to hang on to what she could.

"You don't what?"

"I don't think of him that way."

"Then why go out with him? Where's that logic?" His voice was so reasonable, so quiet, not yelling, but she knew what he was doing. Pressuring her to do things his way. Soft and gentle or strong and loud, the end result was the same.

"You want me to call it off," she taunted, mainly to bait him, to see what he'd do.

He shrugged. "Actually, I think *you* want to call it off. But it's your decision to make."

She wasn't going to be fooled. "But you're trying to make me do this. You're trying to get what you want."

"What do you want, Rose? What do you really want?"

"I don't know."

"Yes, you do. If you're not happy with what you're doing, stop doing it."

"I'm not doing anything."

He laughed, and it wasn't a nice laugh. "You're building the dream house, your anatomically correct man-mate, a convertible that you can drive with the top down, so that you can smile and wave and watch the world from behind a sealed cellophane package."

Her head jerked from the sting of the words, as accurate as they were. "That's insulting."

"Not if it's true. You're not her, Rose. You're tearing yourself up, building this world that's all peaches and cream, but that's not you."

That's not you. Someone else deciding who she was, who she wasn't. Rose clenched her hands. "You're just saying that because you wouldn't be a part of it."

"I don't want to be a part of that."

He was lying. She knew it. Every man wanted the brass ring. They spent years, decades, lifetimes chasing it, hands always outstretched. Men needed to be alpha. They needed to be the provider. And when external forces messed with the primordial ooze that beat within the breast of the male species, they grew unpredictable, irrational, lashing out at whatever was closest. For years she'd watched her father beat her mother because there was never enough.

Maybe Ian didn't want to admit it, but all she had to do was expose the ambition in him that was no different from anyone else's, and she knew just where to start.

"Are you happy, Ian? I listened to you complain about your work. Wouldn't you want your old life back? Wouldn't that make you happy? Why can't people be honest? Why is it so bad to want to be comfortable? To have money? To not worry about things?"

He laughed at that, his face hard. "There's always something to worry about it. I had money. I worried. Now I don't have money. I still worry. It comes with the territory. It comes with life. All your little friends, they deal with the same shit as everybody else. Maybe they gloss it over, maybe a winter tan and capped veneers can hide a lot, but trust me, Rose. I know. It's there."

She thought of Sylvia, thought of their life. They were happy. Ian was wrong. "If you were offered your old job, would you take it?"

"No."

"Tell the truth," she coaxed, because she saw the hesitation in his eyes.

"Maybe," he finally admitted.

Rose pounced. "See? Why is it different?"

"Because that's not the point, Rose. What I choose as a career, or what I don't choose, isn't going to make me eternally happy. I like me now. I like you, Rose. The woman under the cream silk and lace. The real you."

The real you. No, he didn't see the real her. He only saw what she let him see. "How do you know me? We just met."

"I know you like to climb on top of me, I know you like gifts for no apparent reason and I know you're terrified of loud noises. I don't like it when cars backfire, but I don't look like I'm going to throw up. Not like you."

Okay, that wasn't something she had revealed. That wasn't something she wanted him to know, wanted anyone to know.

Ignoring the warnings inside her, Rose brushed the hair out of her face and met those unflinching eyes. There, in those dark depths, just as she'd known she would, she saw the courage lanced onto that vulnerability which had drawn her from the first. Time after time, men had worked to impress her with their might, their power and their absolute superiority. Yet it was that open gash of humanity inside him that tugged at her most, and Ian had the rare strength to let her see it.

He wasn't afraid. She wouldn't be afraid, either.

"You're not like them," she stated, believing it. Behind Ian, a light flickered in the darkened sky, blazed and then burned away. An airplane, or a neon bulb failing, or possibly, the tiny shift of a woman's heart.

"Who?"

Rose stayed silent.

Ian nodded once, tacit understanding.

"I let you lay out the ground rules, Rose. I followed them, but I have one of my own."

"What?"

"You don't think I can soar with the eagles, but Tuesday night we try."

"Tuesday?"

"Compare and contrast with the Doctor of Pediatric Perfection who has the ability to buy you a small country, and who, knowing my luck, is great-looking and also nice."

Rose smiled. "You're very sure of yourself for a man with no food and very little organizational skills."

His mouth quirked, his eyes warm. Tacit understanding. "Now you're being bitchy. But I like it."

"I am, aren't I?" she said, surprised at herself, and a little…pleased. All the snarky opportunities that she'd squandered. All the little pings of satisfaction that she'd never known.

Bowing to the inevitable, she lifted one shoulder, not too much, not too carefree. "All righty, then."

He looked so proud of himself, as if he'd had no doubt he would get his way. Slyly, she swung her purse over her shoulder, and kissed him lightly on the cheek. "I'll see you then," she said, her hand on the door, feeling so much happier than before. Free. It was nice.

"Wait! You're leaving?"

Her face was carefully innocent. "Yes. We're changing things, shaking it up, right? All I wanted was sex, but you said, no, no, no."

She'd got him. Slowly, Ian shook his head, but his eyes were both rueful and respectful. Mentally, Rose cheered.

"You're a bad, bad woman."

She grinned, knowing she'd lost the innocent look, and Mrs. Lane from the Little Princess School of Charm would have howled in disapproval, but honestly, she didn't care. "That I am, but I'll still see you on Tuesday."

FOR THE NEXT TWO DAYS, ROSE worked at the penthouse and contemplated her newly unbalanced world order. Ian stayed in her thoughts, her dreams…her worries. When she was with him, she wanted to believe. Her heart actively functioned as any normal person's would, but her mind wasn't so convinced.

She told herself it was the lack of financial security. She ignored his solidly comfortable apartment, yes, not spacious, but adequate. Cozy. Nicer than hers. And yet… She quickly appraised the opulence of the penthouse, and knew that this could be hers, as well.

By the time she'd addressed two hundred handwritten invitations, she'd convinced herself that because he was dissatisfied with his life, he would eventually be dissatisfied with her. And to further that point, on Sunday, on Monday, he hadn't called. Not once.

It was late in the afternoon, her date with Remy approaching, when Sylvia came home after what must have been a brutal day. Her face was flushed, her hair more mussed than her stylist would like, and her mouth was set in a tight line.

"Bad day?" asked Rose, going for the direct route, putting the stamped invitations in plain sight in case Sylvia fastened the death-glare on her.

"Hell," moaned the countess, falling to the couch and kicking off her heels. "Food pantry donations are down another twenty percent. I checked the bottom line for the Simonov Educational Foundation and it's recovering, but with not as much heft as I want. Then The Teddy Bear Brigade snubbed me, asking Vivian Egan to be chair for the Pathways Out of Poverty Women in

Leadership Luncheon. Can you believe the nerve? Who rules the Pantheon of New York philanthropy? Sylvia Simonov, and that's a direct quote from the *Times*."

"Sorry," answered Rose, and then held up the envelopes. "They're ready to go out."

"And look at you, working your fingers to the bone while I'm wailing about the trials of nothingness."

"They're not nothing. I think everybody has a bad day, but usually you're very happy."

"Blissfully," sighed the countess, pouring herself an iced glass of lemon water.

"And the count," asked Rose carefully.

"Of course."

"How do you know? How are you always so confident?"

"You have to be confident, Rose. You can't let things drag you down. And why am I being such a mooncalf. You have a date, missy. Tonight, if I'm not mistaken."

"Remy," she answered.

"I approve." She took another sip and then glanced in Rose's direction. "And the mystery man?"

Rose hesitated, not sure what to say, not sure what not to say. But in the end, the knowing look in Sylvia's eyes made her choice. "We have a date on Tuesday. His name is Ian."

"And?"

"He's nice."

"Nice, nice? Make you smile, give you flowers, take you to the Bahamas nice?"

"Not that kind of nice."

"You're breaking the mold. For three years, I've watched you with exactly one sort of man. High-class, high-dollar, high-gloss. Still got the tingles from New Year's Eve?"

Rose met her gaze. "They haven't left yet."

"And Remy?"

"He's nice, too."

"He'll make you smile, give you flowers and definitely take you to the Bahamas."

"True."

"No tingles?"

"Not a twitch."

Sylvia poured another glass of water, plopped it onto the desk and Rose promptly retrieved a crystal coaster. "You have a quandary, Rose. A very quandrious quandary, and I'm surprised."

"Because of the mold?"

"High-gloss, high-class, high-dollar, those are tough shopping list items to cross off. Whatever you do, pick what's going to make you happy."

And that was the problem. Rose wasn't exactly sure what happiness was, but she knew what nice was. Nice was smooth music, silky aromas and the quiet veneer of peace. Nice was the steady beat of a man's heart against her own. Happiness was her decision, nice was her decision. All she had to do was wrap her hand around it and shape it into whatever she chose. Maybe the quandary wasn't that bad at all.

THAT EVENING, REMY PICKED her up from the penthouse, taking her to a preconcert reception at Carnegie Hall. A world-famous violinist from a world-famous violinist-factory country was performing a world-famous concerto, and the gilded reception hall was filled with the world-famous of New York.

All in all, it definitely qualified as nice.

Rose made sure to talk up the bachelor auction, and yes, people did seem more enthused with the idea of having live dogs present than live, bid-on-able bachelors, which surprised her. Remy took her arm and introduced her to the governor, one Connecticut senator and the chief of staff from New York-Presby. Rose knew her lines, knew her facial expressions and performed them perfectly.

Rose shook off her moment's hesitation, focused on Remy, focused on her dreams, focused on everything she wanted.

From across the room, Blair Rapaport was holding court with an entourage. When she saw Rose, she waved. Stealthily, Rose checked to see if anyone was watching. When the coast was clear, she stroked her eyebrow with her middle finger and pointed directly at Blair, who never noticed.

"You're having a good time? You seem distracted," asked Remy, his nicely handsome eyes concerned.

"It's quite a turnout. Everyone who's everyone, and some people who aren't anyone at all."

Remy looked over at Blair and grinned. "Why don't you go over and pull some hair or rip some clothes? A catfight would make the papers, and it'd be great publicity for the auction."

"Why do you have to be such a man?"

"At some basic level, Rose, we're all alike."

Little did he realize how wrong he was. Ian wouldn't have suggested that. He would have handed her the champagne to throw in Blair's face.

"Why are you doing this?" Remy asked.

"It's for a good cause. Raising money for the humane society. Hey, what's not to like about that? What sort of person would I be if I didn't care about small animals that can't protect themselves?"

He shook his head. "Not the auction. This," he said, pointing to her and then to himself.

Rose laughed, an elegant sound that resembled bells. "What sort of a woman would I be if I didn't enjoy the company of Manhattan's Most Eligible?"

"He's still got your heart?"

"Who?"

Those nicely handsome eyes narrowed. "The one who you're still getting over."

Mentally she flogged herself, blaming the champagne, not wanting to blame Ian. "I'm doing better," she told him, keeping her face adequately enthused, one strand of hair falling in her eyes.

He stole a kiss but her mouth was cold, her heart was cold, and he might have been nicely handsome, but unfortunately, he wasn't nicely stupid.

When he lifted his head, he met her look. "You make a man want to hope. You make him think he can have you. Make him think those pale eyes will flash with something that resembles life or love. I don't want to hope for things I'm never going to get. I don't have to."

"Don't give up on me yet, Remy. I've been busy, this stuff for the countess, and I want it to work out between us. You have no idea how badly I want us to work out."

"Do you mean that?"

"All my life, I've dreamed of a man like you."

"Rich?"

"It's more than that. It's pretty. Like a dream, but it's not. This is real."

"And where does the man fit into the picture, Rose?"

That made her think for a moment, because she didn't usually have a man in her picture. Usually the princess was alone, asleep or worse. But Rose was learning, coping, hoping. She stumbled, her mind putting words to thoughts, to ideas and to a new set of dreams. The same, yet different.

"They're a set. A yin, a yang. A sun, a moon. For every person, there's a match." She pointed to her heart. "Somewhere in here, there's a piece that's missing, a shadow that needs light, and somewhere out there, is that light."

Softly he touched her cheek. "So why do you look worried?"

At first she schooled her features, but then Rose stopped. "You said you didn't want to hope for things you're never going to get. I don't, either. I used to want things that I never got and it hurt like hell, every day, over and over. I did learn, because sometimes I was a little slow. There are things I will never get. Things I don't deserve."

"Why don't you deserve them?"

She almost lied, but across the room Blair Rapaport was laughing and joking and making a mockery of who Rose wanted to be. "Because I don't have a heart."

Remy put a warm arm around her shoulders and smiled. "It's not so bad. Cardiology is my specialty."

ON THE WAY HOME, ROSE stopped by the pet store window, pulled her coat tighter and stared into the empty glass. All the animals were asleep, snug in their little puppy beds, dreaming of dog biscuits, chasing cars, slow-moving cats and all those things that cute puppies dreamed of.

In the corner of the case, the shadows stirred and she took a step back, hoping it was one of the cute fluffy fur balls who wanted to play and leap and grin with little puppy smiles. Instead, the black creature rose from the corner and crawled into the dim light.

"Get away," she scolded, and he obediently retreated on all four paws, belly dragging the ground. His midnight eyes mirrored her own, wary and weary, disillusioned with the dark corners of the world, the dark closets where black dogs were sent to hide, where little girls were sent to refine their behaviors, where monsters lurked and dreams died a small, quiet death.

Dr. Remy Sinclair was the dream that she'd never thought she could actually possess. Ian Cumberland was no dream. He made her feel, he made her cry, he made her hope.

Slowly she raised her hand to the glass, but the black dog was too smart to fall for her voice once again. He was a wise dog, adapting quickly. Survival.

"You're a good boy," she whispered, knowing he would ignore her. His ears perked, but he lay like stone, not moving in her direction. "I'll see you tomorrow," she told him, and if he were smart, he would know that humans were a coldhearted bunch. But Rose meant what she'd said; she would see him tomorrow, and maybe, if she were brave, she'd bring him a biscuit.

IAN SPENT TUESDAY in the office, working and getting ready for Tuesday night. This time, he was smarter, more prepared. He'd researched Dr. Remy Sinclair—his competition—and realized that on the basis of wealth, looks and contributions to humanity, Ian was toast. However, this was no ordinary ordeal, this was for Rose, and Ian was ready to plan the courtship of a lifetime. Yes, because he wanted her. Yes, he firmly believed that fate had thrown them together, but now there was something new. She needed him.

The only problem being that she didn't know she needed him. But Ian knew. He'd watched her in her sleep, watched the clenched fists and the rapid beat at her throat. He'd seen the mindless obedience in her eyes. Sure, money smoothed the way, it might smother the fear, but it wouldn't conquer it. As a man who used to believe that money could leap tall buildings in a single bound, being with Rose had opened his eyes.

Money wouldn't fix her. Money wouldn't fix Ian, either.

However, he'd made dinner reservations at the Waverly Inn and had arranged champagne on ice at the Crystal Room because yes, money wouldn't fix anybody, but the two-dimensional eagles on his walls were staring at him, prodding him into something that was a little extra.

His two o'clock was Hilda Prigsley, a conversation he was dreading. Ian knew banks, he knew advertising agencies, he knew IT organizations, but how to find a spot for a sixty-year-old woman whose sole talent was typing more than a hundred words per minute? For three hours he scoured the online requests, looking for something, anything that would match. Two hours of searching and useless calls, and he was ready to drink himself into oblivion.

Until his cell rang, and his caller ID said Rose.

Suddenly the impossible was possible, the gray clouds were blue and Neil Armstrong had once held the rock on his desk.

"So are you counting hours?" he started with, hoping she'd laugh, hoping she'd admit that she was.

"Hours to what?" she asked, but he heard the tease in her voice and it cheered him.

"We have a date. That's *D-A-T-E*. A social engagement where two people strive to have lively, sparkling conversation, indulge on a feast that will stagger the palette, and then, if somebody decides that someone else looks pathetically frustrated enough, they have passionate sex wherein souls are shared, stars are touched and in general, both parties are ruined for any future with all other people thereafter."

"I can see you've given this a lot of thought."

"You have no idea, and no, I'm not going to tell you exactly how much thought I've given it, because then you would think I'm the most sexually frustrated man on the planet. And so, Ms. Rose Hildebrande, how are you this most glorious of days?"

"Quite well, thank you. Planning the benefit, trying to get the cook to understand that the count doesn't like asparagus, no matter how artfully she prepares it, and I think I need to hire a dog walker."

"They have a dog?"

"No. But I'm putting dogs in the auction. I need a person who's comfortable with dogs. Do you have anybody?"

Ian glanced at the Prigsley file and sighed. "I don't think so."

"That doesn't sound like the voice of a man anticipating this most glorious of days. I would think that soul-sharing requires a certain amount of happiness."

"Talk to me after I find a job for a sixty-year-old woman from London who can type one hundred and twenty words per minute, and then I'll show you happiness."

"Surely people want that sort of superhuman productivity now?"

"On a typewriter, not a computer."

"Oh. I see your dilemma."

"How's the countess?"

"She's got the hairstylist coming in two hours."

"Rough life."

"She's earned it."

He wanted to ask her about last night, wanted to know if Dr. Dreamboat had touched her, if Ian was going to have to kill him, but he knew all those questions were a bad idea. Instead, he forced a laugh. "I'll pick you up at seven."

"I should meet you."

"I insist. Besides, I love the Bronx."

"You're a nice liar."

"That's totally not a lie. My most favorite thing is in the Bronx."

"What?"

"You."

MISS PRIGSLEY APPEARED precisely at five to two, not that it mattered because five minutes wasn't going to change the outcome.

She settled herself in the chair, her sensible feet planted firmly on the floor, and looked at him with great expectations in her eyes.

"I'm still working it," he explained, and then, to twist the knife even further, she handed him a cookie tin.

"You don't have to do this," he started, pushing the tin back toward her, because she thought he could deliver miracles.

"I don't have to, but I did, Mr. Cumberland. You're working

very hard on my behalf and it'd be awfully churlish of me to not to come up with some small whatnot to keep you in good spirits. So…there's still no takers for this old bird?"

"I won't give up," he promised, picking up his rock, thinking of a story to tell her and immediately realizing he'd told them all before. Her eyes sparkled behind her silver frames and Ian knew she was on to him, and even nicer, she didn't mind.

"You could learn the computer."

"And I could happen on to the winning lottery ticket and buy myself a nice warm flat. It's not me, you see. I need the feel of the typewriter, the keys pecking back at me, one whack of the roller and ding, you're off to the races again. I have to be who I am, and can't be any more."

"Yes, you can," Ian argued, because a person was only limited by the scope of his dreams.

"Mr. Cumberland, if the pool of potential employers can't appreciate who I am, then what good am I to them, trying to be someone I'm not? My great-aunt Hilda, second cousin on my father's side, used to always tell him that not everyone gets to be an astronaut when he grows up."

Ian stubbornly eyed his rock. "But Britain never had a space program."

"That's exactly what my father said, but then she'd fix him with her evil eye and tell him that if Parliament cared two hoots about a little boy's dreams, they'd have funded space exploration long ago, but instead they spent her hard-earned tax dollars on the Concorde, and we all know how that turned out."

With a regretful sigh, Ian stared down at the sheet of paper that had the phone number for the Waverly Inn, and firmly scratched it out.

"Miss Prigsley…"

"My darling boy, you can certainly call me Hilda."

"Hilda…"

"Yes," she asked, eyeing him with an obstinate lift to her brows.

"I'll keep looking. We'll find something."

She gave him a saucy wink and patted his hand. "I know

you will, Mr. Cumberland. You don't know what you're capable of, but I do."

After she left, Ian contemplated the hunk of rock on his desk and glared at the soaring eagles on the wall. He now had a new favorite motivational saying: Until you spread your wings, you'll have no idea how far you can walk.

13

ROSE WASN'T ACCUSTOMED to people in her apartment. It was her space, her domain, and it wasn't so much that it was located in the Bronx—yes, that was some of it—but more, it was the belief that when someone stepped inside they would see all the things that she saw. The blinds that should have been dusted, the sofa slipcover that was ten years out of date and the sad sheen of a solitary woman who had very little life.

However, with Ian, there was no reason to worry about his judgment, to steel for his disapproval; with Ian, she didn't have to care. Which did nothing to explain why she vacuumed like a lunatic, why she made apple pie so the apartment would have that "homey" scent and why she tucked her rabbit carefully out of sight in case it made a grown man laugh.

When the buzzer sounded she checked herself in the mirror. The royal blue dress made her eyes look more vibrant, her makeup was flawless, every single hair was in place but her insides were plunged in mayhem. For a moment, she closed her eyes, searching for her peace, but when she opened them peace had still gone missing.

After she opened the door, Ian was there, black slacks, white polo, Armani coat and scuffed shoes. Breathlessly she waited while his gaze inspected her apartment, passed sightlessly over the slipcover and then ended on her face.

In the twinkling of an eye, Rose forgot the dated slipcovers altogether.

She held out the pie in her hand. "I baked you a pie."

"I think you look better than the pie."

"You don't like it?" she asked, putting the plate back on the table. Baking had been a stupid idea.

"I love it. We'll take it with us," he said, as if everyone carried food while commuting.

"I should have thought—" she started, but he covered her mouth with a kiss.

"I love the pie."

"Enough to drag it around Manhattan—complete with falling crust, gathering flies and strange looks? It's stupid. I won't make you take it." Quickly she stopped rambling. "Next time, I'll bring it to your office."

"Are you sure?" he asked. "It's your decision."

"Positive," she answered, very sure of herself, and she felt like he'd given her the best present ever. Yes, Ian Cumberland was a very sneaky man. She liked it.

They took the subway into the city, and this time she didn't mind the long ride, the swaying train. She stayed fascinated by the glow in his eyes, and yes, his scuffed shoes made her feel oddly comforted.

He asked about her day, carefully avoiding brining up her date last night. She answered him in great detail, trying to impress him with her dog-trainer-interviewing skills and carefully avoiding saying a word about her date last night.

As the lights of the city approached he looked at her, studying her. She put her hand in his, forgetting every ladylike rule in the book. "What?"

"I thought a long time about how to go about tonight," he explained to her. "Plan A was to impress you with the Waverly, champagne at the Crystal Room. But then I realized that you were too cynical for that."

"I was?"

"Oh, yeah. How many times have you been to the Waverly?"

"Seven."

"And where's the fun in number eight?"

Slowly she smiled, her fingers curling over his. "I see your dilemma."

"Instead I opted for Plan B."

"Which is?"

"You think no one can be happy unless they're rolling in money."

"That's about right."

"I'm here to shoot holes through that little mercenary life-theory."

"You can try," she taunted.

"And I will win," he said, pulling her up from the subway seat. "This is where we get off."

The weather had decided to cooperate—the temperature a mild forty degrees—the moon was full and the streets filled with the last of the holiday stragglers. Those gullible fools who didn't want to see the last of the New Year. Like Rose.

They walked to Eighty-Third Street, a street row full of dark awnings and tiny neon signs, and she watched curiously to see where they would land.

She didn't have to wait long. "First," he announced with a flourish, "we have the pièce de résistance of New York City cuisine. That succulent fusion of sweet and tangy that was first perfected in New York, circa 1905, and changed the culinary world forever. May I present the New York slice."

Her mouth fell open, only slightly, before she shut it. "Seriously? You're trying to impress me with pizza?"

Ian was not discouraged at all, one of the things she most adored about him. "And not just any pizza, but the finest the city has to offer. Fontini's."

"I don't know Fontini's."

"That's because, my darling debutante, you've lived a sheltered life. Follow me and let your taste buds discover culinary Utopia."

Inside was a small dining room filled with tables covered in red-checkered tablecloths and topped with straw-wrapped bottles of Chianti. The flowers were yellow plastic and the music was a grainy Frank Sinatra, but there was something special in the air. Garlic. Definitely garlic. Rose began to smile.

"Two slices, Fabrezio. Plain."

"But what if I wanted a salad," Rose blurted out. Not that she wanted a salad, but maybe she wanted the option of a salad. How did anyone know unless they asked?

Fabrezio looked at her, insulted, his voice starting to rise above the crooning strains of "It Had To Be You." "Excuse me, Miss Whoever You Are, here is buffalo mozzarella that does not melt into oblivion, here is fresh basil gently nestled among ripe Italian tomatoes, here is a bubbly crust perfectly cooked in a century-old coal-fired oven... You ask for salad, when I present you with...*capolavoro!*" He slammed his hand on the table, and Rose jumped.

"I'll have a slice," she told him demurely, deciding this was not the place to pick a fight—not that she would, but who knew? Ian looked at her as if the real world was a fine and shining place, and well, heck, tonight the sky was the limit.

After the man left, Ian put a concerned hand over hers. "You're okay?"

Determined not to be intimidated by a surly Italian who didn't like unenlightened plebs, Rose nodded firmly. "Of course. Although if this pizza isn't the greatest thing since sliced bread, I'm going to tell him."

Ian grinned at her proudly. "You'd break his heart."

"I'm a very hard-hearted woman."

"No," he told her, his thumb sliding over her palm, warming her all over. "I don't think you are."

The pizza was as perfect as Ian had said it would be, and when Fabrezio hovered nearby as she took the first bite, Rose smiled graciously. "It's delicious."

"That is all you can say?"

"Magnificent, a tribute to Sicilians everywhere, with cheese that shames my inferior palette."

Fabrezio nodded with approval. "Ian, she's all right. A little prissy, but every woman can be forgiven when she has the face of a Botticelli."

After dinner, they sipped on the wine and he made her tell him about working for the countess. She told him about her secret plan to dunk Blair Rapaport in the East River, and he laughed and made her think she could. She asked about his day, asked about the English typist, but he shrugged and looked away. Rose didn't press, but she wouldn't forget, either. Ian wasn't a man to shrug something off. He buried it inside, just like her, and it worried her to see it.

It was nearly ten when he paid the check and took her hand, leading her back into the night.

"Where now?"

"Dancing at the Rainbow Room," he answered, and she was too polite to tell him how many times she'd been there before.

Two subway stops later, they were outside Rockefeller Center, where they rode the elevator to the sixty-fifth floor. A sign outside read "Gibraltar Reception" and Rose pulled him back. "You didn't tell me we were going to a wedding reception. I didn't bring a gift. I don't even know these people," she whispered.

"I don't know these people, either," he whispered to her.

"Ian!" She looked at him, shocked, *shocked.*

"Rose!" he mocked, looking completely unshocked.

"You can't do this. It's…it's…not done."

"Oh, you are an innocent, but tonight, you get to sample some of my most favorite things. Over the past ten months as I have mastered the art of living responsibly, I have scoped out happy hours, free movie screenings, food samples at Trader Joe's and one really crazy bar mitzvah, sometimes because I missed the social life, and sometimes because it was a kick. It's only one night. Why don't you walk on the wild side?"

"The wild side, yes, but Emily Post will not approve."

His eyes darkened, lit with something wicked and wily.

"There's nothing I have planned that Emily Post would approve of."

Her stomach curled with anticipation, and Rose moved a step closer, drawn to the wild side. "We could just go back to your apartment and have mad, passionate sex and possibly an exchange of souls," she offered in her most seductive voice.

"After we dance," he insisted.

"You're going to make me do this." She was learning to recognize the hard determined face, and it didn't make her freeze the way it used to. Progress.

"I'm not going to make you do this. That would be wrong of

me, but I will be disappointed as hell if you don't," he said, standing his ground.

Oh, that was such a low blow. Admitting the strategy right up front and counting on her to step up to the plate, for him... *No, this was for her, and she knew it.* Rose frowned, scowled, an unattractive face that would cause early wrinkles, all while Ian watched patiently and waited.

He wanted to get his way, wanted her to do his bidding, but he wasn't yelling, or glaring, or worse. He was giving her a choice. Rose bit her lip, the lilting strains filtering outside. She wanted to dance with him, and it only took one small, slightly unbecoming step.

"They won't throw us in jail?"

"For crashing a reception? Nah."

"You're a very poor influence," she told him, needing to make the point that this was really, *really* not done.

His devilish laugh was very little comfort to a woman who liked things in neat packages, with very pretty bows, yet she found herself following, holding his hand, and perhaps her palm was sweating, but Ian didn't seem to mind.

The room was decorated in pink and white, filled with balloons and gleaming silver ribbons. All in all, a neat little package with a very pretty bow. Ian headed straight for the bride, kissed her hand and told her that she shamed almost every woman there with the light of her smile. The bride, a radiant redhead with clashy coral lipstick, blushed and giggled, and when the groom appeared, she looked at Ian, who held out a hand. "Ian Cumberland. Second cousin on her mother's side. But you know, tonight, I think you're the lucky man. Congratulations." He lifted two passing glasses, and pressed them into the hands of the couple.

"A toast, to new beginnings, and to the magic created when two souls merge into one, the Fates playing mischief and forging true love."

Rose struggled to keep a straight face, but ended up stealing a cocktail napkin, bearing the words, Larry and Allison, forever. When Ian wasn't looking, she tucked the napkin in her purse. A keepsake, because she suspected that tonight was a memory she would keep for a long, long time—assuming she didn't get thrown in jail.

The lights dimmed, the spotlights dancing on the floor, the music fell to a slow, soothing song and the room filled with the magic of what could be. Ian took her hand, tucked her into his arms and under the balloons and streaming silver ribbons they slowly circled the floor to a melody that few people were lucky enough to hear. When Ian held her so close, when her missing heart began to stir, it wasn't smoke and mirrors. This wasn't an illusion to her, or the Fates playing mischief.

With Ian, everything was startlingly real.

THE DREAM CONTINUED. Through the night, on the ride to her apartment. Magic floated everywhere he touched. When he looked at her with eyes that saw only the best, she got caught up in the spell of what could be. He kissed her, once, a thousand times, until she couldn't think, couldn't plan, all she could do was feel.

Everywhere his mouth touched her. Her face, her neck, the curve of her breasts, the line of her arm. It was the wine, it was the music, she thought, but she knew that it was him. Laying siege, plotting to possess her. At first she struggled, but then he stopped the siege, holding her close, stroking her hair—comfort. Such gentle comfort.

"Shh," he whispered, his lips on her ear, his mouth slow, insidious, making her forget, taking her under once again. He lingered at her breasts until she was lost. Her body struggled to regain control, but each time he stopped, whispered against her neck, his hands never still, always creating pleasure. Lower he moved, and she could feel her body freeze, feel her muscles tighten. Yet each time he was there with tenderness, comfort, peace and such glorious pleasure.

Weakly her legs parted, craving more, and he was between her thighs, kissing her, his mouth hot and wicked, possessing her, controlling her… Loving her.

Rose could feel the orgasm riding inside her, building, and she needed to explode. But she wouldn't do it, not with him, not like this. She wanted to go alone, she must go alone. But then, when she was sure she had him locked out of her mind, his hand took hers and twined their fingers together, linked. Merged. Joined.

Fate.

When Rose fell, when her body shattered like glass, she wasn't alone. Not this time. His name was on her lips, in her mind and coming to rest in a heart she hadn't known she had.

ROSE WOKE, THE DARK HOVERING around her, and she could hear her mother's angry screech, the hard slap on her thigh, and automatically she froze.

Wouldn't move. Can't move.

The scream rose in her mind, silent, echoing over and over. Her heart was pounding. No crying. Little ladies never cried.

No, she thought, she would be smart.

The hand moved, and she waited for the next slap, steeled for the pain.

"Rose?"

Carefully she listened; the voice was gentle, soothing, floating through the night.

"It's Ian, Rose." She heard him shift away, far away, and she opened her eyes, adjusting to the dim of the night.

He looked so worried, so gloriously perfect, soft hair, softer eyes, and Rose came fully awake.

"I can go," he told her, uncertain, waiting for her.

Always waiting for her.

Rose began to breathe, and inched closer. She took his hand, twined their fingers together, linked, joined, fated.

"I'll be fine," she told him, lying next to him, almost touching, but not quite. Not yet.

It wasn't long before she fell asleep again, and this time when she woke, when she heard the quiet sound of his breathing and her heart froze again, he squeezed her hand once—tender, not hard—and Rose went back to sleep. And this time, she smiled.

THE NEXT MORNING, IAN LEFT early. Not as early as he had planned, Rose thought, smiling to herself as she remembered her well-plotted diversionary tactics. Honestly, relationships were easier than she had realized. She'd worried about losing herself, losing control, but sex was a remarkable equalizer. Men had money and power, and women, well… Mentally she patted herself on the back. Well, women had some tricks of their own.

Rose picked up bagels on the way to the penthouse, mortally insulting Michael, the chef, but Michael would recover. It was a marvelous, blustery day, the sky a clear blue, the trees bare, but spring was out there, waiting in the wings. And spring would come.

When she got to the penthouse, she hung up her coat, walked into the kitchen and grinned, a cheeky grin that Rose would never have attempted before.

"I brought bagels," she announced, plopping the sack on the granite counter.

"Why?" Michael asked, not quite getting the new-improved Rose.

"I thought we could use a change. Shake things up a bit. Don't you think the routine gets stale?"

"No. You like routines, Rose."

"Not today. Today, I'm taking lunch."

"Sylvia's looking for you," he said, with a last disdainful glance at the bag.

Rose waved a cavalier hand and floated to the living room, her mouth coated with True Love Shimmer—smudge-free—and a permanent smile.

"Rose! Rose!"

"In here, Sylvia," she trilled, plucking petals to the steady rhythm of he loves me, he loves me not.

When she spied Rose, Sylvia skidded to a halt. "What is this? My God, do you see that smile? It's the cat that swallowed the canary, swallowed Godzilla, and truly, I don't know what else the cat has been swallowing." She grabbed Rose by the arms, studied her face. "Happiness. Yes, I think they call that happiness."

"Maybe," answered Rose primly.

"Wait, I came here for something. The nuclear brightness of your teeth, the radioactive glow in your eye, they fried my memory. What was it?"

"Plans for the auction, selection for the book club, new dress design from Stella M or massage therapy at three?"

"There's my girl. The auction. We have the dogs?"

Rose could feel the light from her tiara dim. "Are you sure? The Empire wants to charge an extra twenty-grand deposit, plus any additional cleaning and—" Rose rolled her eyes "—fumigation that might be necessary."

"Bastards and crooks. Every one of them. Squeezing the public until they bleed." Sylvia pinched her arm. "Oops. No bleeding. Go for it, doll. How many bachelors do we have in play, ready to be buffed and polished until they shine?"

"Ten."

"We couldn't get twelve."

"Ten creates elitism. A dozen is common. It's the better choice."

"I suppose you're right. You on with the printers?"

"Check."

"Sponsors?"

"Check, check."

The phone rang, and Rose answered. "Simonov residence."

"Yeah, this is Dwayne from Flowers by Dwayne. I need to confirm an address. Sorry about the trouble, but we got this new kid, and honestly, you should see the way he scribbles his numbers. I've seen prescriptions that shame him. Anyways, we've got an order for orchids from an…Irene Simonini."

"Anton Simonov," Rose corrected.

"Whatever. Anyways, it's headed for 401 West Seventy-Eighth Street. At least I think that's Seventy-Eighth Street, but 401 ain't on the map, so I'm thinking maybe that's a nine, could be a seven."

Rose glanced up, noticed Sylvia watching. "Let me check the computer," she answered efficiently. As if she needed to check; she knew this address. The computer record was there—901 West Seventy-Eighth Street, Apartment 45G. Blair Rapaport.

Rose smiled at Sylvia, held the phone away for a minute. "An invitation got clogged in the mail. Give me a sec."

"Dwayne, okay, here's the right address. It's 401 East Seventy-Eighth Street."

"That's not a nine? And the *West* seems real clear."

"Nope. Sometimes these things get reversed. Mistakes happen."

"I should fire the kid."

"Don't do that—give him a break. You never know how you can change a life with a little kindness." Or how you could change a life with a mafia hit. One bullet. Was murder really so wrong? Rose looked at Sylvia and nodded stupidly.

"Yeah, guess you're right. Anyways. Have a nice day."

After she hung up, Sylvia shrugged. "It's such a trial to do anything these days."

"I know," agreed Rose, fingering the letter opener. She could tell Sylvia. She could confront the count. She could drench Blair with peroxide, of course—the world would never know the difference. She looked at Sylvia again, opened her mouth, and promptly shut it. *Coward.*

"So, what's my lunch schedule for the day?"

"You're meeting Shelby Fitzsimmons at Diddier Dumas, one o'clock."

Sylvia pulled a face. "It's the pitch for a carbon-offset program. You be there, take notes. Make me seem official and environmentally friendly, because God knows, I'll never convince her."

"Can't make it."

"Does my hearing fail me?"

"Nope. I have a date."

"Remy?" asked Sylvia, her smile approving.

Rose shook her head. "Ian."

Sylvia's smile turned, but the twinkle in the eyes gave her away. "Is your love life going to be interfering with your absolute slavish dedication to this position?"

"Probably."

"Well, hallelujah and pass the mustard. You go, chicky. Take a long lunch. A long, long lunch, but reschedule with Shelby first."

"You're the best," Rose said, and she meant it. Why the count was hell-bent on destroying his marriage to Sylvia, she'd never know, but she was the hired help. She couldn't make a difference. She'd only muck things up more.

The countess fanned herself. "You're a wonderful shot to the old ego." Then her gaze lit on Rose's practical wool suit. "And wear something a little flashier. Tweed is not date material. A little cleavage. There's that black lace bustier in the closet. Put that under the tweed."

"I don't know, Sylvia," Rose started, but Sylvia was dragging her in the direction of the warehouse she called a closet, and then threw a bit of black lace at her.

"Trust me, doll. He won't know what hit him."

14

IAN WAS BUSTING HIS BUTT on the phones, but the world was not feeling the love. The elevator had been broken when he came in. After that he'd spent the morning grasping at straws for Hilda Prigsley. Following three curt "not at this time" responses and one heartless guffaw that was poorly disguised as coughing, Ian wasn't having his best day ever. However, at precisely twelve-seventeen that all changed for the better.

He felt her sneak up from behind, putting cool hands over his eyes. He knew the smell of honeysuckle and he knew those hands. Intimately. "Guess who?"

"Lola?"

Laughing, she planted a tantalizing kiss on his neck. "Jessica Alba."

"Don't tell Lola," he whispered.

After that, her tongue landed in his ear, and oops, she happened to land in his lap. Heroically, he restrained himself from a very inappropriate public display of affection. "Lola deserves everything she gets for ignoring her man."

"Rough day?" she asked, smoothing a hand through his hair while he pretended not to stare down the plump valley of her breasts. Black lace wasn't her usual style. In virginal white, a man could dream, but in sheer black, hell… He stowed his hands to safety and met her eyes.

"How'd you know it was a rough day? The menacing scowl, the brooding gaze?"

"The mussed hair."

Ian scowled, fingering his hair back in place. "Not enough product."

"Don't you dare spoil these artfully tousled locks with chemicals."

"Artfully tousled? Really?" For that, he gave her another kiss. And then one turned into two, and his hand was itching to dive under the silk and explore, but there was a roomful of the seething unemployed waiting for his attention, and deep in his soul, Ian wasn't that cruel.

"What's the problem?" she said, noting his heartrending sigh.

"Well, right now the problem is more of a physical inconvenience than an actual work-related problem."

She studied the glass panels that displayed the crowded lobby, and he knew exactly what was on her very clever mind. "There are ways…" he mentioned casually, not that he would be so crude as to actually suggest it, but if she did, well, hell that was a different matter entirely.

She did consider it, he could see the sensual possibilities churning in her eyes, but in the end her sigh was nearly as heartrending as his. "It's not the location, more the idea that all those people are here seeking gainful employment, and to find selfish pleasure while they're waiting? It feels wrong."

"It's not *exactly* wrong," he told her courageously, his gaze drawn to the mind-popping low edge of the silk.

"Ian," she said, and pulled her jacket together, ripping temptation from his grasp.

"Fine. It's wrong."

"I'll make it up to you tonight," she purred.

His heart leaped; his cock approved. "And with those magic words, all is forgiven. Did you come here just to arouse me, seduce me to the edge of sexual frustration and then leave?"

"I came for lunch." She pulled out a paper sack. "Hot dogs."

Rose looked so happy and thrilled with her choice, that he didn't have the heart to educate her as he watched her take a bite. He nearly moaned. Eventually a blush burned her cheeks, so Ian figured she knew, most likely because she was still sitting in his lap.

Prudently, she moved to the other side of the desk. "Sorry. I actually came to say hello."

"And it was the nicest hello I've had this morning. How's your day?"

For a few minutes she told him about the plans the countess had, the words tripping faster as she talked, and he could see how much she loved what she did. It was good that she had found her niche. His eyes found the rock on his desk. At one time, he'd thought her job was frilly, all societal froufrou, but he'd been wrong.

Funny, everyone took Rose as a lightweight, but she knew what she wanted and went after it with a drive that could put the marines to shame, leaving a lollipop- and rainbows-ravaged landscape in her wake.

"What about you?"

"Miserable," he complained, and then promptly shut up.

Rose, being the people-pleaser she was, noticed. "Tell me."

And so he proceeded to expound on the full extent of his miseries. Rose looked at him with great sympathy, taking his hand, and eventually Ian found himself milking the moment for everything it was worth.

It felt great to pile all his doubts and worries onto someone else. He was truly loving this job, but some days—like this one—the weight was killer, letting everyone dump on him and smiling as if everything was going to be okay. The old days at the bank, the pressures, the rarified air, it all seemed stale now when he compared it to the personalities that needed him here.

At the bank, he'd dealt with computer screens, faceless numbers and legal waivers that absolved him of all responsibility in case, God forbid, disaster struck.

And then it had.

Here, with less than a foot of space between him and his client, he worried all the rocks, all the cheery T-shirts, all the optimism in the world wouldn't be enough.

Like Hilda Prigsley, he thought, and explained the situation in detail to Rose.

When Rose watched him, believed in him, counted on him, all that weight—it felt good. It felt right.

"Why don't you go back to the bank? Go where the air is fresh and guilt-free?"

"I've talked to my old boss. It's a possibility. Maybe."

"That'd be fantastic," she told him enthusiastically. Too enthusiastically.

Ian frowned. "It's not even that close to a possibility."

"I can pull strings. I know people. Actually, I know people who know people."

"Not yet. I'm…happy."

"But for how long, Ian?" It worried him, that panic inside her when she contemplated anything less than a seven-zero bank account. He could stall for a while; he was adjusting to his altered circumstances. But what about Rose?

"I'm happy at least until tonight, unless you're cavorting with Doctor Dolittle." *Who had a seven-zero bank account. Hell, probably eight.*

"My calendar is open," she said and then a gleam came back into her eyes. "How old is she?" she asked, startling him.

"Who?"

"Hilda. Hilda Prigsley."

"She's sixty," explained Ian slowly, curious.

"Would she be willing to learn anything else?" she asked, and he saw where her mind was running.

He rocked back in his chair, wishing it were that easy. "Trust me, I've tried. I could get her computer training, but she doesn't think she can learn new skills."

"Can I talk to her?" she asked, then immediately shook her head. "No. Forget that."

Seeing her interest, Ian was intrigued by the spark in her eyes. "You have an idea?" he asked casually, not prodding, not forcing, not demanding, trying to kindle it before she killed it herself.

"Possibly."

Okay, maybe demanding was going to be necessary. He could ask, probably a couple of times to drag her idea out of her, and there was the off chance that it was something that he hadn't thought of, and then he could try…*to trample all over her plan.*

Her plan, not his. Not going to do that, he thought, digging through the files on his desk before triumphantly pulling out Hilda's file. Rose merely watched him, warily, not saying a word.

Ha. Ian cracked his knuckles, punched the speaker button on his phone and dialed.

Two minutes later, he had Hilda's okay to talk to another counselor. The very talented Rose Hildebrande, who the firm used on occasion for their most special cases. Ian scribbled Prigsley's phone number down on a piece of paper and handed it to Rose.

Rose stared at the paper, and then looked at him. "I can do this? You don't mind. If you…"

Ian cut her off before she handed the file back to him. "I've tried, Rose. I don't know what else to do, and honestly, the woman's getting tired of me. Oh, she doesn't say anything, but you can tell. I'd appreciate your help," he encouraged, willing her to try.

Her teeth dug into her lips before she realized what she was doing and stopped. "I'll do it." Then she checked her watch and stood up, dusting crumbs from her skirt. "I should go. I have some things to do for the countess. We could meet at your place about eight. I'm thinking we'll eat in."

Then, with a wicked glimmer in her eyes, she leaned over his desk, black lace gaping anew, exposing a treasure of creamy white flesh that begged to be plundered. Mindlessly, Ian swallowed, sitting on his hands, lest they plunder away. "You're heartless, heartless, I say."

"I know," she said, planting a saucy kiss on his mouth and left.

And how the hell was a man supposed to work after that?

Two snowy nights later, Rose found herself sitting on the uncomfortable steel of the bleachers at the RAC. She kept wanting to squirm, find a comfortable spot, but she was too well trained, and Ian was watching her. Not like her parents, but worried. Ian cared like a person should. He must have sensed her nerves—he always did—and he twined their fingers together.

"What if they don't like me?" she asked, tucking her hair behind her ear, managing a furtive wiggle at the same time.

"You're very likable."

"I'm not as likable as you think."

"You won't be the problem."

Somehow that made her feel better. "Why not?"

"I neglected to mention this earlier, but they're high maintenance. Both of them." His gaze kept scanning the aisle, and Rose wished she could distract him.

"I'm sensing a trend," she told him in her bitchiest, most judgmental voice, but the sweat was starting to trickle down her neck.

"I don't want there to be a trend. What does that say about me? Do I seek out people who are high maintenance? Am I high maintenance, and by the way, the correct answer is no."

He turned to her, and his eyes were remarkably calm for such a big faker of anxiety. Very smooth, she thought, noting that it worked. Her nerves were already starting to calm, and she slid closer to him, snuggling under his arm. "You're very sexy when you're nervous." *And when you're trying to protect me,* she thought, but she kept that to herself because it felt so nice.

"That was a good answer. It dodged the bullet and made me hot all in one sentence. Why do I continually underestimate you?"

She gave him her best, most innocent Mary Jane look. "Me?"

Not falling for it, he kissed her, and she forgot about trying to appear innocent, her hand curling toward his thigh, just under the coat….

"Geez, Ian. Can you show a little respect here? Minors are present."

Rose broke off and got her first glimpse of Beckett and Phoebe. Phoebe was short, with slightly frizzed chestnut hair, clear gray eyes that shone behind her glasses and a distressing flair for frumpy clothes. Beckett was a foot taller than Phoebe, his clothes were equally awful, but the arrogant granite in his face reeked of money.

Under Phoebe's critical stare, Rose fought the urge to squirm once again. Failed. Ian caught her hand and held tight.

Quickly he performed the introductions, and Rose plastered her best, most implacable smile on her face. She'd been through worse. She'd survived. But she knew Ian was watching her, knew he worried, and she didn't want to disappoint him.

"You're Rose?" Beckett asked, and Rose nodded once.

Beckett nodded once, and then some silent milestone had been passed. Beckett and Ian plugged into the game, and Rose was left to bond with Phoebe.

Oh, God.

"Why are you here?" asked Phoebe, soft enough that Ian couldn't hear.

And thus, twenty questions had begun, but Rose had no idea what the correct answers would be. Social chitchat, pithy bons mots and heartfelt eloquence on the state of world hunger, sure, that she could recite in her sleep. But this black-ops mission on the state of Rose's heart, or lack thereof, was almost as bad as what she'd endured as a kid. No. Not really.

Rose steeled her spine, lifted her chin and threw back her shoulders, determined to do this right.

"Ian asked me," Rose replied, which wasn't the right answer, but she suspected that flawless makeup and the ability to explain the Continental style of fork etiquette weren't going to cut it with Phoebe. When all that failed, Rose's fallback position was vapid bubblehead.

"You're going to be nice to him now?" Phoebe asked, not falling for vapid bubblehead, and Rose blinked, feeling a pit spread in her stomach. Apparently Phoebe knew things. Phoebe knew what Rose had done to Ian, and she wasn't so quick to forgive. Unfortunately, or perhaps fortunately, females weren't nearly so gullible as men.

The first reply on her tongue, those fail-safe responses to be pulled in case of emergencies, weren't going to work. Rose was not going to blow this. She was not going to let her rigid personality ruin the very first, very best relationship of her life. Carefully she struggled to find the right words. "I don't deserve him, but he always sees the best in things, including me. There are a lot of things that aren't going to be easy for him, because where most people want two steps forward, I'll go forty steps around and then sideways until a sane person would give up. He doesn't give up, and I don't want to give up, either."

"What about the other dude?"

"What other dude?"

"Dr. McDreamy?"

"Remy?"

"Exactly how many Dr. McDreamys do you know?"

"One," lied Rose. Phoebe wouldn't understand.

"And have you broken it off with him?"

Rose wasn't sure if that was any of Phoebe's business, because she hadn't even told Ian, but the look in Phoebe's eyes said that death was possible, so Rose decided to tell her the truth.

Talking to Remy hadn't been easy. It had felt like a breach of all of her dreams. She'd taken out her military strategy books and could find absolutely nothing that covered the proper way to lose a war. Eventually, she had met him for drinks—at the Waverly. And when she'd walked away, she knew she'd done the right thing.

"I told him yesterday."

Phoebe stared, but Rose didn't blink and she didn't look away, not once. Eventually, Phoebe nodded, and Rose resumed normal breathing function again.

Another milestone passed.

"I like the sweater," offered Phoebe, "but I think our society is way too preoccupied with this concept of the superficial—looks, money. I don't think that's important? How 'bout you?"

Rose felt the strong urge to crawl under the seat, but Ian glanced her way, checking to see if she was okay. She shot him a reassuring smile, and was brought back to when she nine—the disastrous piano concert where she'd taken second and her mother had never forgotten. Thoughtfully, Rose stared at the ceiling, a considering expression on her face.

"Looks, money, intelligence, talent. All these things are gifts, raw materials that we can choose to better humanity. There are a lot of people who waste these talents, who use them for their own gain, and that's wrong. But no, I don't think that looks or money are a curse. I think, with the right attitude, an awareness of the needs of the world around us, they can be a force for good."

"That's some great bullshit."

Rose blushed. "Little Princess School of Charm. Rule Number Three Hundred Seventeen: You are a caretaker of the earth and the sisterhood that is womankind."

"Sucked for you, didn't it?"

"Yeah," agreed Rose. Her mother had counted on lace, ribbons and flowing tawny hair to be enough. That, Rose had in abundance. The inner beauty thing—that her mother had tried to beat into her. Gee, and why hadn't that worked? Rose managed a tight smile.

"Beckett's loaded. It makes him miserable."

"It doesn't have to be a burden. For a lot of people, money's security."

"Yeah, Ian used to think that, too. He's happier now."

Rose glanced over, watched the men cheering, laughing. Sure, for the moment, he seemed happy, but eventually he'd get beaten down, just like her. It always happened. "He wants his old job back."

Phoebe pushed at her glasses and frowned. "Nah. He's saying that because that's what he thinks he thinks. He's found his home. He's good at it."

"It wears him down," answered Rose quietly.

"Don't like that? Want him back the old way, loaded and stress-free?"

"Banking is highly stressful," defended Rose. "In a few months, he'll be back where he belongs."

Phoebe coughed. "If he's not, are you going to stick around, or does he get a cutesy kiss-off letter with a heart over the *I?*"

"I made a mistake. I learned from it. I don't…" Rose stopped, bit her tongue.

"What?"

"It's not what you think. I've been around a lot of poverty and I've seen what it does. It sounds so all-fired romantic to you, big ole families sitting around the kitchen table playing board games."

Ian turned, "Everything okay?"

Phoebe laughed. "Oh, yeah."

Ian looked at Rose. "Yeah?"

"Sure. No big here," she said, and for a little while, she tried to follow the game. Phoebe and Beckett argued about his clothes, about her nachos, about the game, about the everything, and Rose watched, studying the easy fighting, the impulsive behaviors, the mild insults that everyone seemed to accept.

In the third quarter, Phoebe spilled a drop of cheese on her linen shirt, and Rose kept checking, kept looking, her eyes drawn to the spot. Phoebe didn't seem to care, and Rose told herself it wasn't her place.

Eventually Phoebe noticed the mark, taking a napkin and grinding it into the thin material.

Not smart, not smart at all. Quickly Rose pulled the stain-stick from her bag, efficiently shooing Phoebe's hands away, and then worked the material in gentle strokes, not grinding. "You'll kill your shirt," Rose explained, as processed orange turned back to white.

Phoebe pulled at the shirt, admiring Rose's results. "You do that well."

"Always prepare for the disasters."

"A survivalist at heart?"

"Yes."

"I've never seen a survivalist that does such a great job with makeup. It's really natural. Not all fakey-fake."

"If you went with a darker tone for your blush, something in a coral, I think it'd go great with your hair."

"Are you giving me makeup tips?"

"No." Determined, Rose sat on her hands. "Yes. Yes, I'm giving you makeup tips." She leaned over and handed Phoebe a compact and blush. "Try it. It'll be very flattering. The lights in here are fluorescent. The worst for skin tone, but in candlelight, it'll be awesome."

Beckett turned, and his jaw dropped. "You're putting on makeup? At a basketball game?"

"Is there a law?"

"No." He peered closer. "It looks good."

Phoebe twisted toward Rose and smiled, apparently noticing the lost expression on her face. "You don't know basketball at all, do you?"

"Not a clue."

"Okay, see, the guys there, the ones in red, that's Rutgers. You want to cheer for them."

"Got it."

"And when the other team steals, you shout out, 'you suck.'"

A few minutes later, when the team in white stole the ball, Rose stood up, "Go!"

Phoebe nodded sadly, noting the male heads turning around Rose. Beckett saw her face, laughed. "It's going to be tough breaking her in."

"But she's really excellent when it comes to spot removal," Phoebe teased.

Rose was beautiful, polished, elegant and had a magical touch with makeup, but sometimes those gorgeous blue eyes were sad, looking at the world as if she'd been locked out. Ian had never been drawn to gorgeous and polished before. He usually laughed it off, but not this time. Phoebe could see the way he watched Rose.

Phoebe leaned over and whispered to Beckett. "I think he's in deep trouble."

"It's the abyss. It's a scary-ass thing, but you can't avoid it."

Phoebe covered his hand gently. "I don't know why that touches my heart, but it does."

FOUR DAYS LATER, ROSE WAS scrutinizing her apartment, adjusting the flowers, checking for dust under the refrigerator and straightening the paintings on the wall four times. No matter how often she righted them, they always looked a little off.

Tonight was her first night with Hilda, her first night as job counselor extraordinaire. Ian had warned her that Hilda was stubborn, but Ian had no idea what stubborn truly meant. Rose could do this.

At the sound of the buzzer, Rose took a deep breath and straightened her pink silk jacket. For Ian, she would do this.

Thirty minutes later, she was ready to scream. Oh, Hilda Prigsley was a darling. Charming, jovial and completely convinced that she could never learn anything. Rose had started out trying to explain that truly a computer was no big deal, and if Rose could learn it, then anyone could. Hilda laughed, gray curls bobbing, and explained that she was too old.

When further coaxing and then bribery failed, it was time to bring in the heavy artillery.

"Let's do this. I'm going to sit here, and you don't have to lift a finger. Just watch. Maybe you'll lose some of the fear."

"It's not my fear that's causing the problem, dearie. I'm an old dog, and new tricks aren't my cup of tea." Then she gave out a hoot of laughter.

Patiently, Rose pulled out the laptop, sat it on the coffee table and opened the lid. "Okay, so here we go. The first thing is to power it on. There's a little button or a switch or a lever or some contraption that you push and then the lights will start to flicker. They showed me how to do this just yesterday, and it was so easy. So…" She fumbled around the computer case. "Where was that switch?" For five minutes Rose poked every key and every button—except the most important one. "I know it's here."

Hilda sat, arms crossed, her eyes politely blank.

Rose smiled apologetically. "Sorry. Sometimes it takes me a bit to get going. After five, the brain shuts down."

Hilda coughed discreetly, not saying a word.

"It's a really big button…I think."

After another ten minutes, Hilda's foot began to tap, and Rose ran a hand through her hair, fighting the urge to run to the mirror and fix it. No, she would endure, she would thrive and in the end, Ian would be desperately proud. "I'm so embarrassed, but this is a new machine, and I'm not used to it. Would you mind taking a stab? Sometimes another set of eyes…" Rose pulled her very best, uncertain face.

"I don't see how I can be any assistance," argued Hilda.

Rose looked at her, hurt and dismay oozing from her very being. "I don't know what I'm doing. I don't know why I thought I should. I should just go back to perfume spritzing and leave this for someone more capable. When I was little, my parents didn't believe in technology—they thought idle hands would produce the devil's work. We spent a lot of time churning butter, making up our own entertainment because television was the worst sin of all. Two years ago I finally broke down and bought a TV. It's like a brave new world. But computers? They're the last bastion of technology. The Evil

Empire. I know my mother would be turning over in her grave if she could see how I've shamed her. But I'm determined to do it. I won't be beaten down." Her hair fell into her face, and she placed a delicate finger on her forehead. Incapable Woman Broken By Life.

Hilda was unmoved for a solid two minutes, but after Rose added a pious heavenward glance, the woman came and sat next to her. "Now, dearie, don't slight yourself. We'll tackle this bloody machine, and if two women can't conquer the beastie thing, then, Bob's my uncle."

Rose sniffed. "Are you sure? I'm such a failure."

"And don't you be so hard on yourself," she encouraged, with a motherly pat on the hand. "So we're looking for a button?"

"I think so. A large one."

At first, Hilda hit the enter key, and Rose fixed her hands in her lap. Hilda laughed, and then poked shift. Rose stayed granite-still. Eventually, she hit the power button and Rose had to internalize the whoop of joy.

"Aha! The lights are flashing! I think you've done it."

Hilda pushed at the bridge of her wire frames. "Do you, now?" She leaned in close, watching as the bootup sequence started and the words rolled across the screen. "I think we did. My goodness."

It took another two hours of abject failure and Rose whacking herself on the head—sometimes painfully—before Hilda showed Rose how to properly hold her fingers on the keyboard and then discovered the differences between insert and delete. Rose twirled her hair around a finger, looking breathlessly enthralled with each new revelation.

Eventually it was nearing midnight, and Hilda was fighting back a yawn. Rose took pity on the woman.

"It's getting late, and I'm keeping you up. You're such a sweet lady, helping me here. You must be exhausted."

Hilda waved a hand. "Shush. Not a peep from you. It was all great fun."

"Can you come over tomorrow?" asked Rose, shooting a dark glare at the laptop.

"Oh, Rose, I'm not sure," Hilda answered, pursing her mouth

like a fish. Rose knew that look, that defeatist spirit, but not anymore. They were conquering insecurities left and right.

"It's more the moral support, Hilda. When you're here, I'm sure I can do anything. It gives me courage." In case that didn't cut it, Rose placed an earnest hand over her heart.

"You're sure? An old woman like me?"

"I think you're fabulous," answered Rose, and that was true. The woman had a heart that was twice as big as most, and obviously couldn't stand to see someone in need.

Hilda giggled, and pulled her handbag over her arm. "I suppose I could. I have a cribbage game, but I'll put that off."

"You're a darling." Impulsively, Rose gave her a hug, surprised by the motherly feel of the embrace.

"Tomorrow at seven?"

"Make it six-thirty," said Rose. "I have to learn how to work the printer. It could take days."

Hilda tapped at her arm. "And you will."

Rose blushed charmingly. "We will. Two little troopers managing the dark forces together."

"We'll do it for Ian," Hilda announced with cheery pluck, and Rose now understood why he worked so hard to find her a place. Hilda only needed that one little shove in the right direction, and Ian had recognized that in her. He was good at that, recognizing those who needed the push.

Rose smiled to herself. Everyone needed a little push. Even Ian.

THE NEXT TWO WEEKS, ROSE spent her days at the penthouse and her evenings with Hilda, but her lunch hour belonged to Ian. Every time she saw Ian, her mouth opened, wanting to gush about Hilda's progress. She was well disciplined, though, and when Ian asked about Hilda, she'd shrug with disappointment, and say they were still working on it.

Sometimes they spent the hour at his office, sometimes they grabbed a sandwich and rode the ferry, and sometimes, oh, lucky day, they went to his apartment. Those stolen moments were magic, and he'd ask why he couldn't see her that night, and Rose would hide an elusive grin.

On their last night in computer hell, Hilda was emptying out her purse and out popped a biography on the English royal family.

"Is it good?" asked Rose, making polite conversation, curious because the prosaic Hilda with sensible shoes didn't seem the starstruck type.

"They certainly got some of the facts right, but they tried to build the whole business into some penny dreadful. Wasn't quite the truth, although I suppose it makes for good reading, and a brisk business at the shops."

"You're an expert?"

"Four years at Windsor. Not that it was Buckingham Palace, but it was a far sight better than the bowels of Highgrove."

Rose opened her mouth, quickly closed it. "You worked for the royal family?"

"The queen's aunt," Hilda answered with a brisk bob of her head. "I was a young thing, full of all sorts of dreams and it was my first job out of university."

"Why didn't you tell Ian?"

"It was a long time ago, and if I mention it, people expect me to spill all the tawdry doings, and I'm not a gossip. Not by any stretch of the imagination. It was why I lasted so long. Hilda Prigsley knows when to keep her lips zipped."

Rose looked at the woman in a new light. "Hilda, I think we've all underestimated you."

The woman gave her a saucy smile. "They always do."

IT WAS MIDMORNING at the penthouse, when Rose found the perfect moment to talk to Sylvia. Ian was a firm believer in fate. But Rose knew the hard truth of the world, that you had to make your own fate, your own opportunities, and this morning, bless the monarchy, Rose was going to make Ian's day, and by extension, Rose's day, as well.

Sylvia had finished a coffer-filling meeting with the Simonov Foundation, and was reading over the financials—never her favorite chore—when Rose pounced. "Sylvia, I have a friend who's looking for something similar to my role. Do you know anyone who needs a personal assistant?"

The countess glanced up from her schedule, thinking. "Not many. Kylie McMullen chased off another one last week, but between you and me, I wouldn't sick my worst enemy on that woman. She's got a tongue like a pit viper. Why they couldn't inject BOTOX into her mouth and freeze it permanently, I haven't the foggiest. You wouldn't want a friend working there, unless you're planning some sort of personal revenge, and Rose, darling, you don't have a vindictive bone in your body."

Rose twirled her pen between her fingers, all sophisticated wisdom. Not an easy look for her, but today, she managed it. "No, this woman needs someone....*special*. She's got a...past and I wouldn't want to throw her just anywhere."

"What sort of special?" asked Sylvia, sliding the financials aside. Rose took the papers, filed them on the desk.

"It's very hush-hush, so I can't really say. She's British and there are a lot of things that she's not allowed to say about her prior employer." Rose paused, waited, let the countess draw her own conclusions.

Sylvia's eyes grew saucer-wide. "She worked for Madonna?"

Rose kept her smile small, dangling the carrot oh-so carefully. She peeked around the room as if prying ears might be nearby. "Bigger," she whispered.

"Bigger?" Sylvia braced a hand on the piano. "How bigger?"

"I can't say anything, and she can't, either, but..." Rose began humming "God Save the Queen," and Sylvia fell back against the cushions, clutching her heart.

"I have to have her."

"Sylvia..."

"It would be the coup of the year. Are you kidding?"

"Well, yes, you could do that, but Sylvia, you are a countess, and royalty and titles, well, they become common if you have too much in one household. People would talk, say you're being flaunty. You need to pay it forward. You have to be generous with your absolute fabulousness."

"Rose," pleaded Sylvia.

"Sylvia," warned Rose.

"Why do you have to be such a little do-gooder? Can't a

woman have some vices? A selfish twinge of superiority in order to flaunt her lifestyle about the other, less worthy members of her acquaintance?"

"You'd be friends with Bitsy Mortimer if that was true. Every time you see her, she invites you to her club."

"Stuffy little aristocrats with their argyle socks and outdated membership policies."

Rose folded her arms across her chest because as much as Sylvia wanted to be the ruling elite of the New York social diaries, she didn't have the suck-up-edness.

Eventually, Sylvia heaved a sigh. "Rosie, you're a smart doll, keeping me on the straight and narrow."

"You have to be careful. Plus, she can't talk about it."

"Surely there are a few little tidbits she could share—just with me?"

"Not even with you."

"Well, then. If she can't talk about it, it's not nearly as fun. And I'd get frustrated. The stress level would be atrocious."

"Exactly."

Sylvia picked up her address book, thumbing through names. "Give me ten minutes, and we'll have ourselves a Manhattan-style bidding war. Any perks that she needs? A condo in Miami, flextime, her own personal assistant?"

Rose pulled out her phone, prepared to let Hilda in on the good news. "Let me make a call and we'll find out."

IT WASN'T THE MOST FULFILLING day of Ian's life. Every call was a dead end; every interview not a good fit. And then he had to tell the client that he was sorry, not to give up hope. Something was just around the corner.

It was after six; he was packing up for the day and had planned to kidnap Rose, no matter how busy the auction was keeping her. Today, he needed to hold her, needed to bury himself inside her, needed to make her smile. When he did that, when her eyes lit up, it gave him that same top-of-the-world feeling that he craved. He was about to pick up the phone and call when Mrs. Prigsley appeared in his doorway.

"Good evening, Mr. Ian. And how are you this fine day? I brought you an extra tin today," she told him, presenting him with a tin of biscuits, all wrapped with a sensible yellow ribbon.

Ian frowned, confused. "Did we have an appointment?" He sat down, pulled off his coat. "I must have forgotten. Where are we?"

Hilda remained standing, bouncing up and down on her heels. "As for 'we,' I wouldn't speak to that, but as for 'me,' I'm off to work."

Amazed, Ian gave the woman a once-over, noticed the extra glow in the face. "You found a job?"

"I did indeed. All because of your counselor extraordinaire. Although between you, me and the wardrobe, she's not all that good with machines. Poor dearie. It was the blind leading the blind for a bit, but I found myself a book and we muddled through, and studied some, and just this afternoon, I received a job offer from a Mrs. Elizabeth Carlyle. A PA," she added proudly.

"PA?"

"Personal assistant. I've quite a lot of lingo to brush up on, but I'm getting the 411." She leaned in confidentially. "That's information, you know."

Ian grinned, feeling better than he had all day. How had Rose done it? "You'll do great."

"I think so. You're sweet on her, Mr. Ian?"

"That's the understatement of the year," he told her, because sweet didn't begin to describe the swelling in his heart, the clarity in his vision. His life hadn't ended postlayoff, and his life hadn't been lived prelayoff. A man wasn't defined by a title or a paycheck, but instead how well he loved.

Ian loved.

"Just don't let her near the computers," Hilda advised.

And Ian made a properly concerned face. "No. I won't."

15

HE SHOWED UP IN THE BRONX with roses. He considered daisies, orchids, daffodils, lilies, but then realized that there was no more perfect flower. Soft petals, elegant symmetry, and enough thorns to make her deadly.

She looked at the flowers, looked at his face and beamed. "You found out."

"I suppose you're very proud of yourself."

"I am. You think you're the only one that can rescue the world?"

"I imagined all sorts of bad things about you—froufrou evenings with Dr. Buckeroo Bonzai," he told her, taking a definitive step into her apartment. "Long carriage rides in the park, flights to Paris."

"You have a wild imagination," she told him, taking the flowers, laying them aside, her eyes locked with his.

He shut the door, and merely smiled. "You have no idea."

"Dr. Bonzai, he's dead to me." She curled her hands in his hair, lowered his head, but Ian wasn't going to be diverted.

"Dead? How dead?" He tipped up her head and studied her, noting the sparkle in her eye. Happiness. Love. That's what they called it.

"Against you, he never had a chance." She raised her mouth to his, and Ian had the strength of character to feel sorry for the man—but not too long. Rose had that effect. Made him forget about everything but her.

Of their own volition, his fingers lowered the zip on her dress. He hadn't intended this. He'd intended dinner. Ian reminded himself to be careful with her, but her hands slid under his shirt, soft against his heart, and she didn't seem so fragile anymore.

The wispy blue dress fell to the floor, revealing black silk underneath.

"I think you're trying to seduce me, Mrs. Robinson."

"I am," she whispered. His fingers shook as he undid her bra, exposing the pale gold skin, the delicate pink nipples. He took one in his mouth. Her hands tangled in his hair, and Ian decided that dinner was overrated.

He loved her like this. Adrift in pleasure, with her quiet moans that nearly did him in. She was never loud, and he lived for those little sounds that she worked so hard to suppress. It was a challenge to him to make her forget the barriers, to make her let go.

His thumbs slipped underneath the black silk at her hips, then followed the long line of her legs. When she stood before him, he held his breath, because there was no woman as beautiful as this.

Her warm blue gaze met his, liquid, spilling over with things he'd longed to see. Carefully he picked her up in his arms, carrying her to bed. Her arms didn't wait to reach for him, but Ian had other plans in mind. Quickly he stripped, lowering himself to her, his eyes stayed locked with hers, making sure the panic stayed far away. Tonight, he wanted it to be Rose and Ian. No ghosts. No fears.

His mouth tasted the satin of her neck, the elegant line of her shoulder. She closed her eyes, a small smile on her lips.

Lower he went, satisfying himself with one breast, then the other. Lower still to the curve of her hips, but there Ian hesitated, raising his head. Her eyes were open, not so panicked, but not so sure, either.

The radiator hummed, covering the heavy thud of his heart. One beat. Then two. Her teeth sank into her lower lip and she nodded, her body arching in invitation.

Ian didn't waste another beat.

With his hands, he spread her thighs, finding her pink and wet. One finger slid inside her, and he watched her face, her expression sharp with desire. He'd waited for this—ultimate trust.

With each push of his hand, her hips curled upward, urging him on. Her fists curled into the soft down of the duvet, twisting with the same slow rhythm.

For long moments he played and tested, never going too far or too fast, keeping the ghosts far at bay. The sight of her, open, wanting, trusting, was a picture he would never forget.

Slowly he lowered his head, one touch of his tongue to her clit, and her body jerked. His hand splayed over her stomach, gentling her, easing her, and he paused until he felt her relax. This time, he stroked, back and forth, his tongue, his finger, and he felt the tension ease, felt the slow drain of her, heard the quick gasps of pleasure at each touch of his mouth.

Bolder now, he sucked, tasting her honey, hearing the quick gasps grow longer, huskier. Her hips were moving with him now, and he knew she was close.

Ultimate trust.

Her fingers clasped his head, pressing him there, keeping him there.

Ultimate trust.

His hands moved beneath her, lifting her high, and this time, his mouth wasn't gentle, drawing her in, drinking her in.

Her back arched, stiff and tight, and then…

Finally.

Rose fell.

THE NEXT SATURDAY NIGHT, Ian Cumberland was cordially invited to the home of Count Anton and Sylvia Simonov for an evening of fun and festivity, but mainly so that Sylvia could decide if he was worthy.

Rose was a basket case.

That afternoon, she had made a list of suggested topics for them to discuss, prepped him on the appropriate answers and went over his suit choice five times.

Ian was not amused.

"Honey, this is not a huge thing."

"It's huge."

"It's dinner."

"It's my boss, it's the count. It's your shot, Ian," she said, and then immediately shut her mouth.

Of course, he noticed. "What do you mean?"

"Mingle, comingle, mix, this is your world."

"Not really."

"It used to be your world."

"No, Rose," he said firmly. "Is that why you want me there?"

Rose decided it wasn't the time for this discussion. Not yet. "No. I want you to meet Sylvia. I want her to love you. I want you to meet the count because he can do great favors for you."

"I thought you didn't like the count. I thought he was—and these were your words, I wouldn't have been so nice—a cheating son of a gun. I don't want great favors from a cheating son of a gun."

"I don't know that he's cheating. I don't think he's cheating. I think he's thinking about cheating. Blair's just…"

"You're worrying way too much."

"I don't worry. I plan. I organize. I have a strategy."

"Will I doom our entire sexual relationship if I don't have a strategy?"

"Be serious."

"I was serious," he said, then he took her in his arms. "Rose, I'll be fine. You'll be fine. We'll be fine."

"We'll be fine?"

"Perfect."

"You'll wear the gray suit with the blue-striped tie?"

"Of course," he said, wisely choosing not to argue.

DINNER WAS FABULOUS, IAN WAS fabulous and Rose was starting to breathe normally.

"I like him," Sylvia whispered. "He's bonkers for you, not that that's any surprise."

Rose fanned her face, suddenly finding herself short of oxygen. "You think?"

"I *know,* honey. But he's not Remy."

At that, Rose winced. "He's worth ten of Remy."

"Not in actual U.S. dollars," the countess reminded her.

"He's very ambitious, and given the right opportunity…" Rose trailed off.

"You want me to say something to Anton?" asked Sylvia.

Rose frowned. "No. Not yet. Give it time."

"He doesn't seem like the impress-his-betters type."

"He doesn't need to. You should see him at the office. He's always thinking, always making connections, hooking up somebody with somebody else. Sometimes we'll be out on a walk, and he gets this look, and he pulls out the phone. And boom. Somebody new is gainfully employed. Ian gets ahead the old-fashioned way. He earns it." She liked to watch him work, liked to see that flash in his face, liked to know that the world was a better place because Ian Cumberland was there.

"Earning it? Quaint, yet slow."

Without the proper incentives that was true, and Sylvia, attuned to the machinations of the female's drive for security, saw the determination in Rose's face. "Be careful, sweetie," she cautioned. "I'm not so sure that he wants to drive in the fast lane. Sometimes things aren't laid out exactly like we wish they were. What do you do if you have to make a choice?"

Rose watched Ian, lifting his glass, chatting with the count. Okay, maybe the two men weren't the best of friends, and Ian was keeping a distance, but there weren't swords at dawn. She just needed to work a little harder. With Ian, there were no nightmares, there were no shadows, life was perfect. And she would do everything in her power to keep it that way.

"I want to be with him, Sylvia. I'm going to hand him the opportunity of a lifetime, just like you gave me. There won't be a choice. In the end, the human condition is predictable in its need for security. Nobody wants to struggle, nobody wants that pain, the yelling, the constant pressure to do more. There won't be a choice for me. It only takes a strategy."

THE PLANS FOR THE BACHELOR auction were proceeding perfectly. She'd verified the menu, triple-checked the reservation list, picked out the music and met with her team of bachelors, reassuring each one that the proceedings were to be conducted with the utmost respect and dignity for their reputation and, also, physical safety.

As for her nights, they belonged to Ian, and the nightmares stayed at bay—at least most of the time. Sometimes he watched her, and she knew he wanted to know, but shrugged it off as nothing, and she stayed quiet. No one was better at keeping quiet than Rose.

Except for maybe Ian. He stopped saying anything about his old job, he stopped checking in with his old boss, and when she asked him—all very carefully, all very discreetly—he shrugged it off casually and stayed quiet.

Empowered by Hilda's success, Rose knew it was time for Cinderella to take the bull by the horns and plant the glass slipper under Prince Charming's nose. It would take careful timing, charm and a devious mind, all of which she possessed in abundance.

She bided her time, writing down her lines and practicing them until she had perfected the delivery with the right amount of sincerity, spontaneity and uncertainty. And one brilliant February afternoon, she cornered the count in his office.

"Mail for you. A ski junket, something official from the State and a letter from home. Sorry, I couldn't translate."

He took the mail, glanced through it and then looked at her when he noticed that she hadn't left. Rose wasn't usually one to hover, and she didn't do it well.

"Yes?"

"Anton, you're on the board at that bank, aren't you?"

"Several."

"So—" she blanked her face, staring in the distance "—you know the head guy, right?"

"I had lunch with the head of Citi this afternoon," he said, which she knew because she'd logged the invitation in his calendar. "Why the sudden interest in finance?"

"Nothing," said Rose, then turned as if to go.

"Rose? Do you need something?"

She hesitated at the door, opened her mouth, closed her mouth, exactly three times.

"Go ahead, tell me what you're after," he urged. Deep inside—impending midlife crisis notwithstanding—Anton was a man who was as softhearted as his wife.

"It's not for me," answered Rose.

"Someone needs a loan?"

Rose looked horrified. "Oh, no. It's Ian. He's doing well. Or…he's managing well, but before… He had this great position as an investment banker. When we first met, he'd go on about how much he enjoyed all the excitement and risk and the reward. And he was good at it, but then—you know, the economy went south and he was laid off. And now he's got this second-rate job, and sometimes I can see how much he'd love to get back in the game, but he's too proud to say anything, and I thought…you have all these great connections."

"It's a very hard time," he told her, stroking his chin thoughtfully.

Not the moment to press. "You're so right. I can't imagine what I was thinking. Of course, you're not a miracle worker. I'm used to seeing you and Sylvia…it's as if anything is possible. I forget," she told him, adding a self-conscious shrug.

"And you think I could wave my magic wand and poof, he's back at the bank?"

"It sounds silly, doesn't it?" Rose ducked her head, chagrin in her voice.

Anton laughed, that hearty, confident laugh of a man who's used to granting favors for the serfs. "For an ordinary man, perhaps. For a Simonov, nothing is beyond reach. Let me make a few calls to Stan. Perhaps I could let him beat me at golf. He doesn't do it very often."

Rose's mouth gaped open charmingly, full of the appropriate wonder and amazement. "You can do that? Really?"

"Sometimes I surprise myself, as well."

"Thank you, so much. I was worried. I didn't want to assume, but you and the countess…you're the best," she told him. The phone rang and he waved her off.

As she walked away, she began to hum to herself, something that sounded suspiciously like bad Ethel Merman.

Ian would never know.

IT TOOK NEARLY A MONTH for the job offer to come through. Three weeks when Rose was on pins and needles, hoping and praying. Every night she spent at Ian's, rearranging his shelves, organizing his closet and conquering a spot on his curtains that was particularly stubborn. Finally—finally!—after all her impatient waiting, Ian called her at work. "Guess what?"

"What?" she asked, closing her eyes, crossing her fingers and thinking every positive thought she was capable of.

"I didn't want to tell you because it might be nothing, but I got an offer from Citi."

Rose hit the mute button and squealed. When suitably calm, she unmuted and cleared her throat. "Doing what?"

"Investment banking in the overseas division. European investors looking for the security of the dollar."

Rose gasped. "Really? Ian, that's fabulous! You must be thrilled," she said encouragingly, because honestly some of the thrill wasn't there in his voice.

"I am," he said. She still wasn't getting all the thrill, however, this was too big an event not to celebrate.

"When do you start?"

"I have to put in notice at the agency first. I think two weeks is fine, but if they need me for longer—I don't know that I'd turn them down." At that, she definitely heard it. Sad.

Rose stopped the happy dance and sat in her straight-backed chair, feet firmly on the floor, posture rigid. "Why aren't you excited about this?"

"I am. I'm thrilled. I mean, wow. It's completely out of the blue. I had talked to my old boss a few months ago, but... I didn't expect anything."

"It's fate," she told him firmly.

"I guess. Anyway, it'll be nice to not have to worry about keeping the heat down at night, although I have to say that as long as you're sharing the covers, I don't mind energy conservation so much."

"If you like, we'll set the thermostat at fifty."

"See, that's my girl."

"You're going to love it. I know it."

"We'll have to celebrate."

"Pizza at Fontini's."

"Really?"

"I'm feeling the urge to harass Fabrezio."

Ian laughed, and she felt the warmth again. She'd made him happy. She'd done that. Rose Hildebrand.

Little Miss Sweet Pea? Not a chance.

A FEW HOURS LATER, IAN WAS sitting at the bar with Beckett, staring into his beer, excited, nervous, but the old spark wasn't there. He looked in the long mirror over the bar, tried for the devil-may-care grin. Sadly, the devil was refusing to care.

"Missing the mano-a-mano ambience? Need some locker-room talk, some politically incorrect jokes, or want to bitch about the women?" Beckett scowled. "I can't bitch anymore. It seems disloyal. You can bitch if you need to, but I know—stop the presses, here—I'm going to keep my mouth shut."

Ian blew out a breath. "I accepted a job offer today."

"Dude, you're back. And can I say it's about time, because I was tired of the 'disgruntled, life-kicked-you-in-ass, we have to tiptoe about your sensitivities' attitude." Then he broke into a grin and lifted his glass. "Just kidding. Congratulations to a stellar new year. May last year's debacle rest in peace."

Ian clinked glasses, drank, but then returned to cracking peanuts between his fingers. "What if I've lost my touch? What if I've lost the edge? I think I'm getting soft, Beckett. I want to sleep late on Saturday. And the *Wall Street Journal?* It's a very depressing paper. I never realized that before."

Beckett studied him, nodded. "It's to be expected. You're not sure if you can live up to overinflated expectations, dreading that the hype is more than what you're capable of."

"That wasn't exactly it."

"It's all rolled up together. Don't sweat it. Jump in, headfirst and prepare to live."

"That would be so much more effective if it hadn't taken you ten years to sleep with Phoebe."

"I had to be sure."

Ian laughed, because Beckett was probably right. This was jitters, nothing more. "You're going to pick up the tab?"

"Dude, you're in high finance again and you're going to stiff me with the bill?"

Okay, some things didn't change. Ian leaned back, contemplated the new world order, and smiled. He looked in the mirror once again. Almost. With a little bit of practice, he'd be fine.

16

THE MANHATTAN OFFICE FOR Employment Displacement was booming, the reception area lined with applicants three-deep. As he made his way through the crowd, Ian avoided their eyes. After nearly a year at the agency, it was the first time he'd ever done that. Undaunted, he manned up and told himself that this wasn't his problem anymore. He was going back to the big time, going to soar with the eagles. However, when he got to his office, the eagle on the motivational picture looked…ticked off.

Ian reminded himself that eagles always looked ticked off. It was their natural state. He shouldn't be taking it personally. Still, two hours later, he got up and moved the picture behind the printer where he couldn't see those two beady eyes glaring at him as if he was betraying some eagle-esque code of honor.

His letter of resignation was typed up and sitting on the desk, awaiting only his signature before he turned it in to his boss.

The files needed to be ordered, notes needed to be drafted, there were calls that he should make in order to transition his caseload to someone else, although they would transition it to Arnie who didn't have enough of the real dogged perseverance to do anybody any good. Sadly, that same never-say-die-I-don't-care-if-I'm-an-asshole quality that made him good in finance, was also a plus in job placement. Who knew?

He was half-way through his first set of notes when Hilda came into his office wearing a rather fetching forest-green dress and bearing the usual tin of cookies. Dragging behind her was a hesitant stick of a man with a tweed cap on his head.

"Mr. Cumberland, this is Mr. Fergus Moore and he's seeking

employment, preferably in the tailoring industry. I said that you and Ms. Hildebrande were top-notch at finding a position, yet he was skeptical. Tell him, Mr. Cumberland."

Ian pushed the cookies back in her direction.

"Hilda, I can't take on the case."

"Of course you can. Compared to my own pitiable situation, Fergus is a foregone vocational conclusion."

"I'm sure he is, but I won't be here."

Her eyes grew huge. "They sacked you? I'll go speak on your behalf. Right now. It's an injustice, it is."

"No, I'm putting in my notice. Two weeks."

"You're quitting, Mr. Cumberland?"

Her shocked dismay hurt more than he expected. "I got my job back on Wall Street. It's a fantastic opportunity."

"Where you'll be mingling with the dregs of the earth?" she said with a huff.

"They're not that bad."

"But your calling is here." She nodded toward the crowd on the other side of the glass partition. "They need you."

"No one is indispensable, not even me. Whoever handles their case will do great." Assuming it wasn't Arnie—or Melinda, who hated people. Why, everybody else was... Almost okay.

"You've disappointed me, Mr. Cumberland. I pleaded and begged with Mr. Moore for a good ten days, promising him ten months' worth of shepherd's pie if he'd only come to talk to you and see the great promise in your face. Tell him, Fergus."

The man held his hat in his hands and bobbed his head. "That she did."

Hilda stared him down, using that same beady, eagle-eyed glare. Once again, Ian failed to live up to expectations. "Well, I suppose this finishes it. Good luck with your life, Mr. Cumberland. And Ms. Hildebrande, would she be able to help Fergus?"

"I doubt it, Hilda."

"I see," she answered, as if everything could be summarized in two words. Actually, it could.

No and *Shit.*

After they left, Ian studied the faces in the reception room, picked up his lucky rock and tossed it up and down, letting the smooth stone weigh in his hand, a Magic 8-Ball telling him all the right answers. Where did he belong? Here? On Wall Street?

As long as it was with Rose, did he really care?

Yes. Yes, he did.

She'd be disappointed if he didn't take the job. What woman wouldn't? And Rose's standards were higher than most. But if he stayed here, they would never starve, they wouldn't lack for shelter, or heat. It wasn't as if he was condemning her to a life below the poverty line.

He was needed.

He liked it here. He belonged here.

He was staying.

Feeling better, he ripped up the letter and threw it away. Relieved, he took a long breath, planting the rock back on his desk where it belonged.

Hopefully, Rose would understand.

IAN SEARCHED FOR THE RIGHT time to say something to Rose, but every time she looked at him with those blue eyes that were now full of hope and excitement, he couldn't do it. There were so many pieces to Rose that he didn't understand, and he kept waiting for her to trust him, but she didn't, and he wasn't sure she ever would. It wasn't the world's best relationship. In many ways it flew in the face of everything he wanted in a relationship, but since he had important things that he didn't want to tell her, either, he couldn't blame her for keeping the bad things at bay.

However, Ian wasn't Rose. In the end, he knew that motivational posters didn't do crap, shit happened, and that sometimes people couldn't abandon their high ambitions no matter how badly you wanted to hope. He couldn't run away from this any longer.

Tonight, he'd carefully planned what he needed to say, figured out the perfect phrases to make her understand that he liked working where he was. He liked what he did; there were people who depended on him, and he couldn't go back. Not now, not ever.

But it didn't matter how often he practiced the trite affirmations in his head; there was a sinking in his gut, in his heart, because he knew this wasn't going to go down well.

They were sitting on the couch, and she was laughing at the late night shows, touching him as if he were the mightiest man on the planet. When she lifted her face, shining with happiness, he opened his mouth and then kissed her as if he never would again.

"Ian?" she asked, but he didn't say a word.

Carefully he undressed her, memorizing the feel of his hand on her skin, the scent of honeysuckle teasing his mind. In this, she trusted him. Somewhere, they'd passed the point of battles and tactics, and when he thrust inside her, he could see the love flaring in her eyes.

She never said the words, and neither did he. Ian was fast learning that words were useless things when compared to what the heart knew.

He took her hand, their bodies joined, eyes locked, and slowly they moved together, tenderness, passion, love.

Afterward, he held her, a little tighter than normal, a little more possessive than what he usually dared, and she trailed a soft finger on his face.

"You seem different," she said, and he brought her hand to his lips, kissing it softly. When he first met her, when he first kissed her, it was her beauty that had stolen his breath. But her beauty was the least of what was Rose. She had a tentative courage that her scars couldn't mask. A cynical heart that hadn't quite forgotten how to believe. And a generosity that was destined to hurt her. People looked at Rose, and assumed. Ian had made that mistake, as well. But because of her, Ian had learned to look beneath the surface for what was real.

Now he was different. He was different because of her.

THE NIGHT OF THE AUCTION, Rose wore a sea-foam green silk—simple, elegant, not too much glitz. Being glitzy while asking for contributions never gave a favorable impression. Her makeup was flawless, the hotel staff was buzzing like bees, but the pit in her stomach kept growing. The countess was watching, Ian was watching, the most eligible bachelors were watching, and everyone expected her to perform perfectly.

At one time, she'd have pulled off a flawless show without a wince. She'd endured a pipe against the back with nary a scream, she'd been thrown into that goddamned closet for days, and yet she smiled as if she didn't have a care. A little girl learned not to care. She learned not to dream.

Ian caught up with her behind the staging area, rubbed her hands. "You're sweating."

"I know. It's a terrible habit." She searched for a napkin to get rid of the offending evidence.

"Rose. You'll be fine." His eyes approved of her, warmed her, thrilled her. She took a deep breath, but then from the other side of the room came the furious barking of a dog.

The napkin in her hand flew to the ground.

"You shouldn't have brought in the dogs," Ian told her, retrieving the fallen cloth, and he wished he could retrieve her fallen sanity just as easily.

"It was Sylvia's idea. I can do this, Ian. It's silly to be afraid of dogs."

"Have you been bitten before?"

It was the first time he'd specifically asked about her fears, and instinctively a lie sprang to her lips, but instead she opted for some bit of the truth.

"No. I had this great dress. My parents had spent a fortune on it. This huge dog, a monster, he jumped up. He was just being friendly, but the dress… The dirty paws ruined it and my mother wasn't happy."

Ian pulled her close, stroked her neck—a lot of comfort for a ruined dress, and she wondered how much he guessed. Still, she'd changed. Grown.

"I have to go," she told him.

"I'll be in the back," he said, giving her a kiss for luck, and then he disappeared, leaving Rose to pull this off. Alone.

Behind the main ballroom was a staging area, filled with tailors, hair designers and ten of New York's most eligible bachelors, dashing in their black tuxes, donating their social services for the benefit of the butt-ugly canines on the other side.

Sometimes people surprised her.

She eyed the dogs on the leashes nervously. Slowly, she approached the beasts as if she weren't terrified, though not foolish enough to get within dress-destruction range. Once bitten, twice shy.

The shelter had brought out the lively ones, the ones that jumped and yelped and wanted to get into people's faces, thinking people would be happy and wouldn't scream.

"You're doing a great thing," said a voice from behind her.

It was Remy, darling, dashing, richer-than-Trump Remy, who had asked absolutely nothing of her. Ever.

"So are you. You don't even seem nervous. The ladies are going to break the bank to have a night with you."

He even blushed charmingly. Sadly, it was true. The man had no flaws. "I've gotten over the fear. You're a fabulous cheerleader. And look at those faces. How can I turn my back on that?"

"Remy…"

He stopped her in midsentence.

"He's the one, isn't he?"

Rose nodded apologetically.

He took her face in his hand, tilted it up and smiled. "I've never seen a woman try so hard to make something out of nothing."

"It wasn't nothing," she insisted, not wanting to insult him, not wanting to annoy him, not wanting to make him mad.

He raised his brows, but she stood her ground. "It wasn't. You're a good man."

"And you're a good friend," he said, marvelously calm.

"Thank you for not being angry."

"You showed up in my life at the right time. Mother wants me to find someone appropriate. You were appropriate."

"You have someone 'inappropriate'?" she guessed.

"She's a waitress."

"Tell your mother to take a hike," said Rose, the woman who'd never told anyone to take a hike.

"I think I will."

"What's her name?"

"Steph."

"It's a nice name. Go get her, Remy. Don't wait too long."

"And what about you, Rose? Who is he? I don't think there's a man who couldn't love you."

"His name is Ian, and he's honorable, and loving, and strong and he makes me believe there's hope in the world."

"So…"

"It's complicated."

"That complicated?"

The poodle barked, and Rose's hand shot out to whatever would support her. In this case, Remy. "It's only a dog."

And that was Rose's world. Full of secrets that weren't meant to be told. It wasn't a world she wanted to share. In the past, she'd thought she could, that she could act her way into happiness, but not anymore.

"It's not always easy, Remy."

He shrugged in understanding. "No. I guess not."

THE BALLROOM WASN'T THE MOST perfect venue for black-tie accompanied by a melee of dogs, but Sylvia pulled it off. The auctioneer, imported direct from Christie's, was a short, pudgy man with a dour smile and a wicked gavel-rap that made Rose flinch at regular intervals.

But the auction finished without a hitch. Ten handsome bachelors, ten squealing winners, two dozen dogs straining at the leash and one smug, slutty Blair Rapaport.

It was right before dessert when Blair approached.

"I got the flowers from Anton. I wanted you to know."

"Your adventures in botany aren't my concern," Rose told her, striving to be polite. She snagged a glass of cabernet, needing something in her hands. Preferably a weapon.

"He asked to meet me tonight. I'm going to win."

Rose stepped up, face-to-face. "I'll tell him about the bet. I'll tell the countess. Honestly, you can't imagine her when she's mad. There's dragon fire in her eyes, and she'll rip you a new one before you can say ouch."

Blair only laughed. "I love pissing you off, Rose. You have

these fuming heaves like you've been pricked in the ass with a pineapple. But you would never do a goddamned thing."

A dog barked, and Rose jumped. Blair laughed, and for Rose that was it. Her arm spazzed, and oops, she threw the cabernet right onto Blair's previously pristine dress.

"You bitch!" Blair shrieked, while Rose graciously handed her a napkin.

"The stain's going to be killer to get out. And your mascara is running. If you used waterproof, it wouldn't be a problem. And look at the count—oh, my—he looks horrified."

He didn't, but Blair checked just the same, and Rose quietly rocked on her heels.

"You think this is done."

"For now," answered Rose, her heart pounding, but she hid it, just as she always did.

Two seconds later, Rose realized how much trouble she'd stirred. Blair stalked toward the trainers, grabbed the leashes and in a great show of bad taste—threw them to the floor. Two dozen dogs charged through the dining room, women shrieking, bachelors scrambling, while Rose watched in horror.

She took a step back, away from the chaos, away from the noise.

A German shepherd loped toward her, a happy smile on his doggie face, and Rose felt the double-time thud from her heart, the sweat on her palms, her neck, but she planted her heels firmly on the ground. *Not going to run, not going to run.*

The dog rose on his great doggie paws, his black eyes shining happily, and in slow motion she saw him lunge. At her.

Thankfully, Rose fainted.

17

IAN FANNED HER FACE, trying to get blood circulating, trying to get her to wake up. Eventually, yes, thank God, the lashes flickered and the pale blue eyes worked to focus.

"You okay?" he asked, rubbing her hands together.

"The dogs. The room. The people. Oh, God. Blair." She sat up on the couch, stared in confusion.

"You're in the manager's office, Rose. They're gone."

"How?"

He wisely skimmed over the more chaotic parts and focused on the end results. "The countess took over. Flawlessly, by the way. You should have seen her, the concierge had some doggie treats and she herded them onstage and stood there, two dozen dogs sitting at her heels like some Joan of Arc among the hounds. Honestly, it was awesome."

She whopped herself on the head, once, twice, until he grabbed her hand again, making her stop. "I wanted to do this, Ian. I wanted to do this right. I wanted to do it great. I thought I could get over the Giant Monolith of Roseness. She said I'd never do a goddamned thing. She was right."

Ian held her close, feeling her tremble, feeling the shivers. "Until you threw the wine on her?" he reminded her, because she needed to hear that, needed to know that she had done something. Something kick-ass.

"You saw?"

"A lot of people saw. My table broke out in applause."

"Really?"

He gave her an encouraging smile. "Rose, it's never as bad as you believe. She deserved it."

"I should tell the count I'm onto him. I should tell Sylvia. I should…"

"You'll figure it out. For tonight, I think the count's virtue is safe."

He helped her to her feet just as Sylvia burst into the room, the door slamming behind her. "Rose! You're good?"

"I'm good."

"Thank God, I thought you had died. You looked so white, your eyes were like saucers. And you know this is going to hit Page Six. Throwing wine at Blair. Every man in the place was waiting for hair to rip and clothes to fall off. Honestly, I couldn't have done it better. What did she say to you?"

Rose glanced toward Ian, seeking guidance, but truth be told, he wasn't the best one to be dishing out advice on how to break news.

So he waited.

She opened her mouth, and then the count appeared in the doorway.

"She's not very nice," Rose answered primly. "She said some very rude things about you. I didn't approve." Then Rose gave the count a dark glare. "I don't approve."

"Pshaw." Sylvia waved a hand. "Do you think I let that little twat bother me? Let it go, Rose. You'll be better tomorrow. Ian, take her home, will you?"

Ian nodded and the couple watched them leave. Ian relieved, and Rose, well, Rose seemed disappointed, and she didn't deserve to be disappointed. Not tonight. She'd done great things tonight.

"I should have told her. I wanted to say something, but I couldn't."

Quickly Ian made up his mind. "Stay here a minute, would you? You look like you could use some water."

He ran down the hallway, caught the count as they were nearing the door.

"Sir? A second?" Ian shot an apologetic glance at the countess. "Sorry. Boring financial stuff."

As soon as they were alone, he started in, winging it all the way.

"It was quite the auction tonight."

"With Sylvia, it is always an adventure."

"She's amazing. Rose is really fond of her. She's been a good friend, as well as a boss. That's pretty rare. You must be very proud of her."

"I am, yes. This is what you wanted to say?"

"Give me a sec—it's not so easy. Not that it's my business, but I see these great, long marriages, and—you know how I feel about Rose—it makes me think about how relationships take a lot of work."

"I've been married to Sylvia for twenty-five years. It's not as hard as it seems."

Ian whistled. "Wow. Twenty-five years. Don't you get…stifled? Bored?"

"Never," answered the count, who'd probably never been doubted in his entire life.

"That's really noble with all the…talent that falls into your lap."

The count's eyes narrowed, arrogant, infallible and not to be tweaked. "You have something to say?"

"You're a bet, sir."

"I beg your pardon?"

"Blair. It's a bet, nothing more. She told Rose. It's been bugging her—Rose, not Blair—because she wanted to tell you but she didn't think it was her place. It's not my place, either, but you should know, before you do something that's less than smart."

Pissing off a Russian count was probably something less than smart, as well, but sometimes less than smart had to be done.

Anton pulled at the collar of his coat, his eyes flashing to black. "It is none of your concern, nor is it your place. I expected more gratitude and less…disrespect for a man whom you're indebted to."

Slowly Ian lifted his head, the angry words sinking home. "I wasn't aware I owed you any favors."

"I was wondering about that. You didn't seem the sort. She came to me for you."

"Who?" he asked, not that he didn't know.

"Rose."

It hurt more than he would have expected. It would have been less painful if it were her lack of faith in him. Hell, she probably thought she was doing him a favor.

But in his heart, he knew exactly why Rose had done this. She didn't have a choice.

"I don't need your favors. I don't need a new job."

His smile was coldly polite. "Apparently Rose disagrees."

"I won't presume to speak for Rose."

"Yet you do so before? Suddenly, it's not easy, is it?"

No, it wasn't easy. Ian touched his forehead in salute. "Touché."

"As much as it shames me, I thank you for your concern, warning a foolish man before I ruin something that is very valuable to me. I love her. I will not tarnish that. My choices, they are much easier than yours. Go home, Ian. You have some decisions of your own to make."

ON THEIR WAY BACK TO his apartment, Ian kept a cheery smile on his face, while a storm raged in his gut. At what point was he supposed to step in and demand that she trust him? And how worthless was that? How long was he supposed to live with the mystery that was Rose Hildebrande? His heart told him to wait forever. His brain told him that once he let her know that he was turning down the job, his wait would be over. But not yet.

That night, he woke up to the sound of her shrouded scream and he reached to touch her, then stopped himself.

He knew the routine, knew the code. He didn't know why there was a code; he didn't know why there was a routine, but he knew that what haunted her in her dreams kept her trapped in it. And now, he was trapped there, too.

"Rose. It's Ian."

Her eyes opened and she shot up in bed. He saw the fear first, then recognition flared back into place.

He took her hand, and she curled into his arms. "Stupid dreams," she said, her laugh shaky, forced.

"It's all right now," he murmured, burying his face in her hair. Honeysuckle.

"I'm so glad you're here. It's easier. So much nicer."

"What happened, Rose? I don't want to ask. I keep hoping you'll give me a clue, some idea of what I should do, what I shouldn't do, but…"

At that, she lifted her head, her body stiff, her eyes now nervously awake.

"It's nothing," she lied, and she kissed him, as if she loved him, as if she needed him, as if she trusted him. Ian wanted to press her, but her hand closed over his cock, stroking, tempting, and he didn't want to think about nightmares, or jobs, or long-delayed resignation letters.

He only wanted this.

ROSE KNEW SOMETHING was wrong. At first, she'd been convinced it was her. That she'd put her foot in her mouth, complained too much, demanded too much, and so she'd cleaned his apartment—twice, but the uncomfortable belief remained. Something was wrong.

It was a stunning March Saturday afternoon when he discovered her with a can of scouring powder and pine cleanser, and he took them away.

"Let's go out to eat tonight," he said, and they ended up at the same restaurant where they'd started. It should have thrilled her, but the taut lines in his face made her nervous.

He'd arranged the same table by the kitchen, a bottle of champagne, and this time when the flowers were brought in, the two dozen white roses were delivered to her.

The pit in her stomach only grew.

Desperately she searched the depths of his eyes, looking for that spark of hope and optimism, needing it, but tonight it'd gone missing. It hadn't dawned on her how much she'd come to depend on that spark.

The steward opened the champagne and poured two glasses. Ian touched his to hers.

After the man left, Ian broke the silence. "When I saw you here that night, I'd never had a shock like that, never met someone that made me swallow my tongue. When you look at me with that faith shining in your eyes, everything falls away, Rose. You make a man feel like he can do anything, conquer anything. But I don't want anything, I don't need anything. Everything I need is here. It's you."

They were words she'd waited to hear from him for days,

months, longer than a lifetime. Her hands began to shake, and she didn't want to be here in this damned restaurant with a thousand staring eyes.

"No one's ever needed me before," she told him, which meant "I love you," but he probably wouldn't know that unless she said it. Carefully she laid the napkin over her hands, stilling the noise, stilling her nerves.

"I have to tell you something," Ian began, his voice serious.

She didn't like the regret in his gaze. Ian never regretted anything. Rose regretted her entire life—until she'd met him.

"I'm not going to take the job," he said, and she exhaled, beginning to breathe once again. That wasn't so bad.

"It's the wrong company, isn't it? That can be fixed. I can fix it."

"How?"

"It's a different world, Ian. If you're connected to the right people, anything can be fixed."

Slowly it dawned on her that he knew what she'd done. Strangely enough, she'd never considered this conversation before, but she sensed it would go badly.

Exactly like this.

"You talked to the count. He told me."

"Yes. I wanted to give you something."

"You should have asked."

"You would have said no," she told him, needing to point that out.

"Damn right, I would have said no," he answered, and his fingers tightened over a spoon, harmless, anger carefully controlled.

Rose winced. He noticed, and a shadow of sadness rolled over his face. Perfect. She'd put him back on Rose-alert. Lately she hadn't been so great at hiding her feelings, hiding her fears. "You want this. You told me you missed your old job."

"I thought I wanted this, Rose. But I don't. I like where I am. I don't want the high ozone anymore. The world changed. I changed, too."

"Okay," she answered in an agreeable voice, but her hair was in her eyes, and her back was hardening into its default ladylike position.

No.

Rose pushed her hair away, met his eyes, never wavering, never blinking. She didn't back down, not once.

Words came to her tongue, words she'd never spoken in her life. *I love you. I'll stay with you, whatever you choose. Whatever you do. Don't leave me. Please.*

They were easy words to say. So much easier than anything she'd ever said before. So much easier than what she'd ever been through. She'd survived hell, this was a walk in the park.

His eyes flickered. That same defensive vulnerability that had affected her before. The defiant bravado that shouted: "Go ahead. Get it over with so that I can move on with my life."

But he didn't think she could move on, and something small and fragile within her, died.

"I haven't changed," she told him, because she hadn't. She hadn't changed a damned thing.

"I think you have."

"Some. Not enough."

"Why, Rose? You're not greedy, you'd never have a maid, and you'd never let anyone else touch your laundry. That isn't who you are."

"No. But money can buy anything. It's power. Control. The dreams go away, because you have it all. When you live up there in the penthouse, no one can touch you. You're invulnerable to the rest of the world."

"Only if you're made of stone, Rose."

"It's not a bad thing," she defended, because stone was a material of myriad uses. She wouldn't be sane if she hadn't been stone. She wouldn't be alive if she hadn't been stone.

"So, do I take you home and you write on the mirror again?" he asked. And somehow in this conversation, somehow in this relationship, she'd not only lost all the hope in herself, but she killed it in him, as well. Another one of those myriad uses of stone. It protected, it destroyed.

"I love you," she told him, which was so much more composed than "You make me want to believe. I almost did."

However, Ian was too smart to be sidetracked or flattered by mere words. He waited, knowing what else was there, and she longed to tell him how badly she ached to be somebody new. But she'd molded herself into a statue to survive. And statues didn't change, didn't move. They stood timeless and immobile. For a second she let herself drift, let her shoulders sag, but in the end, her posture was ruler-straight; her chin could only angle at a perfect ninety degrees.

"Please take the job," she asked, her voice carefully polite.

"No."

"You're going to force me to pick?"

"Yes."

"I can't."

His eyes flashed, shuttered, the hurt hidden so completely. Then he downed his glass and the vulnerability there was gone. His gaze was hard and flat. Stone. "Do you want to order dessert?"

"No. I think I should go."

"I think that'd be best."

Carefully she stood, walking on eggshells. As she glided out, she didn't hear Ian. And he mustn't have moved. Not once.

18

THE RAC WASN'T THE SAME. The Knights were on a losing streak, Phoebe and Beckett were happy as clams, and Ian did his duty buying Beckett's beer and letting Phoebe steal his nachos.

She swiped a chip and he watched the cheese dribble on her shirt. Rose would have insisted on making it clean.

"You seem glum tonight, Ian. Why are you glum?" she asked.

"I'm not glum," he replied, eyes now glued firmly on the game.

"Phoebe, let him alone," Beckett warned her, Mr. Sensitivity in Training. Ian nearly smiled.

"He should know he has friends. We're the Three Musketeers, and even though Athos and Aramis are doing the deed, the basic dynamic doesn't change."

Ian looked at her. "Now I'm glum."

Beckett whopped Phoebe on the arm. "Told you."

Ian lifted his glass, drank, and the Knights delivered a three-point shot with a mighty swoosh and cheer. Ian smiled, beamed full of good cheer and nonglumness.

"See? Everything is looking up."

Beckett sighed. "I'll get you a beer. This time, it's on me."

FOR THREE WEEKS, ROSE lived in a fog. Sylvia asked about Ian, Rose shrugged her shoulders casually and told her things didn't work out. Sylvia wasn't fooled, but for the first time ever, she didn't pry.

Every day, Rose worked from early in the morning until the sun had long set at night, walking home from the subway station, wishing the Fates would have pushed a little harder, wishing that she was a little stronger.

It was a warm May night when she passed by the pet store and waited for the puppies to come out and cheer her up. The court jesters of the animal world, designed to make her laugh.

She stood in front of the glass and waited, and when nothing stirred, she rapped carefully. Once. Twice.

Eventually the hay shifted and the shadows began to stir. The puppies were gone, most likely taken to a loving and caring home, and it was only the big black hulk who was eyeing her carefully from his solitary position, safe in his cage.

She lifted a hand, placed it on the glass, but the smart dog stayed immobile.

"Hey," she said, watching his ears perk at the sound.

He barked, but Rose didn't jump. Her hand stayed on the glass, and the midnight eyes watched her with interest. Watched her with hope.

"I'm sorry," she whispered to him. "You shouldn't be alone."

Warily, he lifted his head, still not making a move in her direction.

"I don't want to be alone," she told the dog. "I could do this, couldn't I?"

The dog stared at her, dark unblinking eyes that cowered at monsters, that knew the silent tears in the night. The dog wouldn't push her. The Fates wouldn't push her. Even Ian wouldn't push her anymore.

There was no one left but Rose.

Little Princess School of charm hadn't covered how to abandon every survival rule she'd known. They hadn't taught her how to trust. She needed to trust him. She could trust him. Her heart knew it. Her very real, very alive, very still-beating heart.

Warily, she lifted her chin to a perfect ninety degrees, and gave a sad smile to the animal. "It took so much out of me. My dreams. My courage. But there's something left, something good." Her smile grew a little stronger, a little surer. "I hope."

WHEN IT CAME TO PLOTTING a strategy there was no one better than Rose. She had disappointed Ian, she had disappointed herself, but no more. He needed to believe in fate again, in the meddling gods that pushed them together, and when she focused on what he needed, it made the hard parts easier. She did trust him. She knew that. All she lacked was the courage to take that one small—okay, it was a huge one—step.

She'd seen all of Ian. The strong, the noble, the angry and the vengeful—and after all of that she knew she loved him. She wasn't afraid. She'd never been afraid. Not of Ian.

And that thought cheered her, kept her focused on the plan.

She decided that she was going to play on the "hand of God" angle. In her mind it was all worked out. She's coming to talk to him, they step into the elevator, she begins to speak, she starts to apologize, he isn't happy, but then ooops—the elevator stalls, stuck, and he has to listen to her. A captive audience. And she convinces him. She puts back the glowing optimism in his eyes, the belief that they were not just meant—but *fated* to be together.

In the end, she didn't care what job he did. Yes, she was terrified, but for the first time in her life, she wasn't going to let the shadows rule her life.

Rose took a deep breath. This was for Ian.

She made a call to Manny, the maintenance supervisor in the building. A bribe didn't work, but then she explained what she required and why, and bless his darling romantic heart, they were set.

From here on out, it was up to Rose, and nobody could deliver like Rose.

She wore blue jeans and a trim-fitting T-shirt that clung nicely, but casually. Her makeup was light, almost nothing. She needed a look that said that the old Rose Hildebrande was over, and she could be anything she wanted, including casual.

The speech was done. There were parts left unwritten because she still couldn't say those words, she didn't want to talk about her past. It shamed her that she never fought back. But she had to hope—today, she had to believe that when she saw Ian, when she stared into his eyes, that she could.

New hopes, new opportunities, a new start.

At exactly nine-oh-seven she was in the building, waiting for

Ian, watching the clock, praying he wouldn't be late, because today of all days, she didn't want fate to interfere.

He appeared, exactly on schedule, and Rose sighed at the sight of him, relief, happiness and the unshakable faith that everything was going to be all right. "Ian!"

He turned, his face wary. "Why are you here?"

She glanced at the clock. Thirty seconds. "We need to talk. I'm sorry."

As if he had all the time in the world, he folded his hands over his chest. "Go ahead."

Another glance at the clock, nine-ten, and panic bubbled inside her. "Your office," she ordered, pushing him toward the elevator.

The doors slammed shut. Exactly on schedule. Perfect.

Once they were in the car, Rose brushed her palms on her jeans, realized what she was doing and stopped. "How are you?"

"I've been better," he told her, looking at her wearily, anticipating that she would hurt him once again.

"You were right," she announced, precisely as the elevator ground to a halt.

19

IAN STARED AT THE BANK of buttons, then back at Rose, not ready to believe that fate struck twice. No, the elevator conked out all the time. Not going to read anything into this at all.

"Are we stuck?" she asked, and he wished he couldn't see that flickering vulnerability in her eyes. He didn't want to hope this time. He didn't want to assume. He didn't want to believe in things that weren't going to come true.

"No. We're not stuck. Sometimes it hangs. Or they're doing maintenance. It'll start in a sec."

Impatiently he punched a button. Then a whole bank of buttons, watching them all light up, but the elevator didn't move.

Rose didn't seem alarmed. In fact, she appeared happy, satisfied, content. Obviously life without Ian was treating her well.

He hit the alarm button. Silence. Did anybody care about safety anymore? Apparently not.

"I think we're stuck," she told him, a blinding glimpse of the obvious, if one was inclined to latch on to the obvious. Ian wasn't there yet.

"I can call," he answered, pulling out his phone.

She jumped toward him, ripped the phone out of his hand. *"No!"* Then she recovered. "Sorry," she answered, returning the phone. "But when life stalls you in an elevator, you have to listen, Ian. You can't argue, you can't fight it. You have to accept it." She was lecturing him, with his own words. He remembered. God knows, it was probably slathered on a motivational poster somewhere.

Feigning a casualness that frankly any idiot could see through, he stuffed the phone in his pocket, reckless hope building inside him once again.

"That's a big change for you."

"I'm learning to embrace the chaos. Look," she answered, spreading her arms wide. "Trapped in an elevator, and I'm not nervous, not panicked, not even a tinge of hyperventilating."

"Nicely done," he told her, and at her tiny smile, he felt the familiar warmth inside him, that tug at his heart that would always forgive her. How could he not.

He loved her.

"I'm sorry about the job plan. I thought you'd be happy, but I should have known better. I should have anticipated it, because I understand you. But I didn't see it, because I couldn't face the things that were inside me." Carefully, she brushed the hair from her eyes, meeting his gaze, staying there. "I don't want to be poor. It terrifies me."

"Why?" He'd never pushed her, never prodded, but it was time.

"I didn't write this part down. Give me a second." She held up a finger, her breathing began to speed up, and he longed to hold her, to reassure her that it was okay. But it wasn't. They needed to do this. She needed to do this, and he was going to have to wait.

Eventually she began to talk. "You knew we were poor?"

He nodded. "You told me that part."

"I lied about some of it," she admitted, her face uncertain. "My parents, my mother, she was never going to win awards for child-hood development. I was such a stupid girlie-girl. I loved the lace dresses, the shiny shoes, the smell of flowers in the air. God, somebody mentioned a rainbow, and I was off to chase it." As she talked, her tone turned hard and cold. Bitter. A lot of bitter for a girl who wanted nothing more than to smell flowers and chase rainbows.

Ian took a step toward her, but she raised a hand. "Don't. If you're too close, I can't do this, and I have to finish. They—my mother—she got this idea about beauty pageants because I was such a perfect little doll, but I was never good enough. Clarinet playing didn't cut it, the other girls smiled a little better, their answers were a little cuter, a little less rehearsed. Mama said I was making excuses for my own failures."

She stopped, sliding down against the elevator wall, and this time, Ian sat beside her, because for too long Rose had stood alone. As a kid, as an adult. He wasn't going to let that happen. Not anymore.

"You don't have to say anything, Rose."

She ignored him, her hands fisted together. He untwisted her hands, cradled one in his own, but she didn't notice, her face white, her skin cold. She didn't look at him. He didn't know where she was, but it wasn't here. It was a long way away, it was wherever she went to when the nightmares came.

"After that it was charm school. She thought that would teach me, and they bet everything that I could be taught. Every day we'd drive down to Charleston in Daddy's old pickup, and Mama would tell me how much they depended on this. How much they depended on me. I watched Daddy hit her, and she said it was because there wasn't enough. She said that if I won, we'd have enough. And I tried. I gave it everything, just to win a crown. It was fake, with glue so cheap you could see it, but when you're eight, nine, it doesn't matter…" She trailed off and her hand tightened, hard and harder still. Her mouth worked, tried once, but nothing emerged.

"What did she do, Rose?" he asked, keeping his anger hidden. Later, he'd let it go, but for now he'd be as calm, as still, as stony as she was.

"She was very careful. She had a plumbers' pipe. It was thin so it wouldn't leave a mark. She hit me when I didn't do good, and it didn't matter how much I won, or how perfect I walked, or how cute my answers were. She kept on hitting me. Over and over." She took her free hand and slapped her thigh. Over and over, and those pale blue eyes were so old, so worn. Gently, Ian covered the hand, stilled it.

Her pulse thudded, and she looked at him, blank for a moment. Then she came back to the present. Back to him.

"She's gone. They're gone. You're here." He cursed the words, stupid words that were meaningless. Ian wanted to help her, to make her believe that everything would be okay, but words jammed in his throat. He wanted to take away the scars, take away the pain, but he was fifteen years too late.

"You don't look surprised."

"No." He'd known. The people who cut the hardest were the people who had bled the most.

Awkwardly she turned her face into his shoulder, needing comfort, but not sure how to ask for it. Ian stroked her hair, her back, tracing lines of bruises that he'd never see. For a second, one infinite second, his hand fisted, but he kept that hand away. Far away. She wouldn't see that from him. Not ever.

Her body slowly relaxed, the tension at ease for now, and she started to speak again. "I thought money made me invulnerable. It was this giant cocoon that kept you separated from all the bad and all the unpleasant in the world. My mother said they wanted to have financial security. She told me how lucky they were to have such a talented little girl that was going to make my father's dreams come true."

"She was making excuses, Rose."

"I know."

"What now?"

She lifted her head, met his eyes, and she saw pain and strength…and love.

"I want to please you, Ian. I want to make you happy. At first, I did it because it was all I knew how to do. And now… It's because I love you. I need to be with you. No matter what you do, or how wealthy you are or aren't, or how secure things are or aren't. You're my rock."

Ian wasn't sure he was well equipped to be anyone's rock. That sort of responsibility weighed heavier than job placement, than billion-dollar transactions, than anything he'd ever tried before, and he found the legal waivers slipping from his mouth.

"Do you want me to take the job, Rose? I'll do it." If it made her happy, how could he tell her no?

She shook her head once. "No. I'll do this. I have to do this."

"You might change your mind. I'm not the most rocklike man on the planet."

"Do you think I can do this?" she asked, in a voice that still couldn't quite hope.

He nodded, because he didn't doubt her for a minute. "Yes."

"I think I can, too. Whatever you have inside you, whatever that irresistible something is that's in the air you breathe, it's contagious, Ian. I watch your face, and I believe I can do that, too. It's why you're so good at what you do. It's why Hilda is right. It's why you have to be where you are. People get better around you. The world gets better around you. It's why I met you that night. It's why I dropped my phone. It's why I don't want to be without you. Somebody, somewhere wanted me to get better."

"You're sure?"

"Please, Ian. I need this. I need you."

He kissed her then, soft, gentle, full of promise, full of love. And somewhere in the skies, in the place where the Fates plotted and planned, Frank Capra was there with a wink and a smile.

IT WAS TWO HOURS LATER before they were "rescued." Rose didn't mind that Manny was late. Sitting there with Ian, it was the best sort of dream. When the doors opened to the lobby, Rose noticed the uniform, noted the badge. "Thank you, Norman."

"Where's Manny?" asked Ian. "He's usually a lot faster than this."

"Not today. The lucky bastard picked a winning lottery ticket and took off last night for Paris."

Rose gaped at the elevator man who looked at her blankly. "Is that a problem?"

"Manny isn't here?"

"Nope."

"The elevator it just...broke? Like that."

"Happens all the time," explained Ian.

Her knees buckled a little, but she recovered. "It just...broke? Nobody flipped a switch, or turned it off or cut a cable?"

"She needs to eat," said Ian, pulling her toward the outside world, a fine May day where everything would be all right.

Norman called after them. "She's not going to sue, is she?"

Ian nudged Rose, noting the pale skin, the astonished blue eyes, but it was a good look for her. Awe. "I think we're going to have to invite Norman to the wedding."

Rose only nodded once. "Whatever you say."

Epilogue

ANXIOUSLY, ROSE STARED around the apartment, checking for telltale dust marks, adjusting the bowls so that they were arranged in a pleasing circular arrangement. This shouldn't be a big deal, but her stomach kept tumbling in great heaves, and she'd checked her makeup four times.

Ian had told her to relax, had told her that she'd be okay, but still… Her eyes checked the clock. They should be back any minute.

The writing secretary was in the corner, white mums spilling from the vase, and the kitchen was not only well stocked, but organized, as well. Two months ago, she'd moved in, and between Ian and her therapist, things were progressing nicely. Today was her first big step, and her palms were sweating like a high-strung pig.

Frustrated, she wiped her hands on her white cardigan. Then she heard the shuffling out in the hall, followed by Ian's soothing voice.

After one last check, she planted herself in the middle of the room, a queasy smile on her face.

The door opened and Ian emerged, towing the giant black monster on a leash.

Immediately he noticed the queasy smile. "You're sure? We're not committed to this."

Firmly Rose nodded, her knees starting to wobble. "Positive. Let him go."

The leash dropped to the floor, and the dog walked slowly, cautiously, a great hulking mass headed straight in her direction. Huge black paws stood in front of her, waiting, but she stood strong—until her breathing started to fail.

"Deep breaths," Ian reminded her. "One. Two."

"I can…breathe." She stared deep into the dog's wary midnight eyes, and felt a crack inside her. Concrete cracking under the sun.

Tentatively she lifted a hand, patted the huge head. For the dog, that was all the invitation he needed. Two bear-size paws landed on her chest and Rose was falling, falling…

The dog was all over her, licking and barking—and completely killing her outfit. There was mud on the floor, the rug would have to be cleaned and awkwardly Rose kept patting him between the ears.

Ian's hands were locked across his chest. "I'm standing here. I'm waiting. Not moving until you tell me to move, but you're white as a sheet, and if you throw up, I don't care what you told me not to do."

Rose met his eyes, and managed a wobbly smile. "He's nice, isn't he?"

"He likes you."

The giant tongue took a sloppy sweep of her face, barked twice and charged straight for the secretary. The flowers crashed to the floor, water spilling on wood, papers flying. Chaos.

"No!" she yelled, just as Ian dived for the leash. At the sharp alarm in her voice, the beast cowered on his belly, eyes expecting the worst.

"I can take him back," Ian whispered.

Unsteadily Rose got to her feet, taking one nervous step after another, until she made her way to the giant animal. Tentatively she reached out and stroked the trembling head. "No," she said firmly. "I think we need to keep him."

"What are you going to call him? Chaos? Hellhound? Terminator?" he asked, as if all was right with the world. It was the thing she loved most. Because with Ian, it always was.

The dog flicked a giant tongue over the palm of her hand, as rough as sandpaper, as strong as stone. "No. I have the perfect name."

Gingerly, she settled on the floor, deluged by dog. Underneath, the panic still lurked, but now there was something new, something warm, something safe. It had taken her nearly twenty-eight years, but she'd finally found home.

Rose looked up at Ian, and his eyes were full of hope and the future. And fate. Never forget the fate thing.

"Kismet," she proudly stated. "We're going to call him Kismet."

* * * * *

THE CHARMER &
HER SECRET FLING
(2-IN-1 ANTHOLOGY)

BY KATE HOFFMANN &
SARAH MAYBERRY

The Charmer

Publisher Alex has never had any trouble
attracting the opposite sex, but he was amazed
to be saved from a snowstorm and then
seduced senseless by sexy Tenley.

Her Secret Fling

Star reporter Jake rubs Poppy the wrong way until
they go on a trip together and the relationship goes from
antagonistic to hedonistic. A secret fling seems delicious...

SPONTANEOUS
BY BRENDA JACKSON

Whenever Kim and Duan meet up, the passion between them is
hot, intense...spontaneous. And things really heat up when Duan
accompanies her to a wedding.

SEXY MS. TAKES
BY JO LEIGH

Start the New Year off with a bang with these three sizzling stories in
one Blazing book!

**On sale from 17th December 2010
Don't miss out!**

*Available at WHSmith, Tesco, ASDA, Eason
and all good bookshops*

www.millsandboon.co.uk

1210/14

2 FREE BOOKS
AND A SURPRISE GIFT

We would like to take this opportunity to thank you for reading this Mills & Boon® book by offering you the chance to take TWO more specially selected titles from the Blaze® series absolutely FREE! We're also making this offer to introduce you to the benefits of the Mills & Boon® Book Club™—

- **FREE home delivery**
- **FREE gifts and competitions**
- **FREE monthly Newsletter**
- **Exclusive Mills & Boon Book Club offers**
- **Books available before they're in the shops**

Accepting these FREE books and gift places you under no obligation to buy, you may cancel at any time, even after receiving your free books. Simply complete your details below and return the entire page to the address below. You don't even need a stamp!

YES Please send me 2 free Blaze books and a surprise gift. I understand that unless you hear from me, I will receive 3 superb new books every month, including a 2-in-1 book priced at £5.30 and two single books priced at £3.30 each, postage and packing free. I am under no obligation to purchase any books and may cancel my subscription at any time. The free books and gift will be mine to keep in any case.

Ms/Mrs/Miss/Mr _____ Initials _____

Surname _____

Address _____

_____ Postcode _____

E-mail _____

Send this whole page to: Mills & Boon Book Club, Free Book Offer, FREEPOST NAT 10298, Richmond, TW9 1BR